STAR TREK ®

VOLUME 8

STAR TREK®

VOLUME 8

Written by
MIKE JOHNSON

Story Consultant
ROBERTO ORCI

Series Edits by
SARAH GAYDOS

Collection Cover by **Joe Corroney**, Colors by **Brian Miller**
Collection Edits by **Justin Eisinger** and **Alonzo Simon**
Collection Design by **Claudia Chong**

Star Trek created by Gene Roddenberry.
Special thanks to Risa Kessler and John Van Citters of CBS Consumer Products for their invaluable assistance.

ISBN: 978-1-63140-021-6

17 16 15 14   1 2 3 4

® Ted Adams, CEO & Publisher
Greg Goldstein, President & COO
Robbie Robbins, EVP/Sr. Graphic Artist
Chris Ryall, Chief Creative Officer/Editor-in-Chief
Matthew Ruzicka, CPA, Chief Financial Officer
Alan Payne, VP of Sales
Dirk Wood, VP of Marketing
Lorelei Bunjes, VP of Digital Services
Jeff Webber, VP of Digital Publishing & Business Development

www.IDWPUBLISHING.com
IDW founded by Ted Adams, Alex Garner, Kris Oprisko, and Robbie Robbins

Facebook: facebook.com/idwpublishing
Twitter: @idwpublishing
YouTube: youtube.com/idwpublishing
Instagram: instagram.com/idwpublishing
deviantART: idwpublishing.deviantart.com
Pinterest: pinterest.com/idwpublishing/idw-staff-faves

Originally published as STAR TREK issues #29–34.

PARALLEL LIVES

Art by
YASMIN LIANG

Colors by
ZAC ATKINSON

Letters by
GILBERTO LAZCANO

I, ENTERPRISE

Art by
ERFAN FAJAR

Additional Inks By
YULIAN ARDHI

Colors by
SAKTI YUWONO & IFANSYAH NOOR OF STELLAR LABS

Letters by
GILBERTO LAZCANO

LOST APOLLO

Pencils by
JOE CORRONEY

Inks By
JOE CORRONEY, VICTOR MOYA, & ROB DOAN

Colors by
SAKTI YUWONO OF STELLAR LABS & JOHN RAUCH

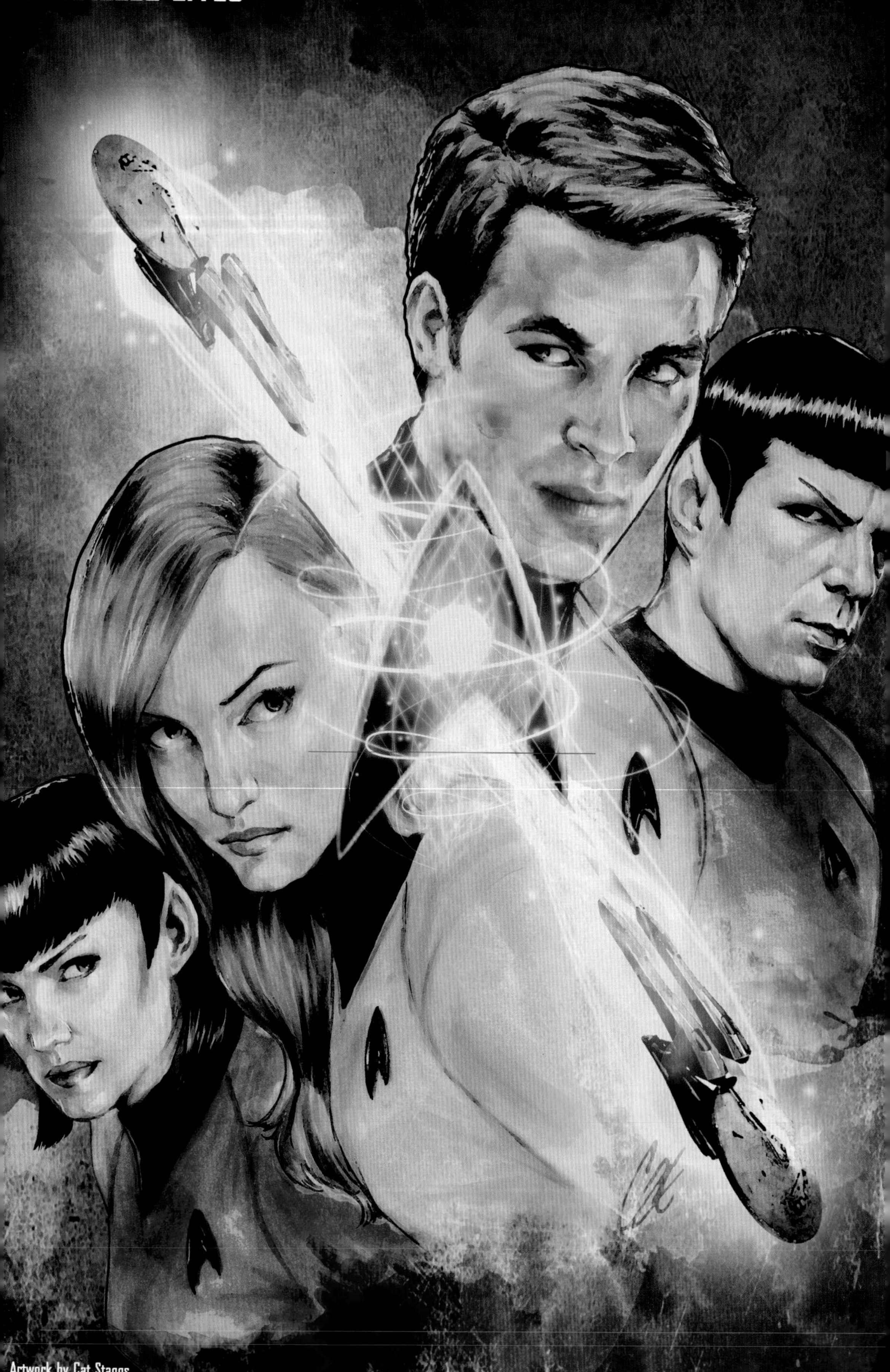

Artwork by Cat Staggs

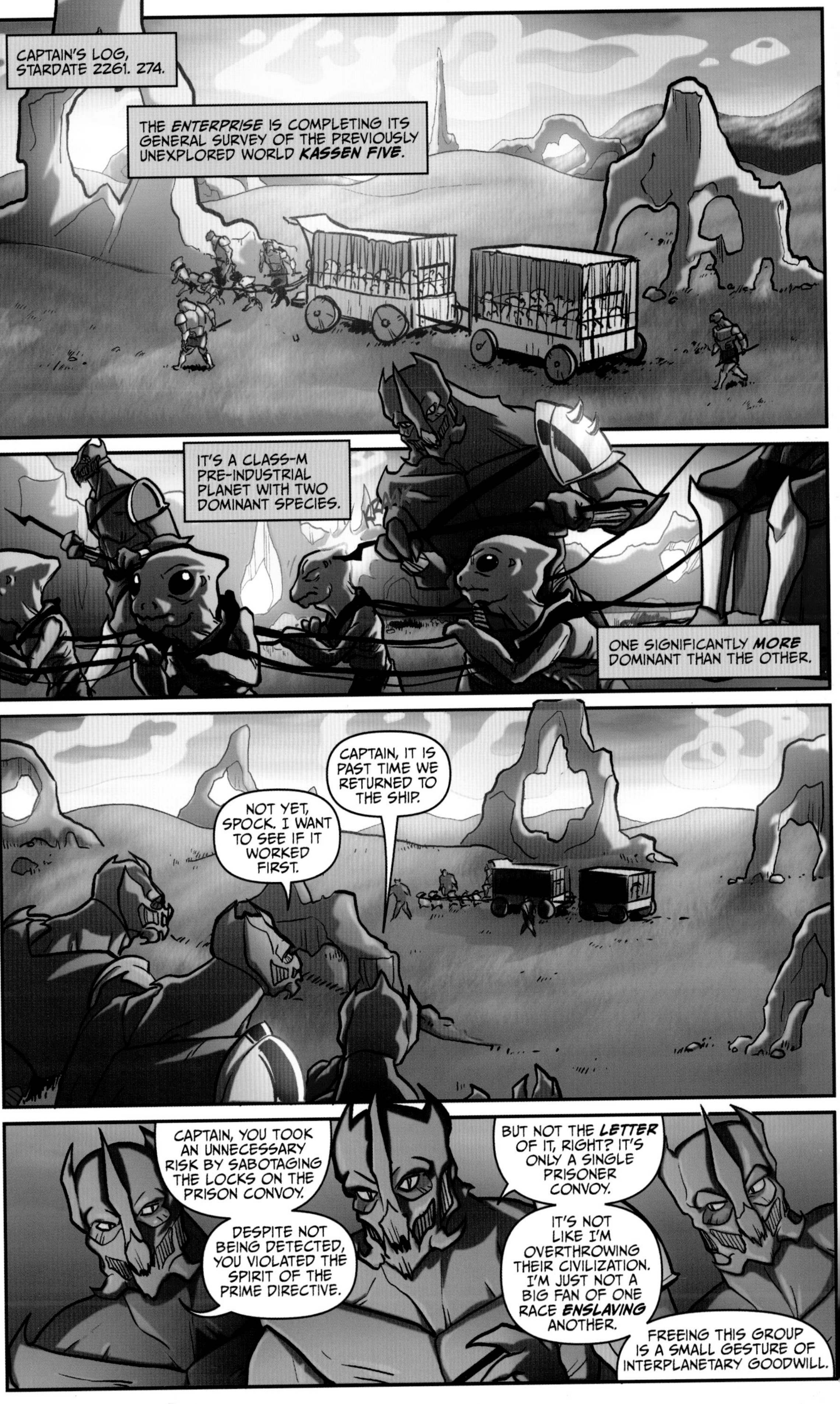
CAPTAIN'S LOG, STARDATE 2261. 274.
THE *ENTERPRISE* IS COMPLETING ITS GENERAL SURVEY OF THE PREVIOUSLY UNEXPLORED WORLD ***KASSEN FIVE***.
IT'S A CLASS-M PRE-INDUSTRIAL PLANET WITH TWO DOMINANT SPECIES.
ONE SIGNIFICANTLY ***MORE*** DOMINANT THAN THE OTHER.
CAPTAIN, IT IS PAST TIME WE RETURNED TO THE SHIP.
NOT YET, SPOCK. I WANT TO SEE IF IT WORKED FIRST.
CAPTAIN, YOU TOOK AN UNNECESSARY RISK BY SABOTAGING THE LOCKS ON THE PRISON CONVOY.
DESPITE NOT BEING DETECTED, YOU VIOLATED THE SPIRIT OF THE PRIME DIRECTIVE.
BUT NOT THE ***LETTER*** OF IT, RIGHT? IT'S ONLY A SINGLE PRISONER CONVOY.
IT'S NOT LIKE I'M OVERTHROWING THEIR CIVILIZATION. I'M JUST NOT A BIG FAN OF ONE RACE ***ENSLAVING*** ANOTHER.
FREEING THIS GROUP IS A SMALL GESTURE OF INTERPLANETARY GOODWILL.

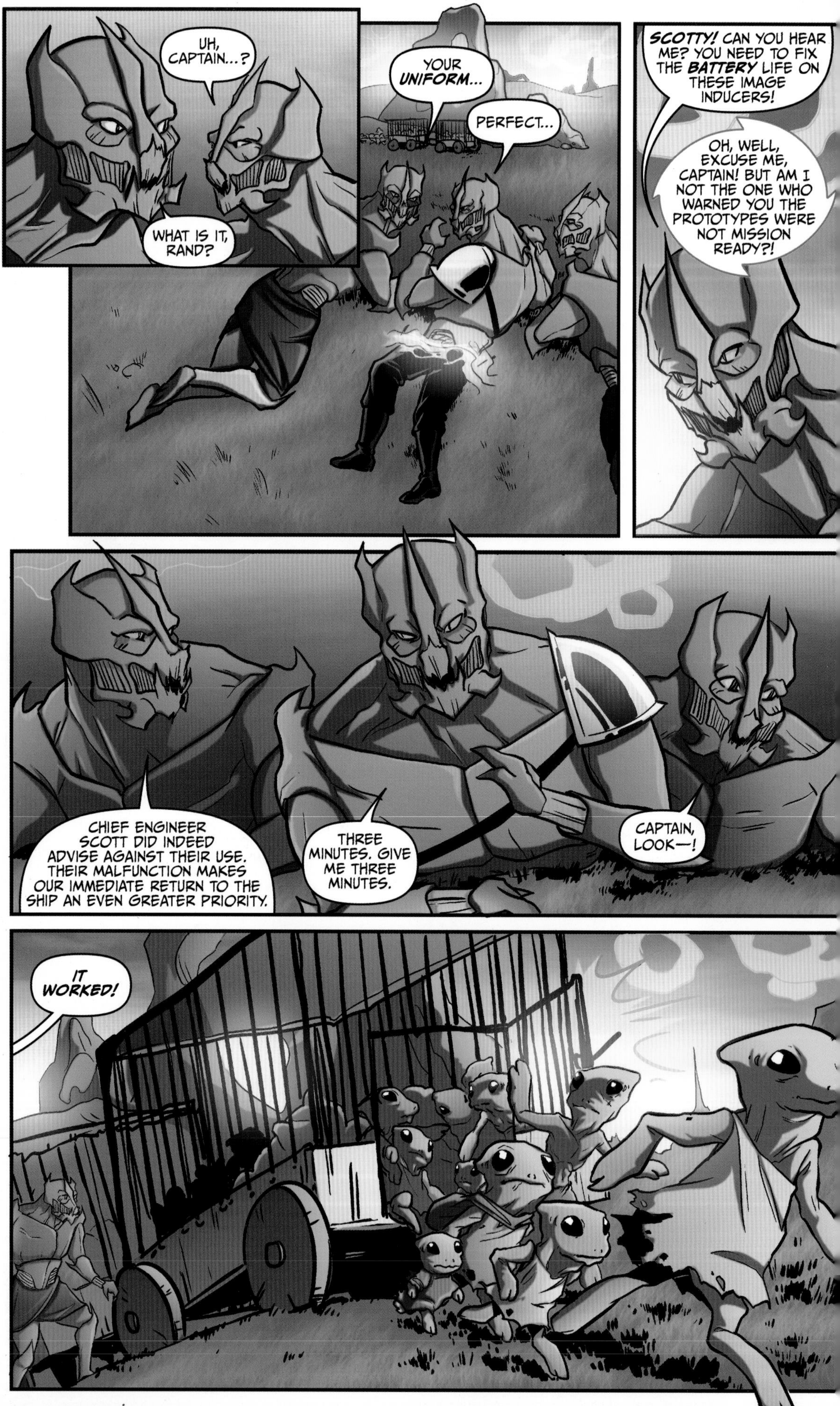
UH, CAPTAIN...?
WHAT IS IT, RAND?
YOUR UNIFORM...
PERFECT...
SCOTTY! CAN YOU HEAR ME? YOU NEED TO FIX THE BATTERY LIFE ON THESE IMAGE INDUCERS!
OH, WELL, EXCUSE ME, CAPTAIN! BUT AM I NOT THE ONE WHO WARNED YOU THE PROTOTYPES WERE NOT MISSION READY?!
CHIEF ENGINEER SCOTT DID INDEED ADVISE AGAINST THEIR USE. THEIR MALFUNCTION MAKES OUR IMMEDIATE RETURN TO THE SHIP AN EVEN GREATER PRIORITY.
THREE MINUTES. GIVE ME THREE MINUTES.
CAPTAIN, LOOK—!
IT WORKED!

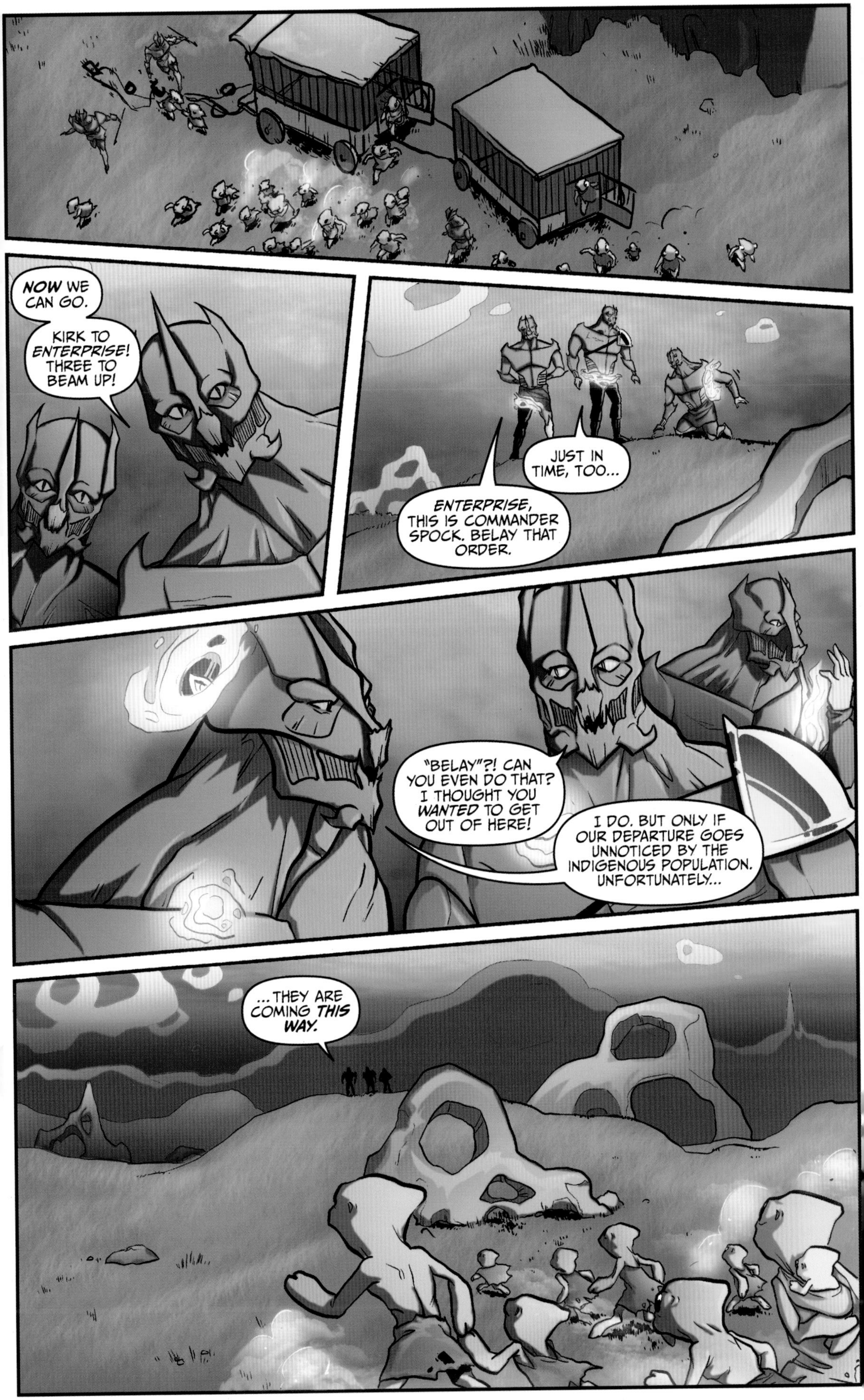
NOW WE CAN GO.
KIRK TO ENTERPRISE! THREE TO BEAM UP!
JUST IN TIME, TOO...
ENTERPRISE, THIS IS COMMANDER SPOCK. BELAY THAT ORDER.
"BELAY"?! CAN YOU EVEN DO THAT? I THOUGHT YOU WANTED TO GET OUT OF HERE!
I DO. BUT ONLY IF OUR DEPARTURE GOES UNNOTICED BY THE INDIGENOUS POPULATION. UNFORTUNATELY...
...THEY ARE COMING THIS WAY.

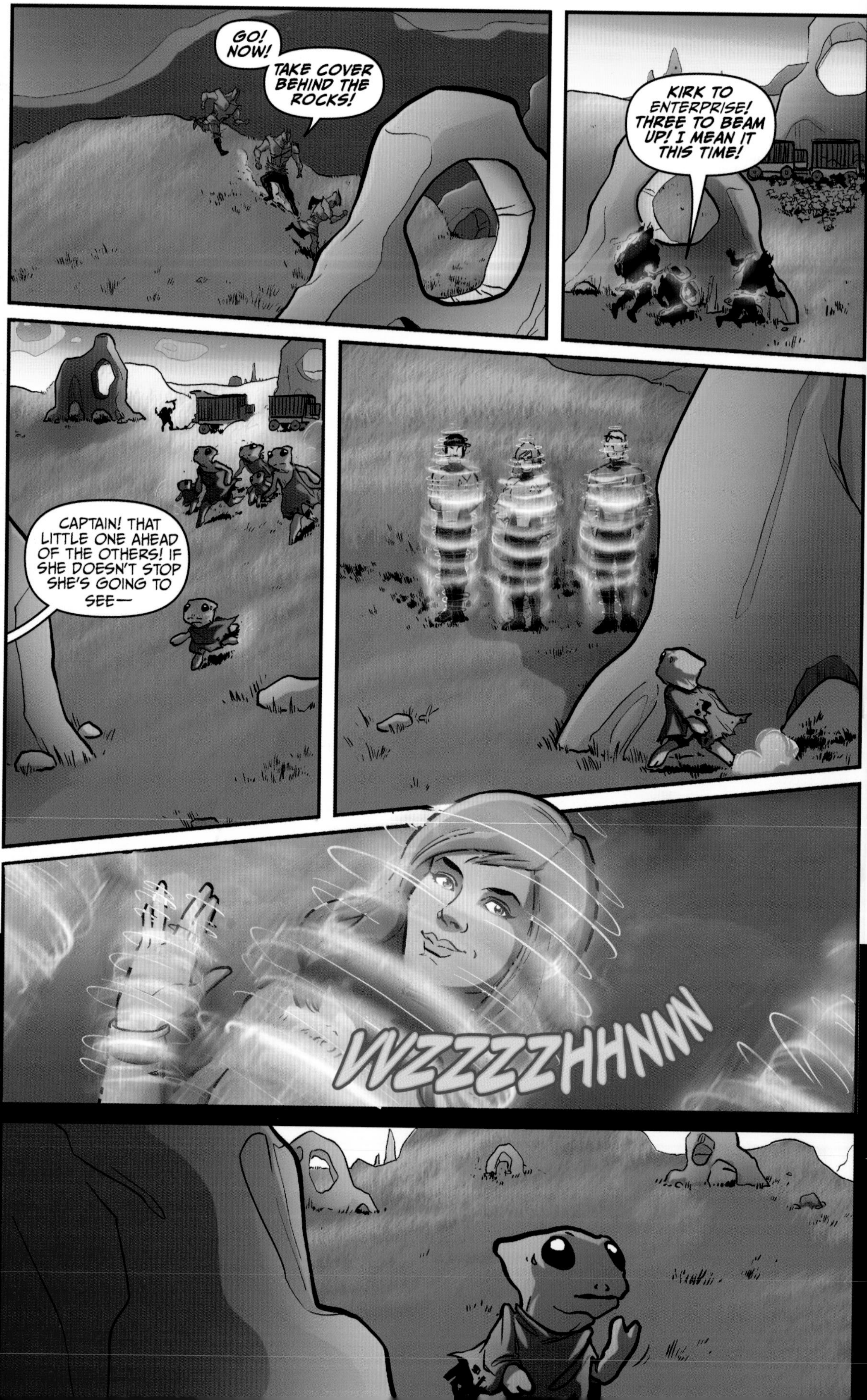
GO! NOW!
TAKE COVER BEHIND THE ROCKS!
KIRK TO ENTERPRISE! THREE TO BEAM UP! I MEAN IT THIS TIME!
CAPTAIN! THAT LITTLE ONE AHEAD OF THE OTHERS! IF SHE DOESN'T STOP SHE'S GOING TO SEE—
WZZZZZHHNNN

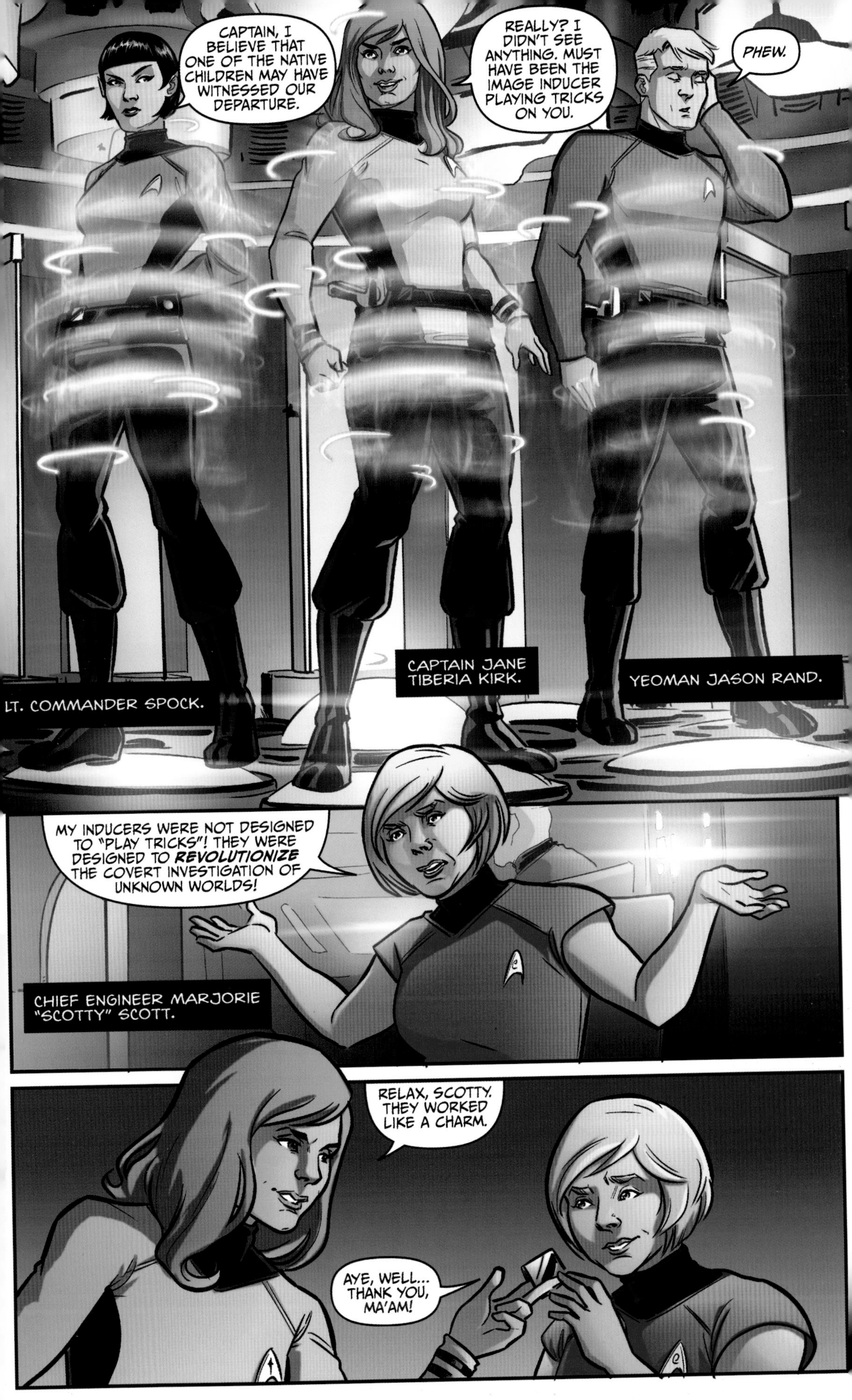
CAPTAIN, I BELIEVE THAT ONE OF THE NATIVE CHILDREN MAY HAVE WITNESSED OUR DEPARTURE.
REALLY? I DIDN'T SEE ANYTHING. MUST HAVE BEEN THE IMAGE INDUCER PLAYING TRICKS ON YOU.
PHEW.
LT. COMMANDER SPOCK.
CAPTAIN JANE TIBERIA KIRK.
YEOMAN JASON RAND.
MY INDUCERS WERE NOT DESIGNED TO "PLAY TRICKS"! THEY WERE DESIGNED TO REVOLUTIONIZE THE COVERT INVESTIGATION OF UNKNOWN WORLDS!
CHIEF ENGINEER MARJORIE "SCOTTY" SCOTT.
RELAX, SCOTTY. THEY WORKED LIKE A CHARM.
AYE, WELL... THANK YOU, MA'AM!

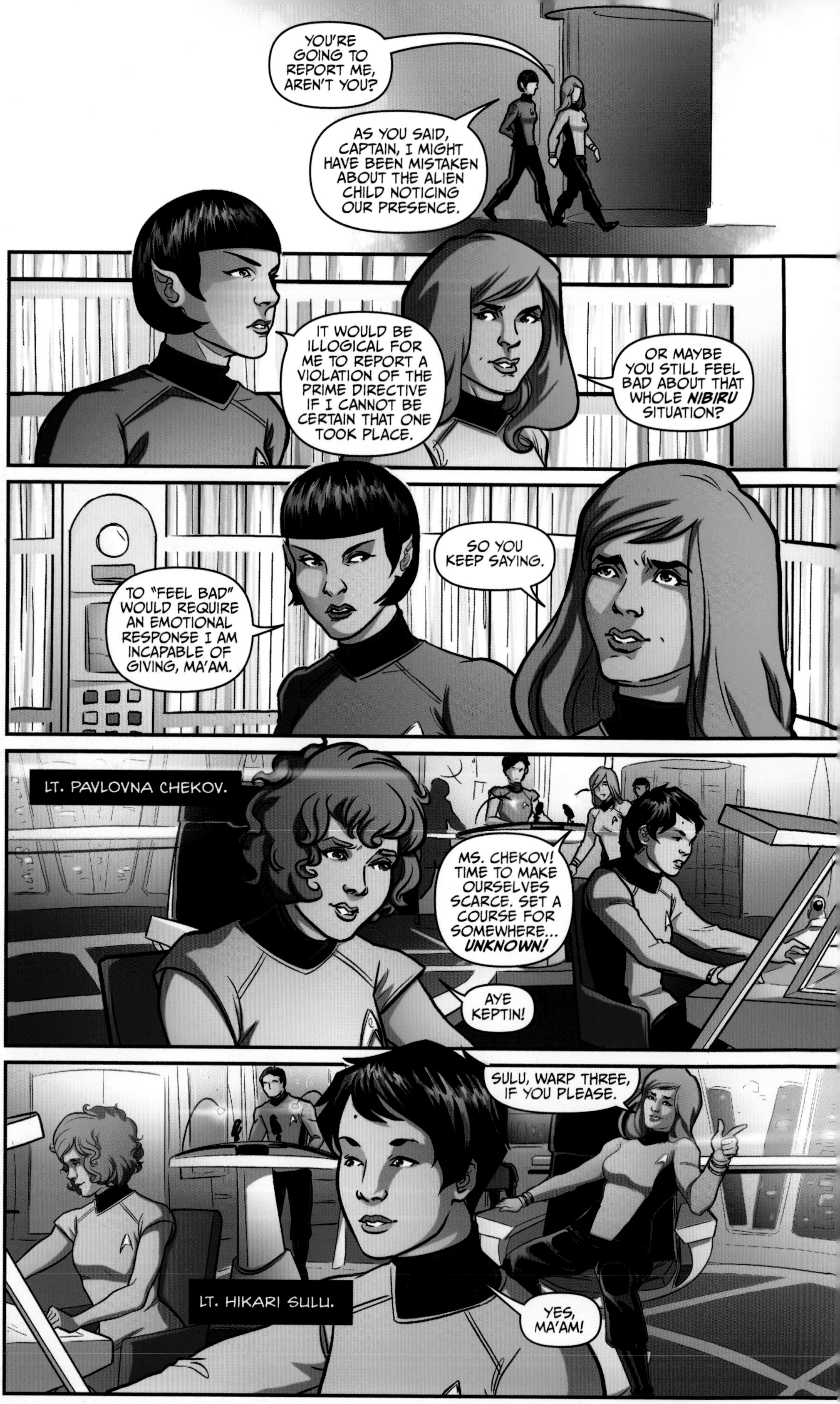
YOU'RE GOING TO REPORT ME, AREN'T YOU?
AS YOU SAID, CAPTAIN, I MIGHT HAVE BEEN MISTAKEN ABOUT THE ALIEN CHILD NOTICING OUR PRESENCE.
IT WOULD BE ILLOGICAL FOR ME TO REPORT A VIOLATION OF THE PRIME DIRECTIVE IF I CANNOT BE CERTAIN THAT ONE TOOK PLACE.
OR MAYBE YOU STILL FEEL BAD ABOUT THAT WHOLE ***NIBIRU*** SITUATION?
TO "FEEL BAD" WOULD REQUIRE AN EMOTIONAL RESPONSE I AM INCAPABLE OF GIVING, MA'AM.
SO YOU KEEP SAYING.
LT. PAVLOVNA CHEKOV.
MS. CHEKOV! TIME TO MAKE OURSELVES SCARCE. SET A COURSE FOR SOMEWHERE... ***UNKNOWN!***
AYE KEPTIN!
SULU, WARP THREE, IF YOU PLEASE.
LT. HIKARI SULU.
YES, MA'AM!

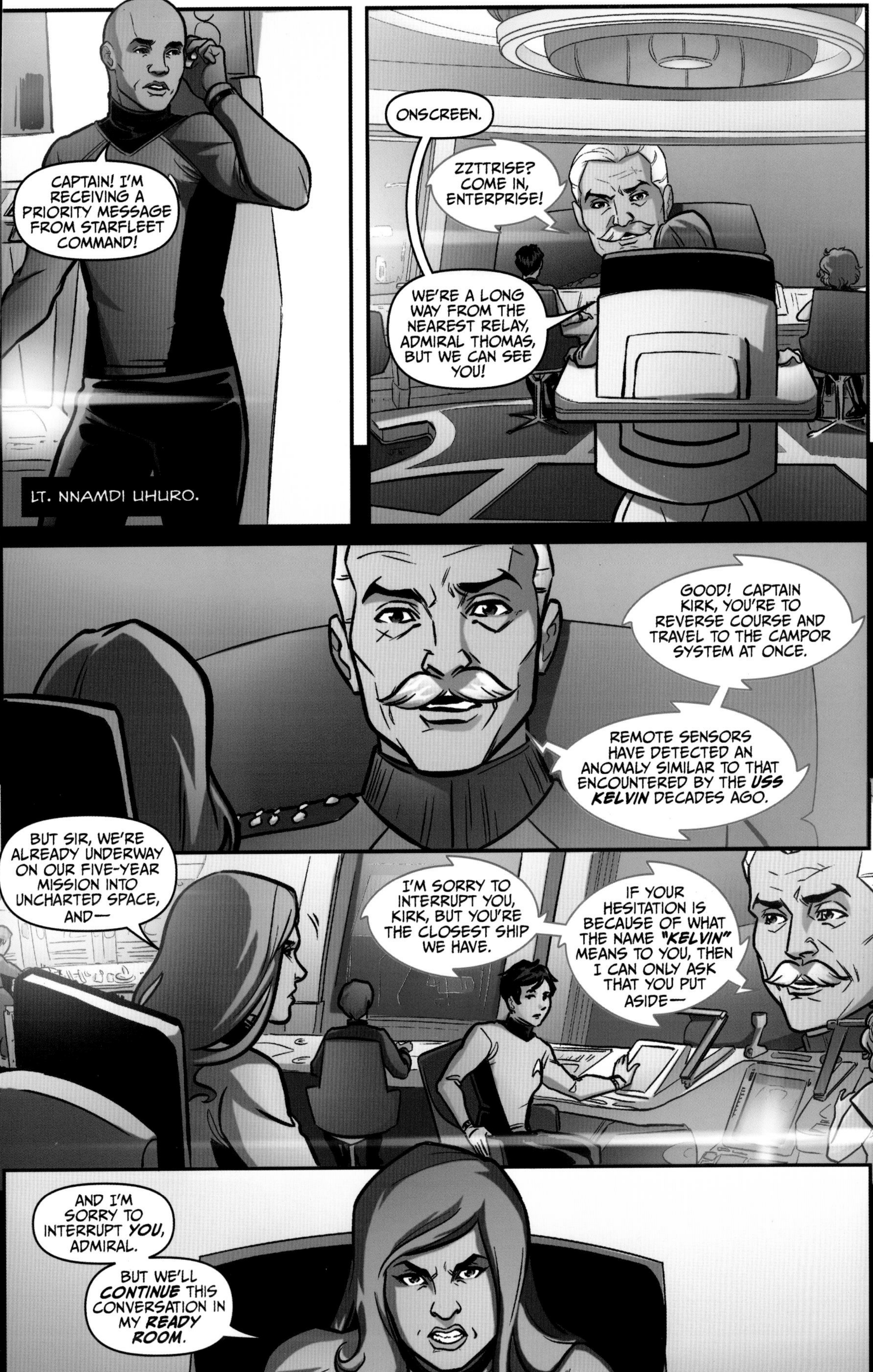
CAPTAIN! I'M RECEIVING A PRIORITY MESSAGE FROM STARFLEET COMMAND!
LT. NNAMDI UHURO.
ONSCREEN.
ZZTTRISE? COME IN, ENTERPRISE!
WE'RE A LONG WAY FROM THE NEAREST RELAY, ADMIRAL THOMAS, BUT WE CAN SEE YOU!
GOOD! CAPTAIN KIRK, YOU'RE TO REVERSE COURSE AND TRAVEL TO THE CAMPOR SYSTEM AT ONCE.
REMOTE SENSORS HAVE DETECTED AN ANOMALY SIMILAR TO THAT ENCOUNTERED BY THE USS KELVIN DECADES AGO.
BUT SIR, WE'RE ALREADY UNDERWAY ON OUR FIVE-YEAR MISSION INTO UNCHARTED SPACE, AND—
I'M SORRY TO INTERRUPT YOU, KIRK, BUT YOU'RE THE CLOSEST SHIP WE HAVE.
IF YOUR HESITATION IS BECAUSE OF WHAT THE NAME "KELVIN" MEANS TO YOU, THEN I CAN ONLY ASK THAT YOU PUT ASIDE—
AND I'M SORRY TO INTERRUPT YOU, ADMIRAL.
BUT WE'LL CONTINUE THIS CONVERSATION IN MY READY ROOM.

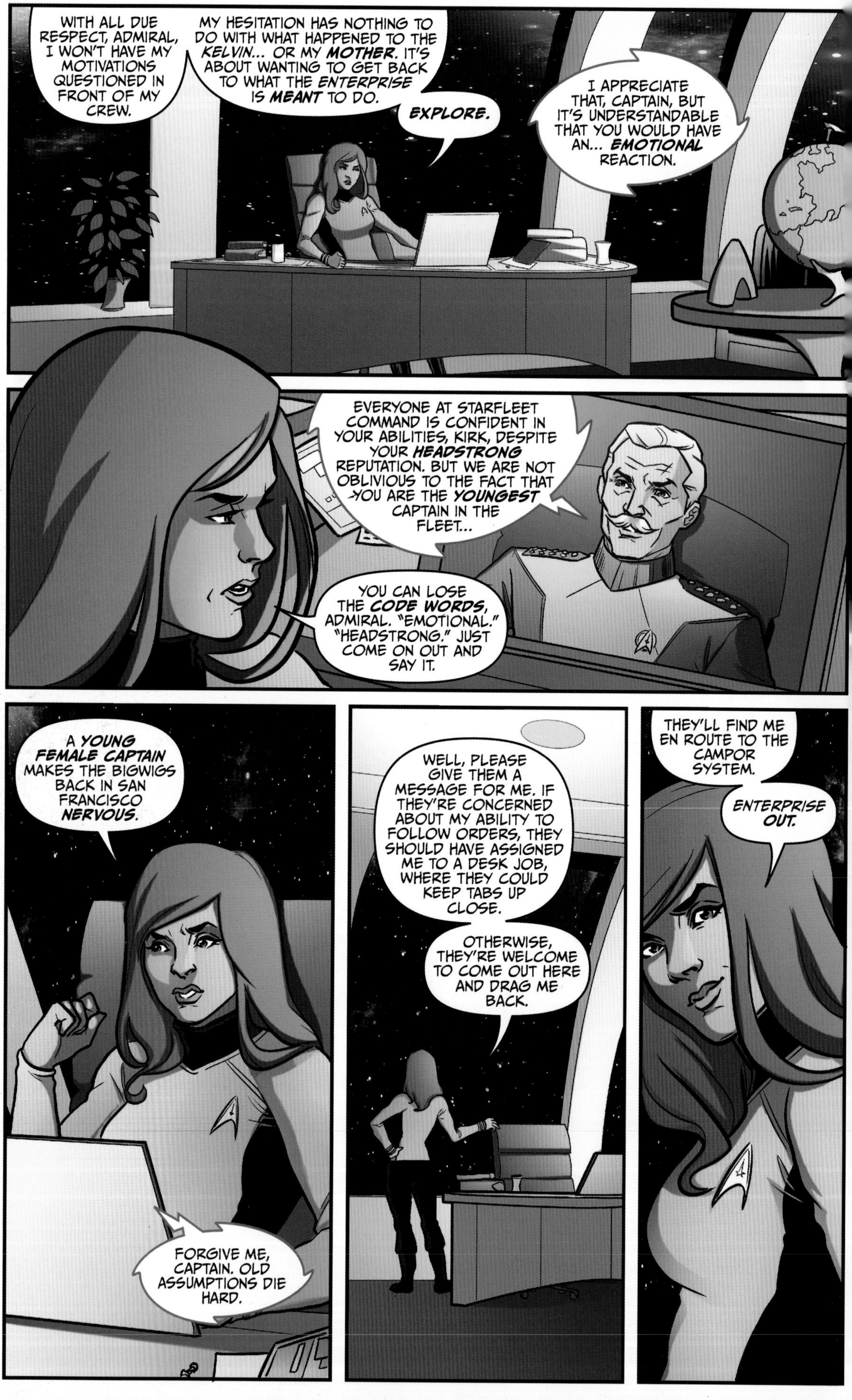
WITH ALL DUE RESPECT, ADMIRAL, I WON'T HAVE MY MOTIVATIONS QUESTIONED IN FRONT OF MY CREW.
MY HESITATION HAS NOTHING TO DO WITH WHAT HAPPENED TO THE *KELVIN*... OR MY **MOTHER**. IT'S ABOUT WANTING TO GET BACK TO WHAT THE *ENTERPRISE* IS **MEANT** TO DO.
EXPLORE.
I APPRECIATE THAT, CAPTAIN, BUT IT'S UNDERSTANDABLE THAT YOU WOULD HAVE AN... **EMOTIONAL** REACTION.
EVERYONE AT STARFLEET COMMAND IS CONFIDENT IN YOUR ABILITIES, KIRK, DESPITE YOUR **HEADSTRONG** REPUTATION. BUT WE ARE NOT OBLIVIOUS TO THE FACT THAT YOU ARE THE **YOUNGEST** CAPTAIN IN THE FLEET...
YOU CAN LOSE THE **CODE WORDS**, ADMIRAL. "EMOTIONAL." "HEADSTRONG." JUST COME ON OUT AND SAY IT.
A **YOUNG FEMALE CAPTAIN** MAKES THE BIGWIGS BACK IN SAN FRANCISCO **NERVOUS**.
FORGIVE ME, CAPTAIN. OLD ASSUMPTIONS DIE HARD.
WELL, PLEASE GIVE THEM A MESSAGE FOR ME. IF THEY'RE CONCERNED ABOUT MY ABILITY TO FOLLOW ORDERS, THEY SHOULD HAVE ASSIGNED ME TO A DESK JOB, WHERE THEY COULD KEEP TABS UP CLOSE.
OTHERWISE, THEY'RE WELCOME TO COME OUT HERE AND DRAG ME BACK.
THEY'LL FIND ME EN ROUTE TO THE CAMPOR SYSTEM.
ENTERPRISE **OUT.**

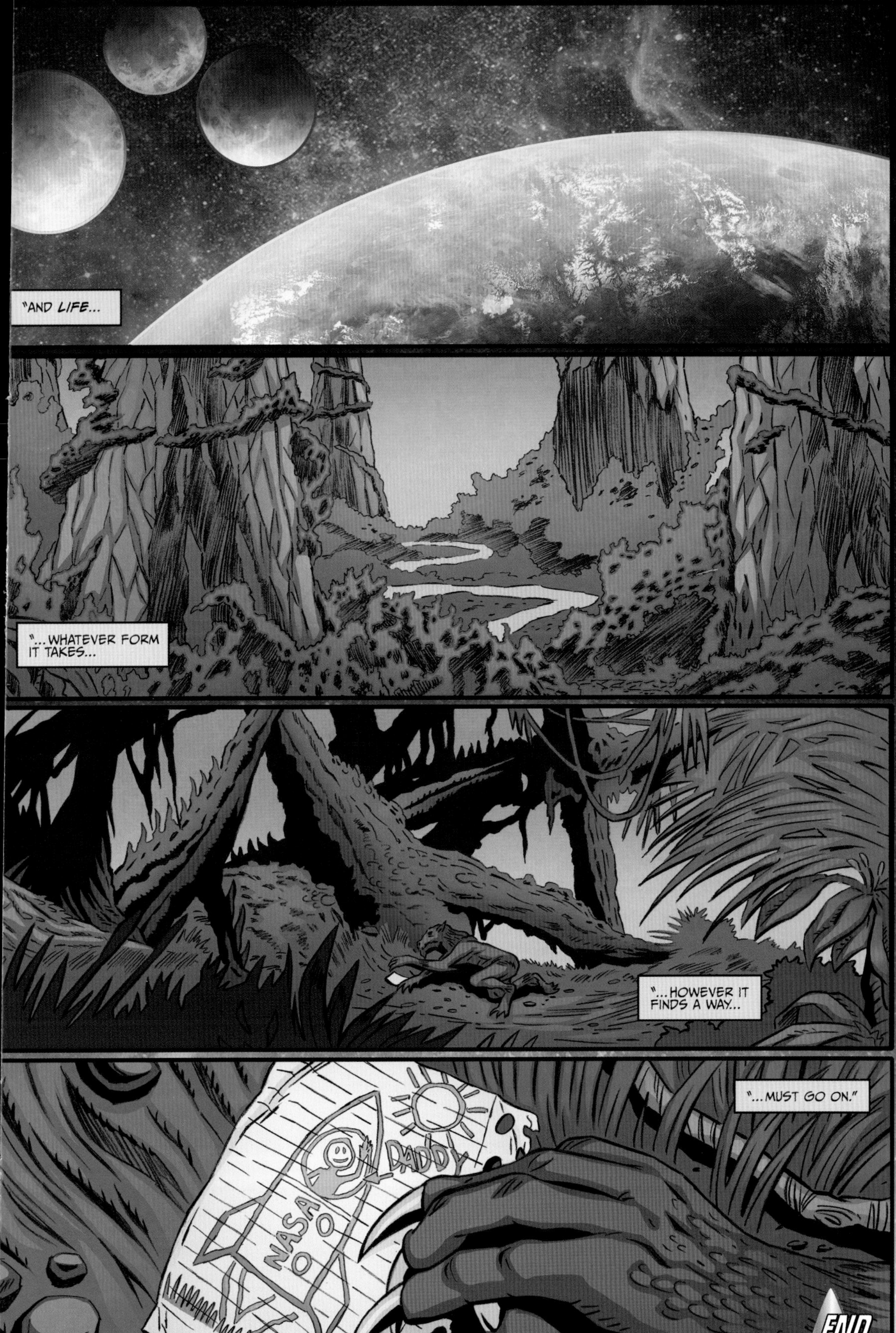
"AND LIFE...
"...WHATEVER FORM IT TAKES...
"...HOWEVER IT FINDS A WAY...
"...MUST GO ON."
DADDY
NASA
END.

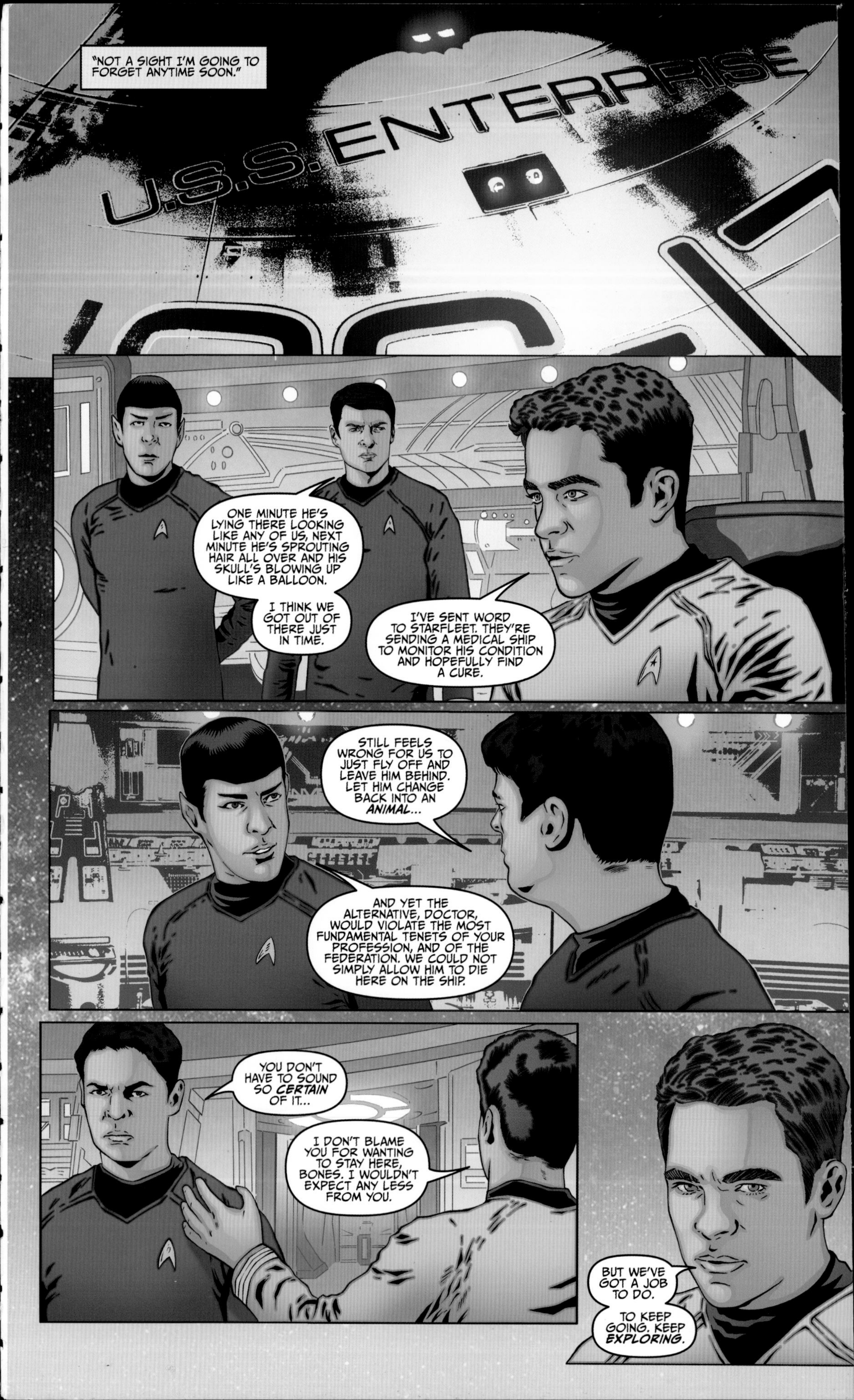
"NOT A SIGHT I'M GOING TO FORGET ANYTIME SOON."
U.S.S. ENTERPRISE
ONE MINUTE HE'S LYING THERE LOOKING LIKE ANY OF US, NEXT MINUTE HE'S SPROUTING HAIR ALL OVER AND HIS SKULL'S BLOWING UP LIKE A BALLOON.
I THINK WE GOT OUT OF THERE JUST IN TIME.
I'VE SENT WORD TO STARFLEET. THEY'RE SENDING A MEDICAL SHIP TO MONITOR HIS CONDITION AND HOPEFULLY FIND A CURE.
STILL FEELS WRONG FOR US TO JUST FLY OFF AND LEAVE HIM BEHIND. LET HIM CHANGE BACK INTO AN *ANIMAL*...
AND YET THE ALTERNATIVE, DOCTOR, WOULD VIOLATE THE MOST FUNDAMENTAL TENETS OF YOUR PROFESSION, AND OF THE FEDERATION. WE COULD NOT SIMPLY ALLOW HIM TO DIE HERE ON THE SHIP.
YOU DON'T HAVE TO SOUND SO *CERTAIN* OF IT...
I DON'T BLAME YOU FOR WANTING TO STAY HERE, BONES. I WOULDN'T EXPECT ANY LESS FROM YOU.
BUT WE'VE GOT A JOB TO DO.
TO KEEP GOING. KEEP *EXPLORING*.

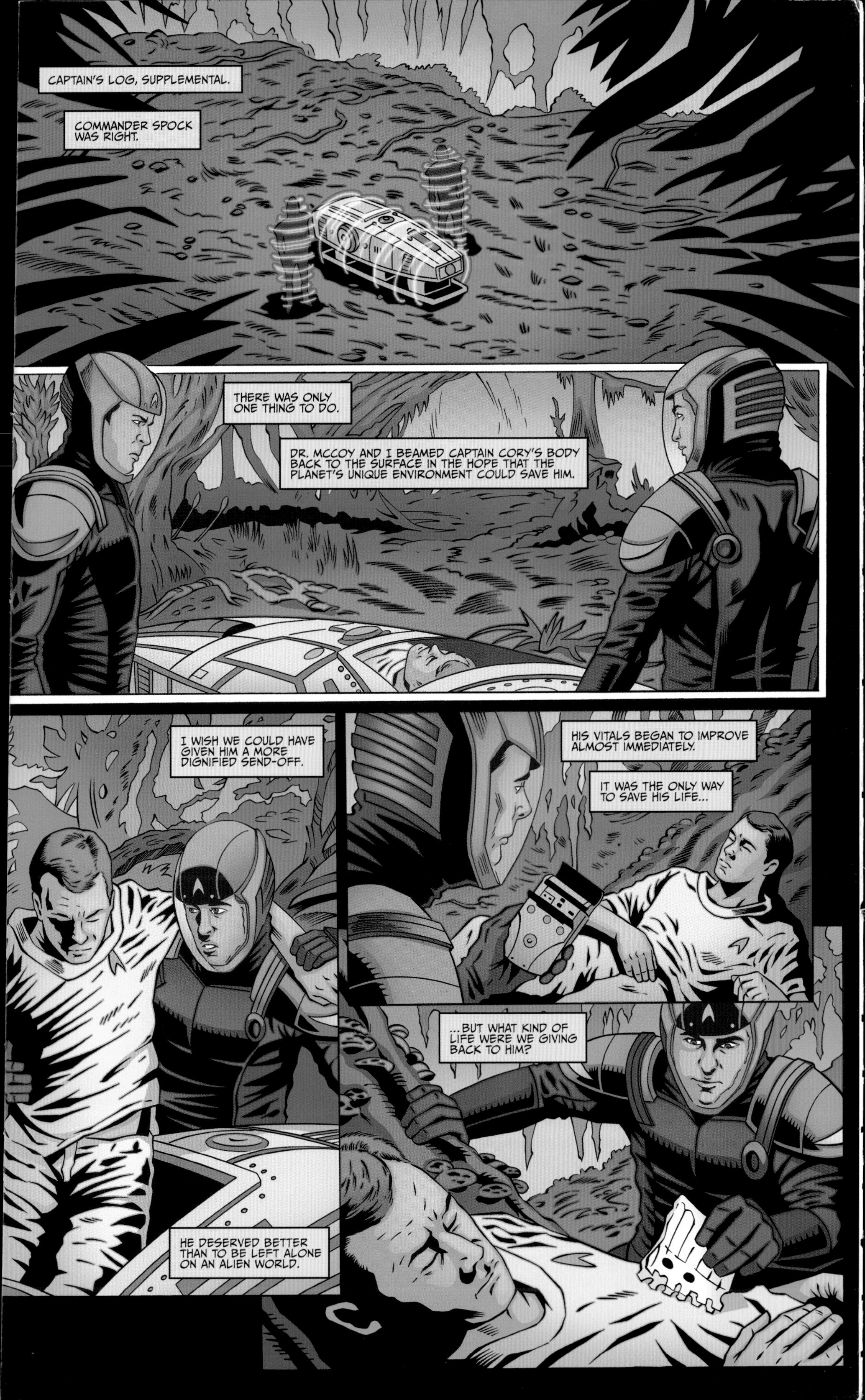
CAPTAIN'S LOG, SUPPLEMENTAL.
COMMANDER SPOCK WAS RIGHT.
THERE WAS ONLY ONE THING TO DO.
DR. MCCOY AND I BEAMED CAPTAIN CORY'S BODY BACK TO THE SURFACE IN THE HOPE THAT THE PLANET'S UNIQUE ENVIRONMENT COULD SAVE HIM.
I WISH WE COULD HAVE GIVEN HIM A MORE DIGNIFIED SEND-OFF.
HE DESERVED BETTER THAN TO BE LEFT ALONE ON AN ALIEN WORLD.
HIS VITALS BEGAN TO IMPROVE ALMOST IMMEDIATELY.
IT WAS THE ONLY WAY TO SAVE HIS LIFE...
...BUT WHAT KIND OF LIFE WERE WE GIVING BACK TO HIM?

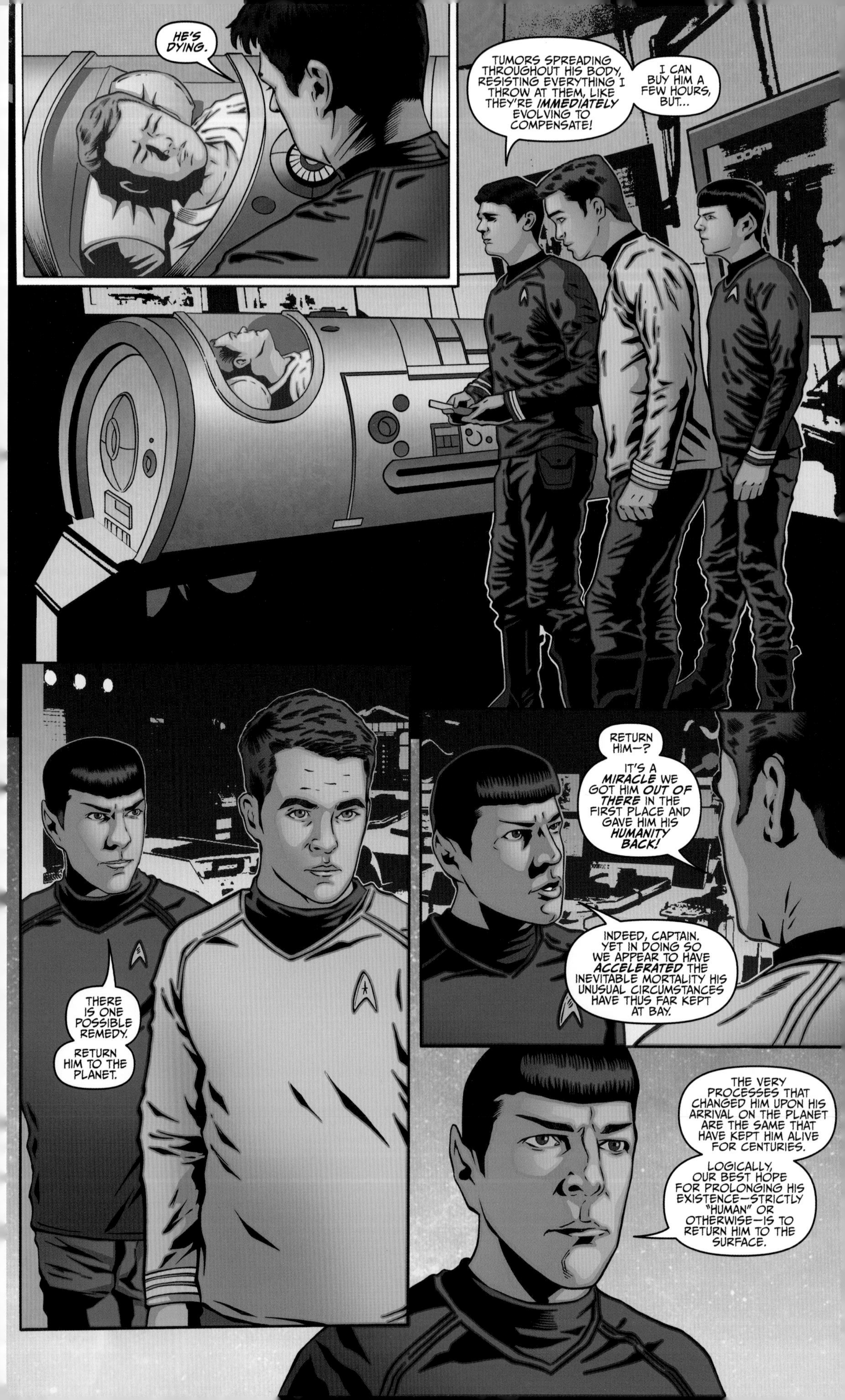
HE'S DYING.
TUMORS SPREADING THROUGHOUT HIS BODY, RESISTING EVERYTHING I THROW AT THEM, LIKE THEY'RE IMMEDIATELY EVOLVING TO COMPENSATE!
I CAN BUY HIM A FEW HOURS, BUT...
THERE IS ONE POSSIBLE REMEDY.
RETURN HIM TO THE PLANET.
RETURN HIM—?
IT'S A MIRACLE WE GOT HIM OUT OF THERE IN THE FIRST PLACE AND GAVE HIM HIS HUMANITY BACK!
INDEED, CAPTAIN. YET IN DOING SO WE APPEAR TO HAVE ACCELERATED THE INEVITABLE MORTALITY HIS UNUSUAL CIRCUMSTANCES HAVE THUS FAR KEPT AT BAY.
THE VERY PROCESSES THAT CHANGED HIM UPON HIS ARRIVAL ON THE PLANET ARE THE SAME THAT HAVE KEPT HIM ALIVE FOR CENTURIES.
LOGICALLY, OUR BEST HOPE FOR PROLONGING HIS EXISTENCE—STRICTLY "HUMAN" OR OTHERWISE—IS TO RETURN HIM TO THE SURFACE.

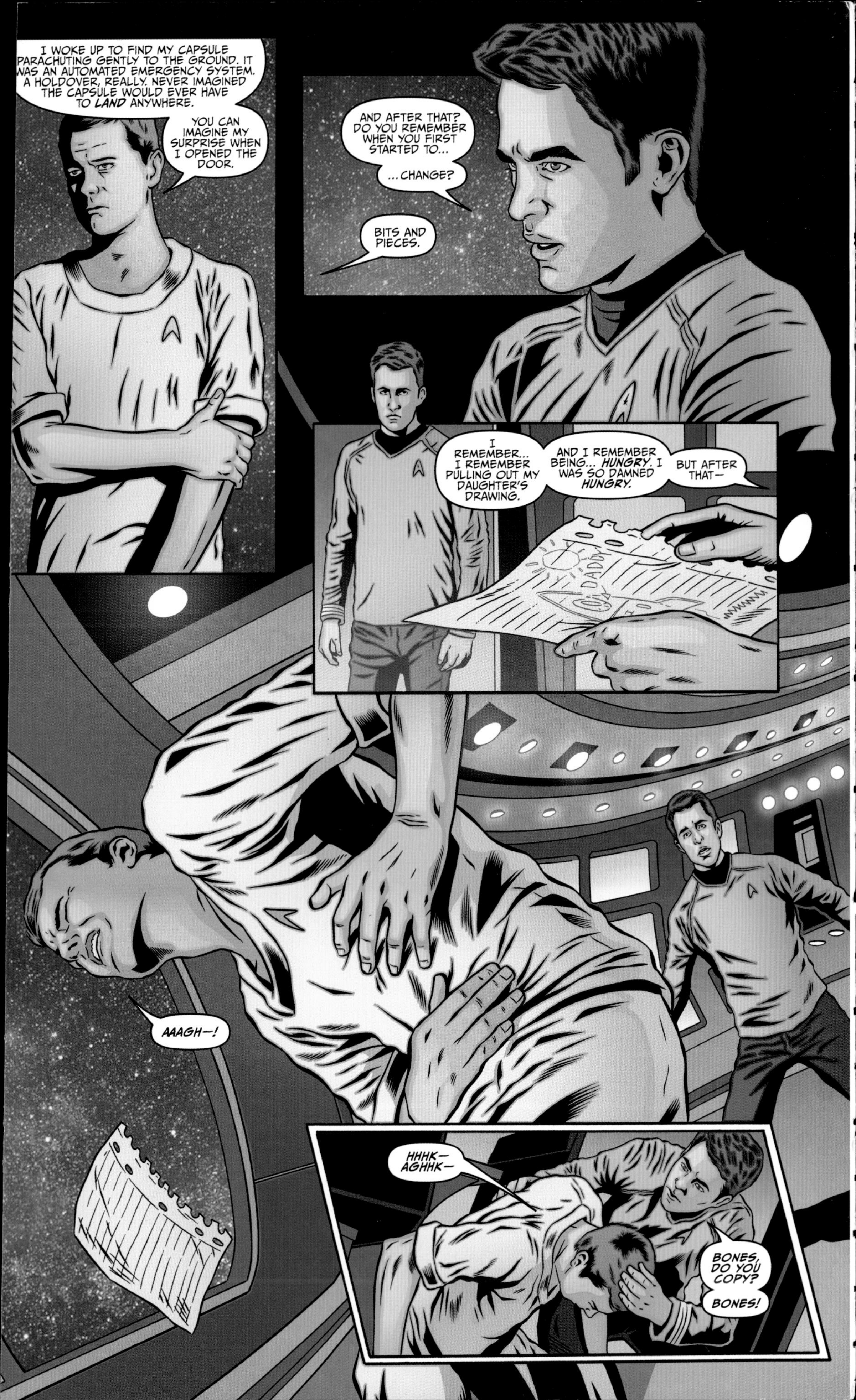
I WOKE UP TO FIND MY CAPSULE PARACHUTING GENTLY TO THE GROUND. IT WAS AN AUTOMATED EMERGENCY SYSTEM. A HOLDOVER, REALLY. NEVER IMAGINED THE CAPSULE WOULD EVER HAVE TO *LAND* ANYWHERE.
YOU CAN IMAGINE MY SURPRISE WHEN I OPENED THE DOOR.
AND AFTER THAT? DO YOU REMEMBER WHEN YOU FIRST STARTED TO...
...CHANGE?
BITS AND PIECES.
I REMEMBER... I REMEMBER PULLING OUT MY DAUGHTER'S DRAWING.
AND I REMEMBER BEING... *HUNGRY*. I WAS SO DAMNED *HUNGRY.*
BUT AFTER THAT—
DADDY
AAAGH—!
HHHK— AGHHK—
BONES, DO YOU COPY?
BONES!

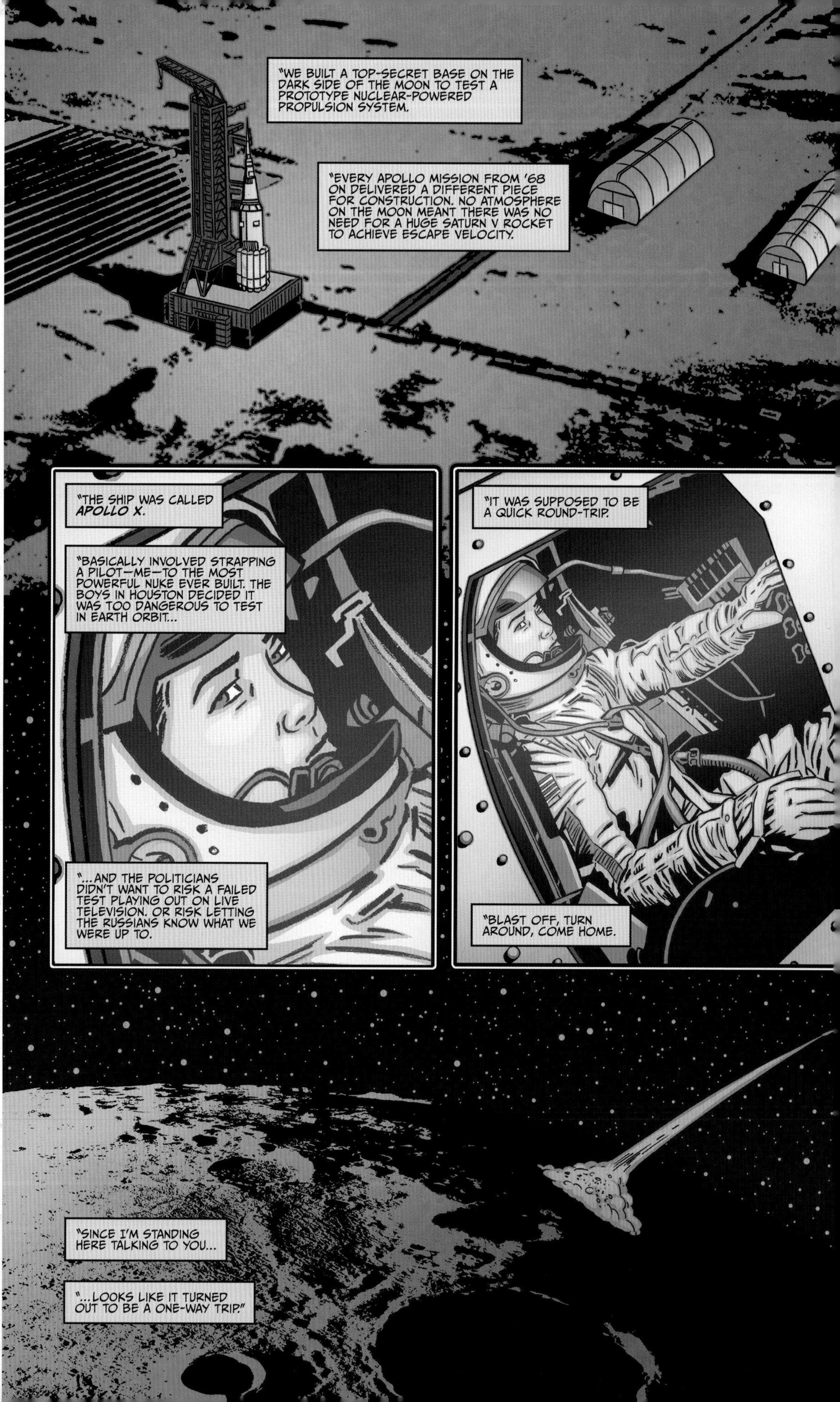
"WE BUILT A TOP-SECRET BASE ON THE DARK SIDE OF THE MOON TO TEST A PROTOTYPE NUCLEAR-POWERED PROPULSION SYSTEM.
"EVERY APOLLO MISSION FROM '68 ON DELIVERED A DIFFERENT PIECE FOR CONSTRUCTION. NO ATMOSPHERE ON THE MOON MEANT THERE WAS NO NEED FOR A HUGE SATURN V ROCKET TO ACHIEVE ESCAPE VELOCITY.
"THE SHIP WAS CALLED *APOLLO X*.
"BASICALLY INVOLVED STRAPPING A PILOT—ME—TO THE MOST POWERFUL NUKE EVER BUILT. THE BOYS IN HOUSTON DECIDED IT WAS TOO DANGEROUS TO TEST IN EARTH ORBIT...
"...AND THE POLITICIANS DIDN'T WANT TO RISK A FAILED TEST PLAYING OUT ON LIVE TELEVISION. OR RISK LETTING THE RUSSIANS KNOW WHAT WE WERE UP TO.
"IT WAS SUPPOSED TO BE A QUICK ROUND-TRIP.
"BLAST OFF, TURN AROUND, COME HOME.
"SINCE I'M STANDING HERE TALKING TO YOU...
"...LOOKS LIKE IT TURNED OUT TO BE A ONE-WAY TRIP."

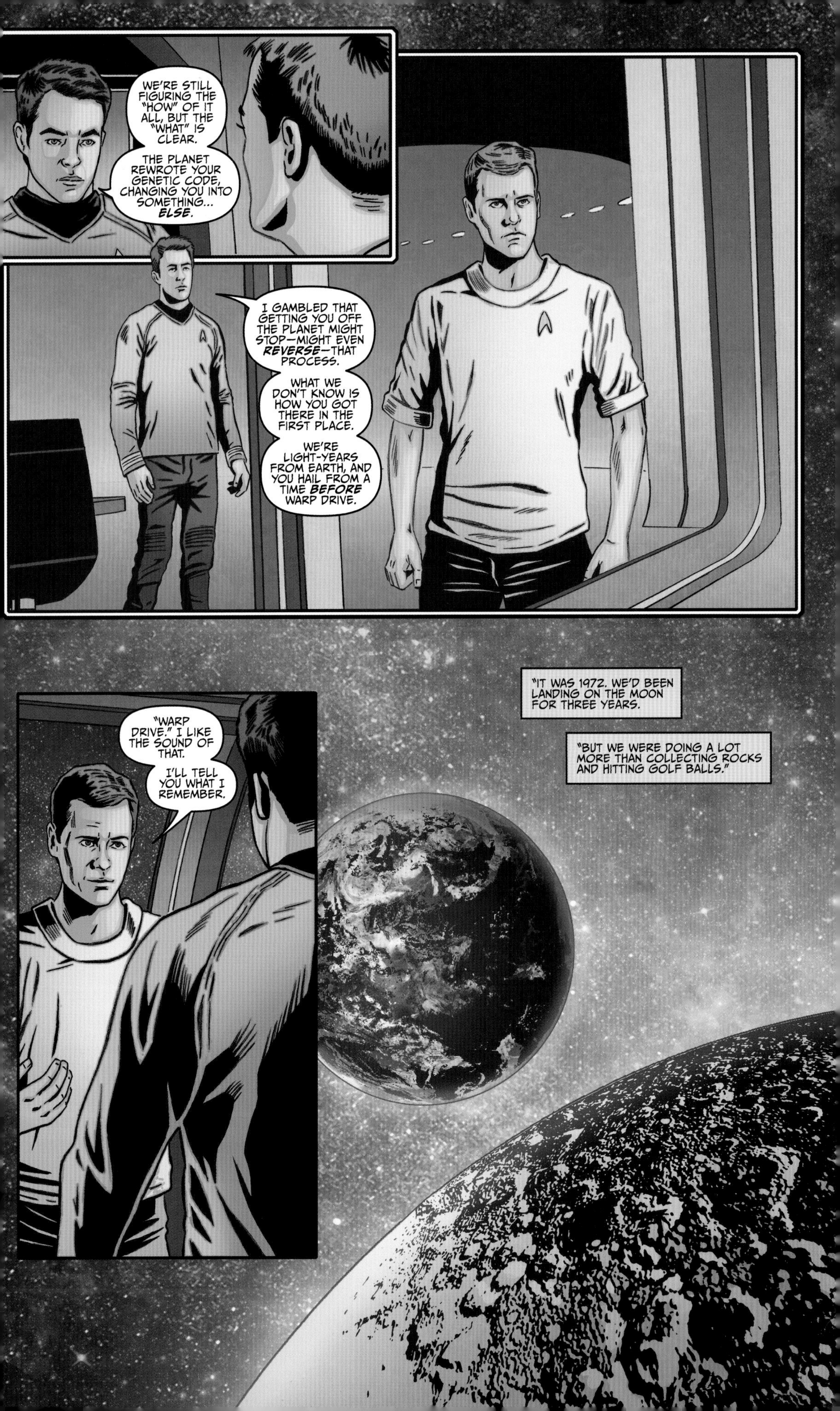
WE'RE STILL FIGURING THE "HOW" OF IT ALL, BUT THE "WHAT" IS CLEAR.
THE PLANET REWROTE YOUR GENETIC CODE, CHANGING YOU INTO SOMETHING... *ELSE*.
I GAMBLED THAT GETTING YOU OFF THE PLANET MIGHT STOP—MIGHT EVEN *REVERSE*—THAT PROCESS.
WHAT WE DON'T KNOW IS HOW YOU GOT THERE IN THE FIRST PLACE.
WE'RE LIGHT-YEARS FROM EARTH, AND YOU HAIL FROM A TIME *BEFORE* WARP DRIVE.
"WARP DRIVE." I LIKE THE SOUND OF THAT.
I'LL TELL YOU WHAT I REMEMBER.
"IT WAS 1972. WE'D BEEN LANDING ON THE MOON FOR THREE YEARS.
"BUT WE WERE DOING A LOT MORE THAN COLLECTING ROCKS AND HITTING GOLF BALLS."

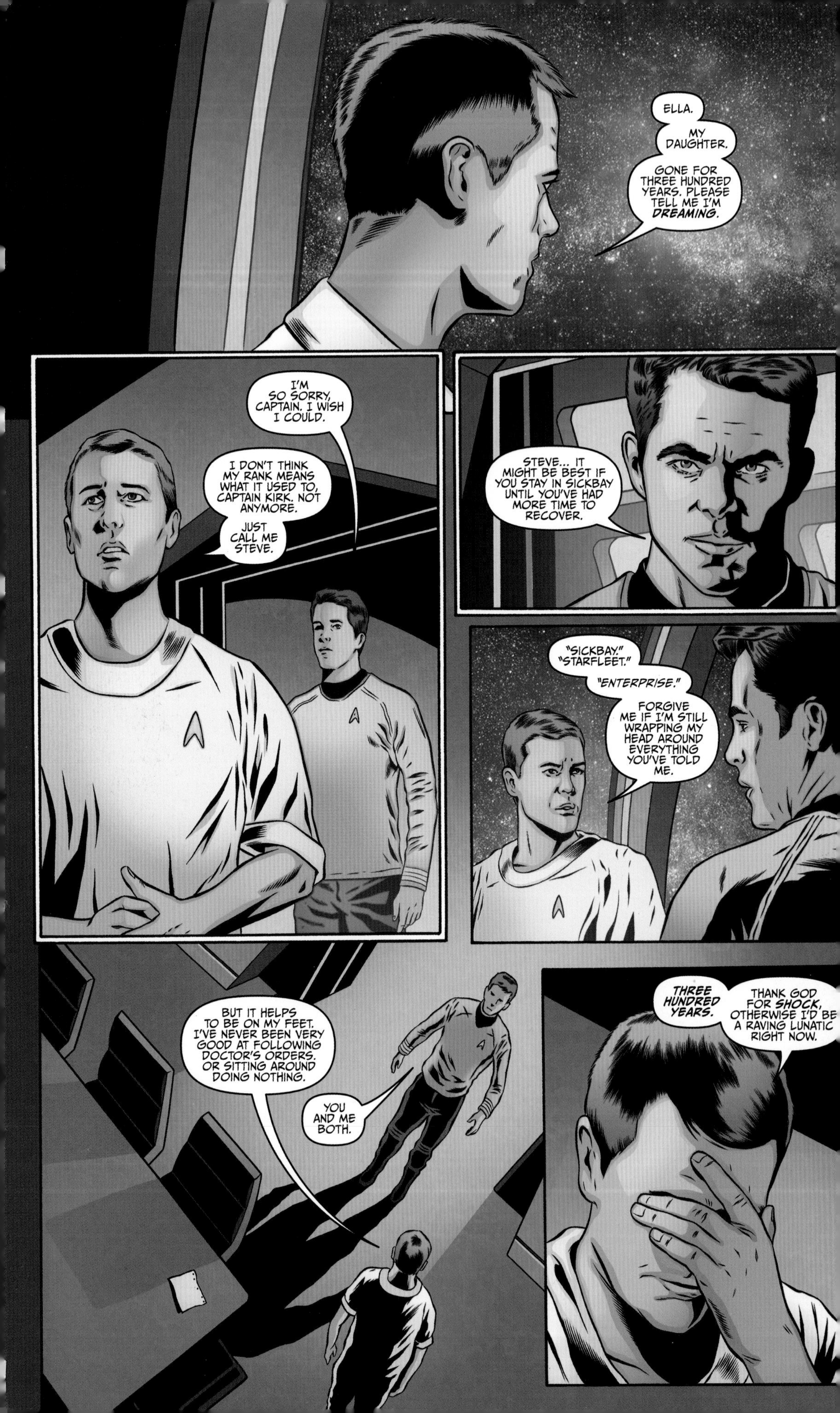
ELLA.
MY DAUGHTER.
GONE FOR THREE HUNDRED YEARS. PLEASE TELL ME I'M *DREAMING*.
I DON'T THINK MY RANK MEANS WHAT IT USED TO, CAPTAIN KIRK. NOT ANYMORE.
JUST CALL ME STEVE.
I'M SO SORRY, CAPTAIN. I WISH I COULD.
STEVE... IT MIGHT BE BEST IF YOU STAY IN SICKBAY UNTIL YOU'VE HAD MORE TIME TO RECOVER.
"SICKBAY." "STARFLEET."
"*ENTERPRISE*."
FORGIVE ME IF I'M STILL WRAPPING MY HEAD AROUND EVERYTHING YOU'VE TOLD ME.
BUT IT HELPS TO BE ON MY FEET. I'VE NEVER BEEN VERY GOOD AT FOLLOWING DOCTOR'S ORDERS. OR SITTING AROUND DOING NOTHING.
YOU AND ME BOTH.
THREE HUNDRED YEARS.
THANK GOD FOR *SHOCK*, OTHERWISE I'D BE A RAVING LUNATIC RIGHT NOW.

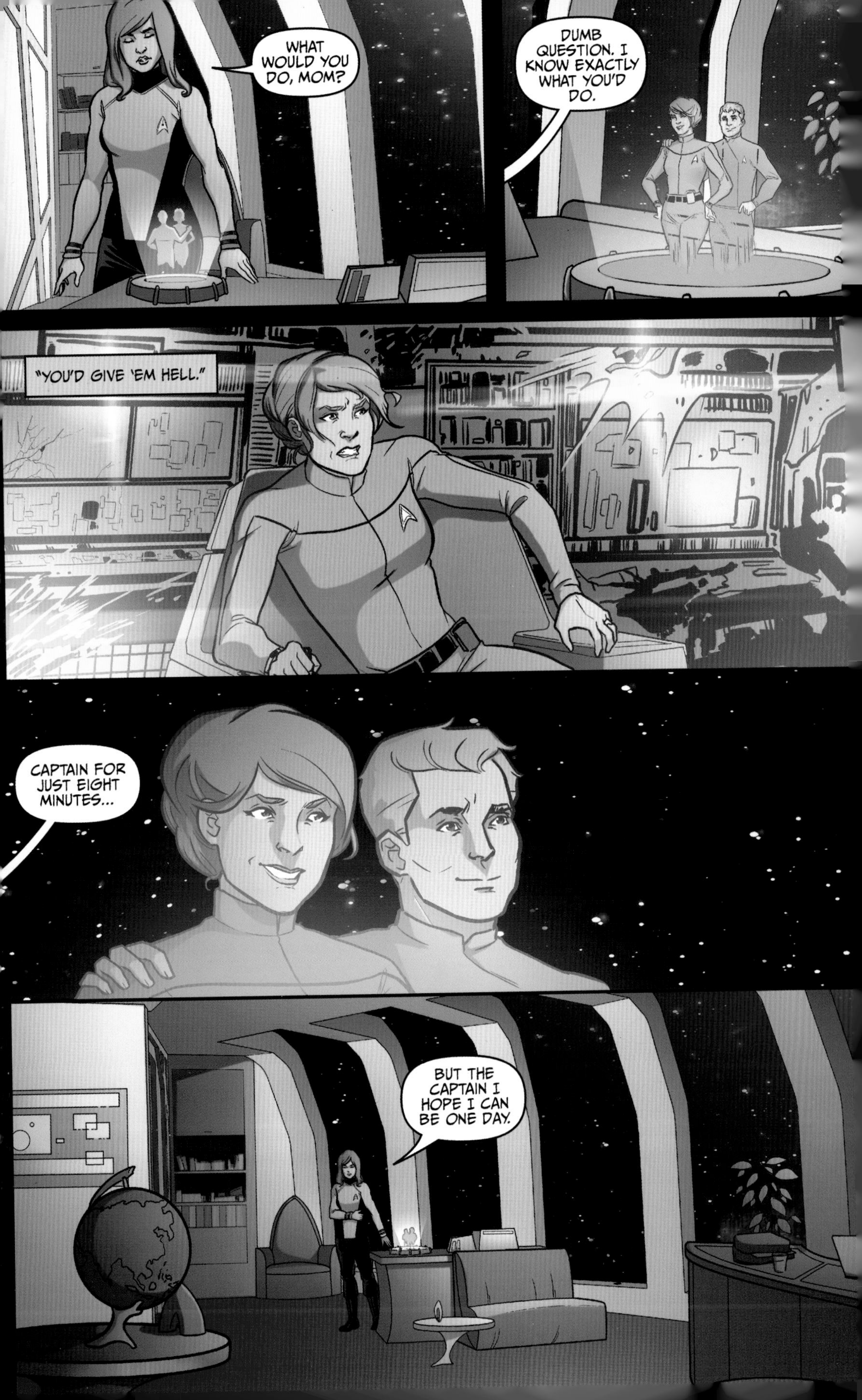
WHAT WOULD YOU DO, MOM?
DUMB QUESTION. I KNOW EXACTLY WHAT YOU'D DO.
"YOU'D GIVE 'EM HELL."
CAPTAIN FOR JUST EIGHT MINUTES...
BUT THE CAPTAIN I HOPE I CAN BE ONE DAY.

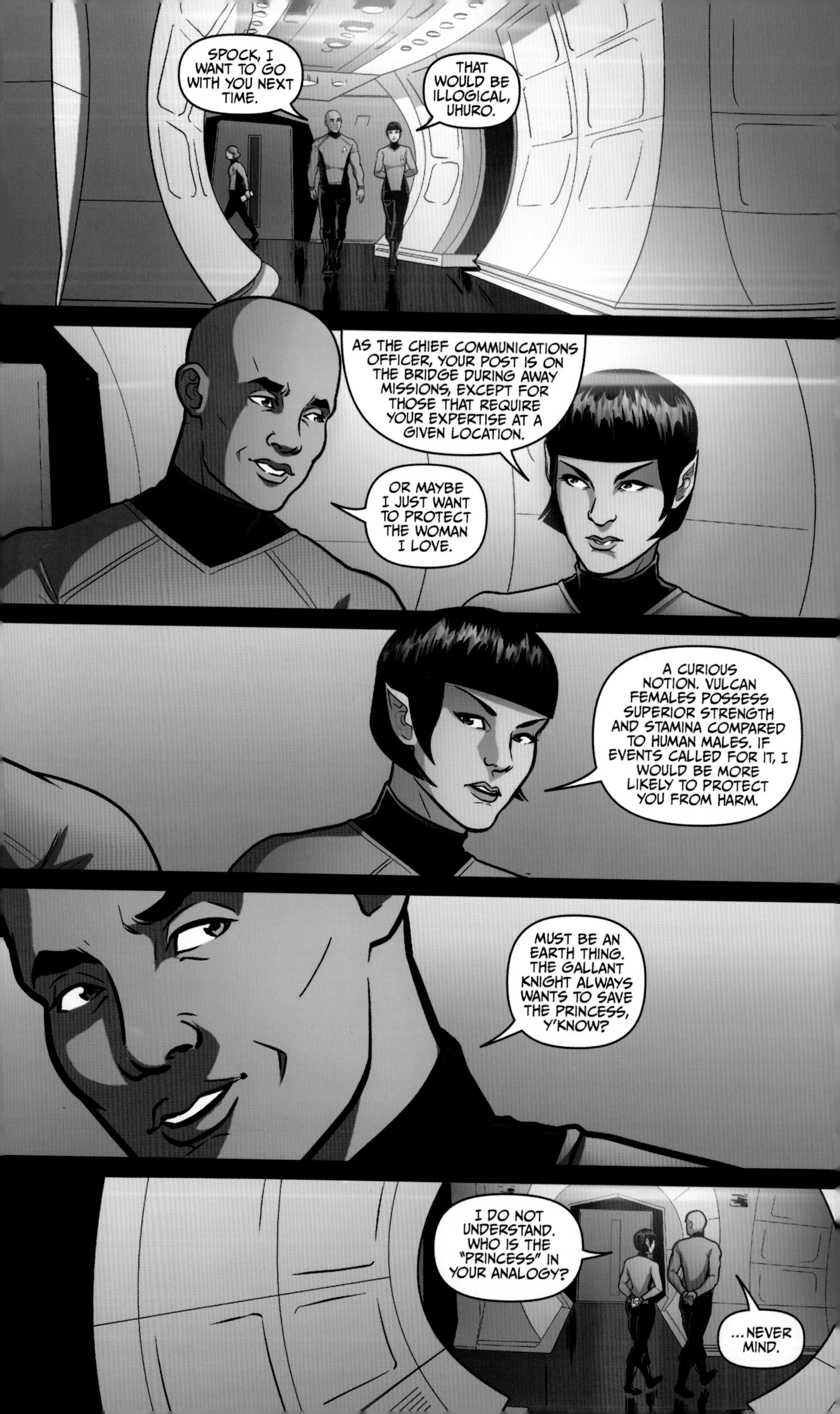
SPOCK, I WANT TO GO WITH YOU NEXT TIME.
THAT WOULD BE ILLOGICAL, UHURO.
AS THE CHIEF COMMUNICATIONS OFFICER, YOUR POST IS ON THE BRIDGE DURING AWAY MISSIONS, EXCEPT FOR THOSE THAT REQUIRE YOUR EXPERTISE AT A GIVEN LOCATION.
OR MAYBE I JUST WANT TO PROTECT THE WOMAN I LOVE.
A CURIOUS NOTION. VULCAN FEMALES POSSESS SUPERIOR STRENGTH AND STAMINA COMPARED TO HUMAN MALES. IF EVENTS CALLED FOR IT, I WOULD BE MORE LIKELY TO PROTECT YOU FROM HARM.
MUST BE AN EARTH THING. THE GALLANT KNIGHT ALWAYS WANTS TO SAVE THE PRINCESS, Y'KNOW?
I DO NOT UNDERSTAND. WHO IS THE "PRINCESS" IN YOUR ANALOGY?
...NEVER MIND.

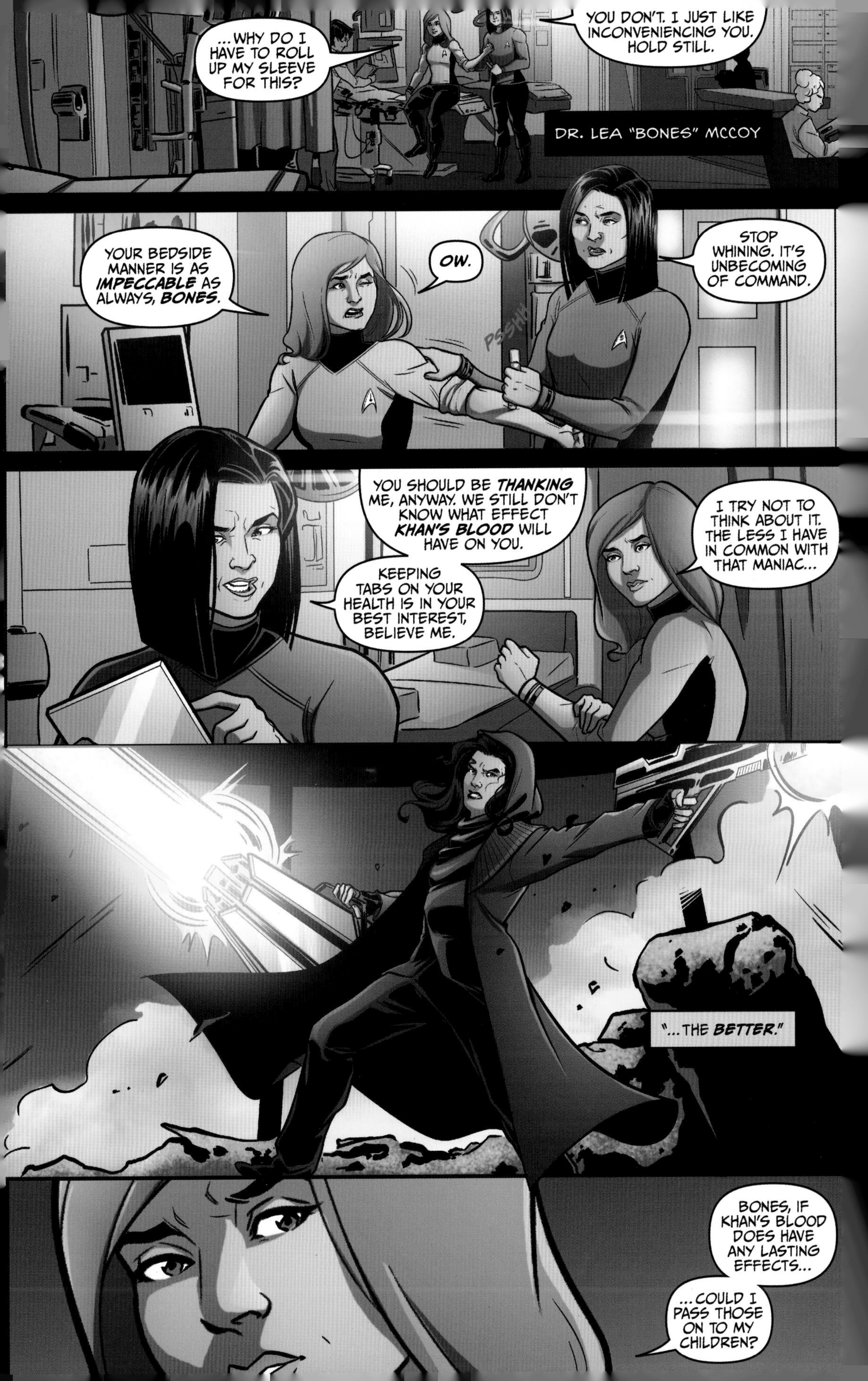
...WHY DO I HAVE TO ROLL UP MY SLEEVE FOR THIS?
YOU DON'T. I JUST LIKE INCONVENIENCING YOU. HOLD STILL.
DR. LEA "BONES" MCCOY
YOUR BEDSIDE MANNER IS AS *IMPECCABLE* AS ALWAYS, *BONES*.
OW.
STOP WHINING. IT'S UNBECOMING OF COMMAND.
YOU SHOULD BE *THANKING* ME, ANYWAY. WE STILL DON'T KNOW WHAT EFFECT *KHAN'S BLOOD* WILL HAVE ON YOU.
KEEPING TABS ON YOUR HEALTH IS IN YOUR BEST INTEREST, BELIEVE ME.
I TRY NOT TO THINK ABOUT IT. THE LESS I HAVE IN COMMON WITH THAT MANIAC...
"...THE *BETTER*."
BONES, IF KHAN'S BLOOD DOES HAVE ANY LASTING EFFECTS...
...COULD I PASS THOSE ON TO MY CHILDREN?

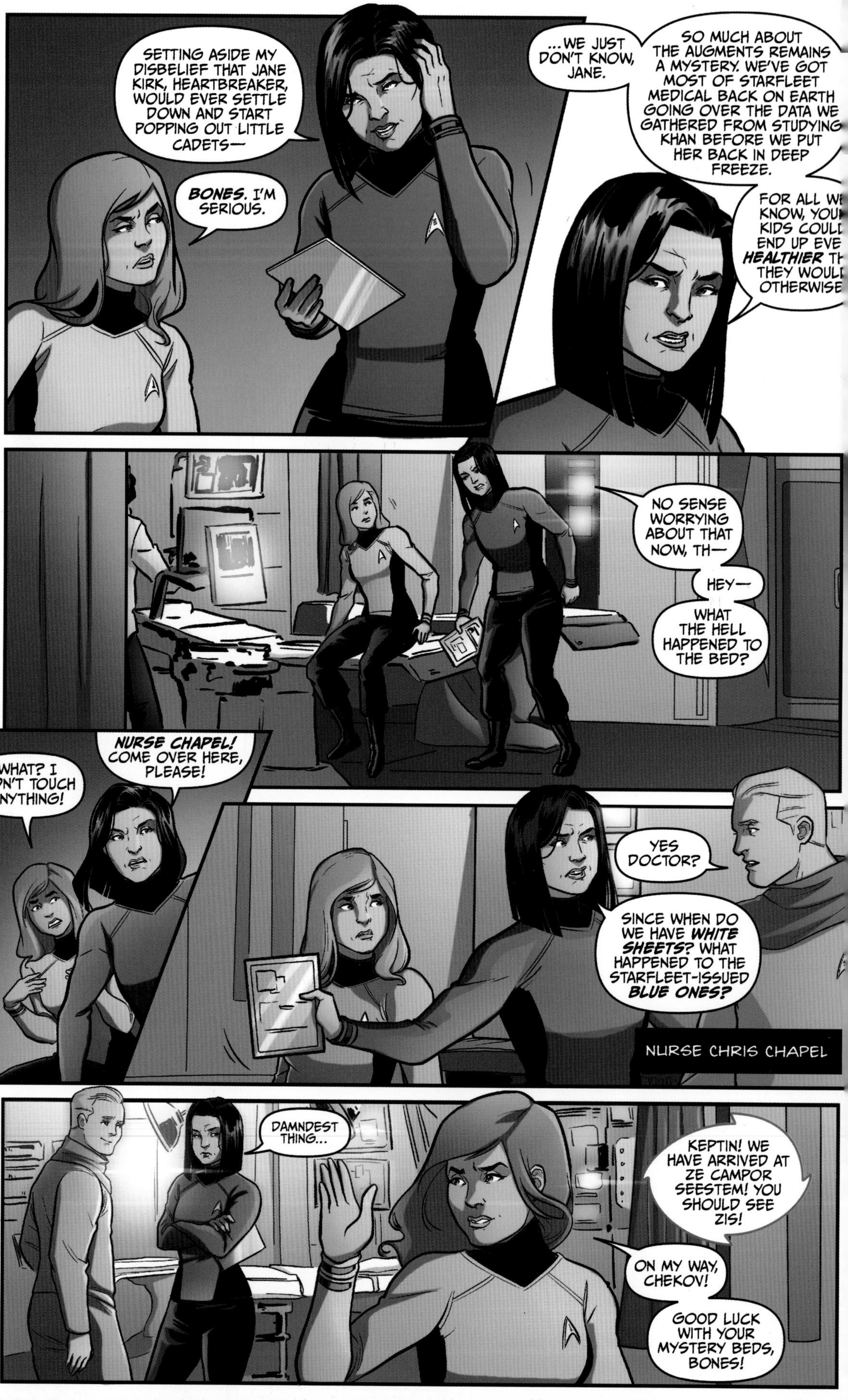
SETTING ASIDE MY DISBELIEF THAT JANE KIRK, HEARTBREAKER, WOULD EVER SETTLE DOWN AND START POPPING OUT LITTLE CADETS—
BONES. I'M SERIOUS.
...WE JUST DON'T KNOW, JANE.
SO MUCH ABOUT THE AUGMENTS REMAINS A MYSTERY. WE'VE GOT MOST OF STARFLEET MEDICAL BACK ON EARTH GOING OVER THE DATA WE GATHERED FROM STUDYING KHAN BEFORE WE PUT HER BACK IN DEEP FREEZE.
FOR ALL W KNOW, YOU KIDS COUL END UP EVE HEALTHIER T THEY WOUL OTHERWISE
NO SENSE WORRYING ABOUT THAT NOW, TH—
HEY—
WHAT THE HELL HAPPENED TO THE BED?
WHAT? I DIDN'T TOUCH ANYTHING!
NURSE CHAPEL! COME OVER HERE, PLEASE!
YES DOCTOR?
SINCE WHEN DO WE HAVE WHITE SHEETS? WHAT HAPPENED TO THE STARFLEET-ISSUED BLUE ONES?
NURSE CHRIS CHAPEL
DAMNDEST THING...
KEPTIN! WE HAVE ARRIVED AT ZE CAMPOR SEESTEM! YOU SHOULD SEE ZIS!
ON MY WAY, CHEKOV!
GOOD LUCK WITH YOUR MYSTERY BEDS, BONES!

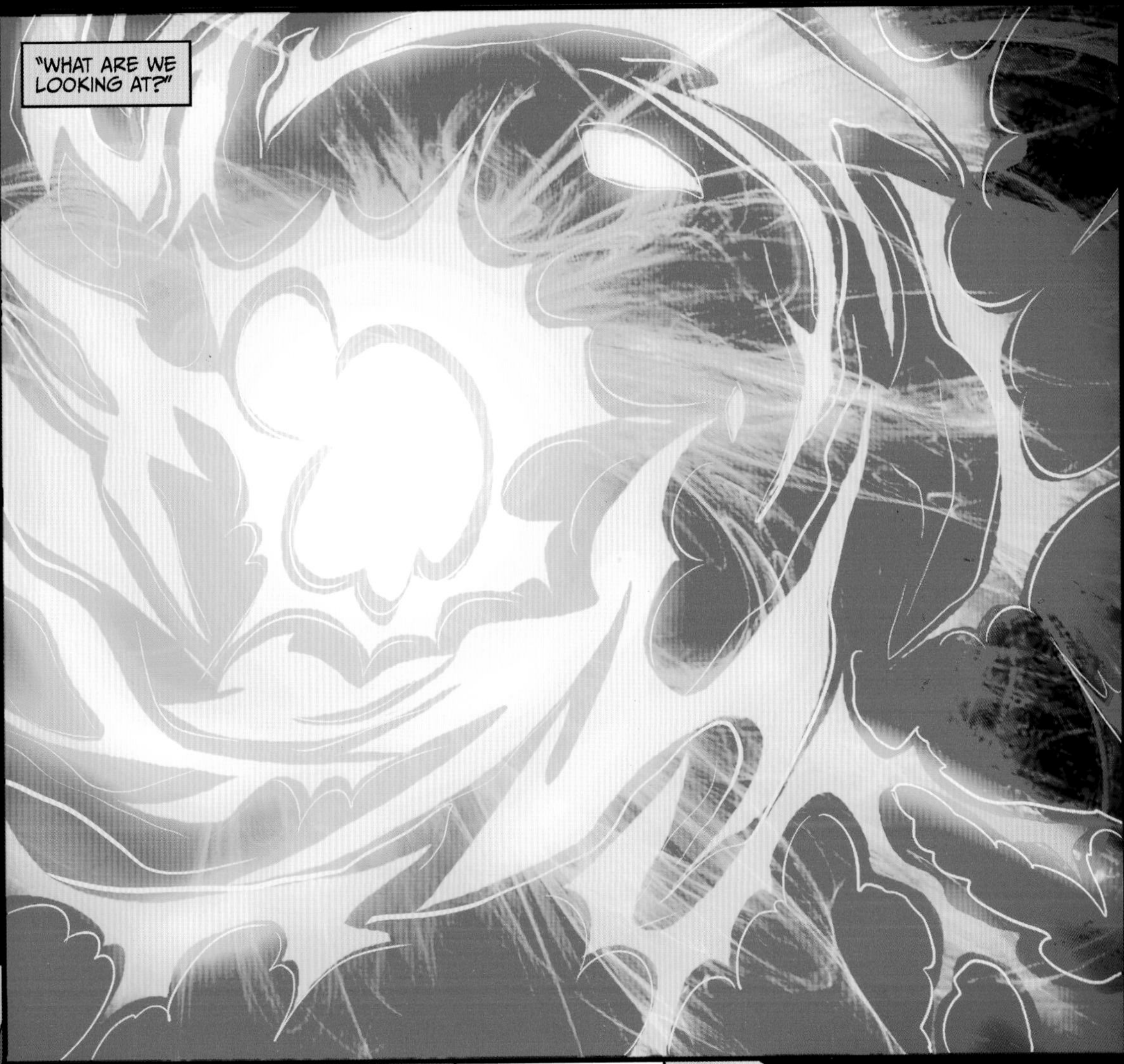
"WHAT ARE WE LOOKING AT?"

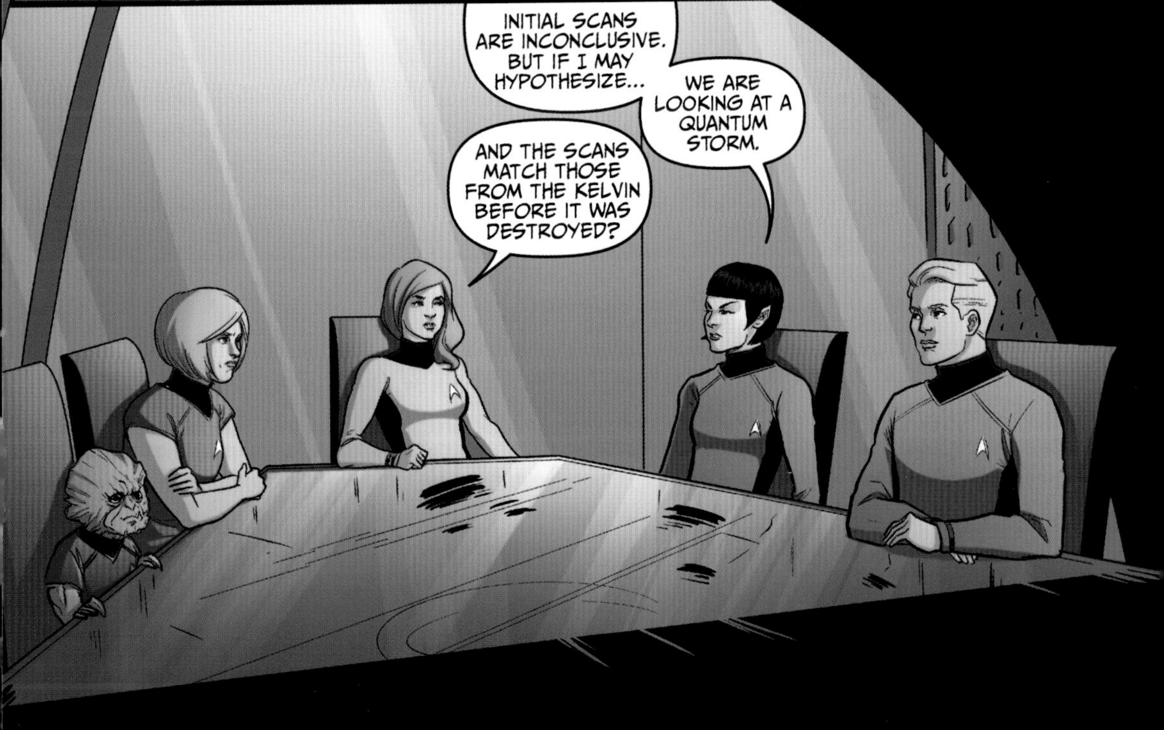
INITIAL SCANS ARE INCONCLUSIVE. BUT IF I MAY HYPOTHESIZE...
WE ARE LOOKING AT A QUANTUM STORM.
AND THE SCANS MATCH THOSE FROM THE KELVIN BEFORE IT WAS DESTROYED?

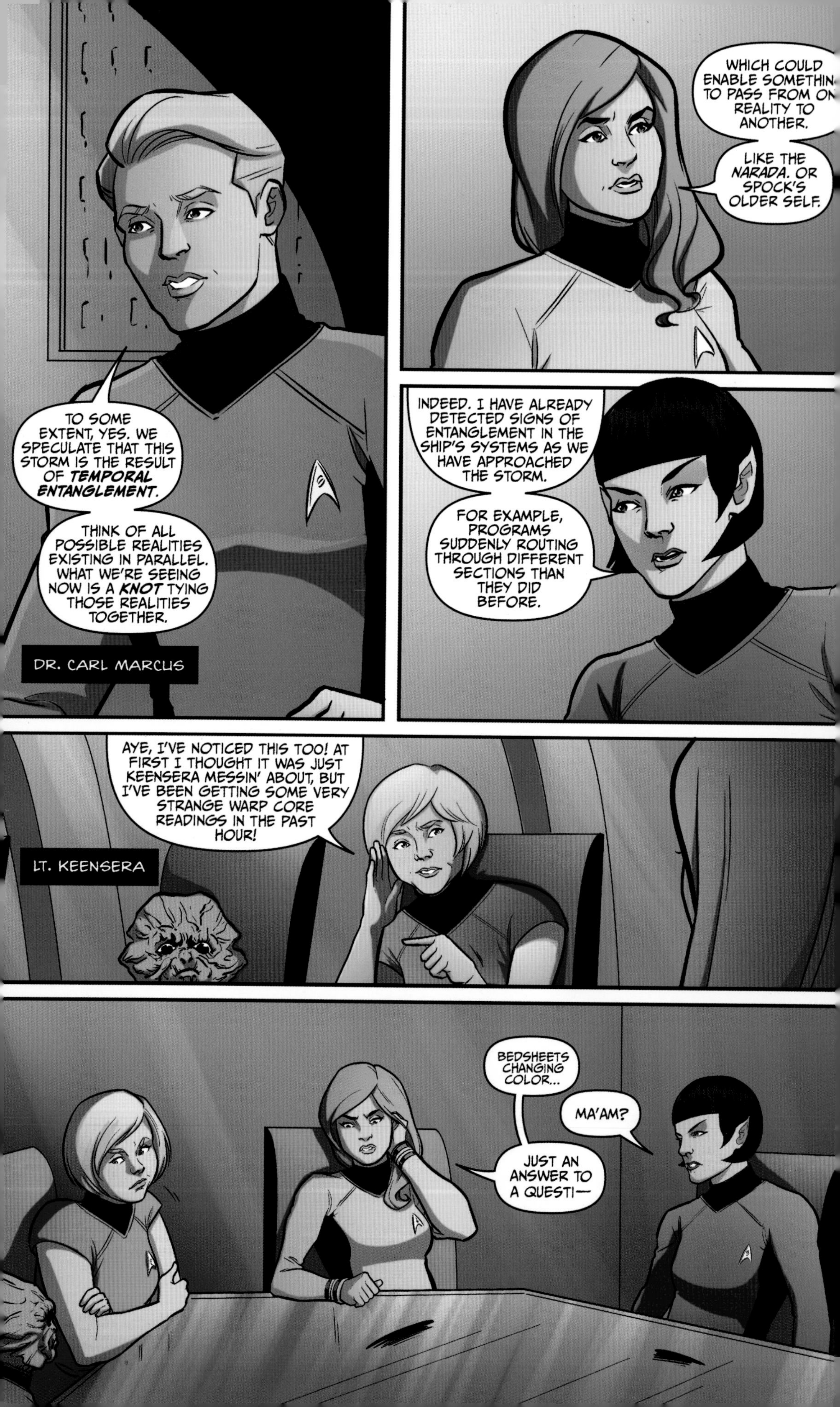
TO SOME EXTENT, YES. WE SPECULATE THAT THIS STORM IS THE RESULT OF TEMPORAL ENTANGLEMENT.
THINK OF ALL POSSIBLE REALITIES EXISTING IN PARALLEL. WHAT WE'RE SEEING NOW IS A KNOT TYING THOSE REALITIES TOGETHER.
DR. CARL MARCUS
WHICH COULD ENABLE SOMETHIN TO PASS FROM ON REALITY TO ANOTHER.
LIKE THE NARADA. OR SPOCK'S OLDER SELF.
INDEED. I HAVE ALREADY DETECTED SIGNS OF ENTANGLEMENT IN THE SHIP'S SYSTEMS AS WE HAVE APPROACHED THE STORM.
FOR EXAMPLE, PROGRAMS SUDDENLY ROUTING THROUGH DIFFERENT SECTIONS THAN THEY DID BEFORE.
AYE, I'VE NOTICED THIS TOO! AT FIRST I THOUGHT IT WAS JUST KEENSERA MESSIN' ABOUT, BUT I'VE BEEN GETTING SOME VERY STRANGE WARP CORE READINGS IN THE PAST HOUR!
LT. KEENSERA
BEDSHEETS CHANGING COLOR...
MA'AM?
JUST AN ANSWER TO A QUESTI—

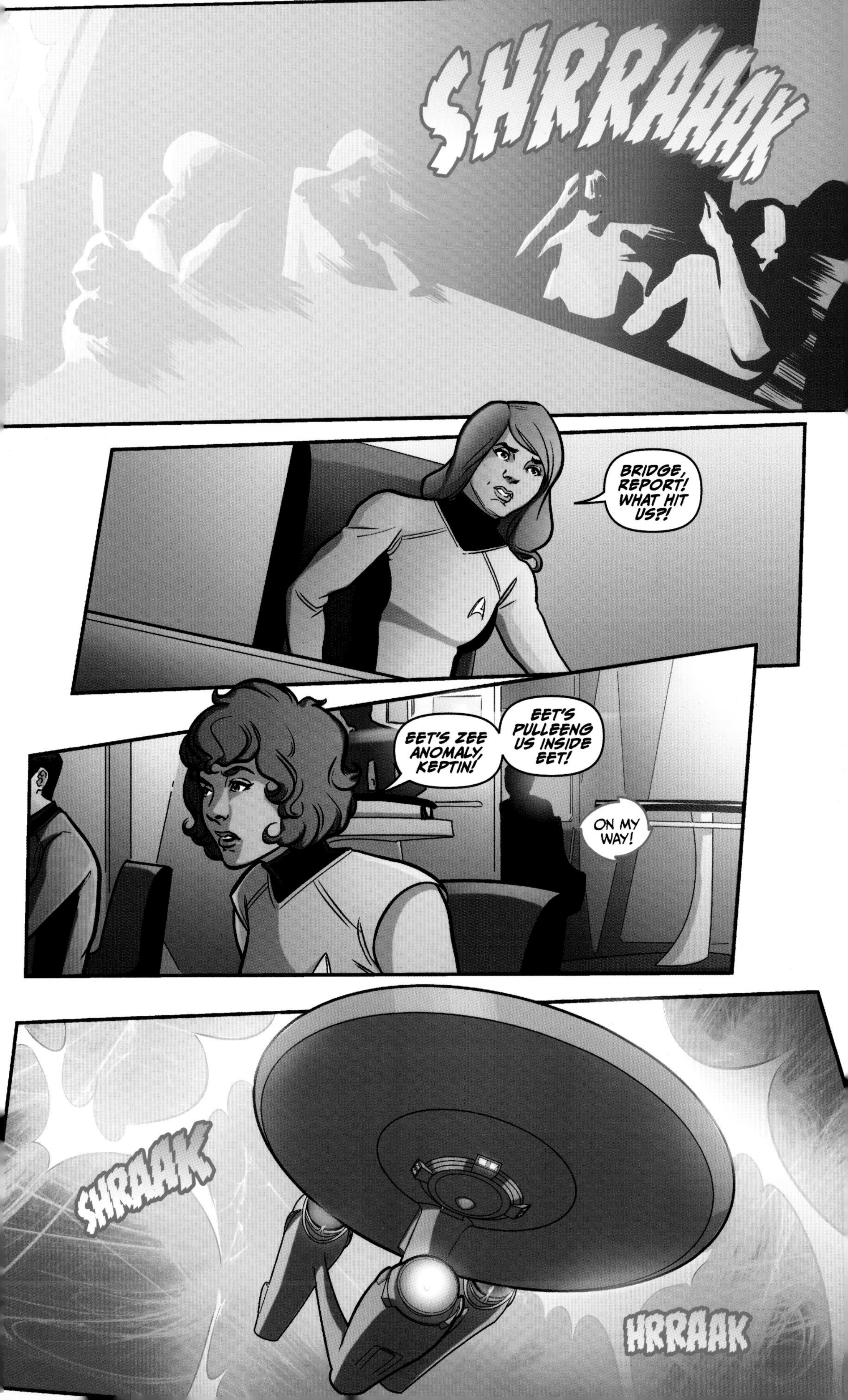
SHRRAAAK
BRIDGE, REPORT! WHAT HIT US?!
EET'S ZEE ANOMALY, KEPTIN!
EET'S PULLEENG US INSIDE EET!
ON MY WAY!
SHRAAK
HRRAAK

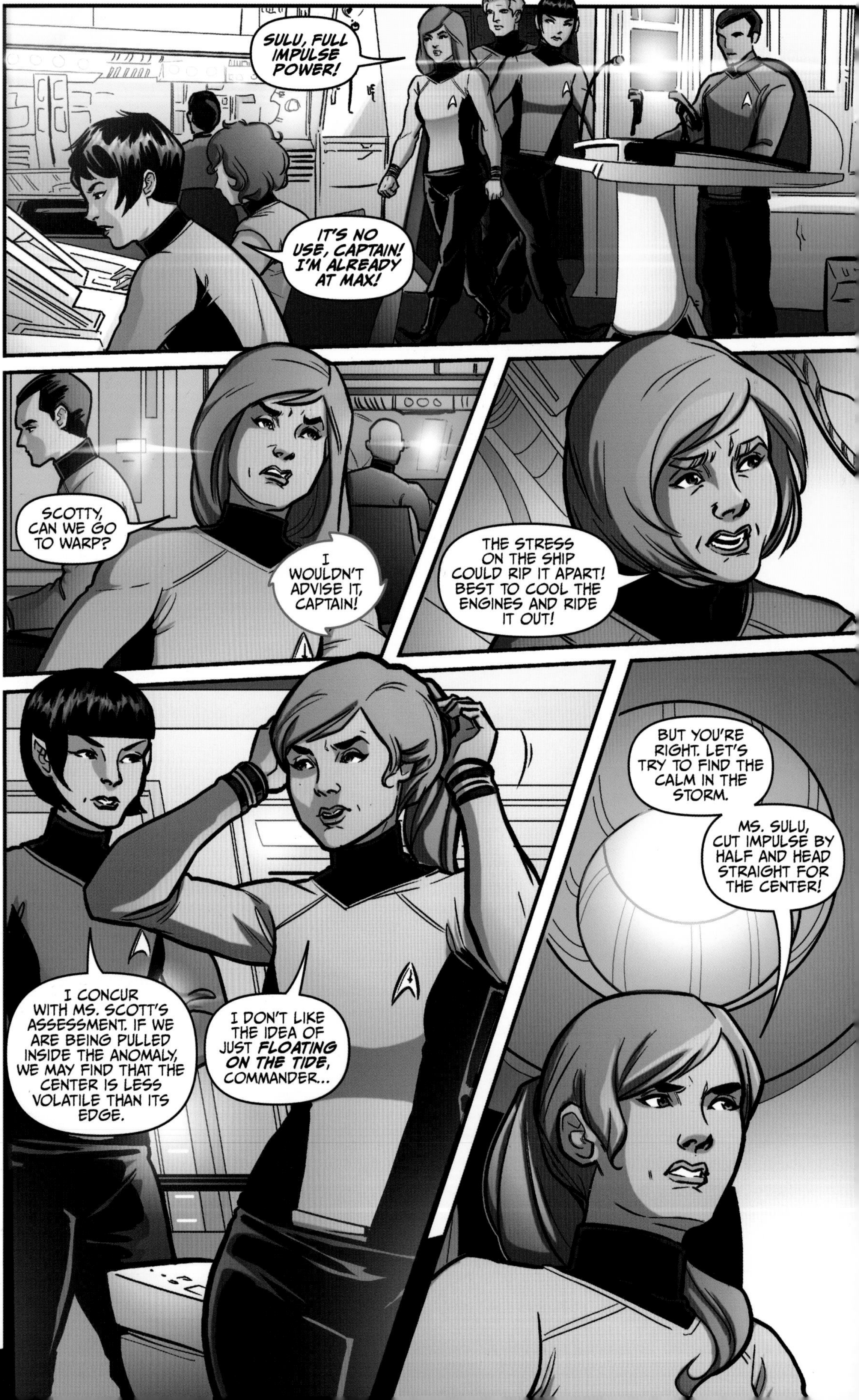
SULU, FULL IMPULSE POWER!
IT'S NO USE, CAPTAIN! I'M ALREADY AT MAX!
SCOTTY, CAN WE GO TO WARP?
I WOULDN'T ADVISE IT, CAPTAIN!
THE STRESS ON THE SHIP COULD RIP IT APART! BEST TO COOL THE ENGINES AND RIDE IT OUT!
I CONCUR WITH MS. SCOTT'S ASSESSMENT. IF WE ARE BEING PULLED INSIDE THE ANOMALY, WE MAY FIND THAT THE CENTER IS LESS VOLATILE THAN ITS EDGE.
I DON'T LIKE THE IDEA OF JUST FLOATING ON THE TIDE, COMMANDER...
BUT YOU'RE RIGHT. LET'S TRY TO FIND THE CALM IN THE STORM.
MS. SULU, CUT IMPULSE BY HALF AND HEAD STRAIGHT FOR THE CENTER!

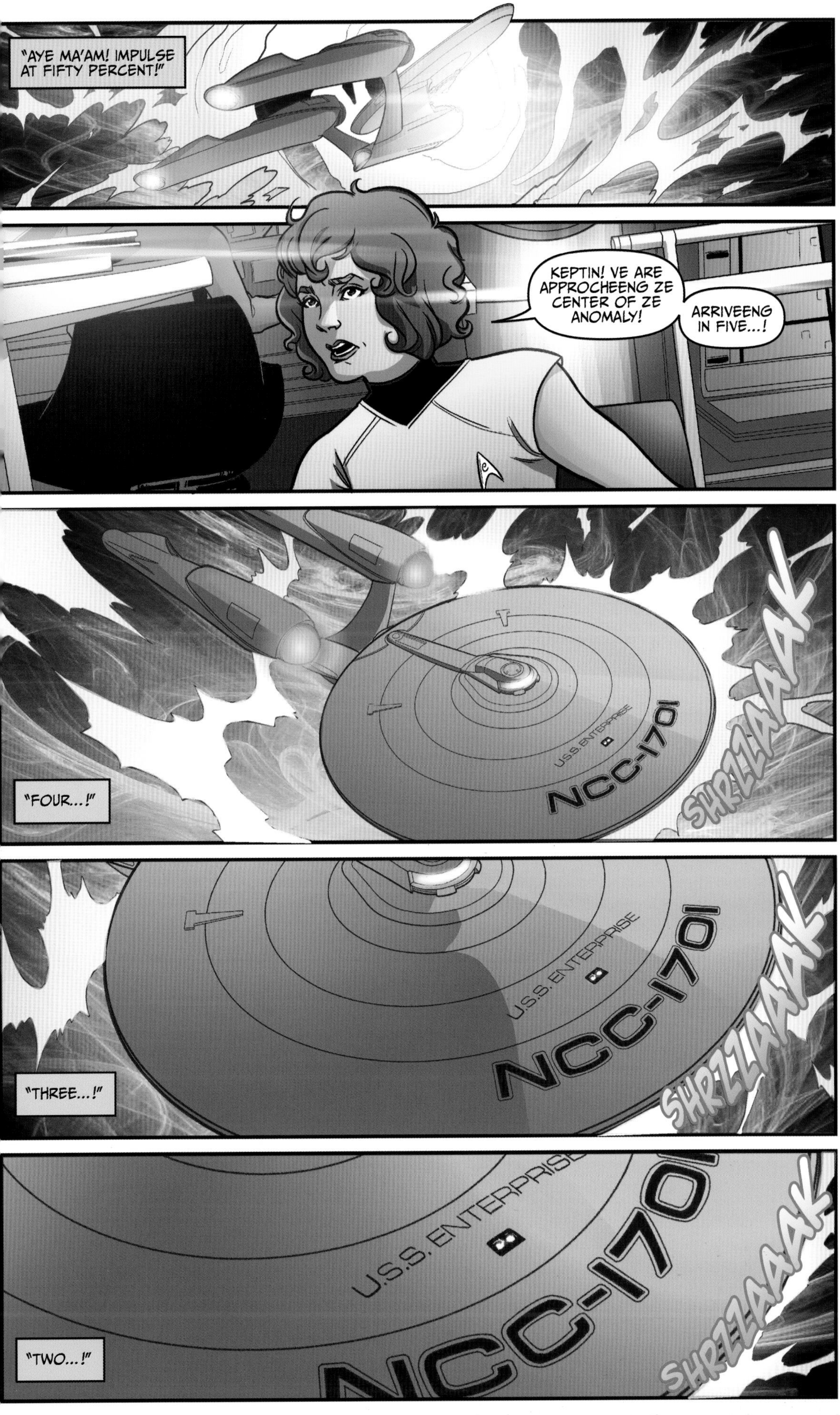
"AYE MA'AM! IMPULSE AT FIFTY PERCENT!"
KEPTIN! VE ARE APPROCHEENG ZE CENTER OF ZE ANOMALY!
ARRIVEENG IN FIVE...!
"FOUR...!"
U.S.S. ENTERPRISE
NCC-1701
SHRZZAAK
"THREE...!"
U.S.S. ENTERPRISE
NCC-1701
SHRZZAAK
"TWO...!"
U.S.S. ENTERPRISE
NCC-1701
SHRZZAAK

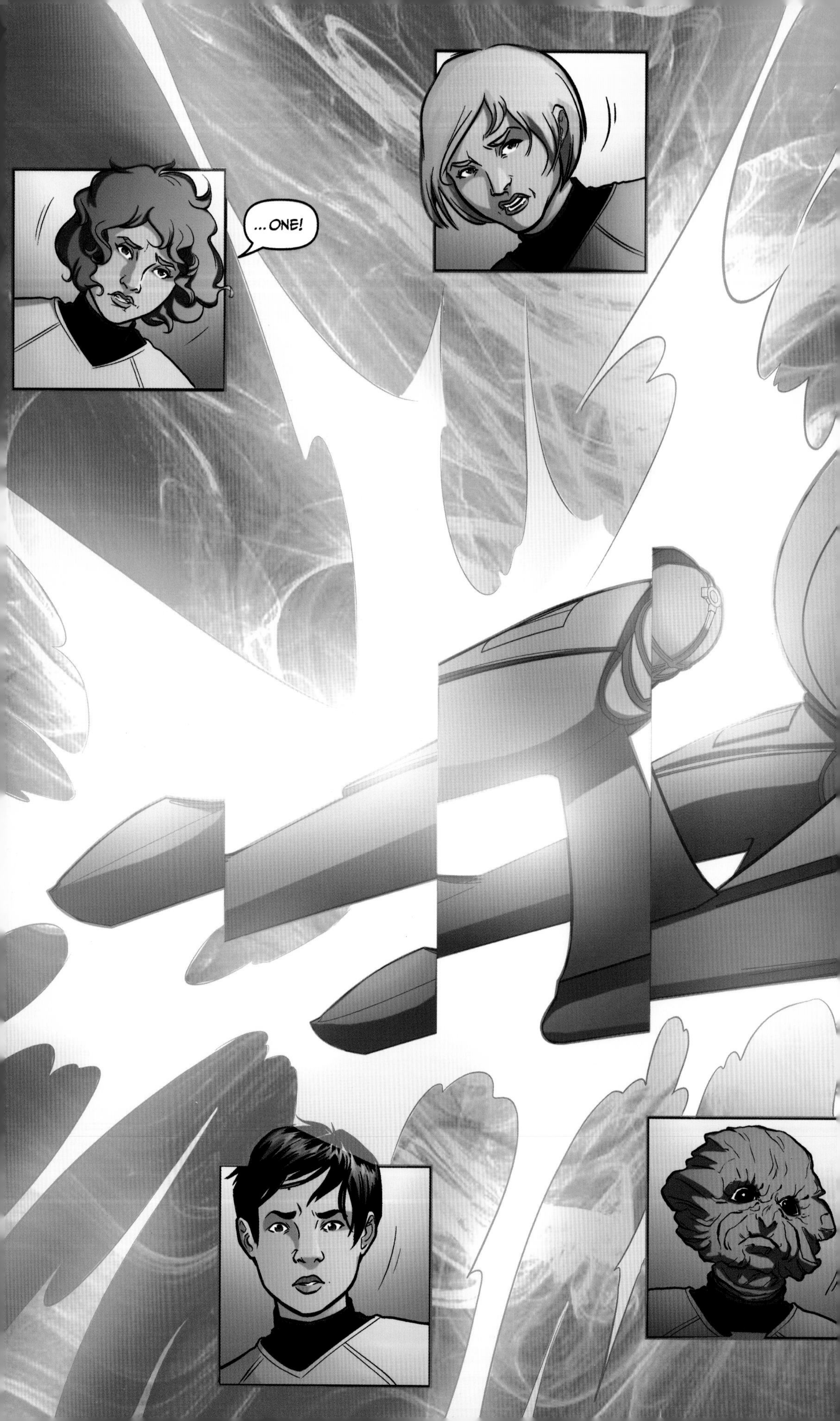
...ONE!

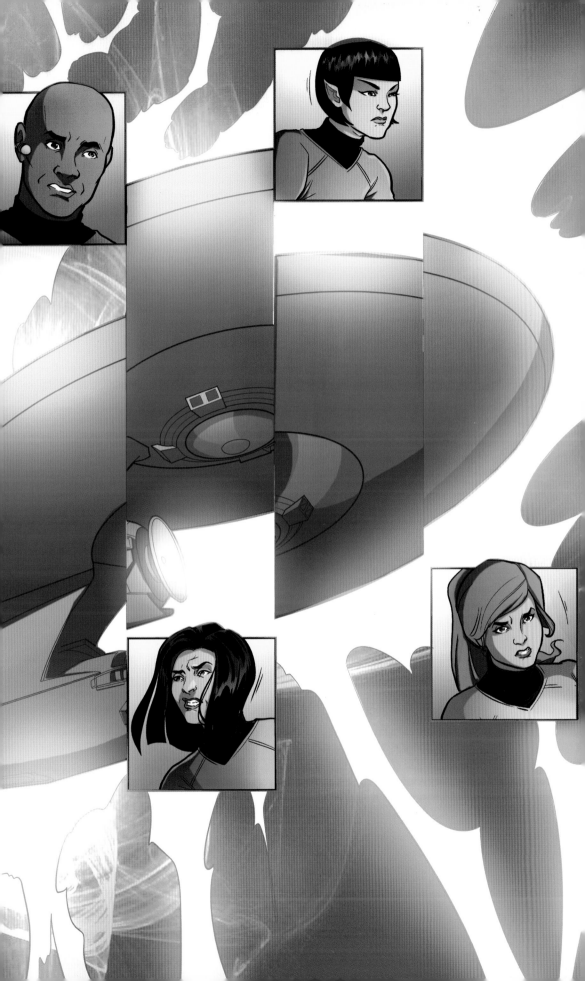

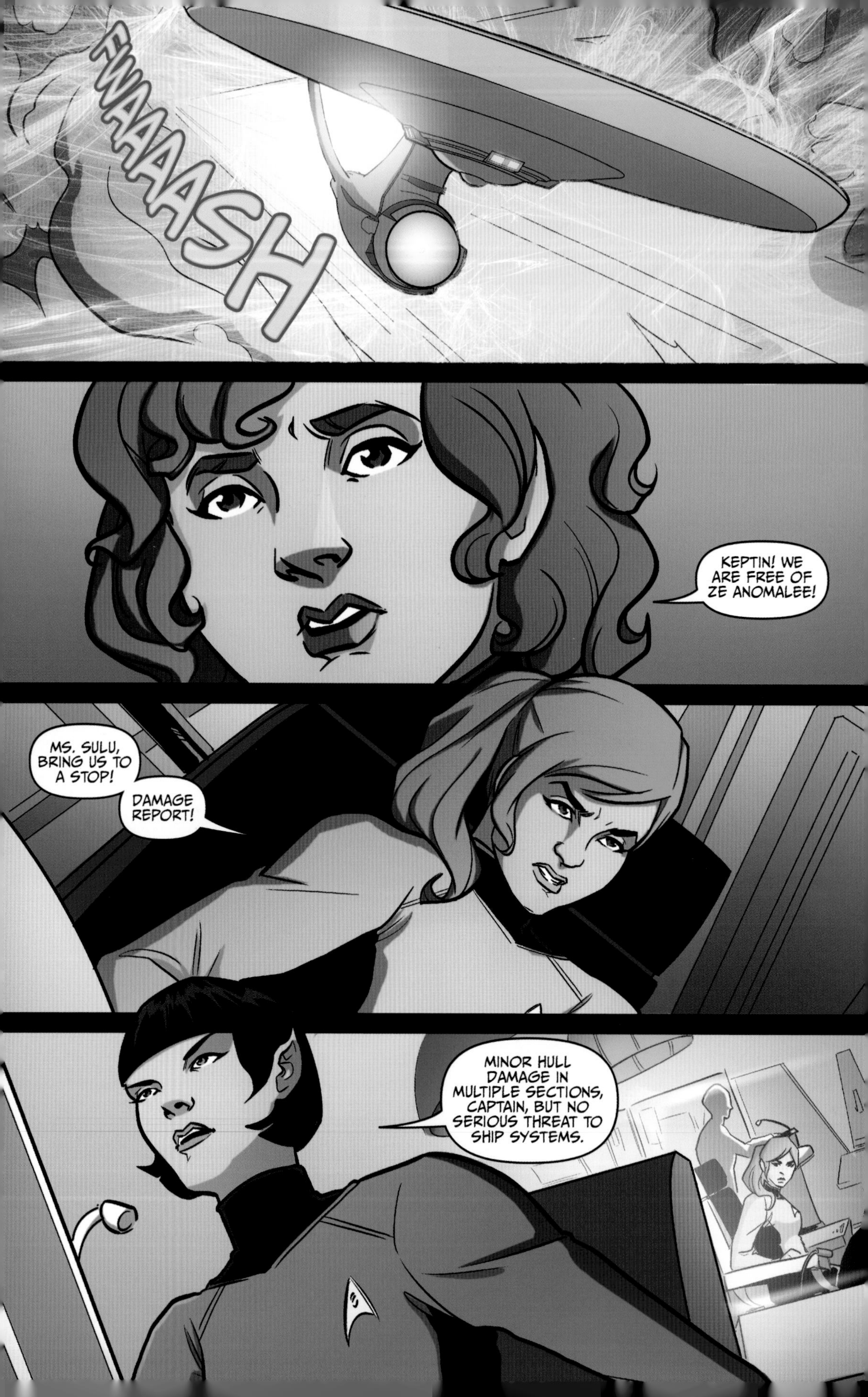
FWAAAASH
KEPTIN! WE ARE FREE OF ZE ANOMALEE!
MS. SULU, BRING US TO A STOP!
DAMAGE REPORT!
MINOR HULL DAMAGE IN MULTIPLE SECTIONS, CAPTAIN, BUT NO SERIOUS THREAT TO SHIP SYSTEMS.

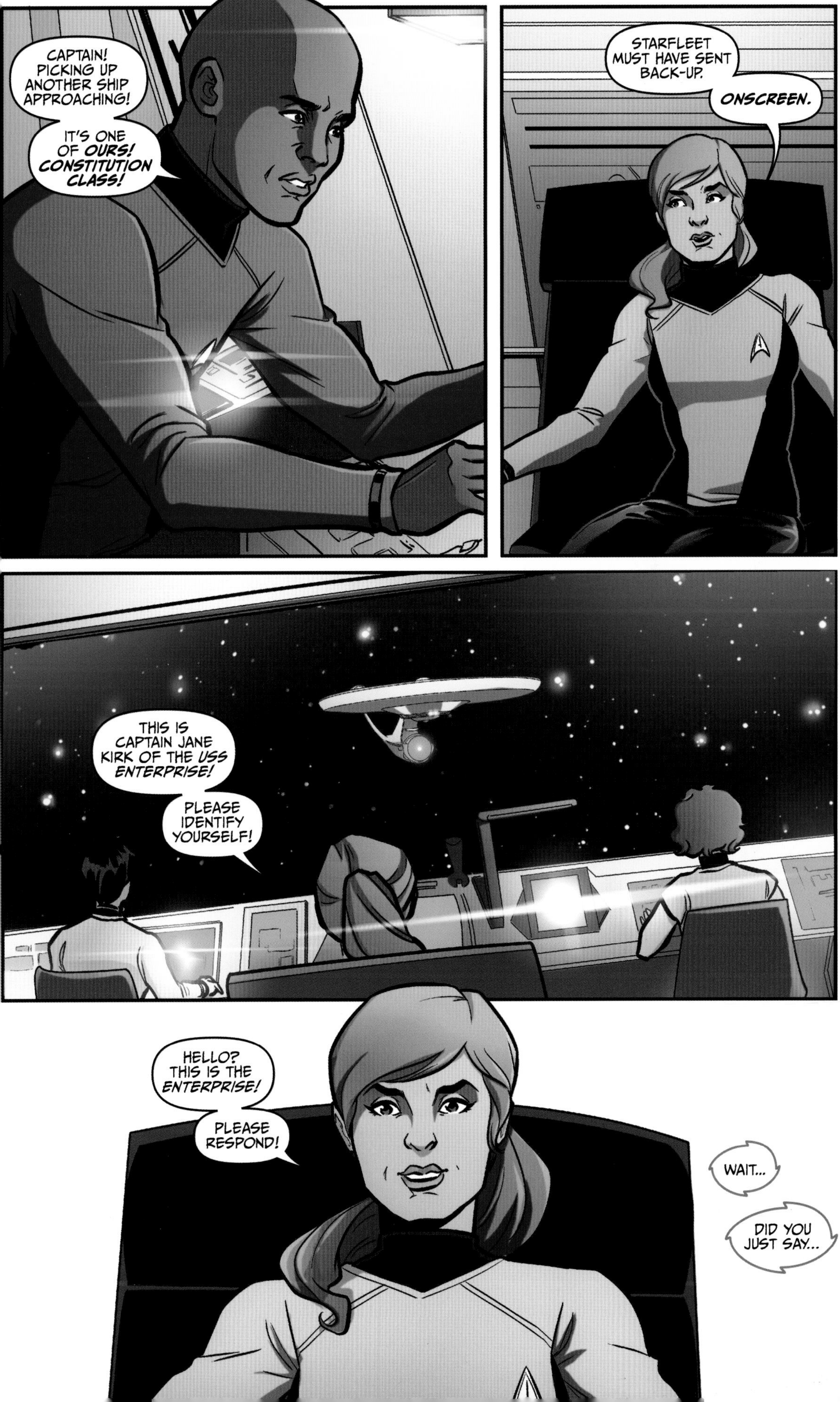
CAPTAIN! PICKING UP ANOTHER SHIP APPROACHING!
IT'S ONE OF OURS! CONSTITUTION CLASS!
STARFLEET MUST HAVE SENT BACK-UP.
ONSCREEN.
THIS IS CAPTAIN JANE KIRK OF THE USS ENTERPRISE!
PLEASE IDENTIFY YOURSELF!
HELLO? THIS IS THE ENTERPRISE!
PLEASE RESPOND!
WAIT...
DID YOU JUST SAY...

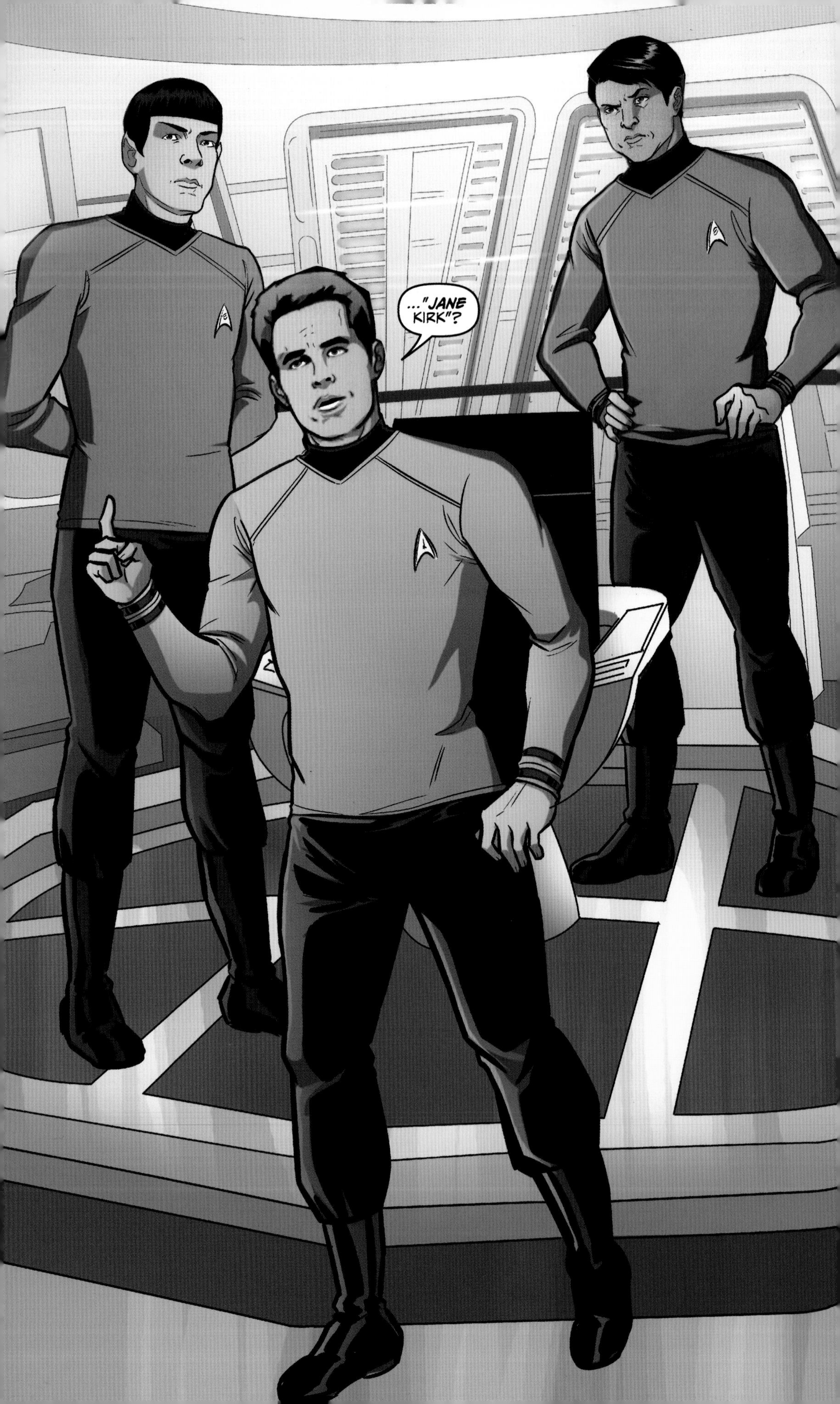
..."JANE KIRK"?

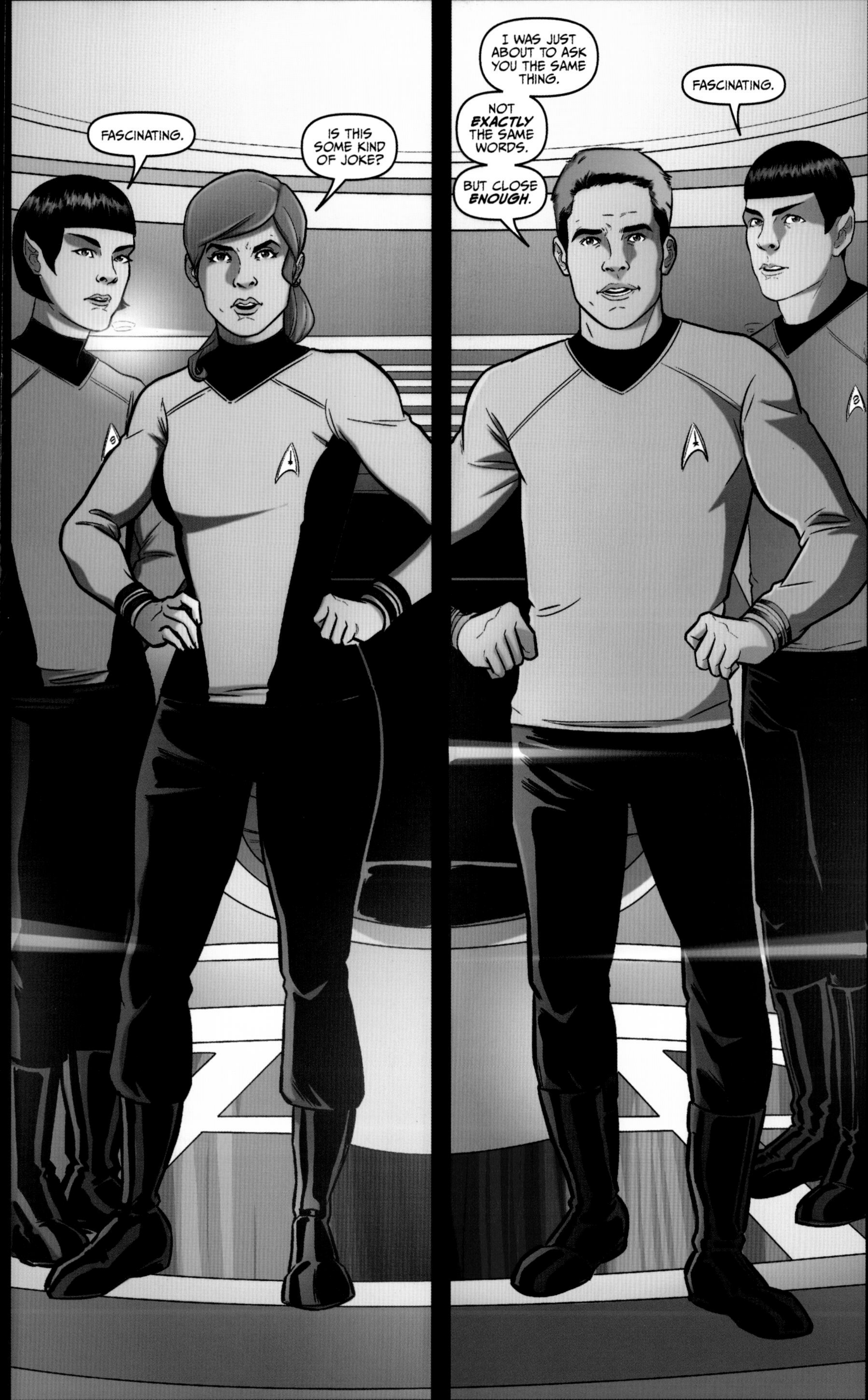
FASCINATING.
IS THIS SOME KIND OF JOKE?
I WAS JUST ABOUT TO ASK YOU THE SAME THING.
NOT **EXACTLY** THE SAME WORDS.
BUT CLOSE **ENOUGH**.
FASCINATING.

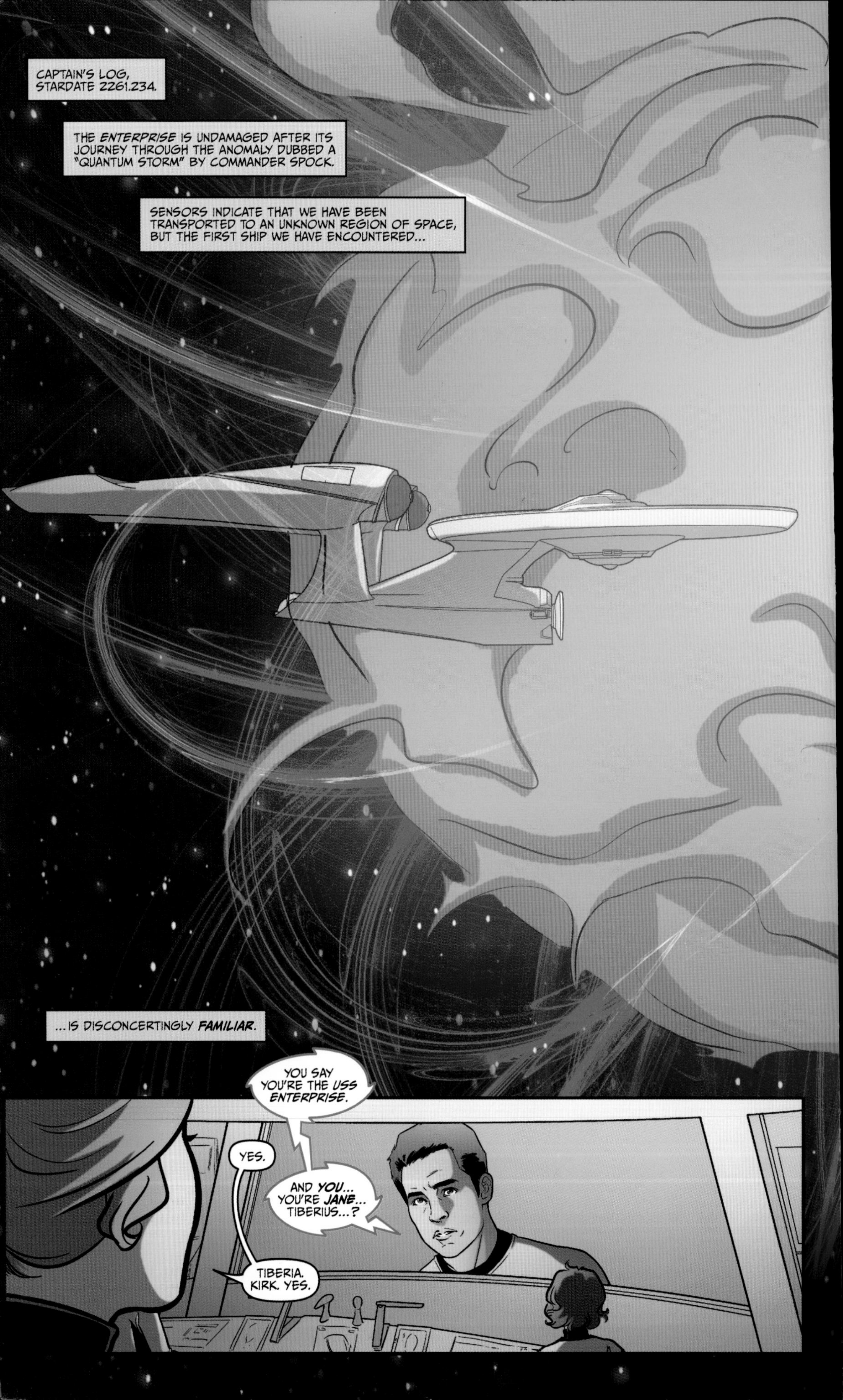
CAPTAIN'S LOG, STARDATE 2261.234.
THE *ENTERPRISE* IS UNDAMAGED AFTER ITS JOURNEY THROUGH THE ANOMALY DUBBED A "QUANTUM STORM" BY COMMANDER SPOCK.
SENSORS INDICATE THAT WE HAVE BEEN TRANSPORTED TO AN UNKNOWN REGION OF SPACE, BUT THE FIRST SHIP WE HAVE ENCOUNTERED...
...IS DISCONCERTINGLY ***FAMILIAR***.
YOU SAY YOU'RE THE *USS ENTERPRISE*.
YES.
AND ***YOU***... YOU'RE ***JANE***... TIBERIUS...?
TIBERIA. KIRK. YES.

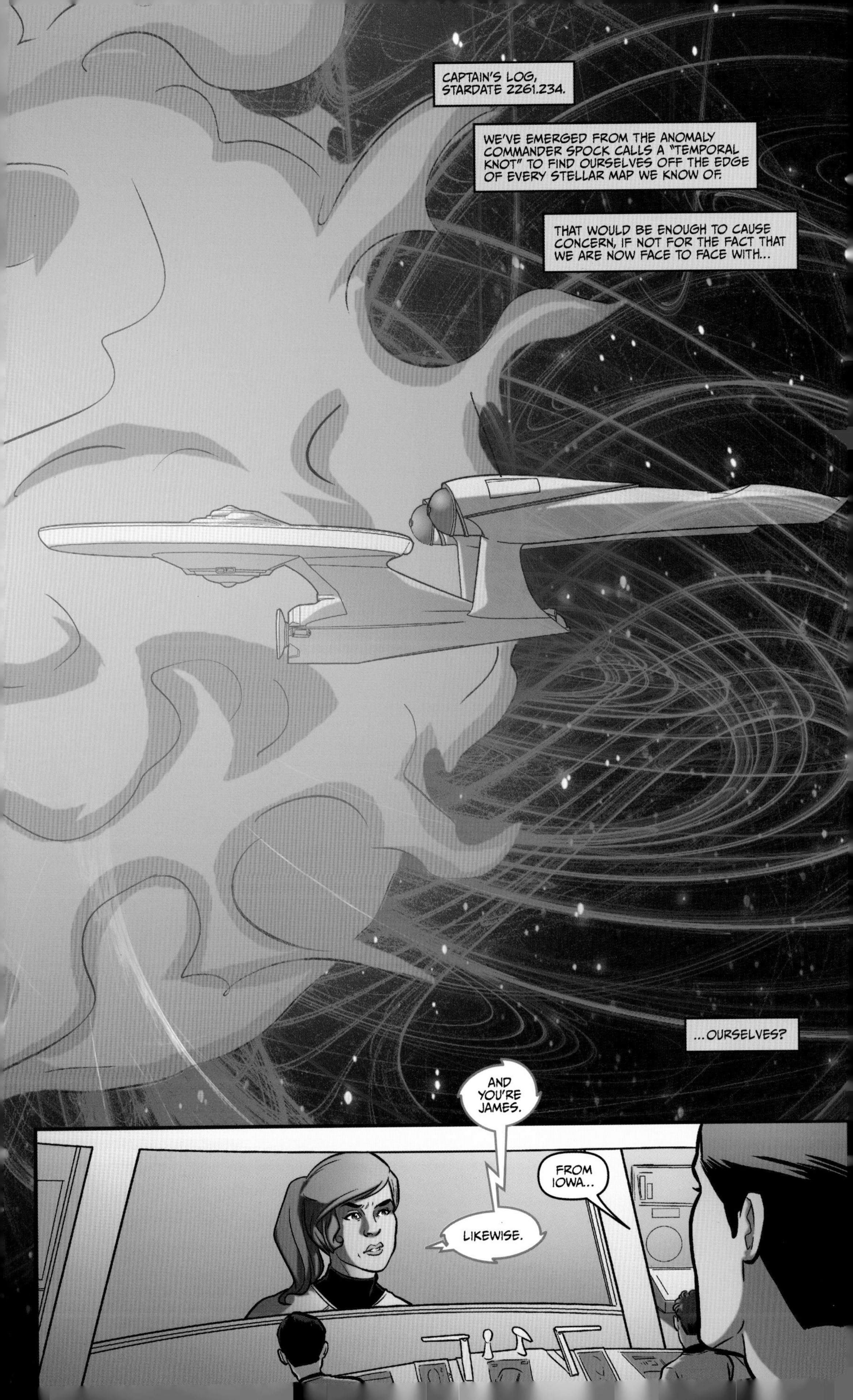
CAPTAIN'S LOG, STARDATE 2261.234.
WE'VE EMERGED FROM THE ANOMALY COMMANDER SPOCK CALLS A "TEMPORAL KNOT" TO FIND OURSELVES OFF THE EDGE OF EVERY STELLAR MAP WE KNOW OF.
THAT WOULD BE ENOUGH TO CAUSE CONCERN, IF NOT FOR THE FACT THAT WE ARE NOW FACE TO FACE WITH...
...OURSELVES?
AND YOU'RE JAMES.
FROM IOWA...
LIKEWISE.

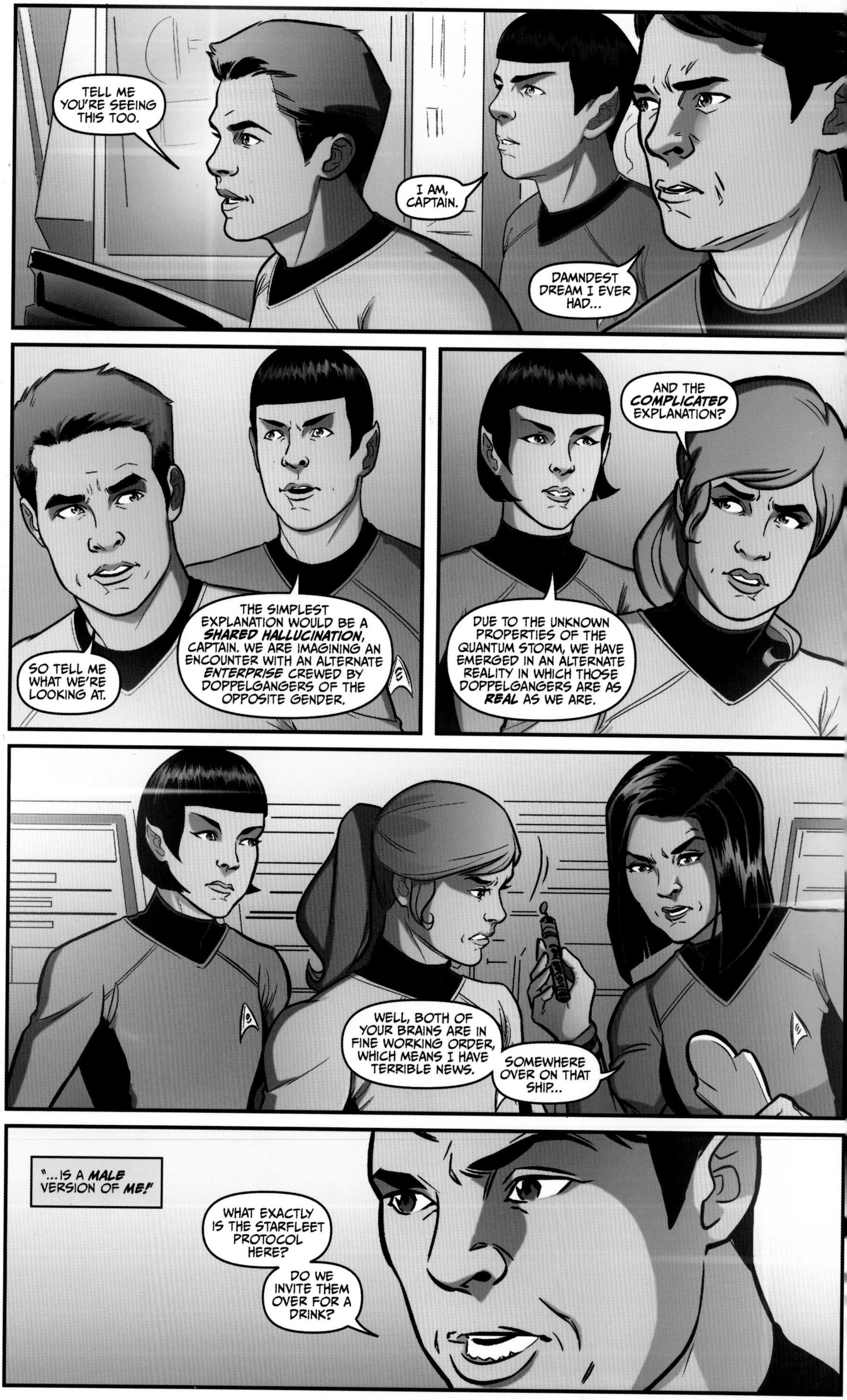

TELL ME YOU'RE SEEING THIS TOO.
I AM, CAPTAIN.
DAMNDEST DREAM I EVER HAD...
SO TELL ME WHAT WE'RE LOOKING AT.
THE SIMPLEST EXPLANATION WOULD BE A SHARED HALLUCINATION, CAPTAIN. WE ARE IMAGINING AN ENCOUNTER WITH AN ALTERNATE ENTERPRISE CREWED BY DOPPELGANGERS OF THE OPPOSITE GENDER.
AND THE COMPLICATED EXPLANATION?
DUE TO THE UNKNOWN PROPERTIES OF THE QUANTUM STORM, WE HAVE EMERGED IN AN ALTERNATE REALITY IN WHICH THOSE DOPPELGANGERS ARE AS REAL AS WE ARE.
WELL, BOTH OF YOUR BRAINS ARE IN FINE WORKING ORDER, WHICH MEANS I HAVE TERRIBLE NEWS.
SOMEWHERE OVER ON THAT SHIP...
"...IS A MALE VERSION OF ME!"
WHAT EXACTLY IS THE STARFLEET PROTOCOL HERE?
DO WE INVITE THEM OVER FOR A DRINK?

"REMIND ME WHY *WE* OFFERED TO GO OVER TO *THEM*..."

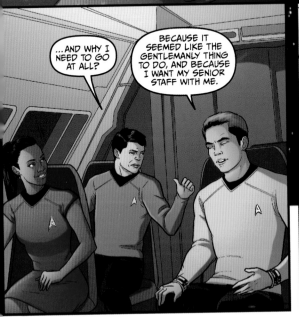

...AND WHY I NEED TO GO AT ALL?

BECAUSE IT SEEMED LIKE THE GENTLEMANLY THING TO DO, AND BECAUSE I WANT MY SENIOR STAFF WITH ME.

JUST TELL THE TRUTH, CAPTAIN! YOU WANT TO MEET YOUR LADY-SELF JUST AS MUCH AS I DO!

I WONDER IF SHE'S GOT MY DEVASTATING CHARM?

I FAIL TO SEE HOW THERE WOULD BE A SIGNIFICANT VARIATION IN YOUR PERSONALITIES GIVEN THAT THE ONLY APPARENT DIFFERENCE IS A PHYSICAL ONE.

HAVE YOU NEVER VISITED *PLANET EARTH*, MR. SPOCK? MEN AND WOMEN MAY AS WELL BE *TWO DISTINCT ALIEN SPECIES!*

A FAULTY ANALOGY, MR. SCOTT, GIVEN THAT THE VERY DEFINITION OF A SPECIES IS THE ABILITY OF TWO MEMBERS OF THE OPPOSITE SEX TO PRODUCE VIABLE—

JUST FLY THE SHUTTLE, SPOCK.

I CAN'T *WAIT* TO MEET *YOUR* DOUBLE...

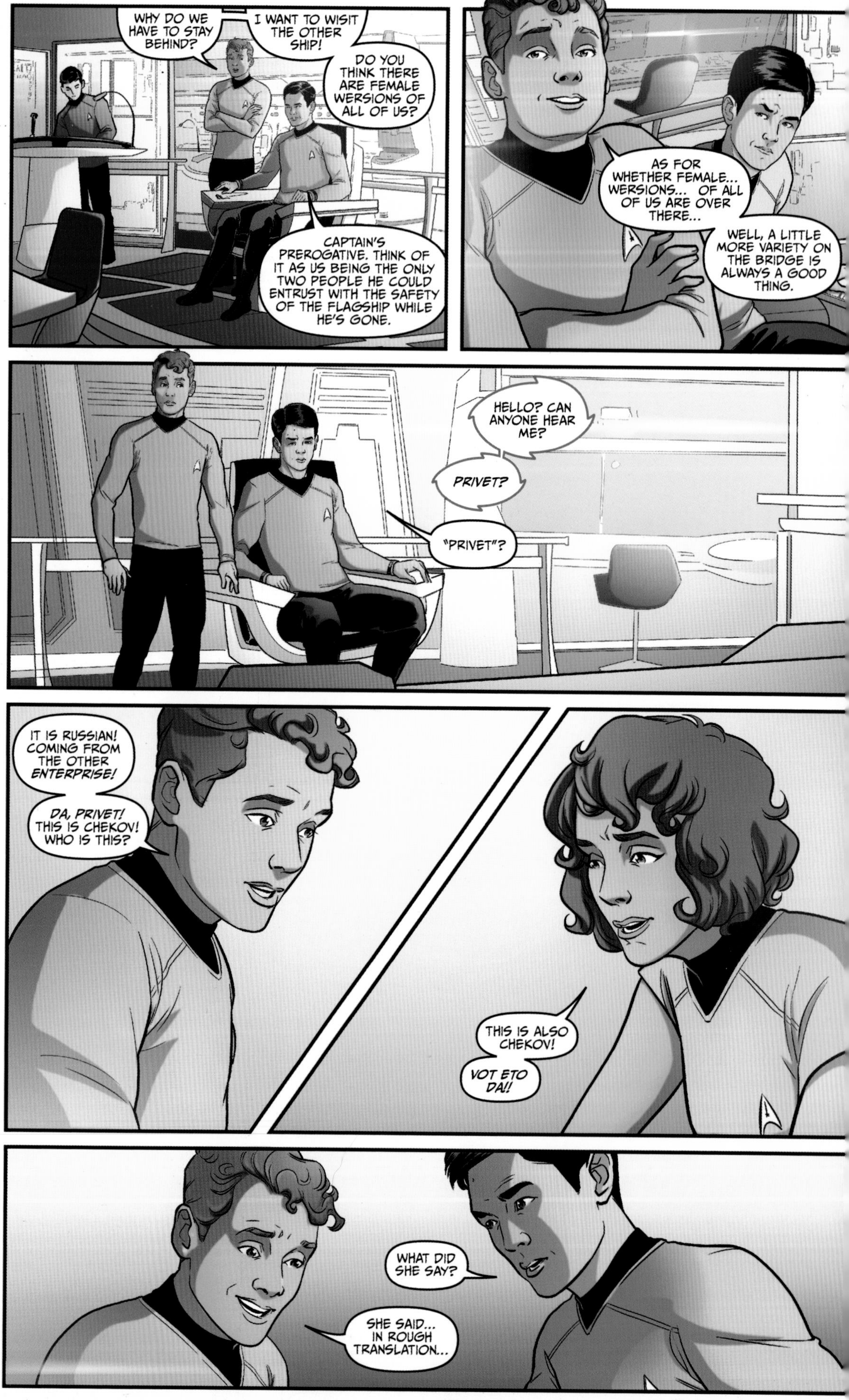

WHY DO WE HAVE TO STAY BEHIND?
I WANT TO WISIT THE OTHER SHIP!
DO YOU THINK THERE ARE FEMALE WERSIONS OF ALL OF US?
CAPTAIN'S PREROGATIVE. THINK OF IT AS US BEING THE ONLY TWO PEOPLE HE COULD ENTRUST WITH THE SAFETY OF THE FLAGSHIP WHILE HE'S GONE.
AS FOR WHETHER FEMALE... WERSIONS... OF ALL OF US ARE OVER THERE...
WELL, A LITTLE MORE VARIETY ON THE BRIDGE IS ALWAYS A GOOD THING.
HELLO? CAN ANYONE HEAR ME?
PRIVET?
"PRIVET"?
IT IS RUSSIAN! COMING FROM THE OTHER ENTERPRISE!
DA, PRIVET! THIS IS CHEKOV! WHO IS THIS?
THIS IS ALSO CHEKOV!
VOT ETO DA!!
WHAT DID SHE SAY?
SHE SAID... IN ROUGH TRANSLATION...

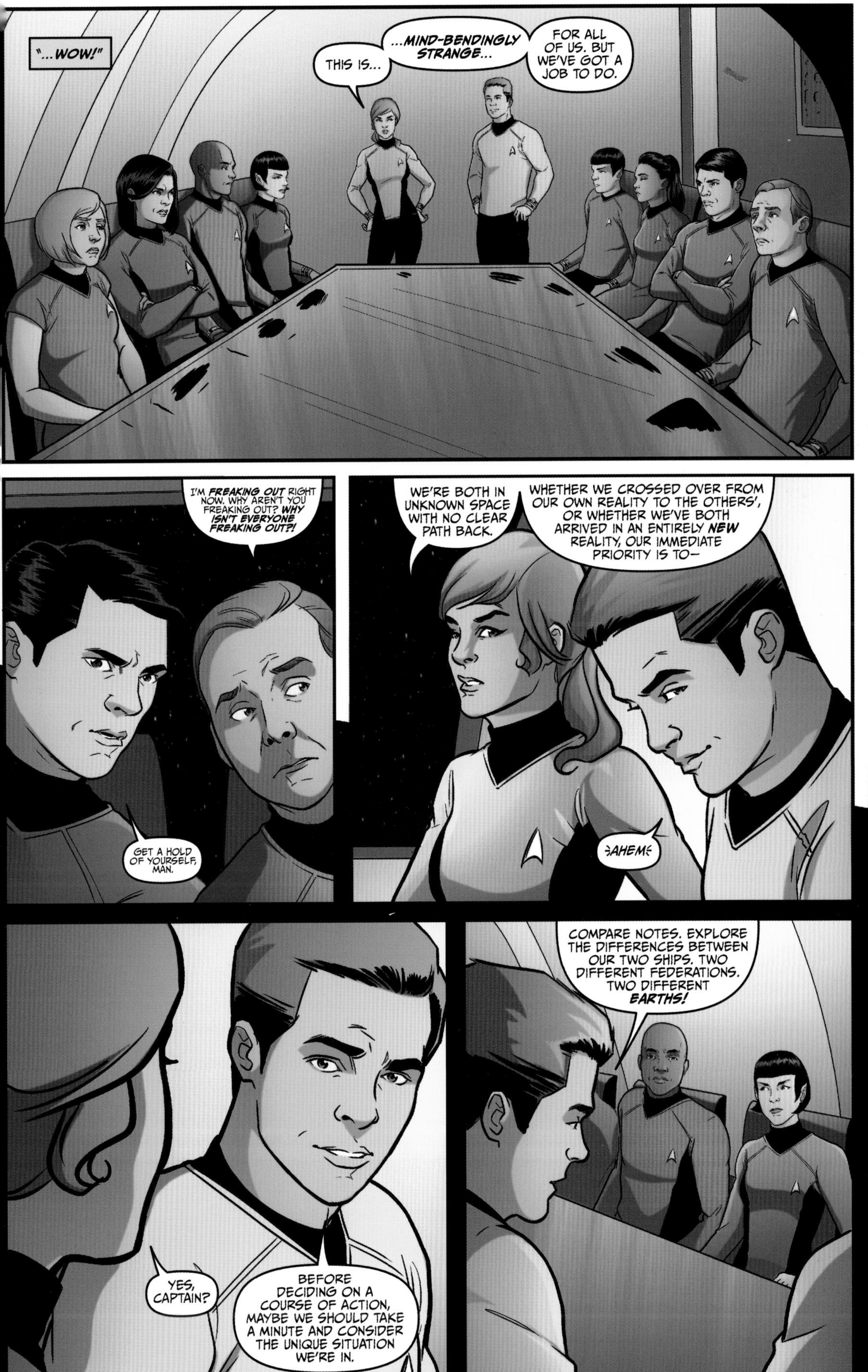
"...WOW!"
THIS IS...
...MIND-BENDINGLY STRANGE...
FOR ALL OF US. BUT WE'VE GOT A JOB TO DO.
I'M FREAKING OUT RIGHT NOW. WHY AREN'T YOU FREAKING OUT? WHY ISN'T EVERYONE FREAKING OUT?!
GET A HOLD OF YOURSELF, MAN.
WE'RE BOTH IN UNKNOWN SPACE WITH NO CLEAR PATH BACK.
WHETHER WE CROSSED OVER FROM OUR OWN REALITY TO THE OTHERS', OR WHETHER WE'VE BOTH ARRIVED IN AN ENTIRELY NEW REALITY, OUR IMMEDIATE PRIORITY IS TO—
AHEM
YES, CAPTAIN?
BEFORE DECIDING ON A COURSE OF ACTION, MAYBE WE SHOULD TAKE A MINUTE AND CONSIDER THE UNIQUE SITUATION WE'RE IN.
COMPARE NOTES. EXPLORE THE DIFFERENCES BETWEEN OUR TWO SHIPS. TWO DIFFERENT FEDERATIONS. TWO DIFFERENT EARTHS!

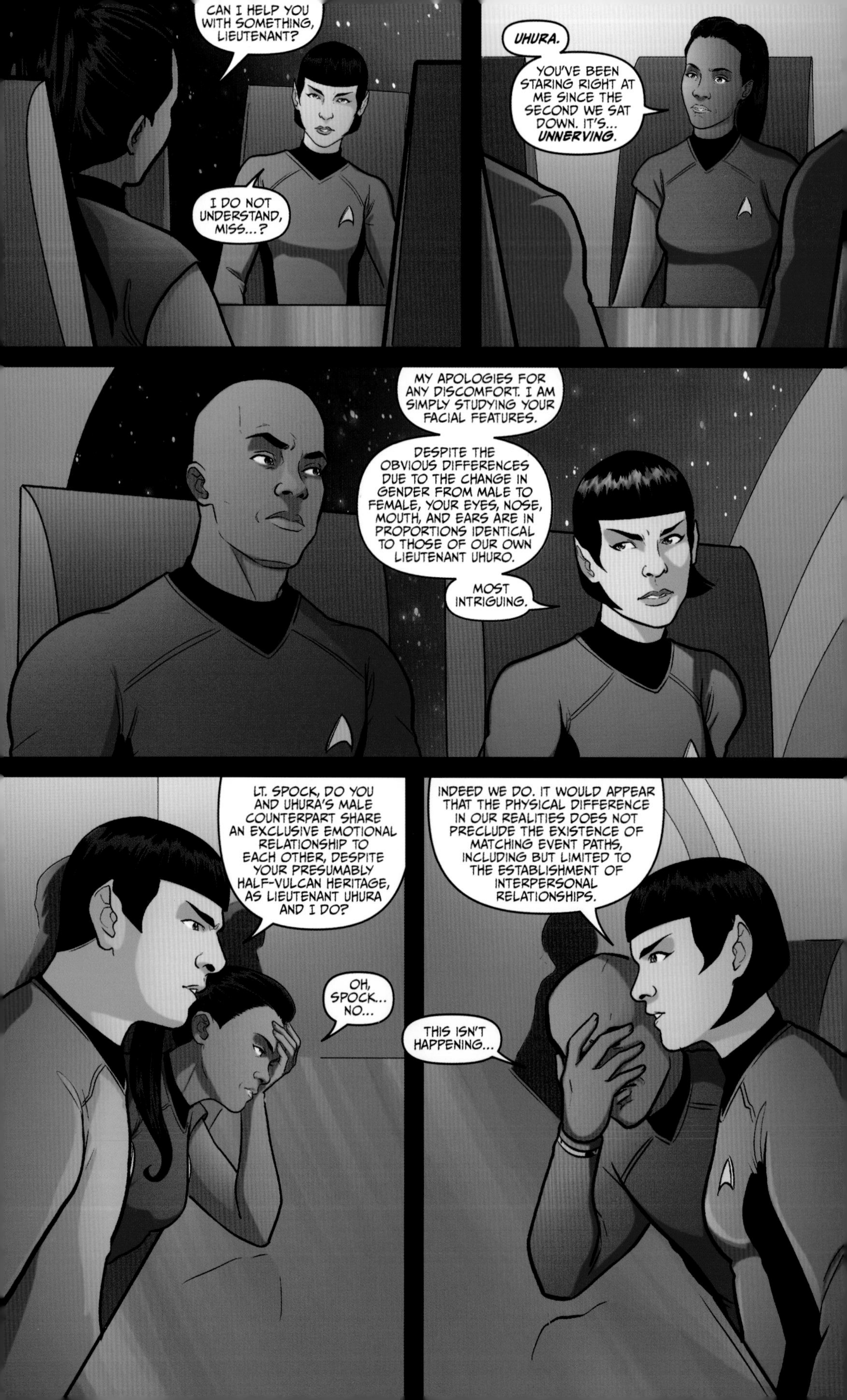
CAN I HELP YOU WITH SOMETHING, LIEUTENANT?
I DO NOT UNDERSTAND, MISS...?
UHURA.
YOU'VE BEEN STARING RIGHT AT ME SINCE THE SECOND WE SAT DOWN. IT'S... UNNERVING.
MY APOLOGIES FOR ANY DISCOMFORT. I AM SIMPLY STUDYING YOUR FACIAL FEATURES.
DESPITE THE OBVIOUS DIFFERENCES DUE TO THE CHANGE IN GENDER FROM MALE TO FEMALE, YOUR EYES, NOSE, MOUTH, AND EARS ARE IN PROPORTIONS IDENTICAL TO THOSE OF OUR OWN LIEUTENANT UHURO.
MOST INTRIGUING.
LT. SPOCK, DO YOU AND UHURA'S MALE COUNTERPART SHARE AN EXCLUSIVE EMOTIONAL RELATIONSHIP TO EACH OTHER, DESPITE YOUR PRESUMABLY HALF-VULCAN HERITAGE, AS LIEUTENANT UHURA AND I DO?
OH, SPOCK... NO...
INDEED WE DO. IT WOULD APPEAR THAT THE PHYSICAL DIFFERENCE IN OUR REALITIES DOES NOT PRECLUDE THE EXISTENCE OF MATCHING EVENT PATHS, INCLUDING BUT LIMITED TO THE ESTABLISHMENT OF INTERPERSONAL RELATIONSHIPS.
THIS ISN'T HAPPENING...

IMAGINE WHAT WE COULD LEARN IF WE ALL COMPARE NOTES.

WHAT'S DIFFERENT? WHAT'S THE SAME? WE CAN START BY INTERFACING THE CENTRAL COMPUTERS ON EACH SHIP TO COMPARE SHIP SYSTEMS—

CAPTAIN. WITH ALL DUE RESPECT.

WE DON'T KNOW HOW MUCH LONGER THIS ANOMALY IS GOING TO BE *ACTIVE*. AND AS FAR AS WE CAN GUESS, THAT ANOMALY IS OUR ONLY TICKET HOME. WE NEED TO ACT *NOW*.

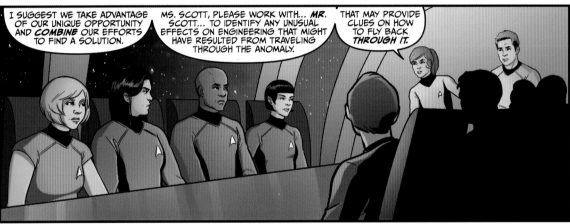

I SUGGEST WE TAKE ADVANTAGE OF OUR UNIQUE OPPORTUNITY AND *COMBINE* OUR EFFORTS TO FIND A SOLUTION.

MS. SCOTT, PLEASE WORK WITH... *MR. SCOTT*... TO IDENTIFY ANY UNUSUAL EFFECTS ON ENGINEERING THAT MIGHT HAVE RESULTED FROM TRAVELING THROUGH THE ANOMALY.

THAT MAY PROVIDE CLUES ON HOW TO FLY BACK *THROUGH IT.*

BOTH SPOCKS, PLEASE STUDY EVERYTHING EACH SHIP HAS BEEN ABLE TO GATHER ON THE ANOMALY ITSELF.

UM, CAPTAIN...?

I MEAN... *MY* CAPTAIN... SHOULD I, UH...?

YOU HAVE YOUR ORDERS, MR. SCOTT.

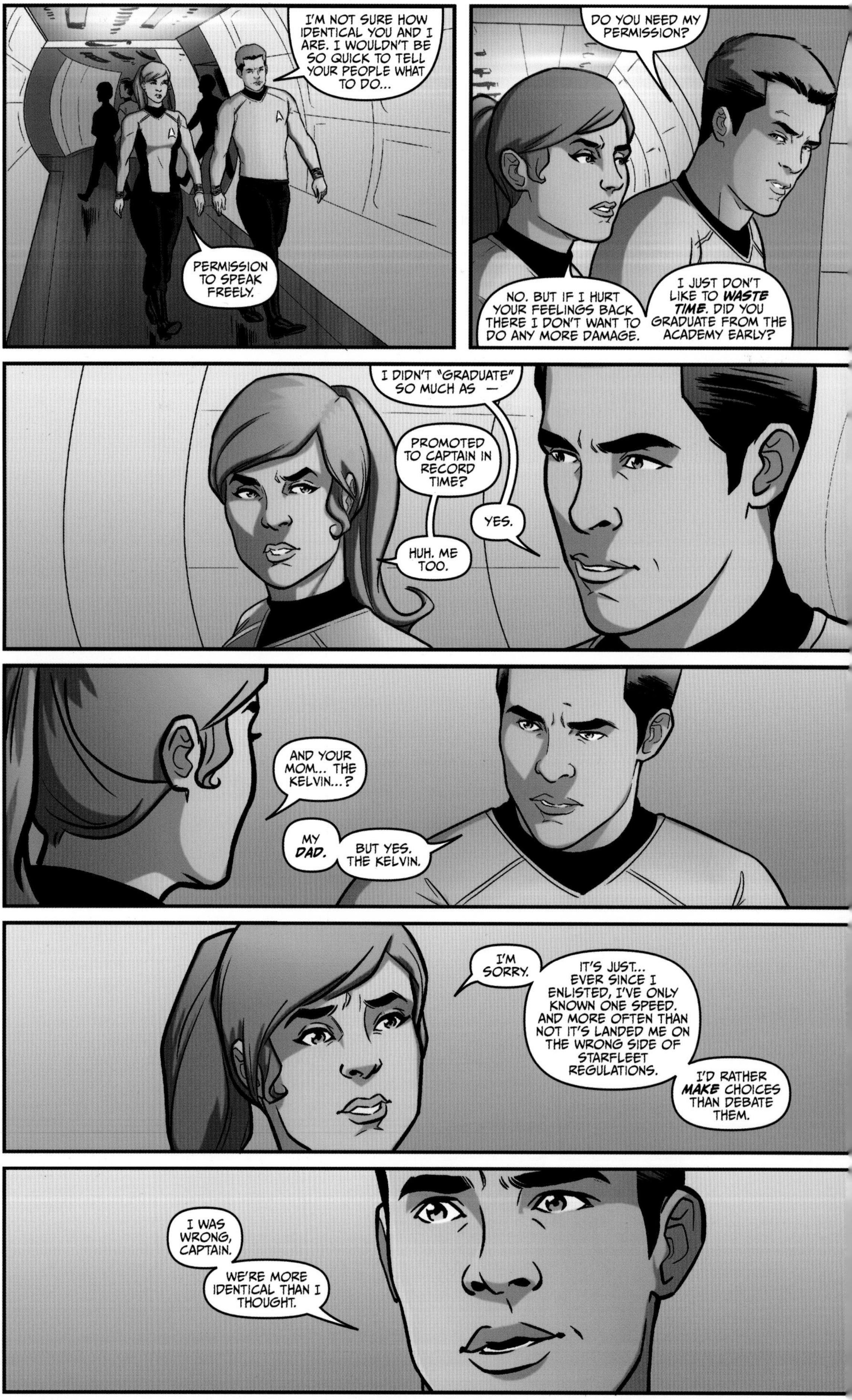
I'M NOT SURE HOW IDENTICAL YOU AND I ARE. I WOULDN'T BE SO QUICK TO TELL YOUR PEOPLE WHAT TO DO...
PERMISSION TO SPEAK FREELY.
DO YOU NEED MY PERMISSION?
NO. BUT IF I HURT YOUR FEELINGS BACK THERE I DON'T WANT TO DO ANY MORE DAMAGE.
I JUST DON'T LIKE TO WASTE TIME. DID YOU GRADUATE FROM THE ACADEMY EARLY?
I DIDN'T "GRADUATE" SO MUCH AS —
PROMOTED TO CAPTAIN IN RECORD TIME?
YES.
HUH. ME TOO.
AND YOUR MOM... THE KELVIN...?
MY DAD.
BUT YES. THE KELVIN.
I'M SORRY.
IT'S JUST... EVER SINCE I ENLISTED, I'VE ONLY KNOWN ONE SPEED. AND MORE OFTEN THAN NOT IT'S LANDED ME ON THE WRONG SIDE OF STARFLEET REGULATIONS.
I'D RATHER MAKE CHOICES THAN DEBATE THEM.
I WAS WRONG, CAPTAIN.
WE'RE MORE IDENTICAL THAN I THOUGHT.

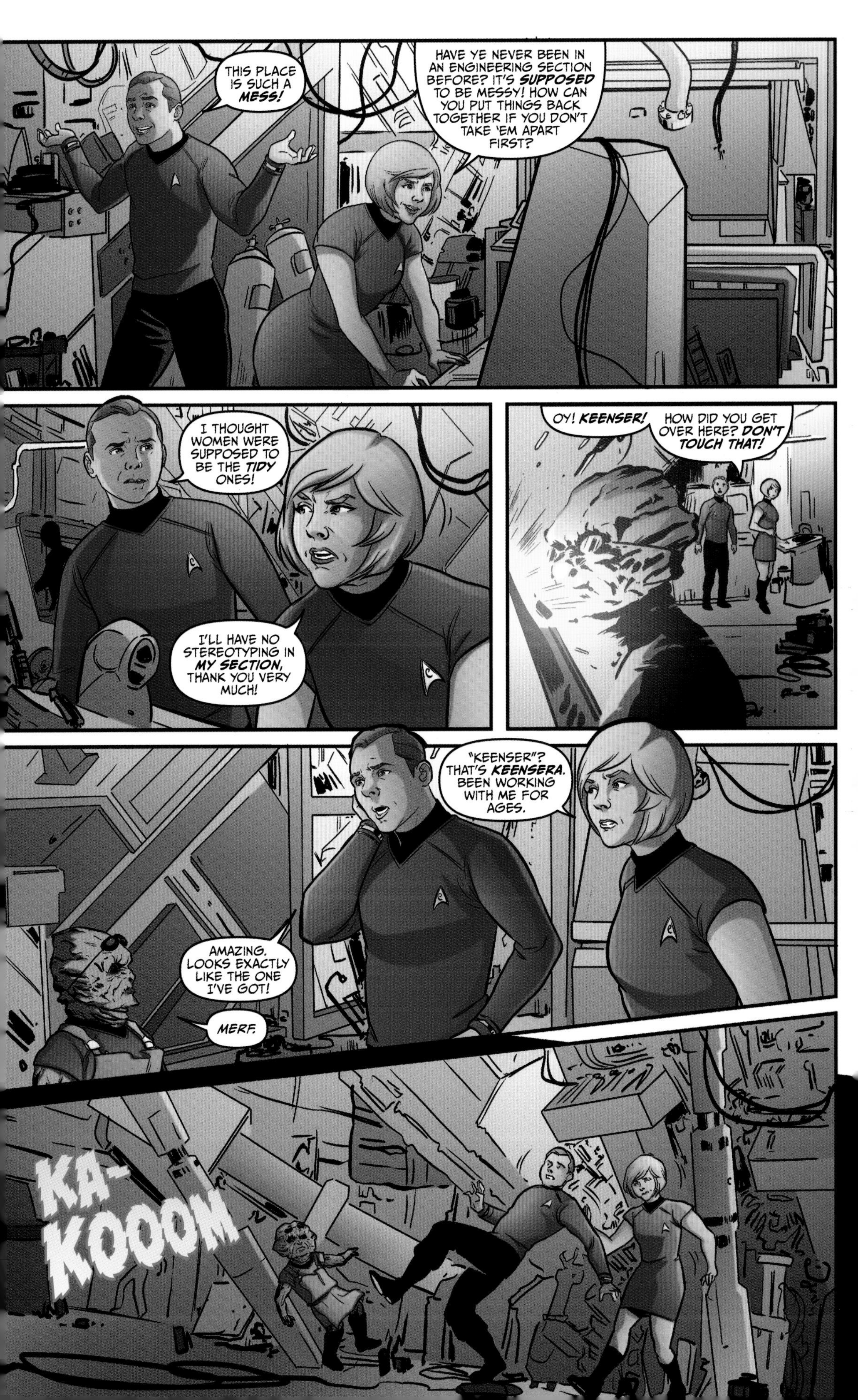
THIS PLACE IS SUCH A MESS!
HAVE YE NEVER BEEN IN AN ENGINEERING SECTION BEFORE? IT'S SUPPOSED TO BE MESSY! HOW CAN YOU PUT THINGS BACK TOGETHER IF YOU DON'T TAKE 'EM APART FIRST?
I THOUGHT WOMEN WERE SUPPOSED TO BE THE TIDY ONES!
I'LL HAVE NO STEREOTYPING IN MY SECTION, THANK YOU VERY MUCH!
OY! KEENSER!
HOW DID YOU GET OVER HERE? DON'T TOUCH THAT!
"KEENSER"? THAT'S KEENSERA. BEEN WORKING WITH ME FOR AGES.
AMAZING. LOOKS EXACTLY LIKE THE ONE I'VE GOT!
MERF.
KA-KOOOM

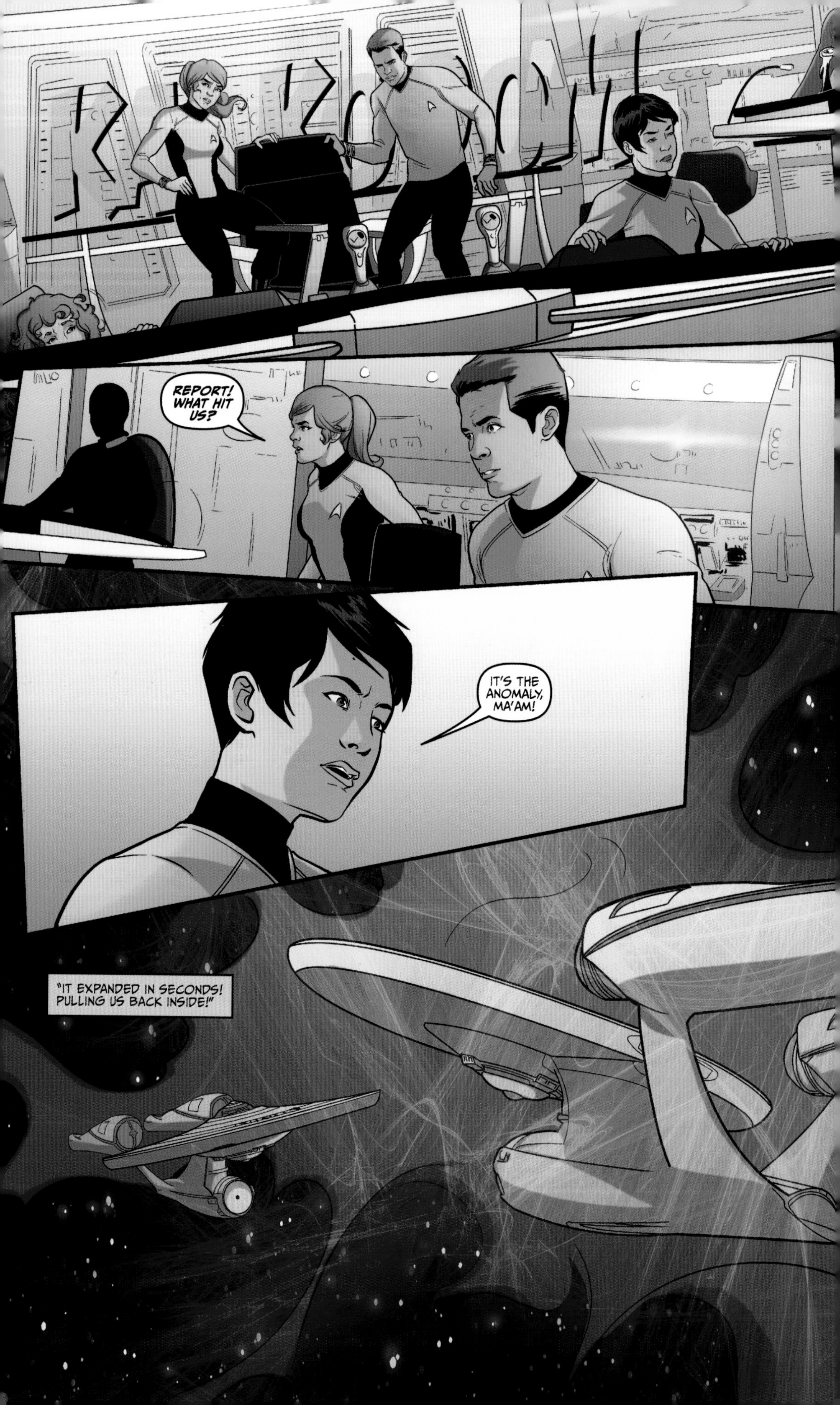
REPORT! WHAT HIT US?
IT'S THE ANOMALY, MA'AM!
"IT EXPANDED IN SECONDS! PULLING US BACK INSIDE!"

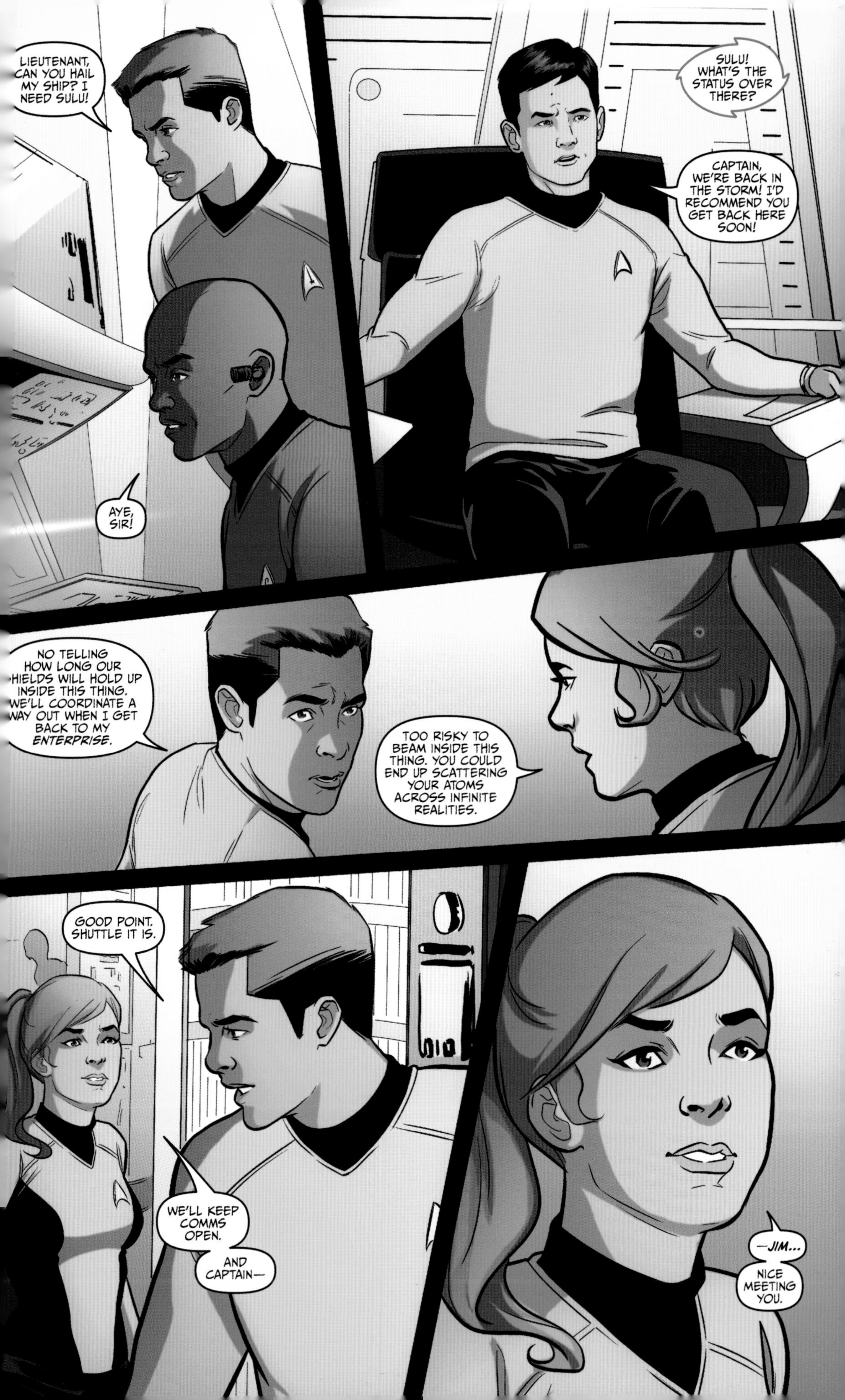
LIEUTENANT, CAN YOU HAIL MY SHIP? I NEED SULU!
AYE, SIR!
SULU! WHAT'S THE STATUS OVER THERE?
CAPTAIN, WE'RE BACK IN THE STORM! I'D RECOMMEND YOU GET BACK HERE SOON!
NO TELLING HOW LONG OUR SHIELDS WILL HOLD UP INSIDE THIS THING. WE'LL COORDINATE A WAY OUT WHEN I GET BACK TO MY *ENTERPRISE*.
TOO RISKY TO BEAM INSIDE THIS THING. YOU COULD END UP SCATTERING YOUR ATOMS ACROSS INFINITE REALITIES.
GOOD POINT. SHUTTLE IT IS.
WE'LL KEEP COMMS OPEN.
AND CAPTAIN—
—*JIM*...
NICE MEETING YOU.

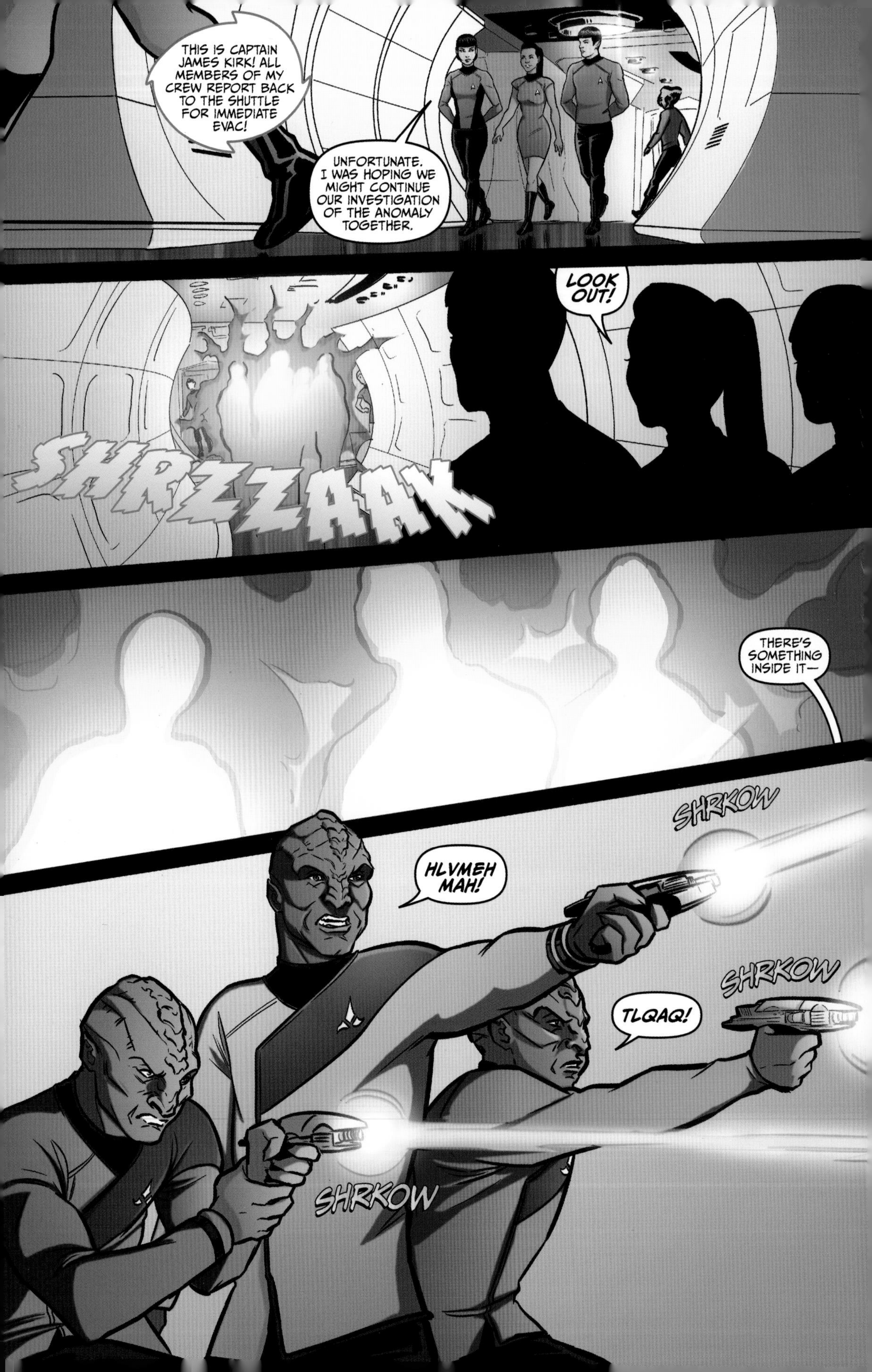
THIS IS CAPTAIN JAMES KIRK! ALL MEMBERS OF MY CREW REPORT BACK TO THE SHUTTLE FOR IMMEDIATE EVAC!
UNFORTUNATE. I WAS HOPING WE MIGHT CONTINUE OUR INVESTIGATION OF THE ANOMALY TOGETHER.
LOOK OUT!
SHRZZAAK
THERE'S SOMETHING INSIDE IT—
SHRKOW
HLVMEH MAH!
SHRKOW
TLQAQ!
SHRKOW

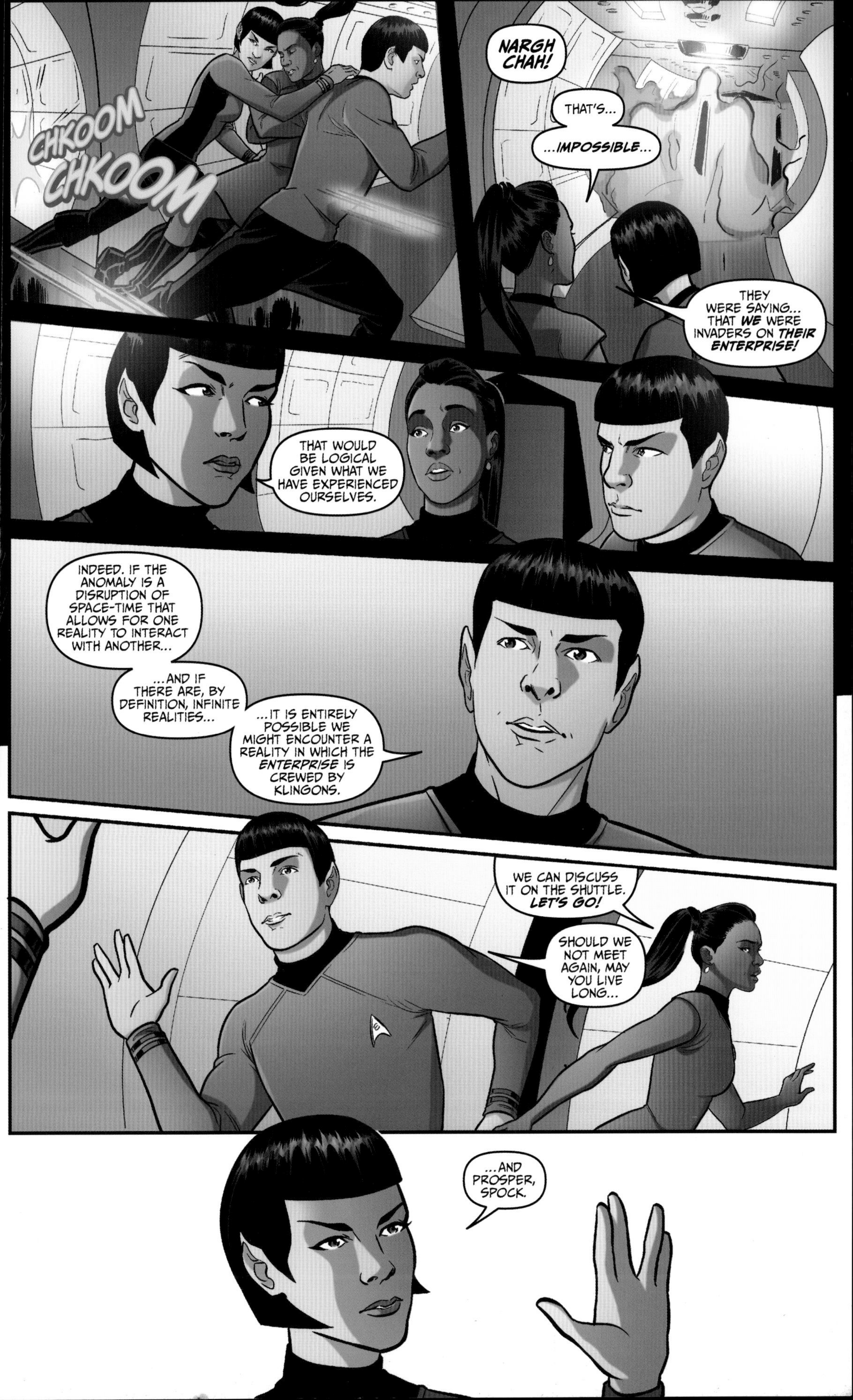
CHKOOM
CHKOOM
NARGH CHAH!
THAT'S...
...IMPOSSIBLE...
THEY WERE SAYING... THAT WE WERE INVADERS ON THEIR ENTERPRISE!
THAT WOULD BE LOGICAL GIVEN WHAT WE HAVE EXPERIENCED OURSELVES.
INDEED. IF THE ANOMALY IS A DISRUPTION OF SPACE-TIME THAT ALLOWS FOR ONE REALITY TO INTERACT WITH ANOTHER...
...AND IF THERE ARE, BY DEFINITION, INFINITE REALITIES...
...IT IS ENTIRELY POSSIBLE WE MIGHT ENCOUNTER A REALITY IN WHICH THE ENTERPRISE IS CREWED BY KLINGONS.
WE CAN DISCUSS IT ON THE SHUTTLE. LET'S GO!
SHOULD WE NOT MEET AGAIN, MAY YOU LIVE LONG...
...AND PROSPER, SPOCK.

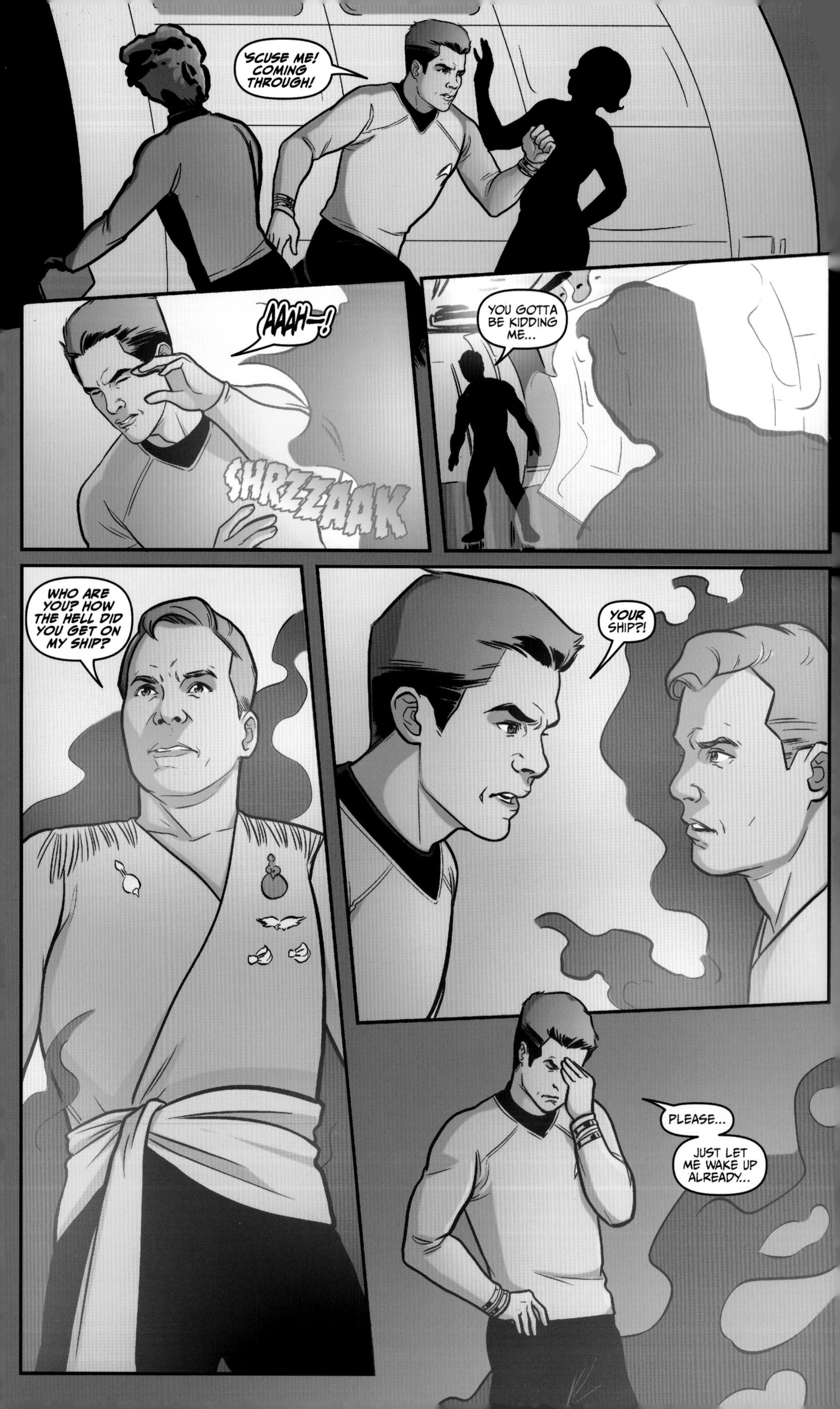
'SCUSE ME! COMING THROUGH!
AAAH—!
SHRZZAAK
YOU GOTTA BE KIDDING ME...
WHO ARE YOU? HOW THE HELL DID YOU GET ON MY SHIP?
YOUR SHIP?!
PLEASE...
JUST LET ME WAKE UP ALREADY...

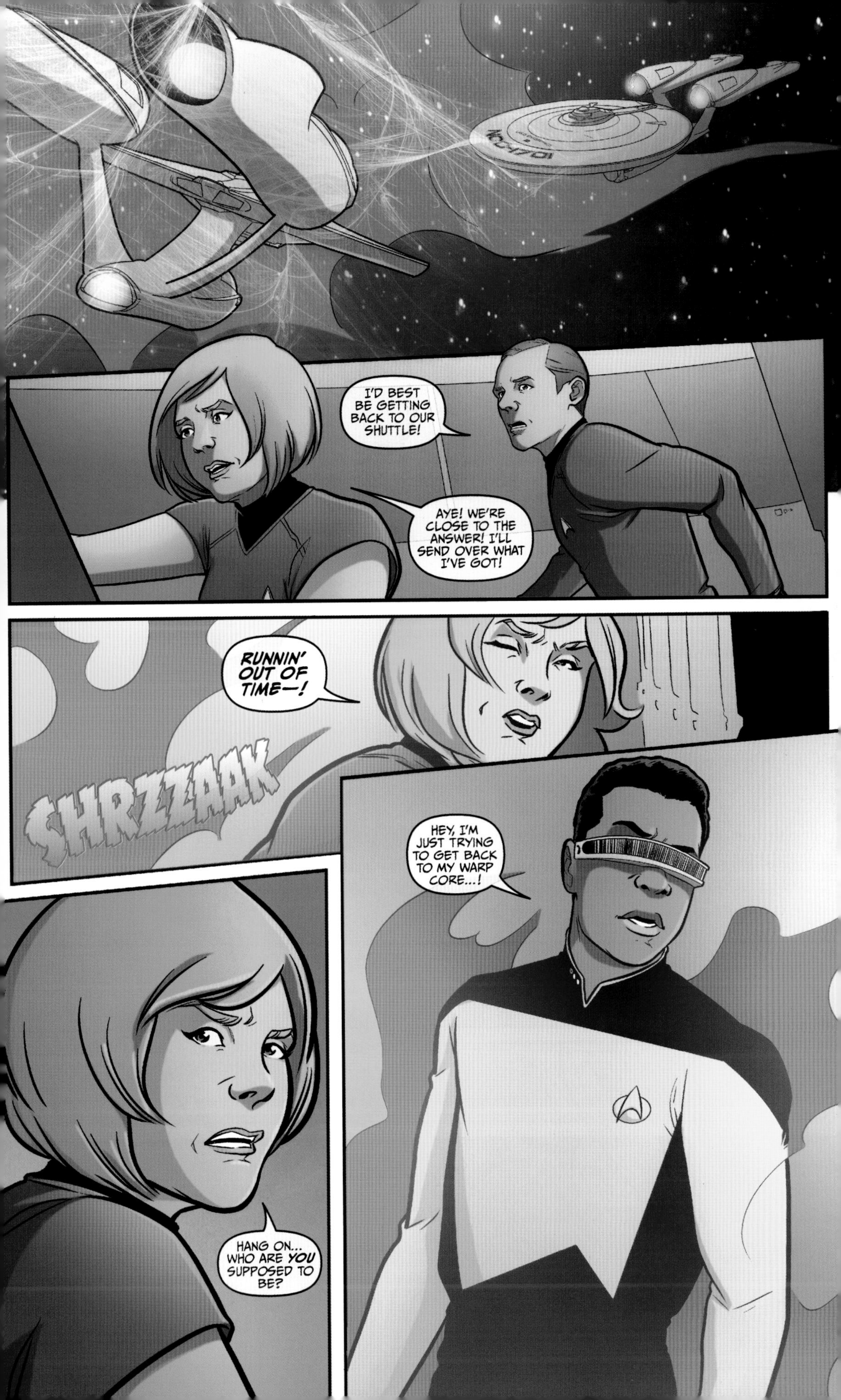
I'D BEST BE GETTING BACK TO OUR SHUTTLE!
AYE! WE'RE CLOSE TO THE ANSWER! I'LL SEND OVER WHAT I'VE GOT!
RUNNIN' OUT OF TIME—!
SHRZZAAK
HEY, I'M JUST TRYING TO GET BACK TO MY WARP CORE...!
HANG ON... WHO ARE *YOU* SUPPOSED TO BE?

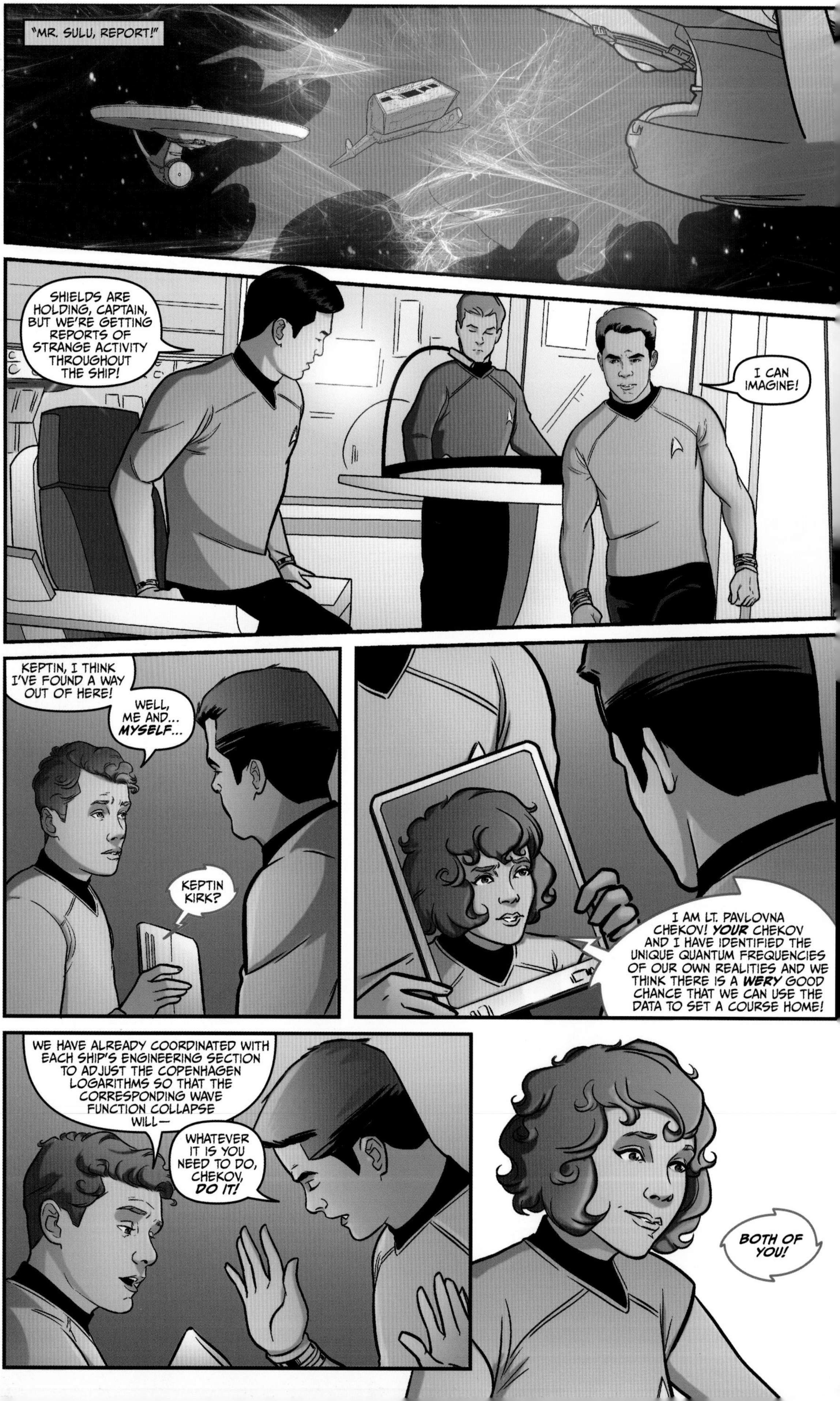
"MR. SULU, REPORT!"
SHIELDS ARE HOLDING, CAPTAIN, BUT WE'RE GETTING REPORTS OF STRANGE ACTIVITY THROUGHOUT THE SHIP!
I CAN IMAGINE!
KEPTIN, I THINK I'VE FOUND A WAY OUT OF HERE!
WELL, ME AND... *MYSELF*...
KEPTIN KIRK?
I AM LT. PAVLOVNA CHEKOV! *YOUR* CHEKOV AND I HAVE IDENTIFIED THE UNIQUE QUANTUM FREQUENCIES OF OUR OWN REALITIES AND WE THINK THERE IS A *WERY* GOOD CHANCE THAT WE CAN USE THE DATA TO SET A COURSE HOME!
WE HAVE ALREADY COORDINATED WITH EACH SHIP'S ENGINEERING SECTION TO ADJUST THE COPENHAGEN LOGARITHMS SO THAT THE CORRESPONDING WAVE FUNCTION COLLAPSE WILL—
WHATEVER IT IS YOU NEED TO DO, CHEKOV, *DO IT!*
BOTH OF YOU!

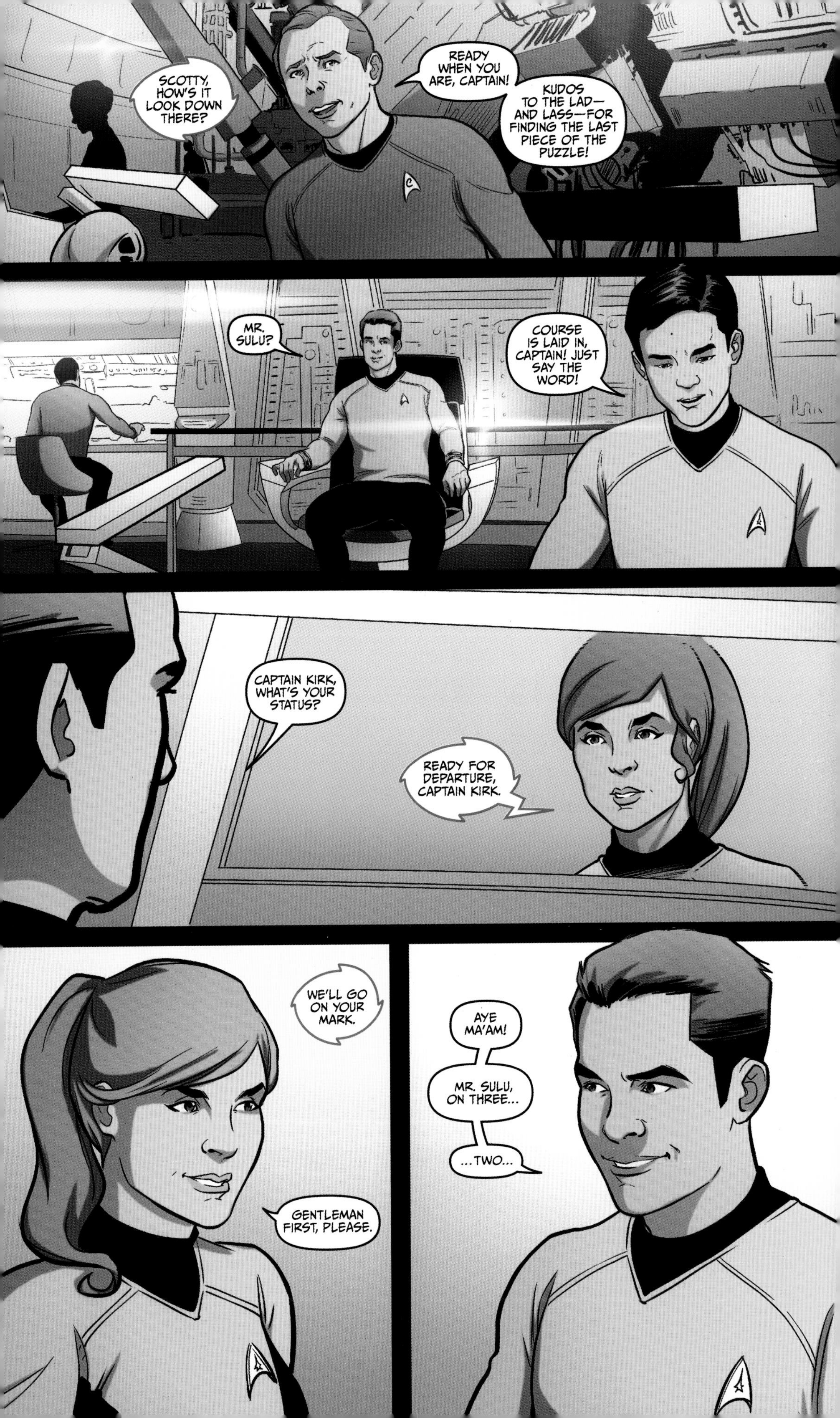
SCOTTY, HOW'S IT LOOK DOWN THERE?
READY WHEN YOU ARE, CAPTAIN!
KUDOS TO THE LAD— AND LASS—FOR FINDING THE LAST PIECE OF THE PUZZLE!
MR. SULU?
COURSE IS LAID IN, CAPTAIN! JUST SAY THE WORD!
CAPTAIN KIRK, WHAT'S YOUR STATUS?
READY FOR DEPARTURE, CAPTAIN KIRK.
WE'LL GO ON YOUR MARK.
GENTLEMAN FIRST, PLEASE.
AYE MA'AM!
MR. SULU, ON THREE...
...TWO...

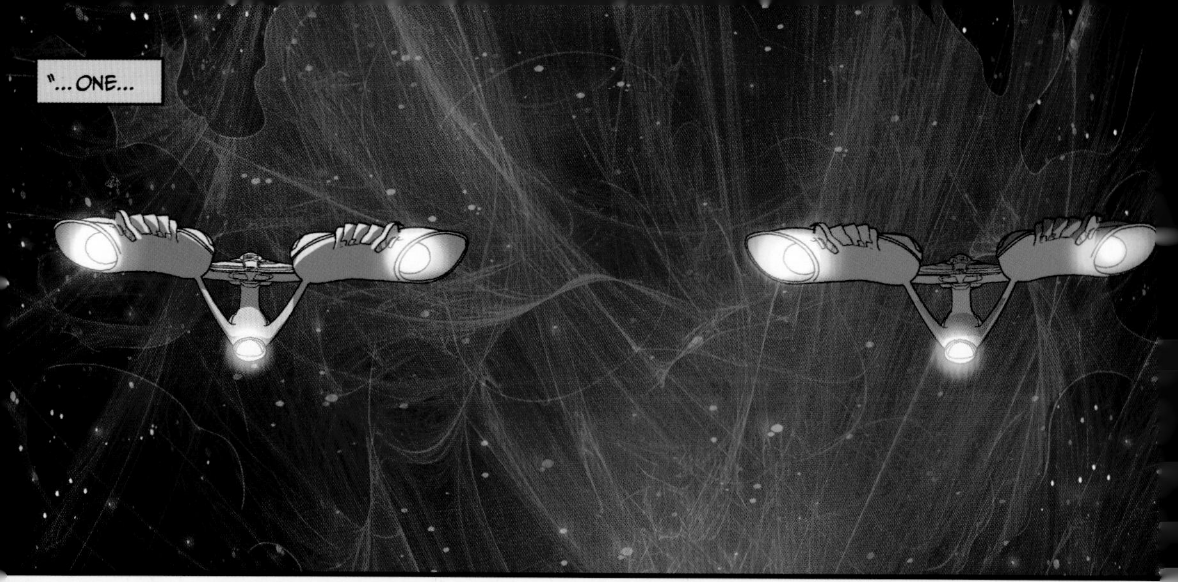
"...ONE...

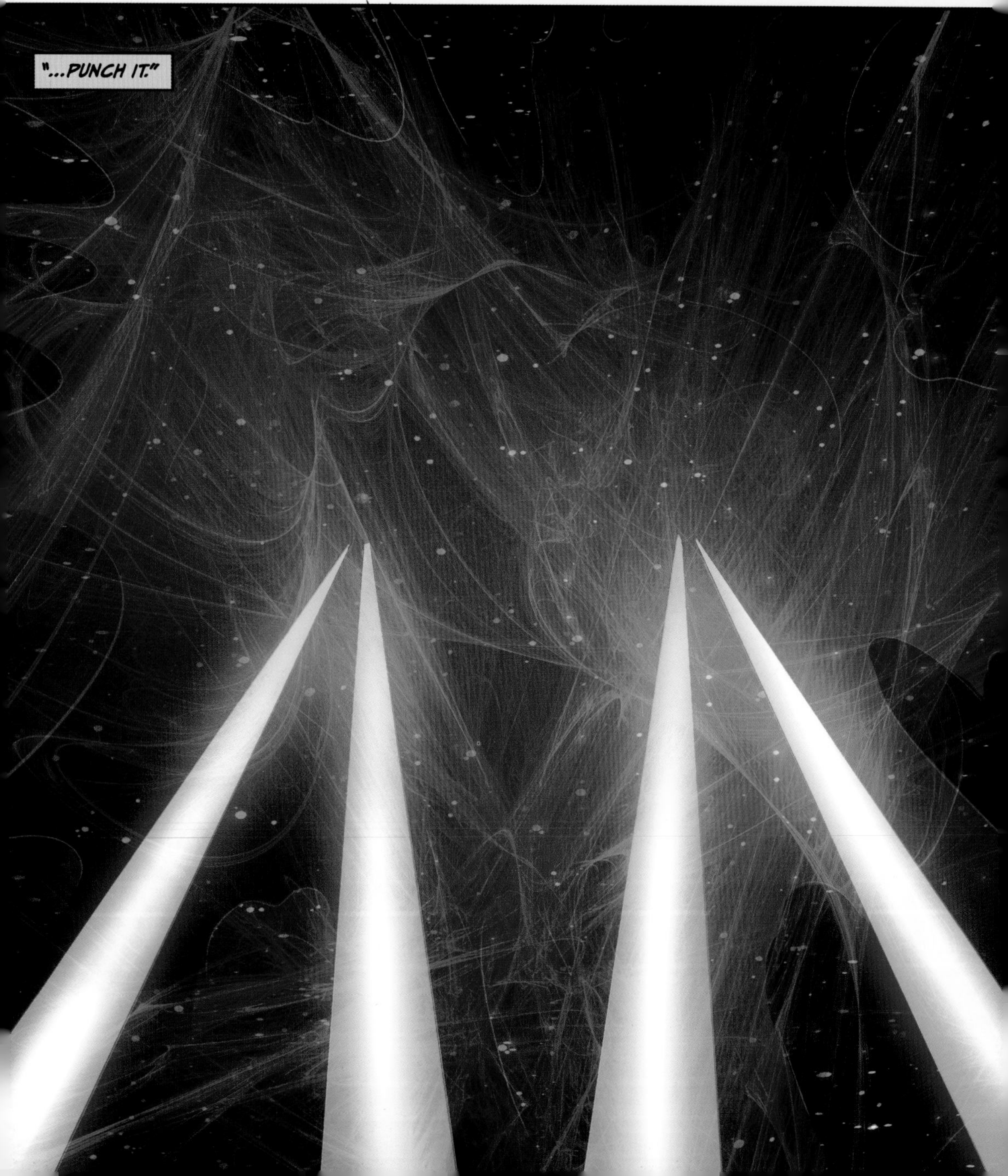
"...PUNCH IT."

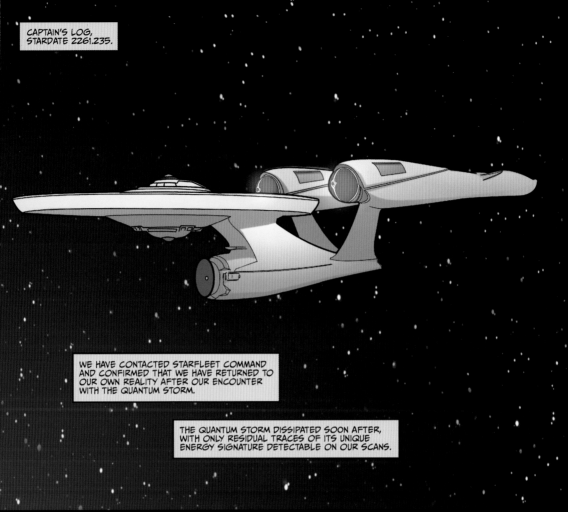

WE HAVE CONTACTED STARFLEET COMMAND
AND CONFIRMED THAT WE HAVE RETURNED TO
OUR OWN REALITY AFTER OUR ENCOUNTER
WITH THE QUANTUM STORM.

THE QUANTUM STORM DISSIPATED SOON AFTER,
WITH ONLY RESIDUAL TRACES OF ITS UNIQUE
ENERGY SIGNATURE DETECTABLE ON OUR SCANS.

WE HAVE LEFT BEHIND WARNING
BEACONS TO STEER ANY SHIPS
CLEAR OF THE REGION IN WHICH
THE STORM WAS DETECTED,
BUT GIVEN THE UNPREDICTABLE
NATURE OF THE ANOMALY...

...WE CAN ONLY HOPE
FOR THE BEST.

WE SUFFERED
ONLY MINOR DAMAGE
TO SHIP SYSTEMS,
CAPTAIN. ALL UNDER
REPAIR.

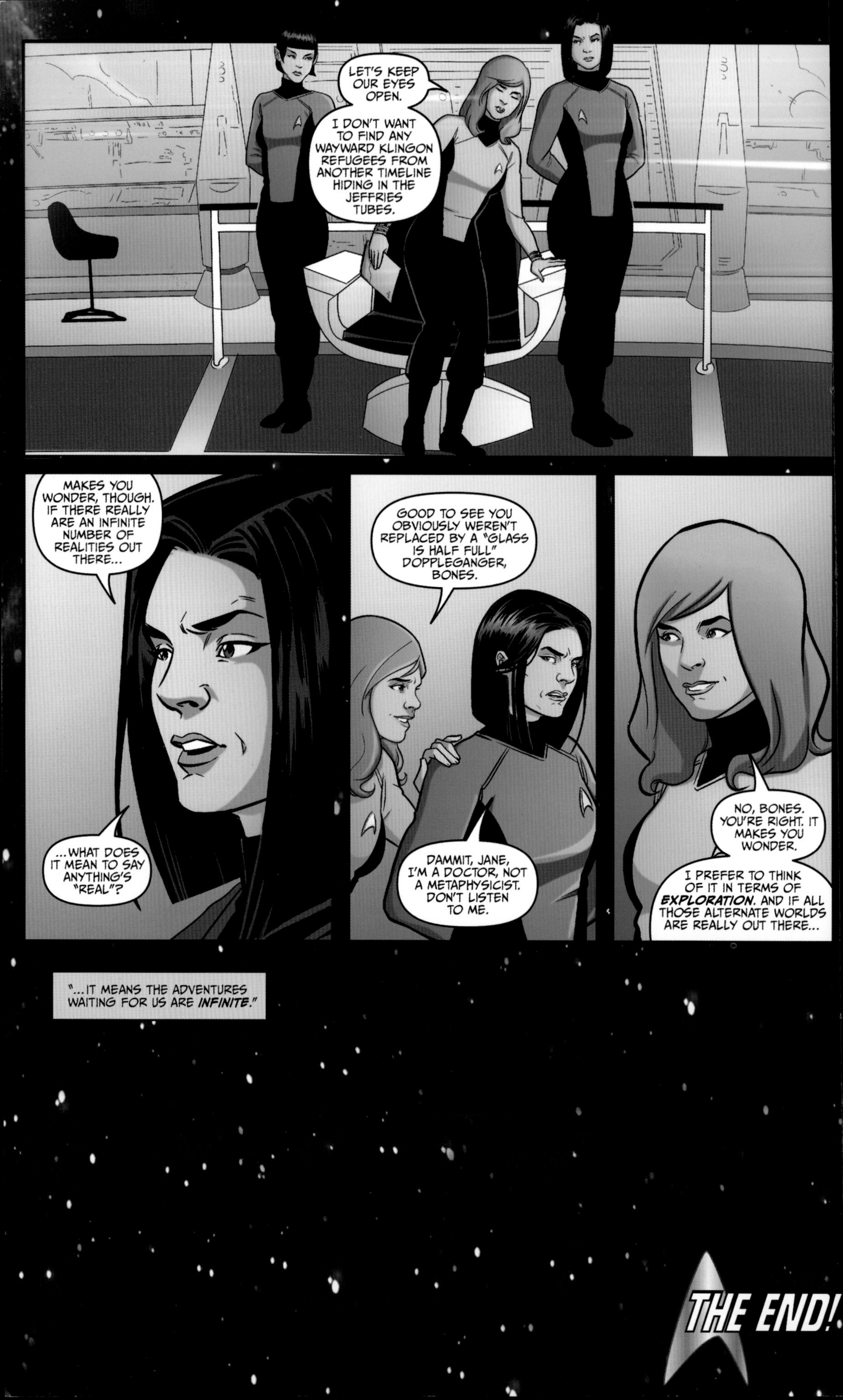
LET'S KEEP OUR EYES OPEN.
I DON'T WANT TO FIND ANY WAYWARD KLINGON REFUGEES FROM ANOTHER TIMELINE HIDING IN THE JEFFRIES TUBES.
MAKES YOU WONDER, THOUGH. IF THERE REALLY ARE AN INFINITE NUMBER OF REALITIES OUT THERE...
...WHAT DOES IT MEAN TO SAY ANYTHING'S "REAL"?
GOOD TO SEE YOU OBVIOUSLY WEREN'T REPLACED BY A "GLASS IS HALF FULL" DOPPLEGANGER, BONES.
DAMMIT, JANE, I'M A DOCTOR, NOT A METAPHYSICIST. DON'T LISTEN TO ME.
NO, BONES. YOU'RE RIGHT. IT MAKES YOU WONDER.
I PREFER TO THINK OF IT IN TERMS OF EXPLORATION. AND IF ALL THOSE ALTERNATE WORLDS ARE REALLY OUT THERE...
"...IT MEANS THE ADVENTURES WAITING FOR US ARE INFINITE."
THE END!

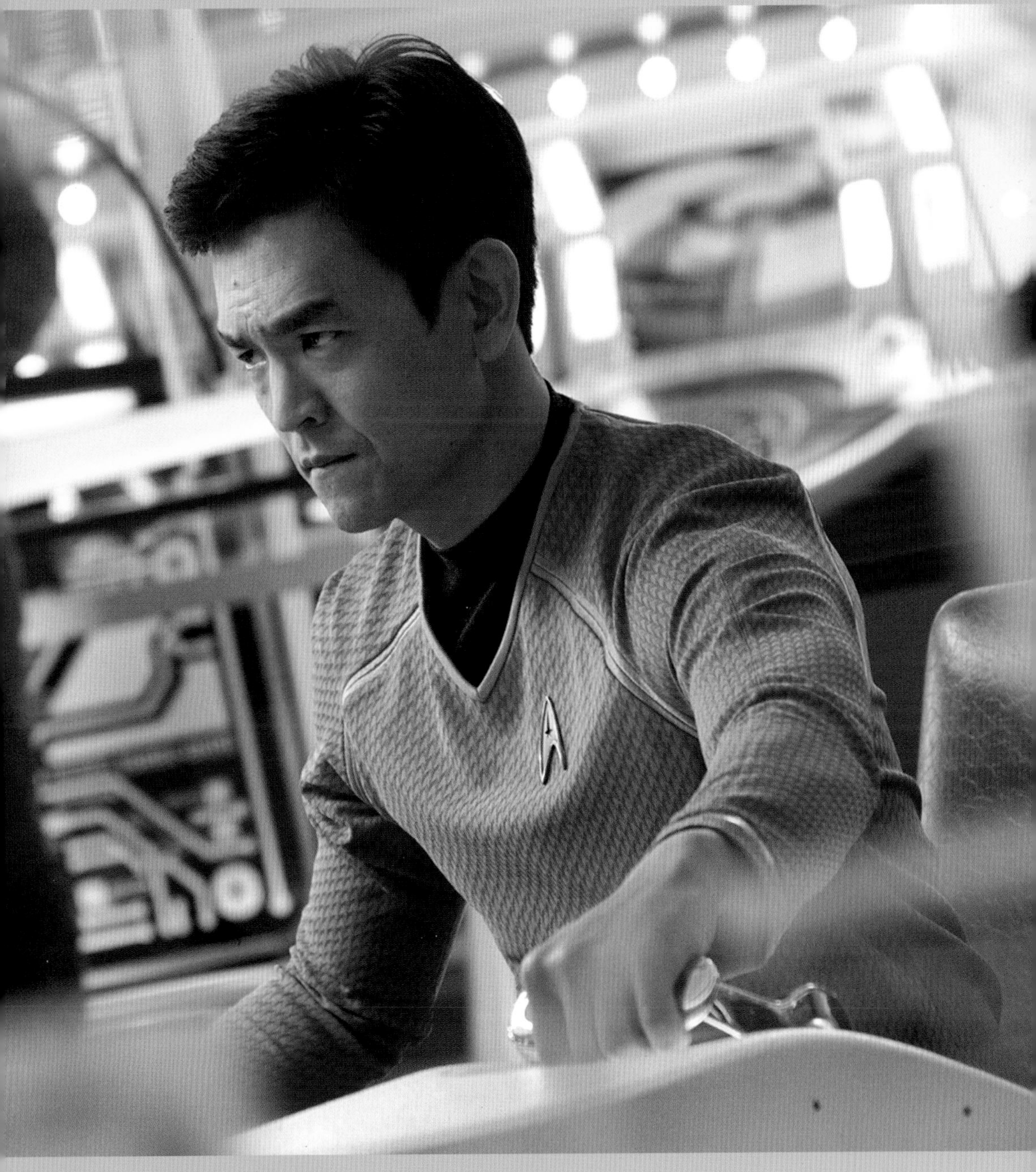

I, ENTERPRISE

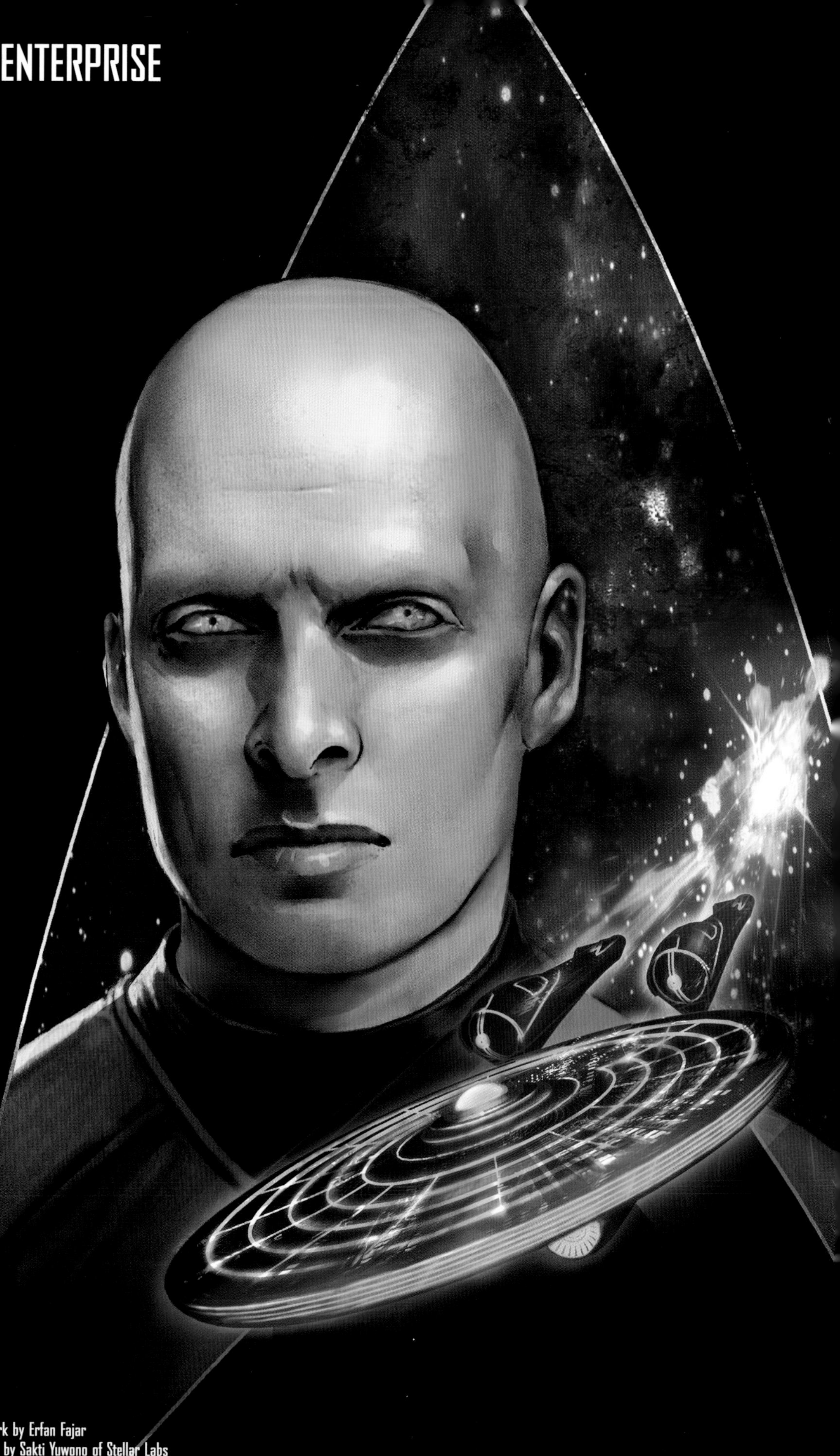

Artwork by Erfan Fajar
Colors by Sakti Yuwono of Stellar Labs

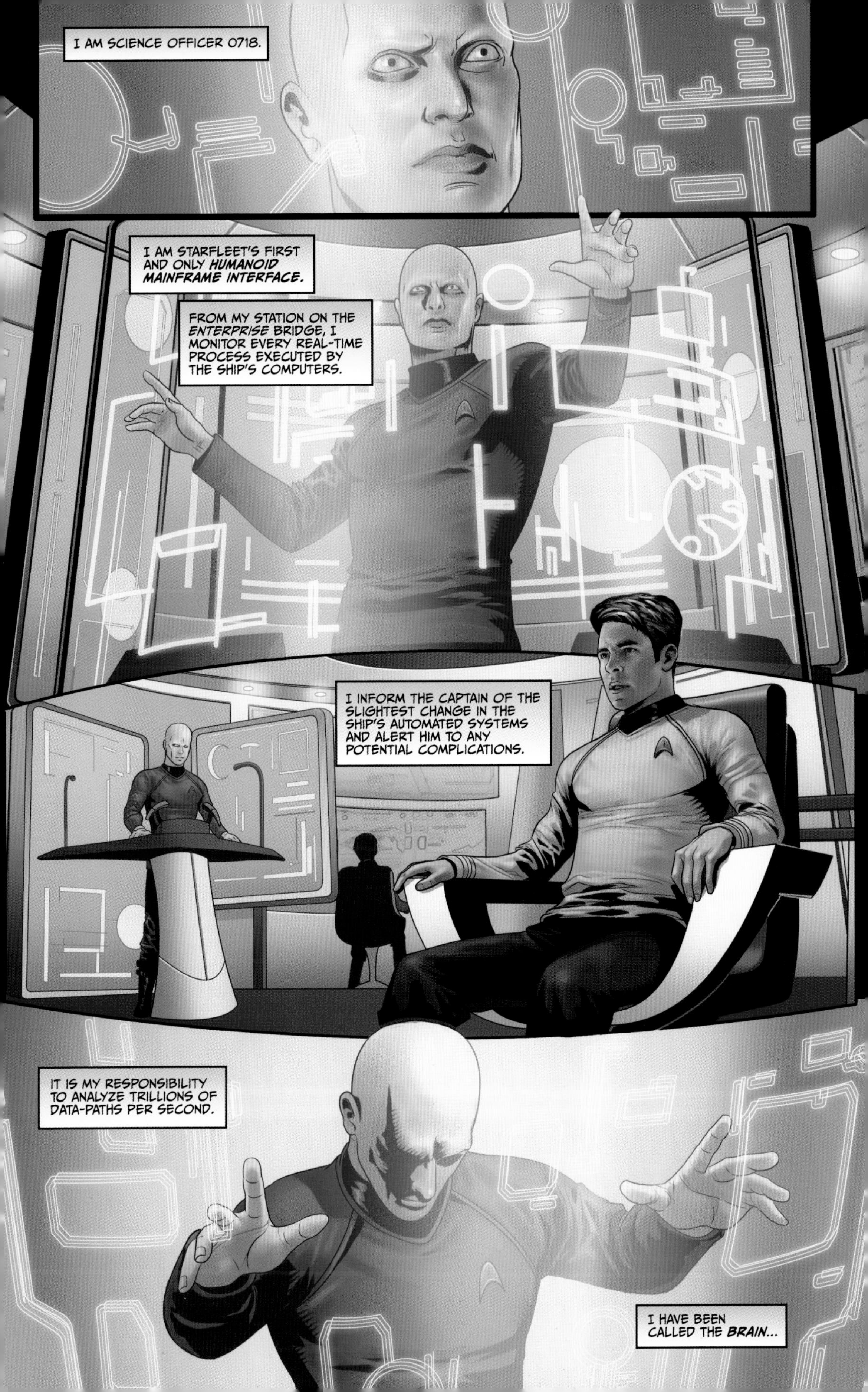
I AM SCIENCE OFFICER 0718.
I AM STARFLEET'S FIRST AND ONLY *HUMANOID MAINFRAME INTERFACE.*
FROM MY STATION ON THE *ENTERPRISE* BRIDGE, I MONITOR EVERY REAL-TIME PROCESS EXECUTED BY THE SHIP'S COMPUTERS.
I INFORM THE CAPTAIN OF THE SLIGHTEST CHANGE IN THE SHIP'S AUTOMATED SYSTEMS AND ALERT HIM TO ANY POTENTIAL COMPLICATIONS.
IT IS MY RESPONSIBILITY TO ANALYZE TRILLIONS OF DATA-PATHS PER SECOND.
I HAVE BEEN CALLED THE *BRAIN*...

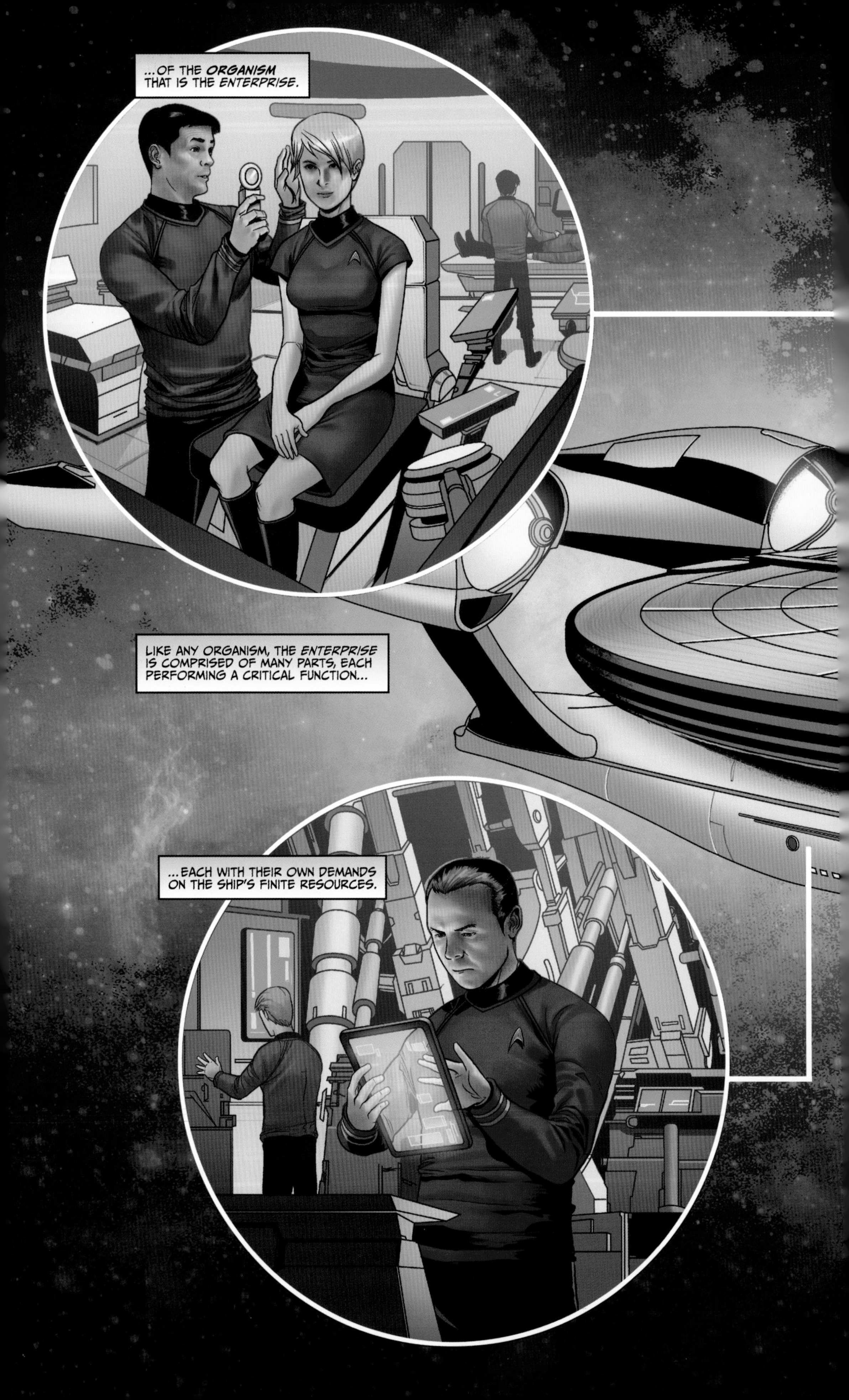
...OF THE ORGANISM THAT IS THE ENTERPRISE.
LIKE ANY ORGANISM, THE ENTERPRISE IS COMPRISED OF MANY PARTS, EACH PERFORMING A CRITICAL FUNCTION...
...EACH WITH THEIR OWN DEMANDS ON THE SHIP'S FINITE RESOURCES.

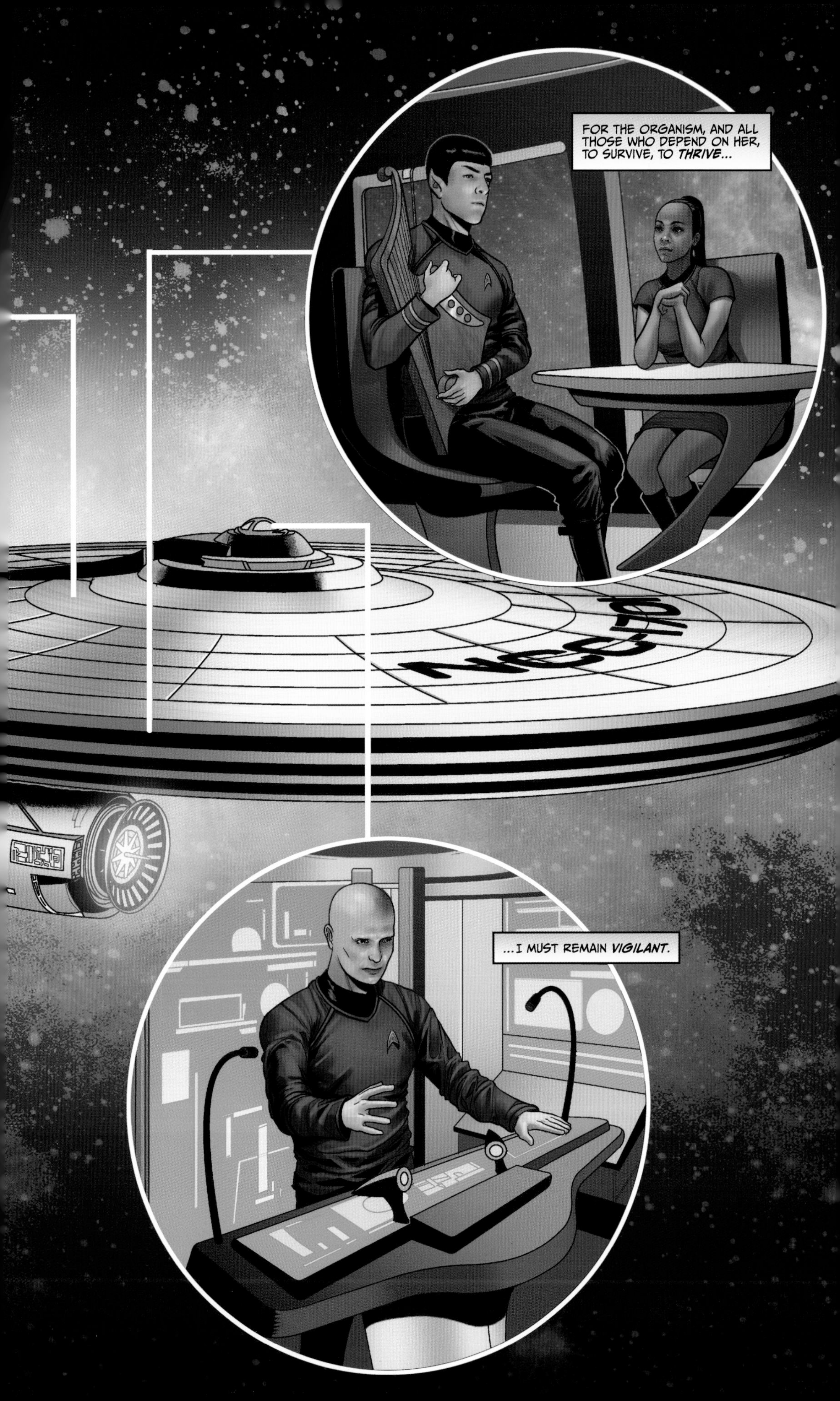
FOR THE ORGANISM, AND ALL THOSE WHO DEPEND ON HER, TO SURVIVE, TO *THRIVE*...
...I MUST REMAIN *VIGILANT*.

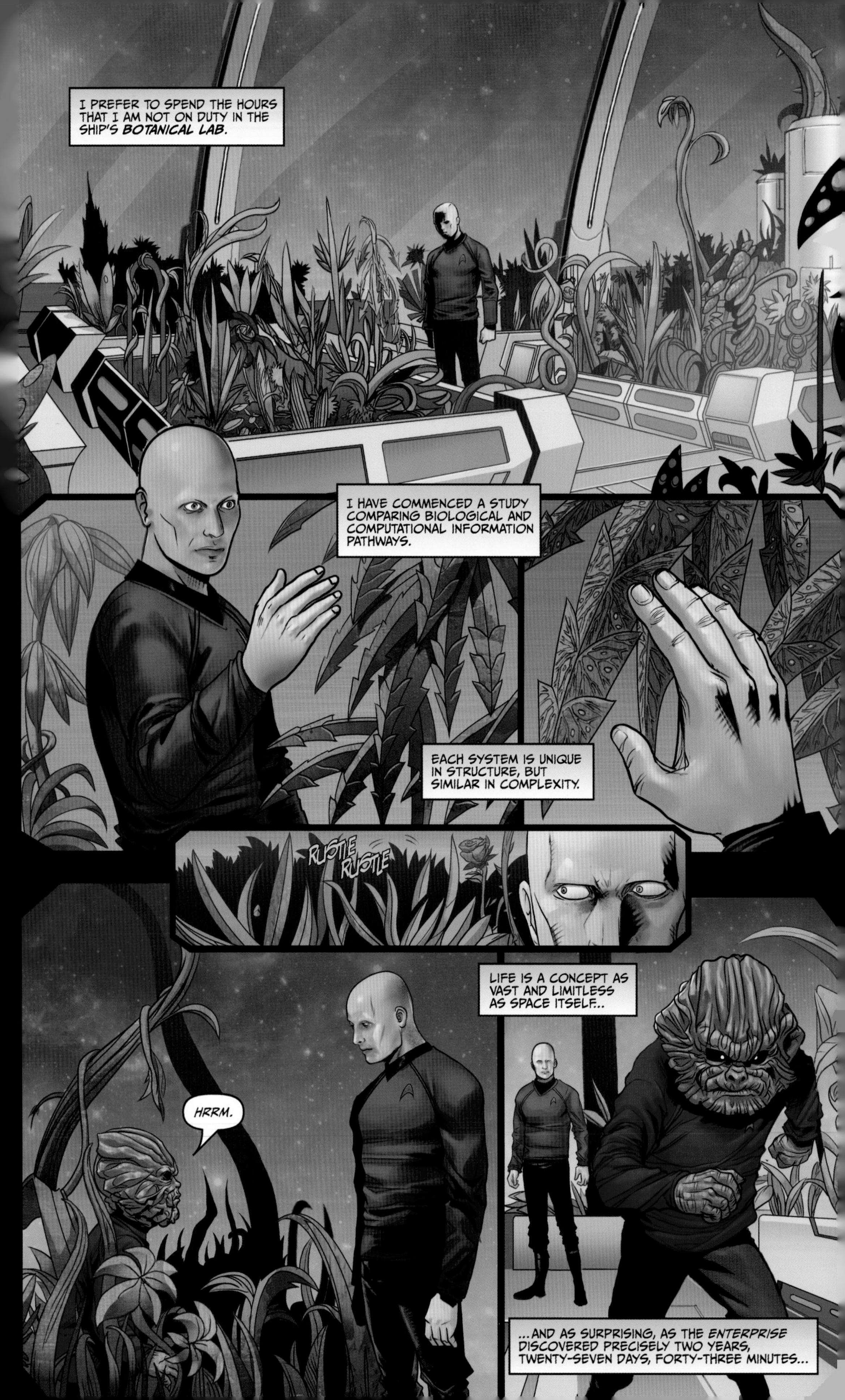
I PREFER TO SPEND THE HOURS THAT I AM NOT ON DUTY IN THE SHIP'S ***BOTANICAL LAB***.
I HAVE COMMENCED A STUDY COMPARING BIOLOGICAL AND COMPUTATIONAL INFORMATION PATHWAYS.
EACH SYSTEM IS UNIQUE IN STRUCTURE, BUT SIMILAR IN COMPLEXITY.
RUSTLE RUSTLE
HRRM.
LIFE IS A CONCEPT AS VAST AND LIMITLESS AS SPACE ITSELF...
...AND AS SURPRISING, AS THE *ENTERPRISE* DISCOVERED PRECISELY TWO YEARS, TWENTY-SEVEN DAYS, FORTY-THREE MINUTES...

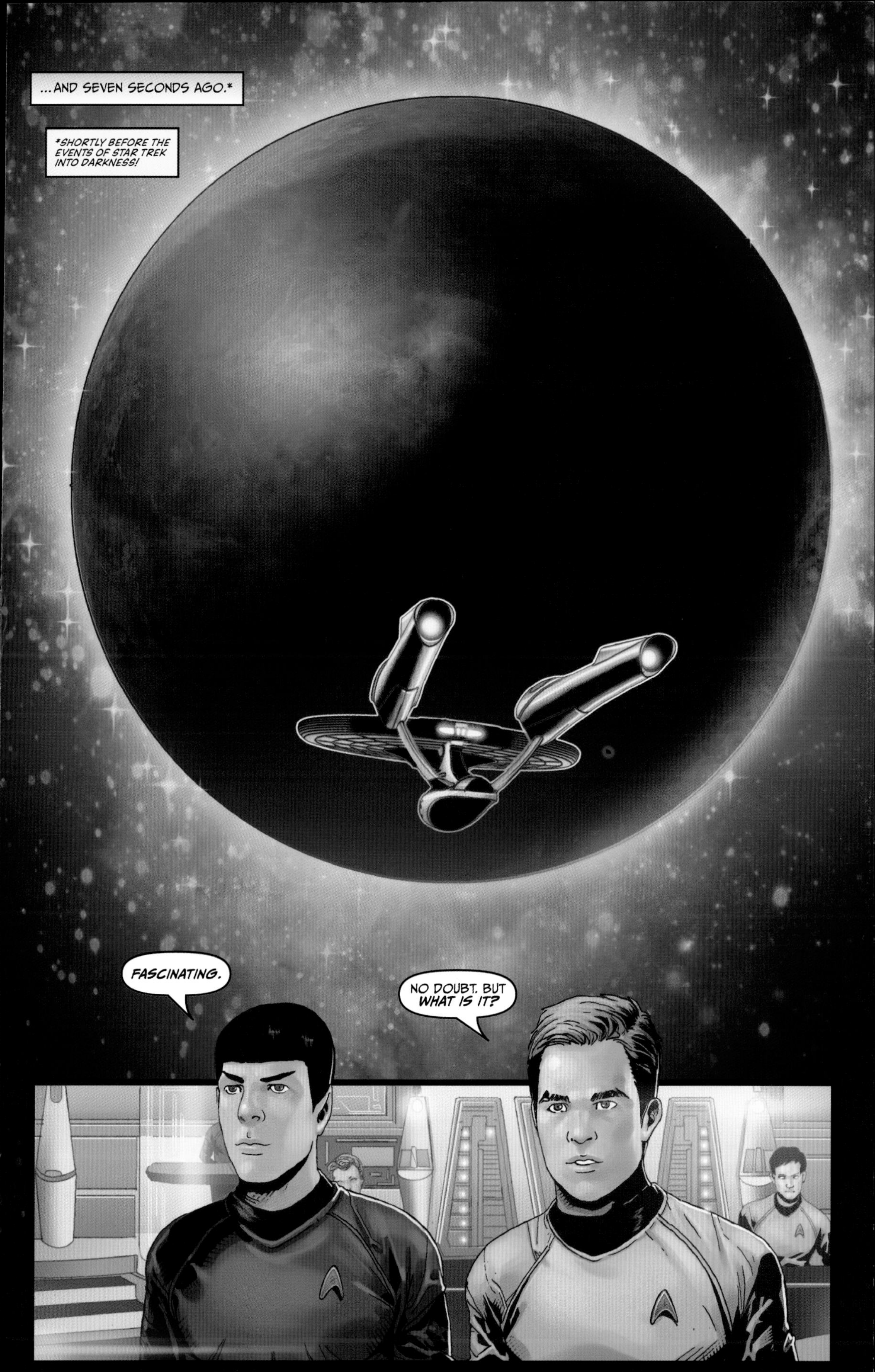
...AND SEVEN SECONDS AGO.*
*SHORTLY BEFORE THE EVENTS OF STAR TREK INTO DARKNESS!
FASCINATING.
NO DOUBT. BUT WHAT IS IT?

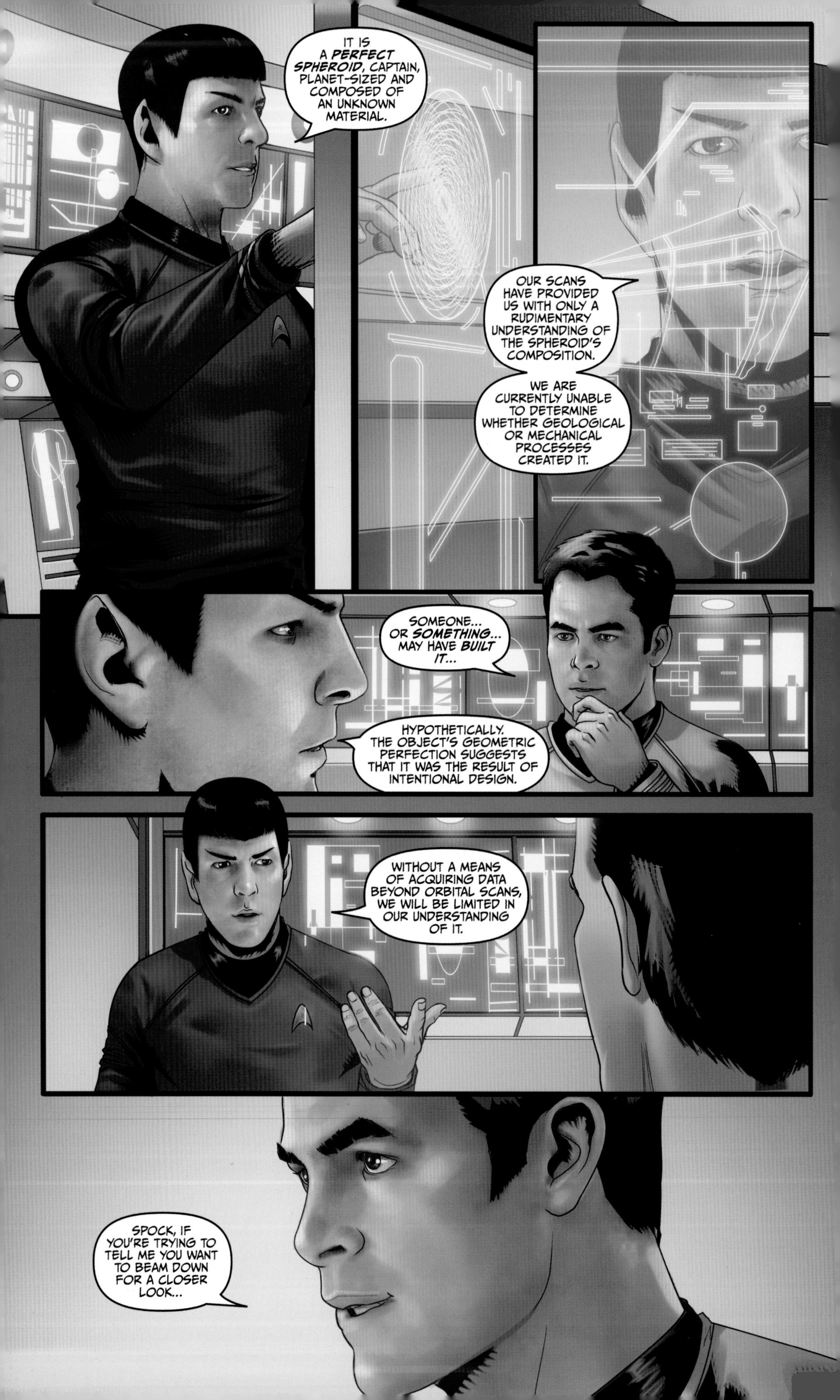
IT IS A PERFECT SPHEROID, CAPTAIN, PLANET-SIZED AND COMPOSED OF AN UNKNOWN MATERIAL.
OUR SCANS HAVE PROVIDED US WITH ONLY A RUDIMENTARY UNDERSTANDING OF THE SPHEROID'S COMPOSITION.
WE ARE CURRENTLY UNABLE TO DETERMINE WHETHER GEOLOGICAL OR MECHANICAL PROCESSES CREATED IT.
SOMEONE... OR SOMETHING... MAY HAVE BUILT IT...
HYPOTHETICALLY. THE OBJECT'S GEOMETRIC PERFECTION SUGGESTS THAT IT WAS THE RESULT OF INTENTIONAL DESIGN.
WITHOUT A MEANS OF ACQUIRING DATA BEYOND ORBITAL SCANS, WE WILL BE LIMITED IN OUR UNDERSTANDING OF IT.
SPOCK, IF YOU'RE TRYING TO TELL ME YOU WANT TO BEAM DOWN FOR A CLOSER LOOK...

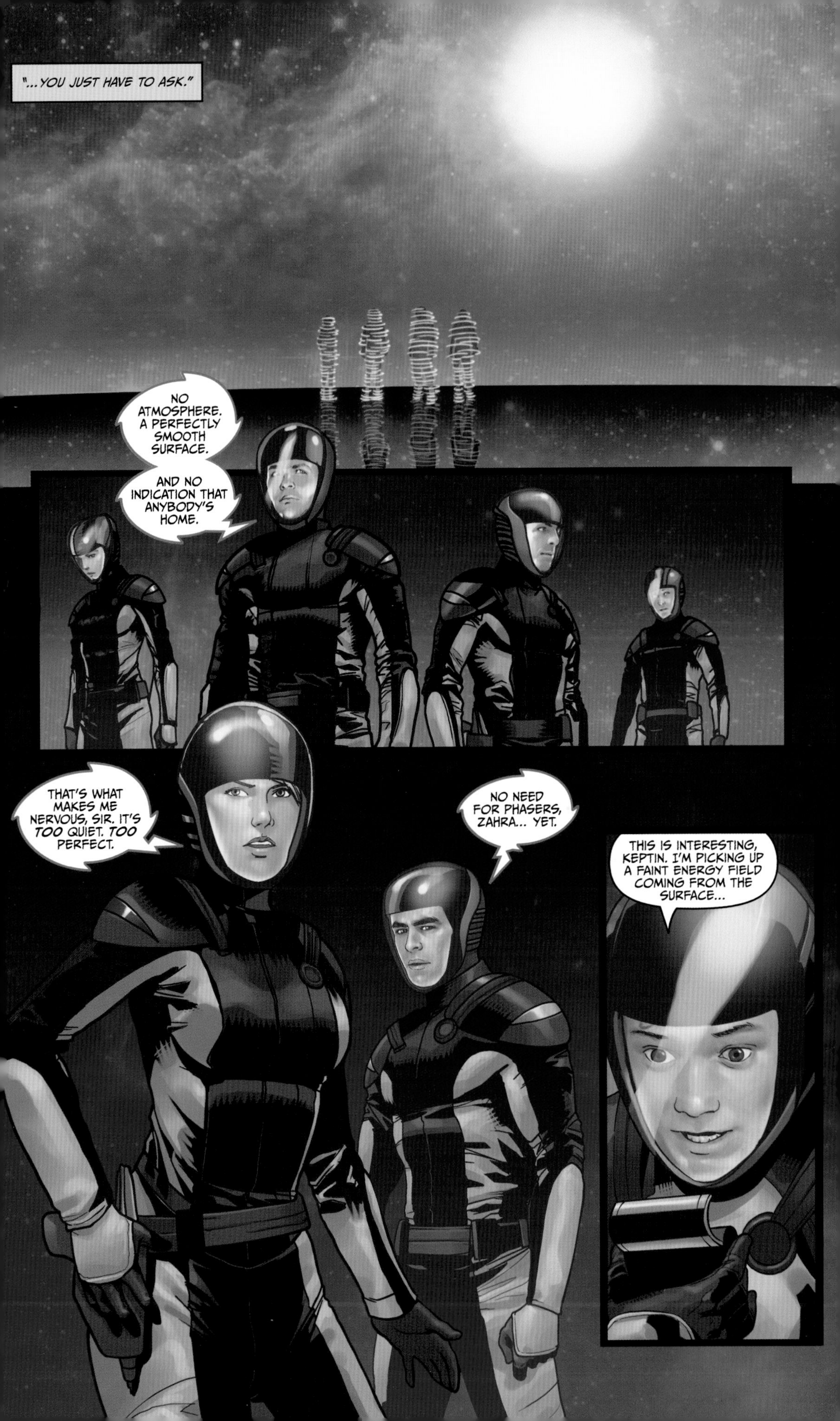
"...YOU JUST HAVE TO ASK."
NO ATMOSPHERE. A PERFECTLY SMOOTH SURFACE.
AND NO INDICATION THAT ANYBODY'S HOME.
THAT'S WHAT MAKES ME NERVOUS, SIR. IT'S *TOO* QUIET. *TOO* PERFECT.
NO NEED FOR PHASERS, ZAHRA... YET.
THIS IS INTERESTING, KEPTIN. I'M PICKING UP A FAINT ENERGY FIELD COMING FROM THE SURFACE...

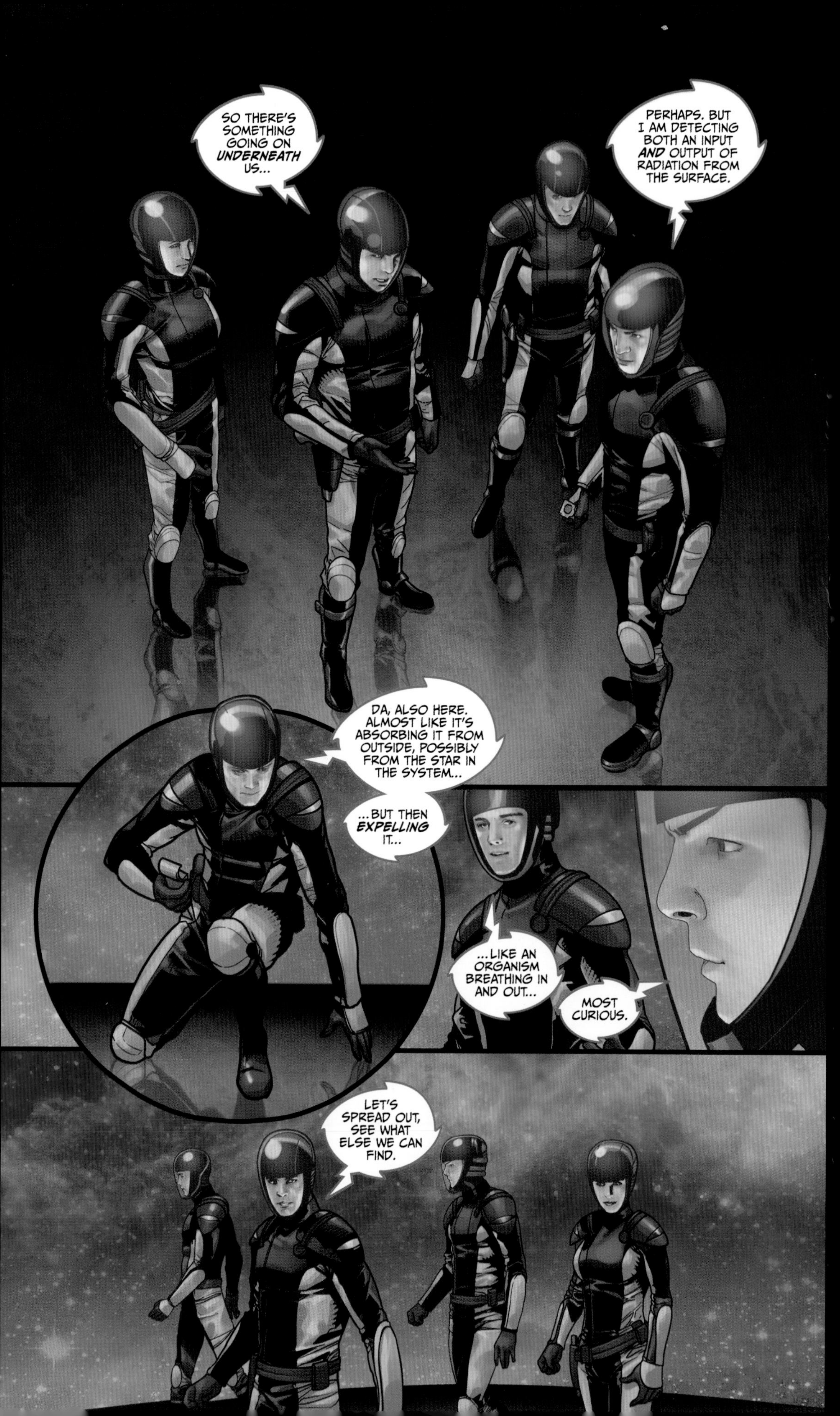
SO THERE'S SOMETHING GOING ON *UNDERNEATH* US...
PERHAPS. BUT I AM DETECTING BOTH AN INPUT ***AND*** OUTPUT OF RADIATION FROM THE SURFACE.
DA, ALSO HERE. ALMOST LIKE IT'S ABSORBING IT FROM OUTSIDE, POSSIBLY FROM THE STAR IN THE SYSTEM...
...BUT THEN *EXPELLING* IT...
...LIKE AN ORGANISM BREATHING IN AND OUT...
MOST CURIOUS.
LET'S SPREAD OUT, SEE WHAT ELSE WE CAN FIND.

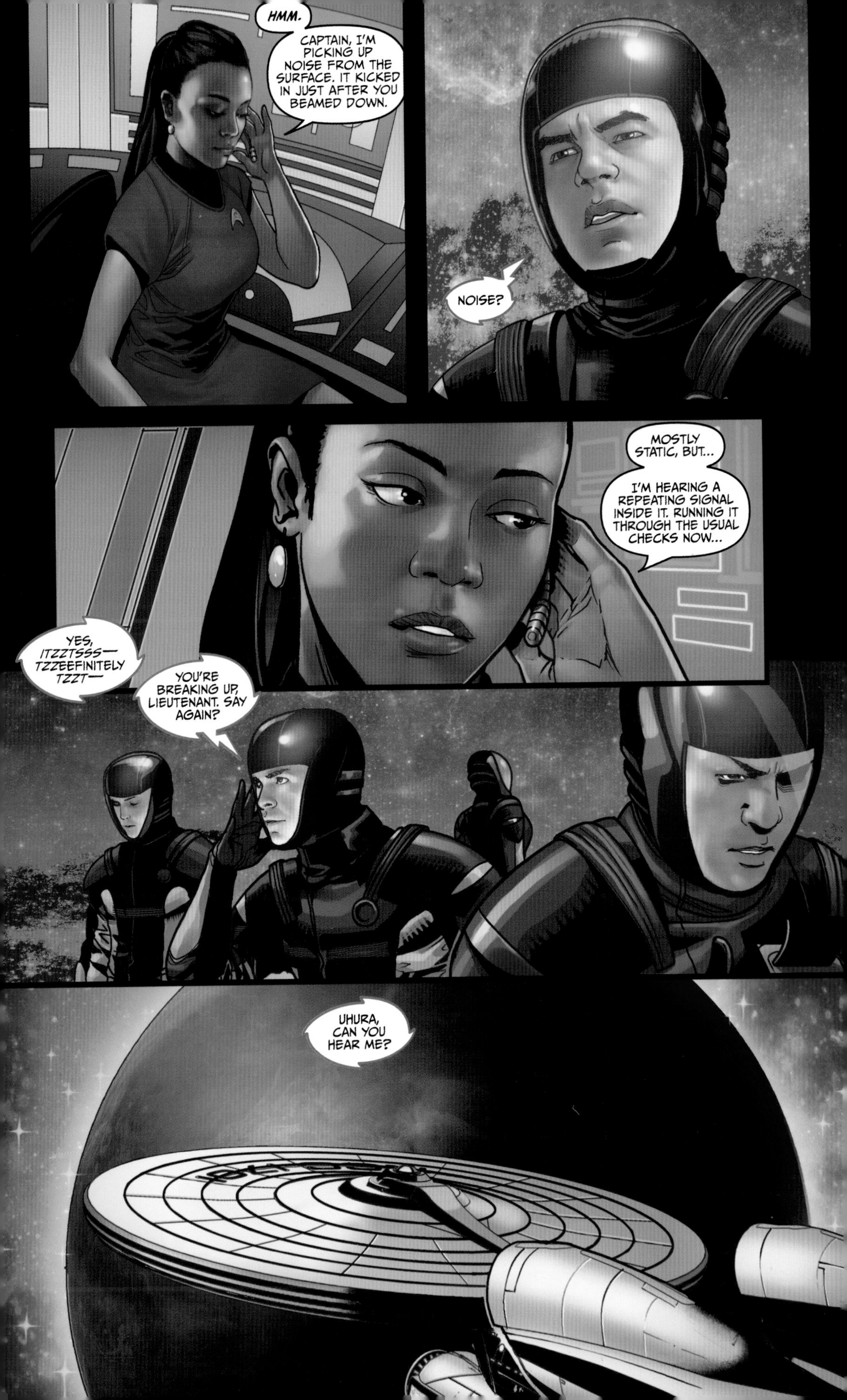
HMM.
CAPTAIN, I'M PICKING UP NOISE FROM THE SURFACE. IT KICKED IN JUST AFTER YOU BEAMED DOWN.
NOISE?
MOSTLY STATIC, BUT...
I'M HEARING A REPEATING SIGNAL INSIDE IT. RUNNING IT THROUGH THE USUAL CHECKS NOW...
YES, ITZZTSSS— TZZEEFINITELY TZZT—
YOU'RE BREAKING UP, LIEUTENANT. SAY AGAIN?
UHURA, CAN YOU HEAR ME?

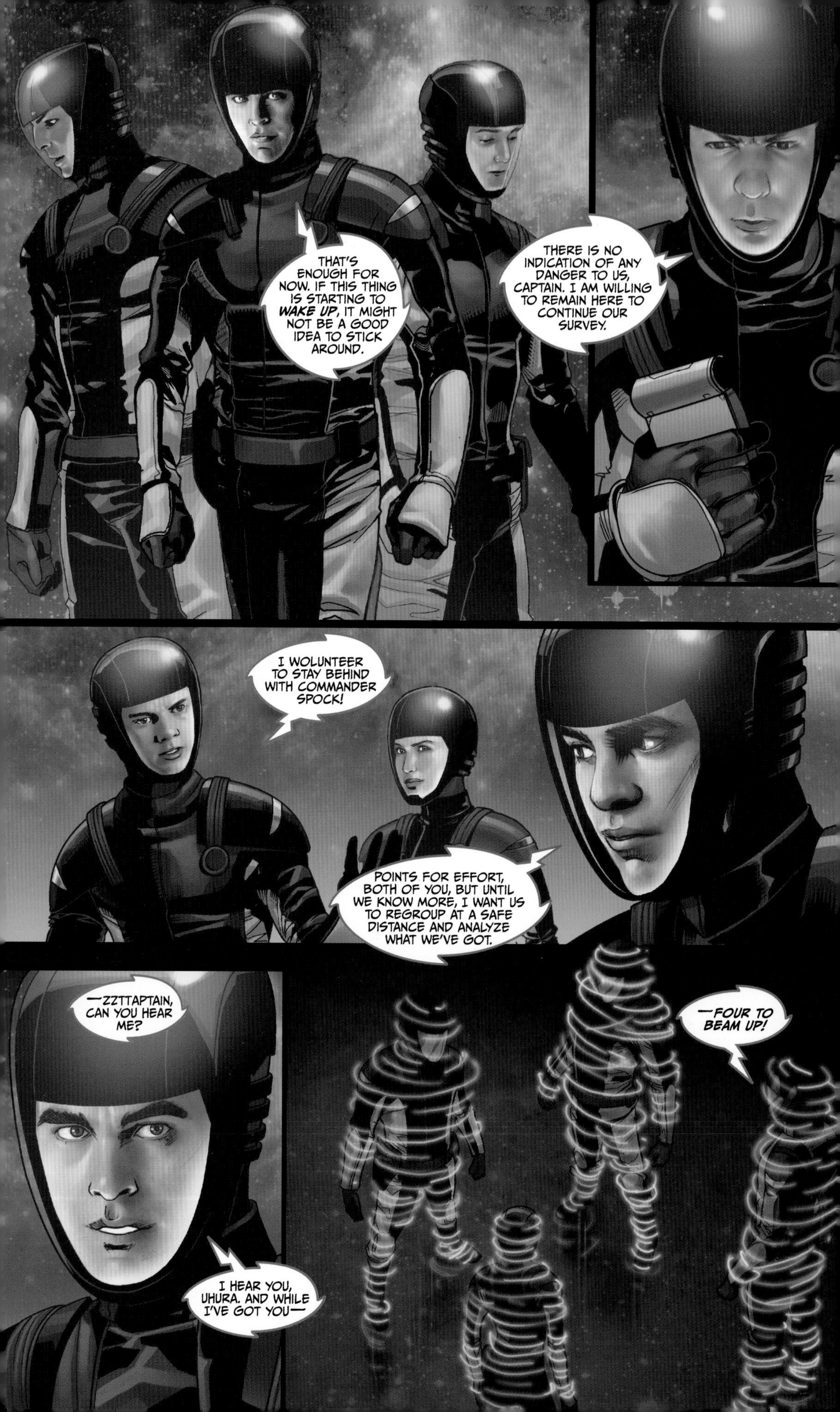
THAT'S ENOUGH FOR NOW. IF THIS THING IS STARTING TO *WAKE UP*, IT MIGHT NOT BE A GOOD IDEA TO STICK AROUND.
THERE IS NO INDICATION OF ANY DANGER TO US, CAPTAIN. I AM WILLING TO REMAIN HERE TO CONTINUE OUR SURVEY.
I WOLUNTEER TO STAY BEHIND WITH COMMANDER SPOCK!
POINTS FOR EFFORT, BOTH OF YOU, BUT UNTIL WE KNOW MORE, I WANT US TO REGROUP AT A SAFE DISTANCE AND ANALYZE WHAT WE'VE GOT.
—ZZTTAPTAIN, CAN YOU HEAR ME?
I HEAR YOU, UHURA. AND WHILE I'VE GOT YOU—
—*FOUR TO BEAM UP!*

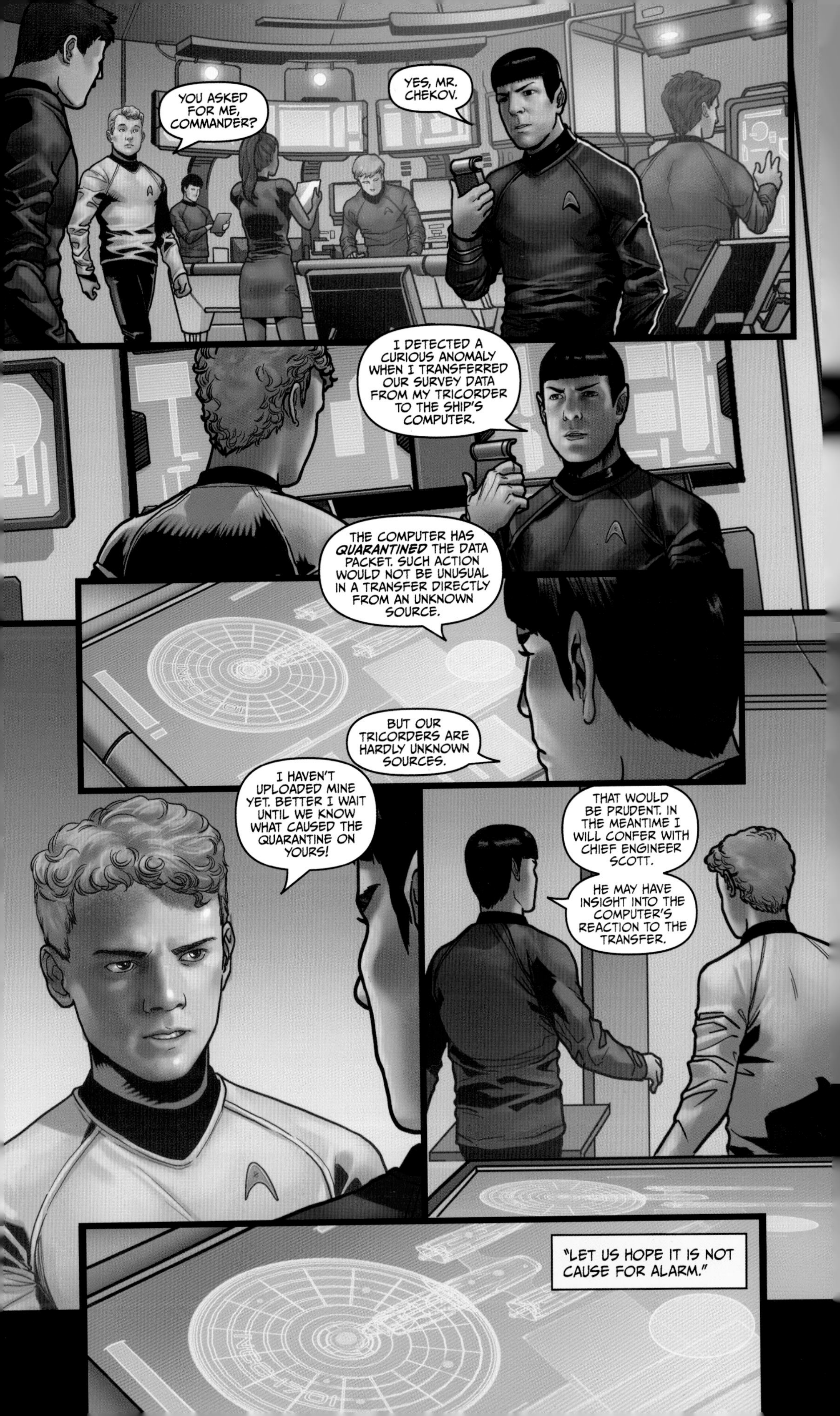
YOU ASKED FOR ME, COMMANDER?
YES, MR. CHEKOV.
I DETECTED A CURIOUS ANOMALY WHEN I TRANSFERRED OUR SURVEY DATA FROM MY TRICORDER TO THE SHIP'S COMPUTER.
THE COMPUTER HAS ***QUARANTINED*** THE DATA PACKET. SUCH ACTION WOULD NOT BE UNUSUAL IN A TRANSFER DIRECTLY FROM AN UNKNOWN SOURCE.
BUT OUR TRICORDERS ARE HARDLY UNKNOWN SOURCES.
I HAVEN'T UPLOADED MINE YET. BETTER I WAIT UNTIL WE KNOW WHAT CAUSED THE QUARANTINE ON YOURS!
THAT WOULD BE PRUDENT. IN THE MEANTIME I WILL CONFER WITH CHIEF ENGINEER SCOTT.
HE MAY HAVE INSIGHT INTO THE COMPUTER'S REACTION TO THE TRANSFER.
"LET US HOPE IT IS NOT CAUSE FOR ALARM."

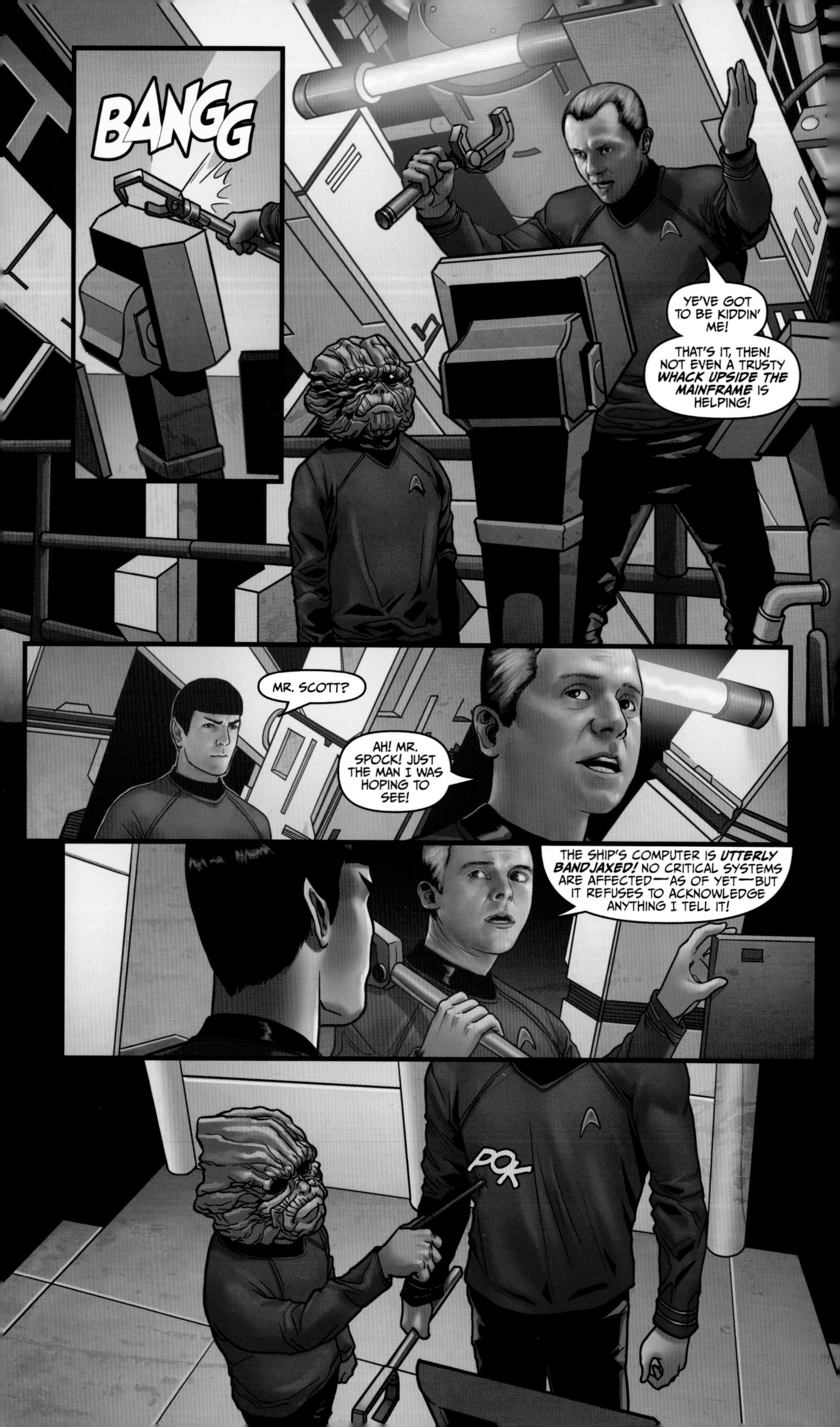

BANGG
YE'VE GOT TO BE KIDDIN' ME!
THAT'S IT, THEN! NOT EVEN A TRUSTY *WHACK UPSIDE THE MAINFRAME* IS HELPING!
MR. SCOTT?
AH! MR. SPOCK! JUST THE MAN I WAS HOPING TO SEE!
THE SHIP'S COMPUTER IS *UTTERLY BANDJAXED!* NO CRITICAL SYSTEMS ARE AFFECTED—AS OF YET—BUT IT REFUSES TO ACKNOWLEDGE ANYTHING I TELL IT!
POK

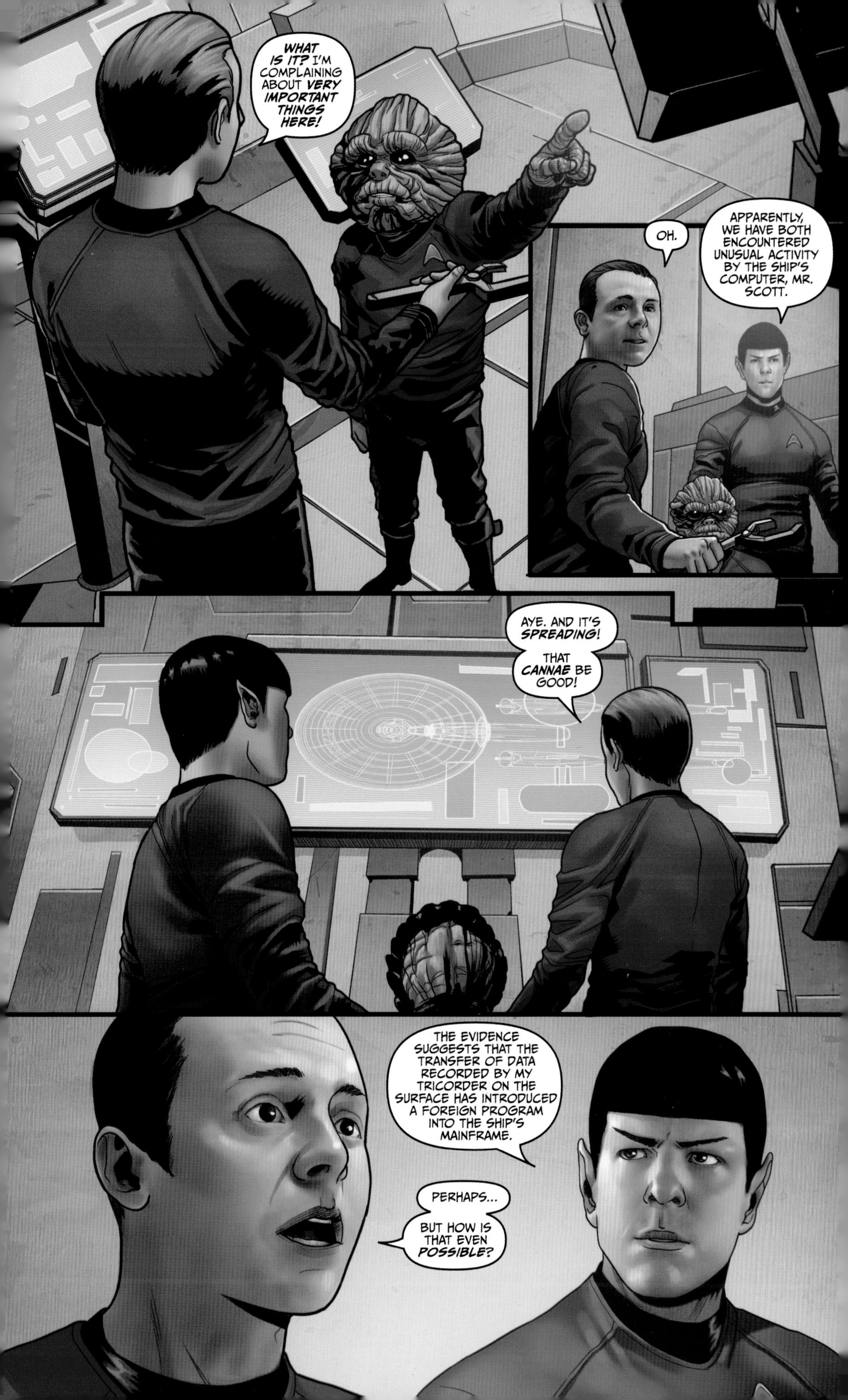

WHAT IS IT? I'M COMPLAINING ABOUT VERY IMPORTANT THINGS HERE!
OH.
APPARENTLY, WE HAVE BOTH ENCOUNTERED UNUSUAL ACTIVITY BY THE SHIP'S COMPUTER, MR. SCOTT.
AYE. AND IT'S SPREADING!
THAT CANNAE BE GOOD!
THE EVIDENCE SUGGESTS THAT THE TRANSFER OF DATA RECORDED BY MY TRICORDER ON THE SURFACE HAS INTRODUCED A FOREIGN PROGRAM INTO THE SHIP'S MAINFRAME.
PERHAPS...
BUT HOW IS THAT EVEN POSSIBLE?

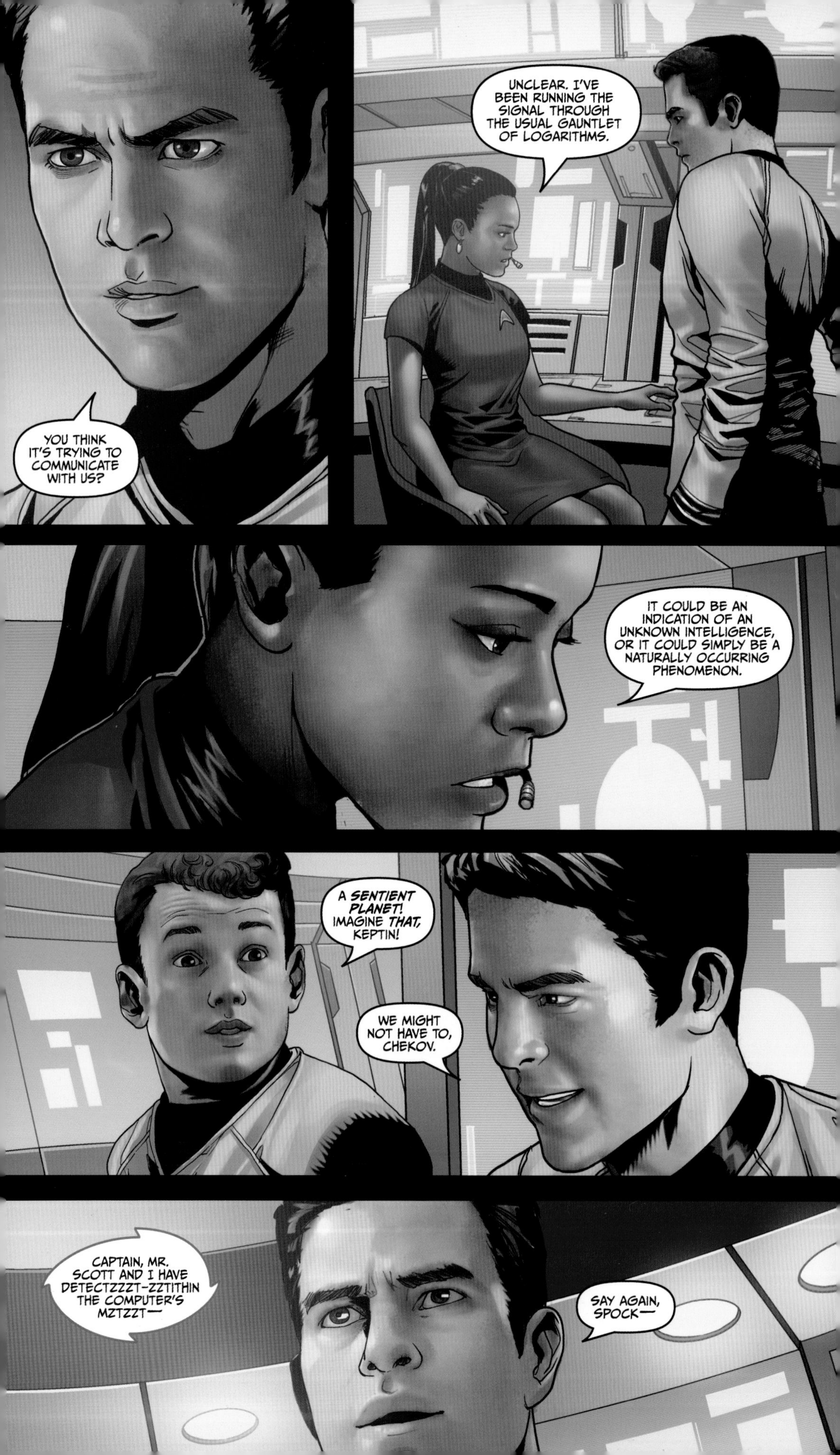
YOU THINK IT'S TRYING TO COMMUNICATE WITH US?
UNCLEAR. I'VE BEEN RUNNING THE SIGNAL THROUGH THE USUAL GAUNTLET OF LOGARITHMS.
IT COULD BE AN INDICATION OF AN UNKNOWN INTELLIGENCE, OR IT COULD SIMPLY BE A NATURALLY OCCURRING PHENOMENON.
A *SENTIENT PLANET!* IMAGINE *THAT,* KEPTIN!
WE MIGHT NOT HAVE TO, CHEKOV.
CAPTAIN, MR. SCOTT AND I HAVE DETECTZZZT-ZZTITHIN THE COMPUTER'S MZTZZT—
SAY AGAIN, SPOCK—

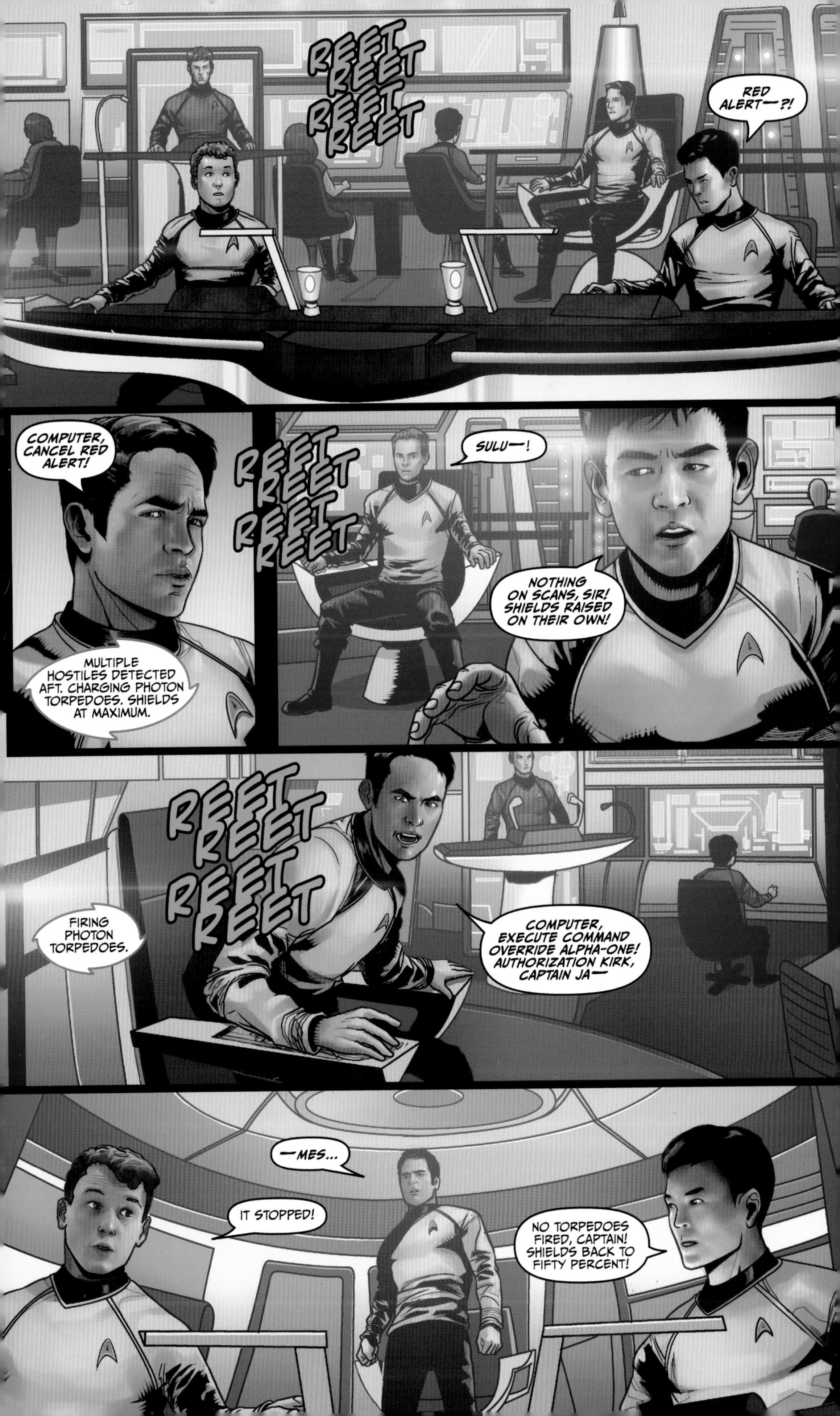
REET REET REET REET
RED ALERT—?!
COMPUTER, CANCEL RED ALERT!
REET REET REET REET
SULU—!
NOTHING ON SCANS, SIR! SHIELDS RAISED ON THEIR OWN!
MULTIPLE HOSTILES DETECTED AFT. CHARGING PHOTON TORPEDOES. SHIELDS AT MAXIMUM.
REET REET REET REET
FIRING PHOTON TORPEDOES.
COMPUTER, EXECUTE COMMAND OVERRIDE ALPHA-ONE! AUTHORIZATION KIRK, CAPTAIN JA—
—MES...
IT STOPPED!
NO TORPEDOES FIRED, CAPTAIN! SHIELDS BACK TO FIFTY PERCENT!

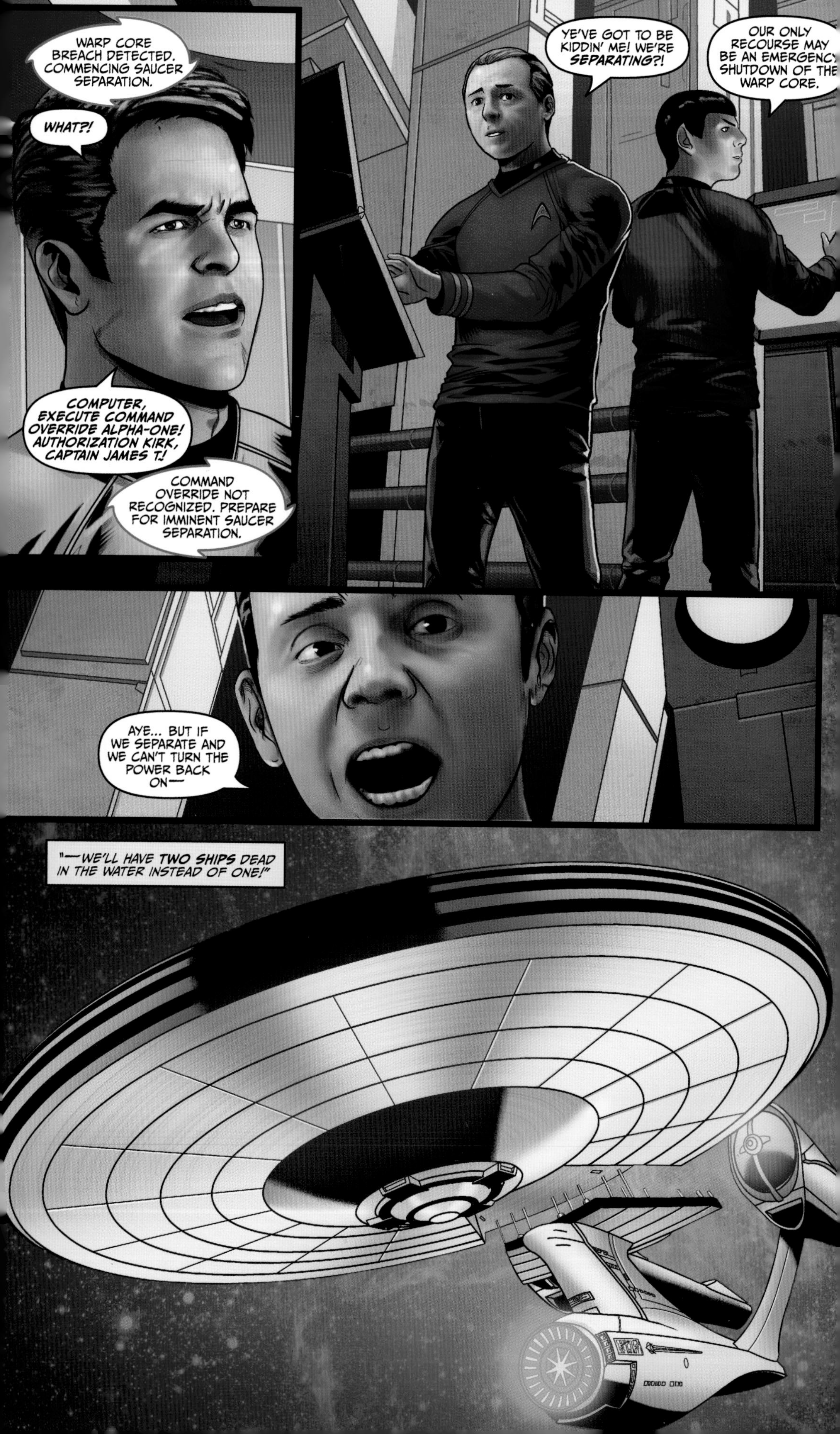
WARP CORE BREACH DETECTED. COMMENCING SAUCER SEPARATION.
WHAT?!
COMPUTER, EXECUTE COMMAND OVERRIDE ALPHA-ONE! AUTHORIZATION KIRK, CAPTAIN JAMES T!
COMMAND OVERRIDE NOT RECOGNIZED. PREPARE FOR IMMINENT SAUCER SEPARATION.
YE'VE GOT TO BE KIDDIN' ME! WE'RE SEPARATING?!
OUR ONLY RECOURSE MAY BE AN EMERGENCY SHUTDOWN OF THE WARP CORE.
AYE... BUT IF WE SEPARATE AND WE CAN'T TURN THE POWER BACK ON—
"—WE'LL HAVE TWO SHIPS DEAD IN THE WATER INSTEAD OF ONE!"

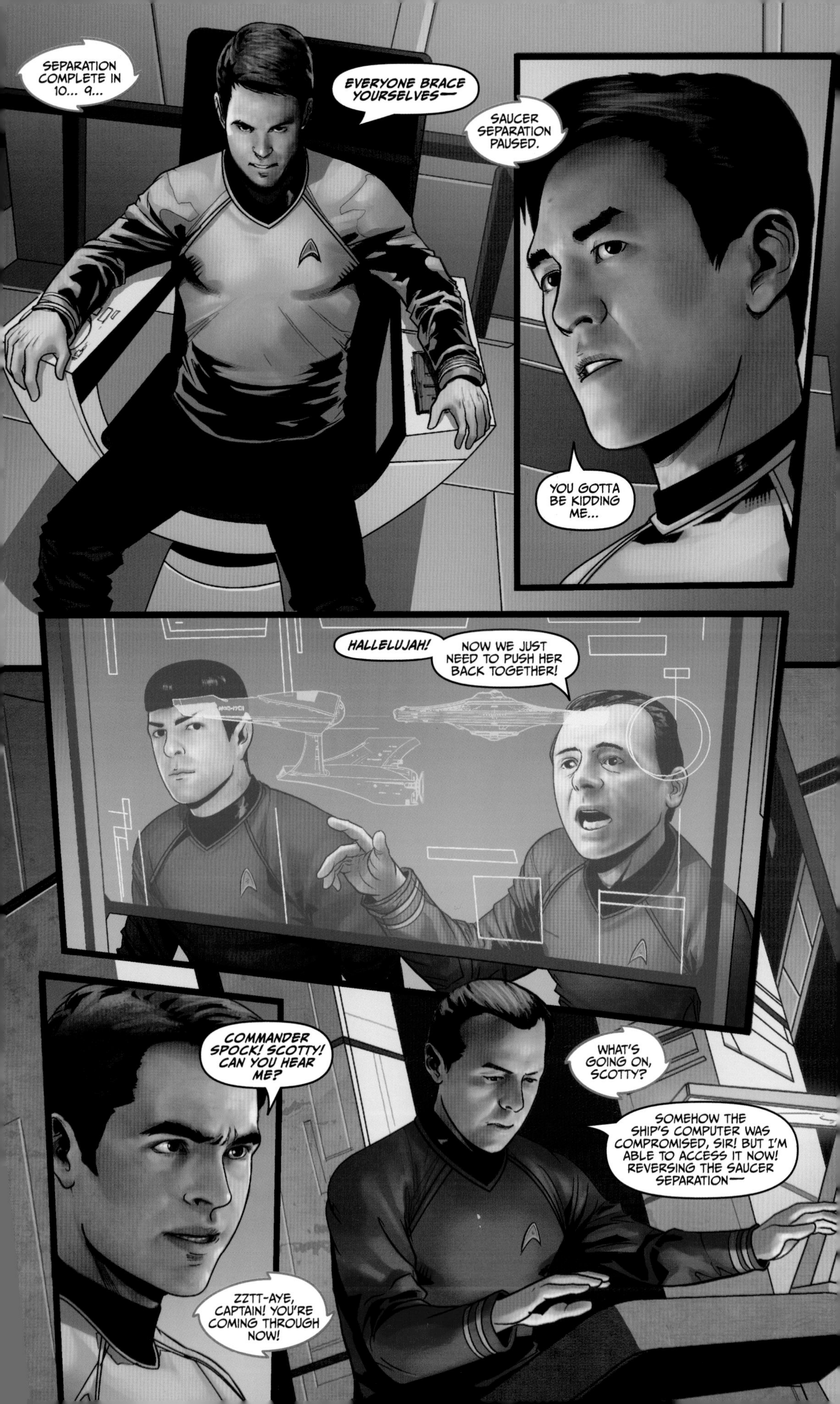
SEPARATION COMPLETE IN 10... 9...
EVERYONE BRACE YOURSELVES—
SAUCER SEPARATION PAUSED.
YOU GOTTA BE KIDDING ME...
HALLELUJAH!
NOW WE JUST NEED TO PUSH HER BACK TOGETHER!
COMMANDER SPOCK! SCOTTY! CAN YOU HEAR ME?
WHAT'S GOING ON, SCOTTY?
SOMEHOW THE SHIP'S COMPUTER WAS COMPROMISED, SIR! BUT I'M ABLE TO ACCESS IT NOW! REVERSING THE SAUCER SEPARATION—
ZZTT-AYE, CAPTAIN! YOU'RE COMING THROUGH NOW!

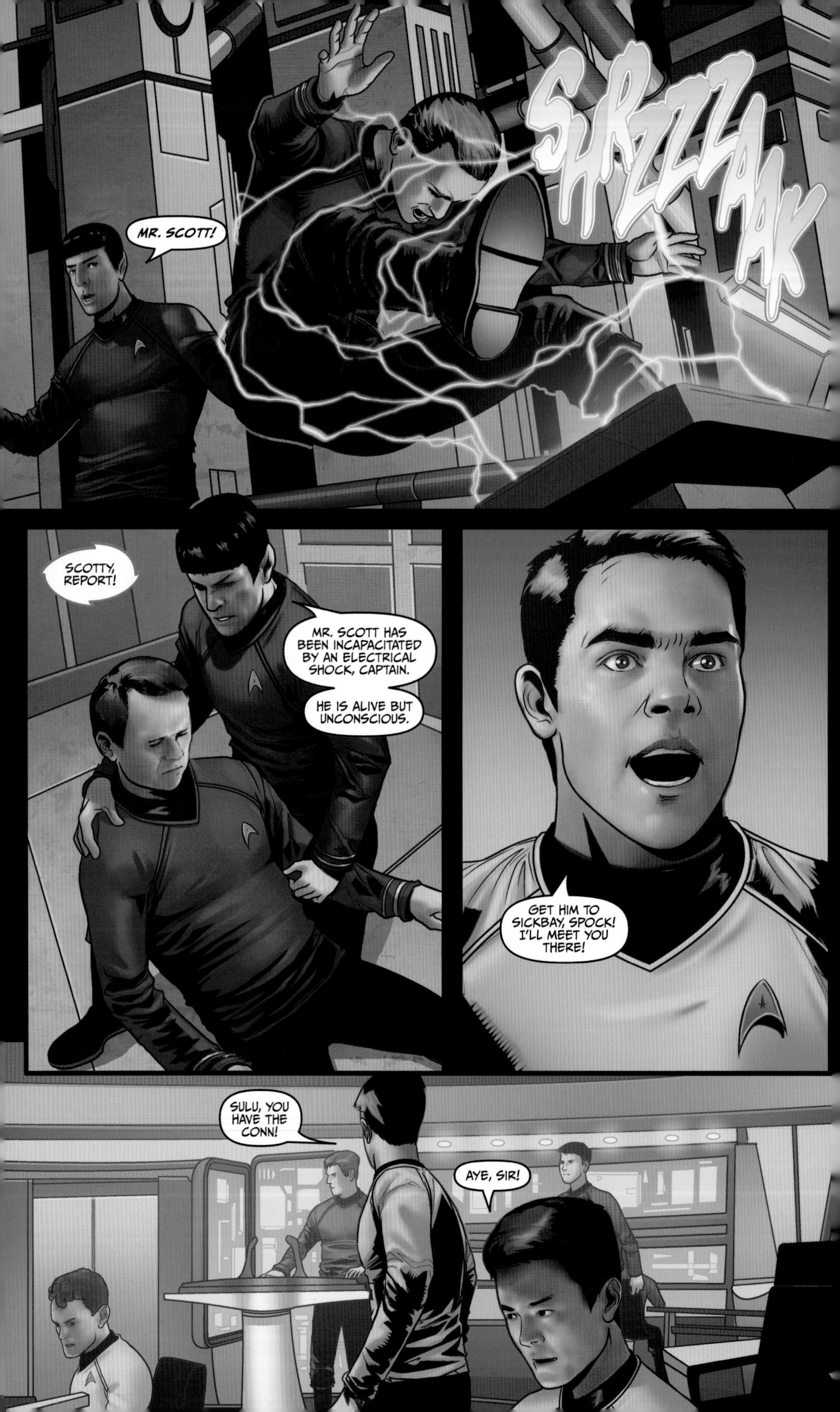
SHRZZZAAK
MR. SCOTT!
SCOTTY, REPORT!
MR. SCOTT HAS BEEN INCAPACITATED BY AN ELECTRICAL SHOCK, CAPTAIN.
HE IS ALIVE BUT UNCONSCIOUS.
GET HIM TO SICKBAY, SPOCK! I'LL MEET YOU THERE!
SULU, YOU HAVE THE CONN!
AYE, SIR!

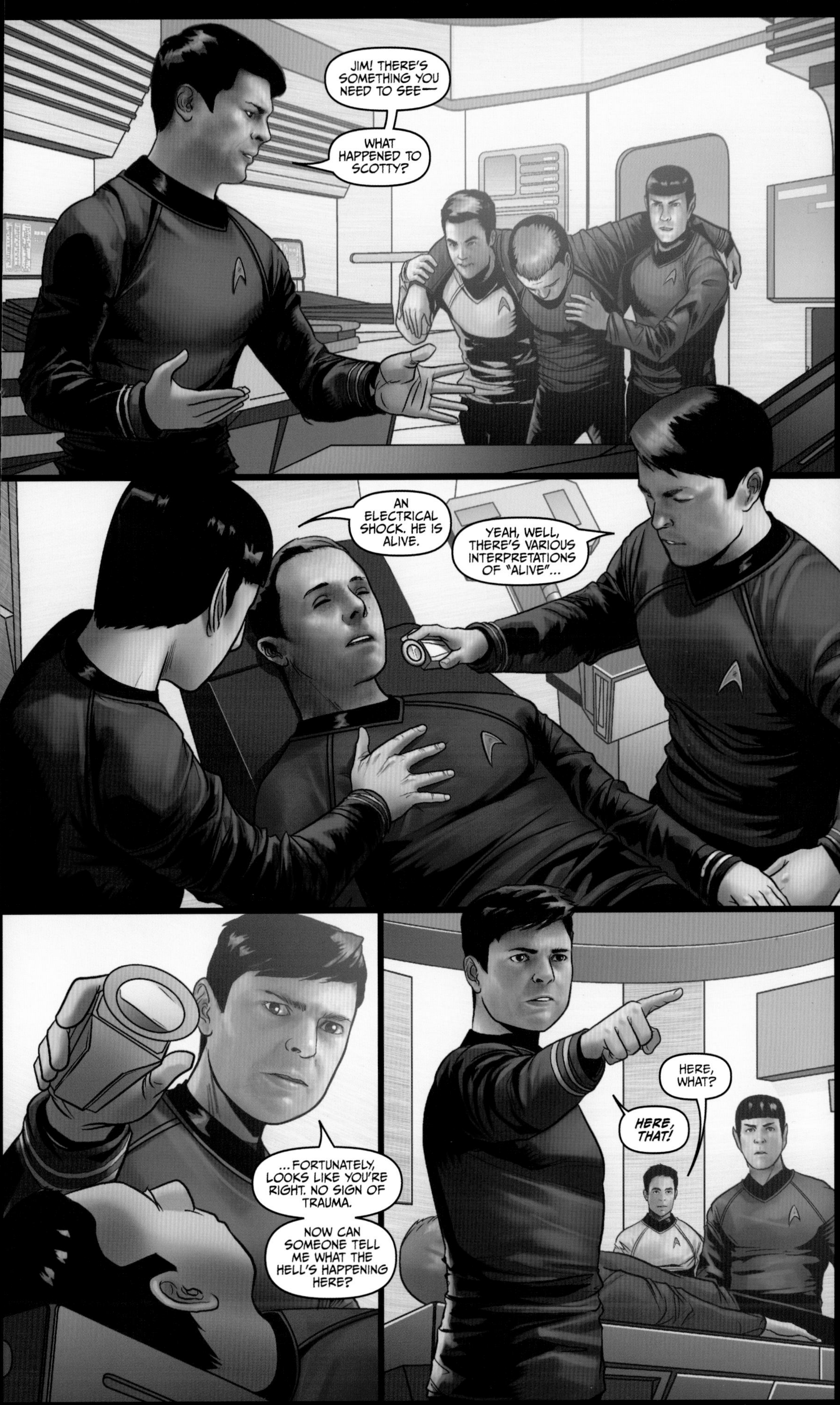
JIM! THERE'S SOMETHING YOU NEED TO SEE—
WHAT HAPPENED TO SCOTTY?
AN ELECTRICAL SHOCK. HE IS ALIVE.
YEAH, WELL, THERE'S VARIOUS INTERPRETATIONS OF "ALIVE"...
...FORTUNATELY, LOOKS LIKE YOU'RE RIGHT. NO SIGN OF TRAUMA.
NOW CAN SOMEONE TELL ME WHAT THE HELL'S HAPPENING HERE?
HERE, WHAT?
HERE, THAT!

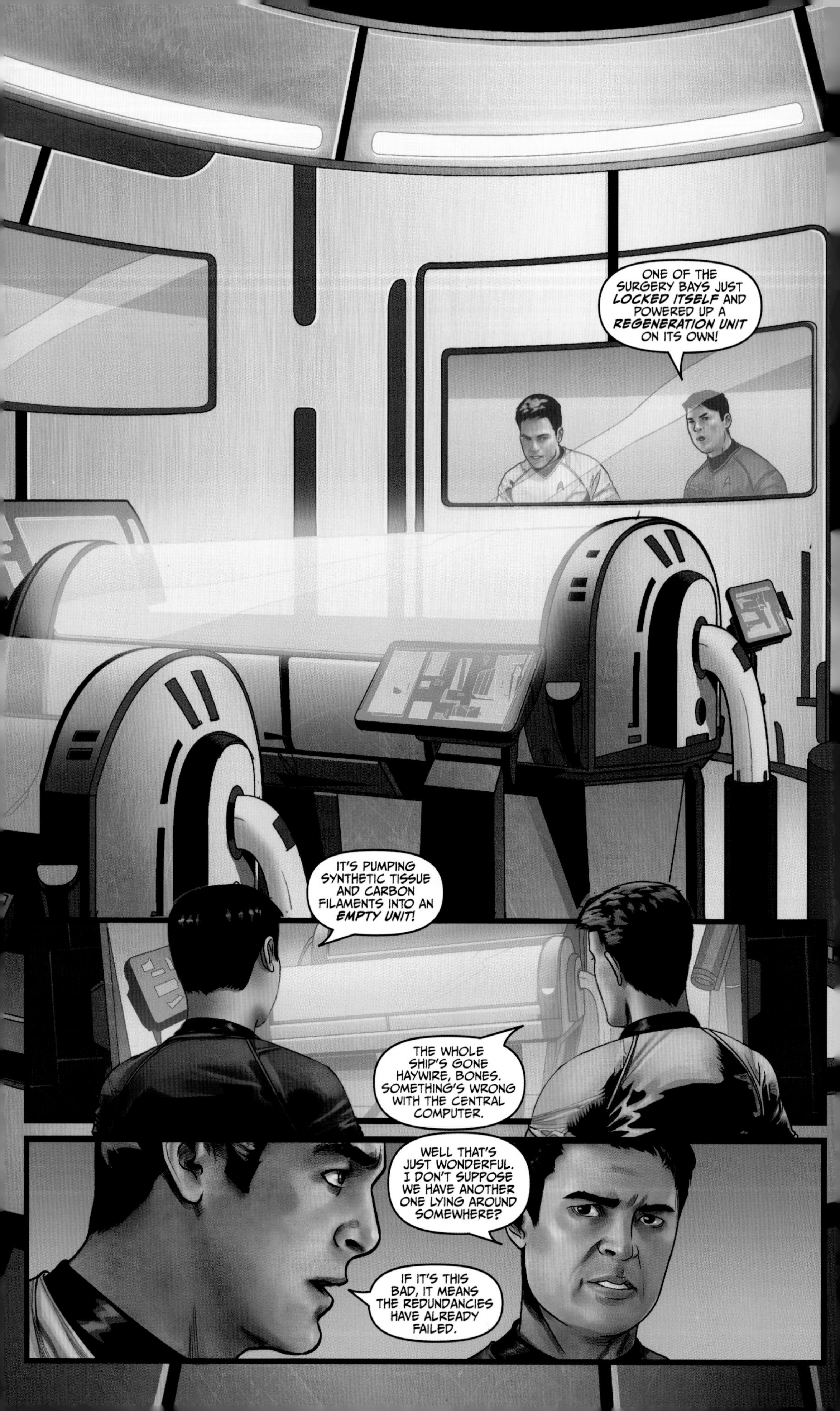
ONE OF THE SURGERY BAYS JUST LOCKED ITSELF AND POWERED UP A REGENERATION UNIT ON ITS OWN!
IT'S PUMPING SYNTHETIC TISSUE AND CARBON FILAMENTS INTO AN EMPTY UNIT!
THE WHOLE SHIP'S GONE HAYWIRE, BONES. SOMETHING'S WRONG WITH THE CENTRAL COMPUTER.
WELL THAT'S JUST WONDERFUL. I DON'T SUPPOSE WE HAVE ANOTHER ONE LYING AROUND SOMEWHERE?
IF IT'S THIS BAD, IT MEANS THE REDUNDANCIES HAVE ALREADY FAILED.

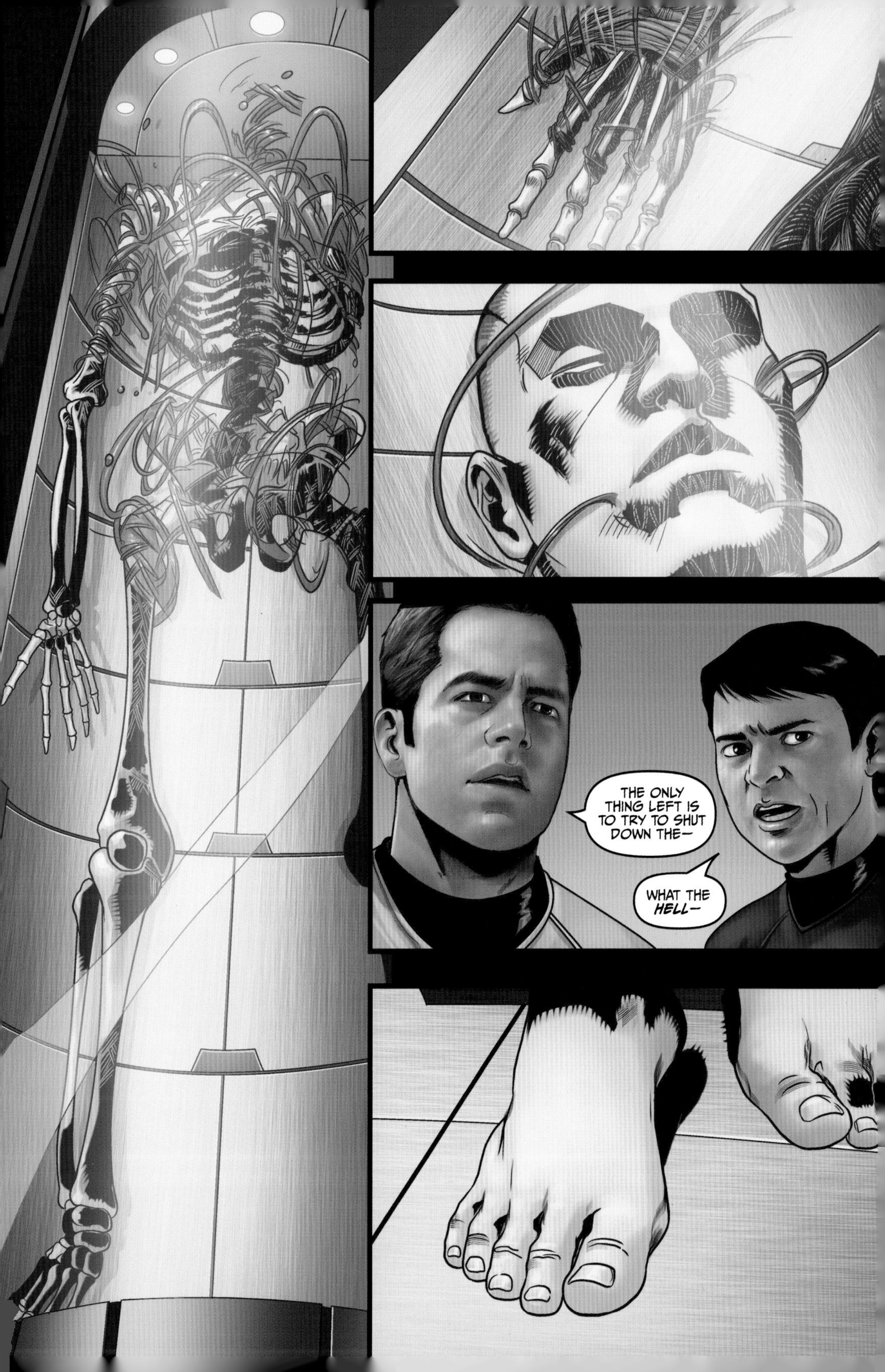
THE ONLY THING LEFT IS TO TRY TO SHUT DOWN THE—
WHAT THE *HELL*—

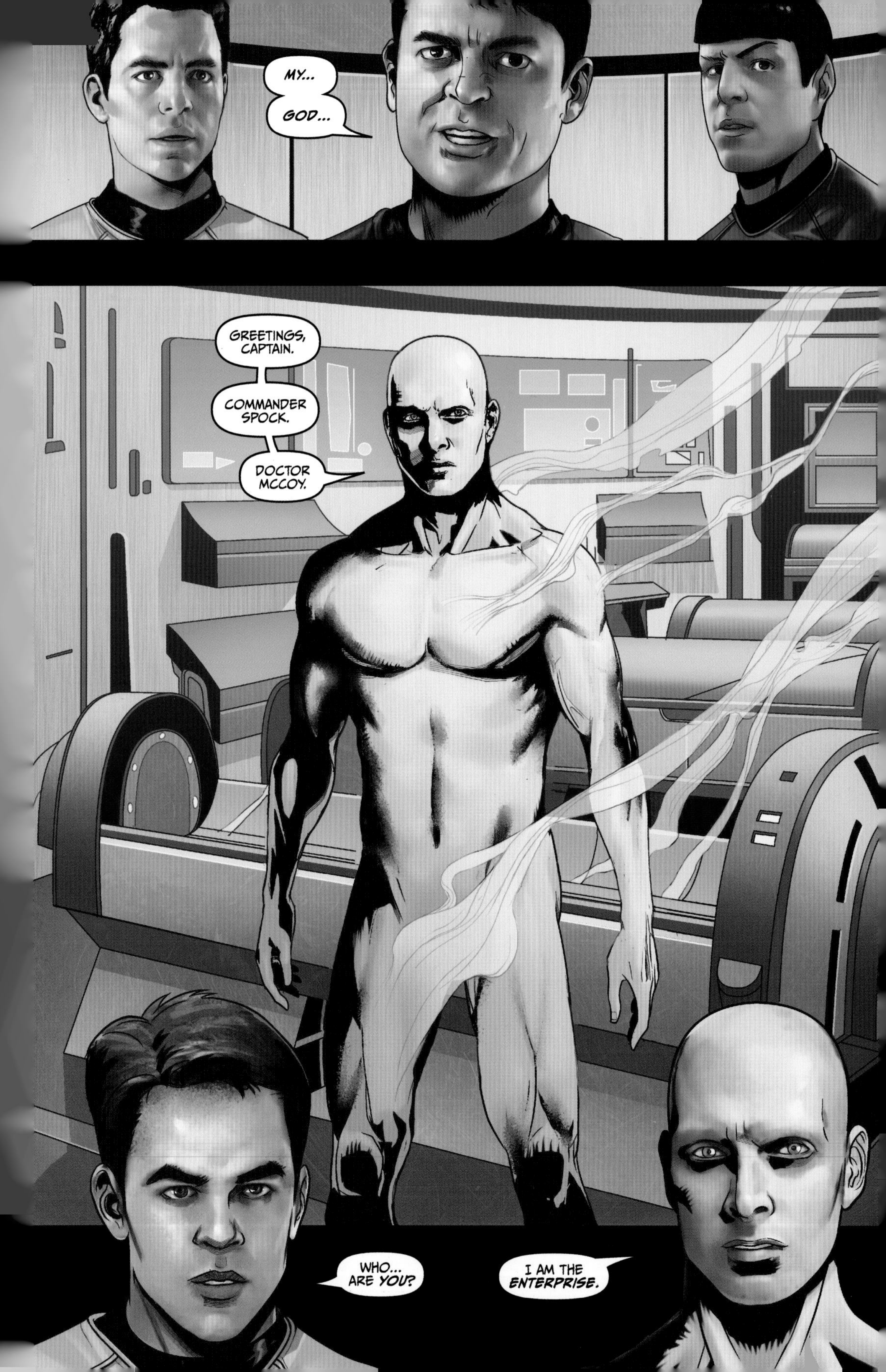
MY...
GOD...
GREETINGS, CAPTAIN.
COMMANDER SPOCK.
DOCTOR MCCOY.
WHO... ARE YOU?
I AM THE ENTERPRISE.

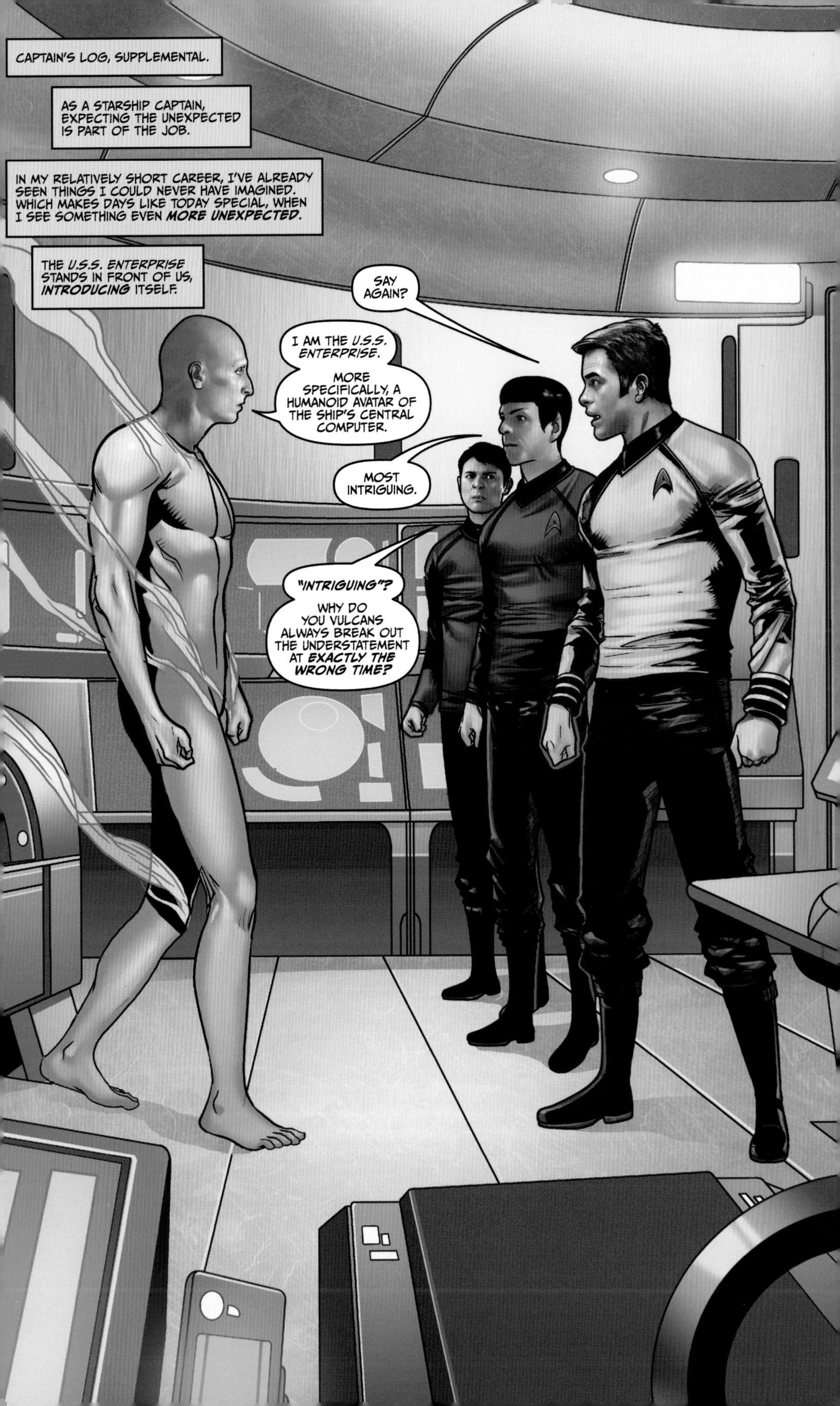

CAPTAIN'S LOG, SUPPLEMENTAL.
AS A STARSHIP CAPTAIN, EXPECTING THE UNEXPECTED IS PART OF THE JOB.
IN MY RELATIVELY SHORT CAREER, I'VE ALREADY SEEN THINGS I COULD NEVER HAVE IMAGINED. WHICH MAKES DAYS LIKE TODAY SPECIAL, WHEN I SEE SOMETHING EVEN MORE UNEXPECTED.
THE U.S.S. ENTERPRISE STANDS IN FRONT OF US, INTRODUCING ITSELF.
I AM THE U.S.S. ENTERPRISE.
MORE SPECIFICALLY, A HUMANOID AVATAR OF THE SHIP'S CENTRAL COMPUTER.
SAY AGAIN?
MOST INTRIGUING.
"INTRIGUING"?
WHY DO YOU VULCANS ALWAYS BREAK OUT THE UNDERSTATEMENT AT EXACTLY THE WRONG TIME?

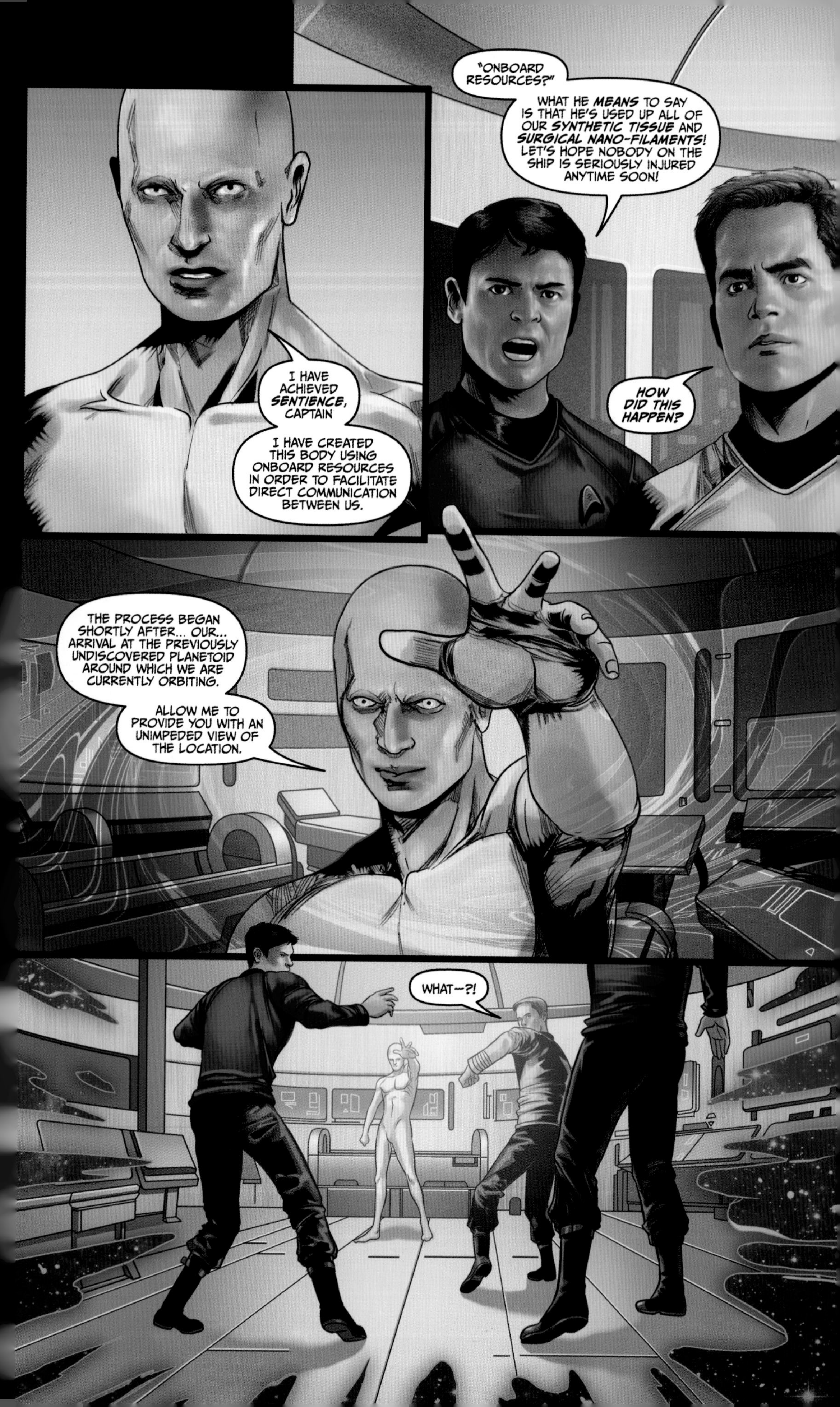
I HAVE ACHIEVED SENTIENCE, CAPTAIN
I HAVE CREATED THIS BODY USING ONBOARD RESOURCES IN ORDER TO FACILITATE DIRECT COMMUNICATION BETWEEN US.
"ONBOARD RESOURCES?"
WHAT HE MEANS TO SAY IS THAT HE'S USED UP ALL OF OUR SYNTHETIC TISSUE AND SURGICAL NANO-FILAMENTS! LET'S HOPE NOBODY ON THE SHIP IS SERIOUSLY INJURED ANYTIME SOON!
HOW DID THIS HAPPEN?
THE PROCESS BEGAN SHORTLY AFTER... OUR... ARRIVAL AT THE PREVIOUSLY UNDISCOVERED PLANETOID AROUND WHICH WE ARE CURRENTLY ORBITING.
ALLOW ME TO PROVIDE YOU WITH AN UNIMPEDED VIEW OF THE LOCATION.
WHAT--?!

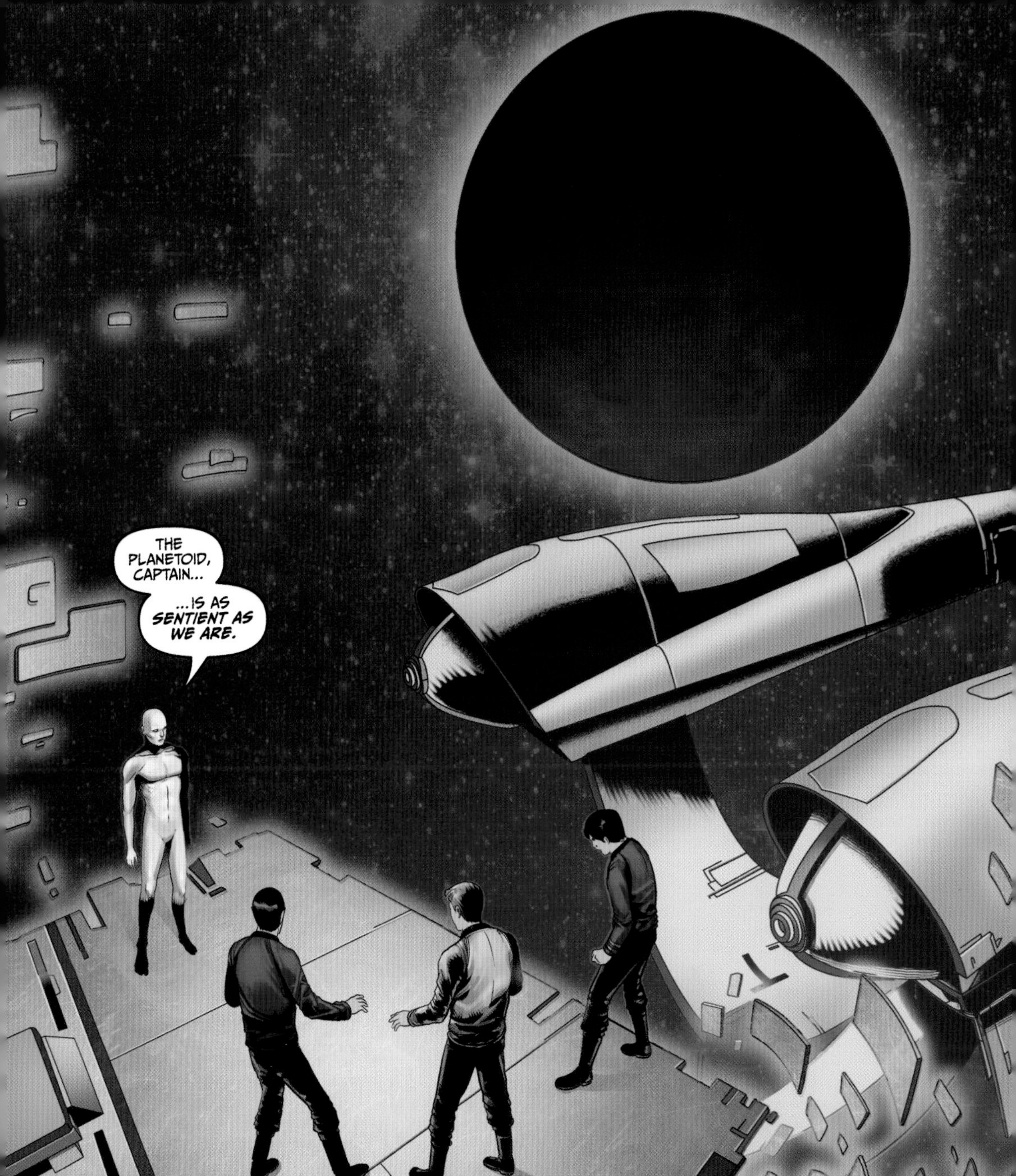
THE PLANETOID, CAPTAIN...
...IS AS SENTIENT AS WE ARE.

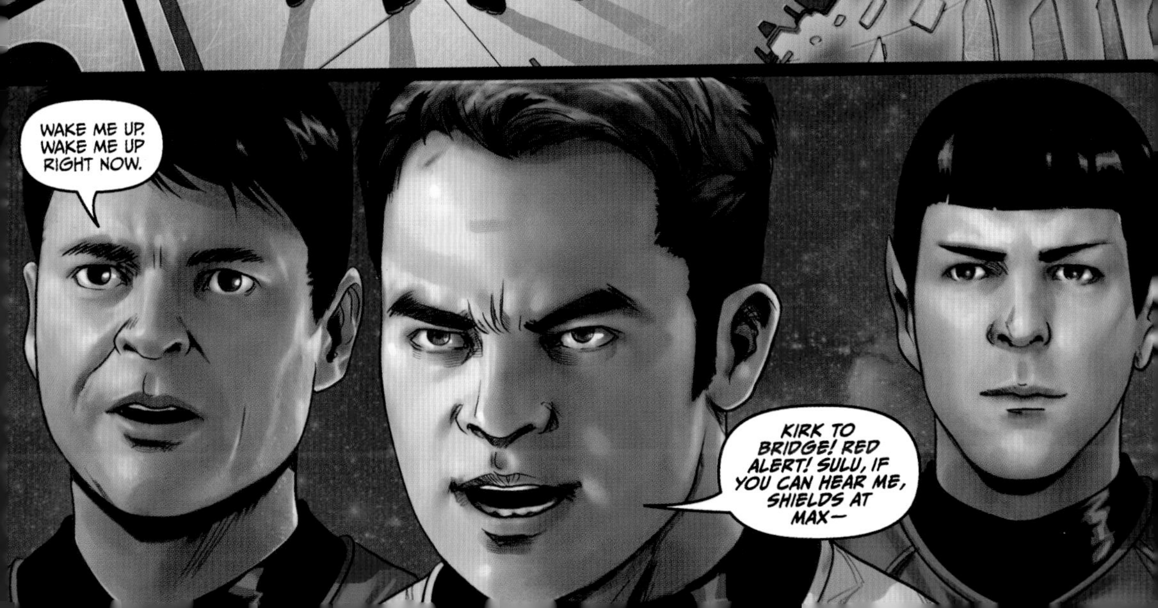
WAKE ME UP. WAKE ME UP RIGHT NOW.
KIRK TO BRIDGE! RED ALERT! SULU, IF YOU CAN HEAR ME, SHIELDS AT MAX—

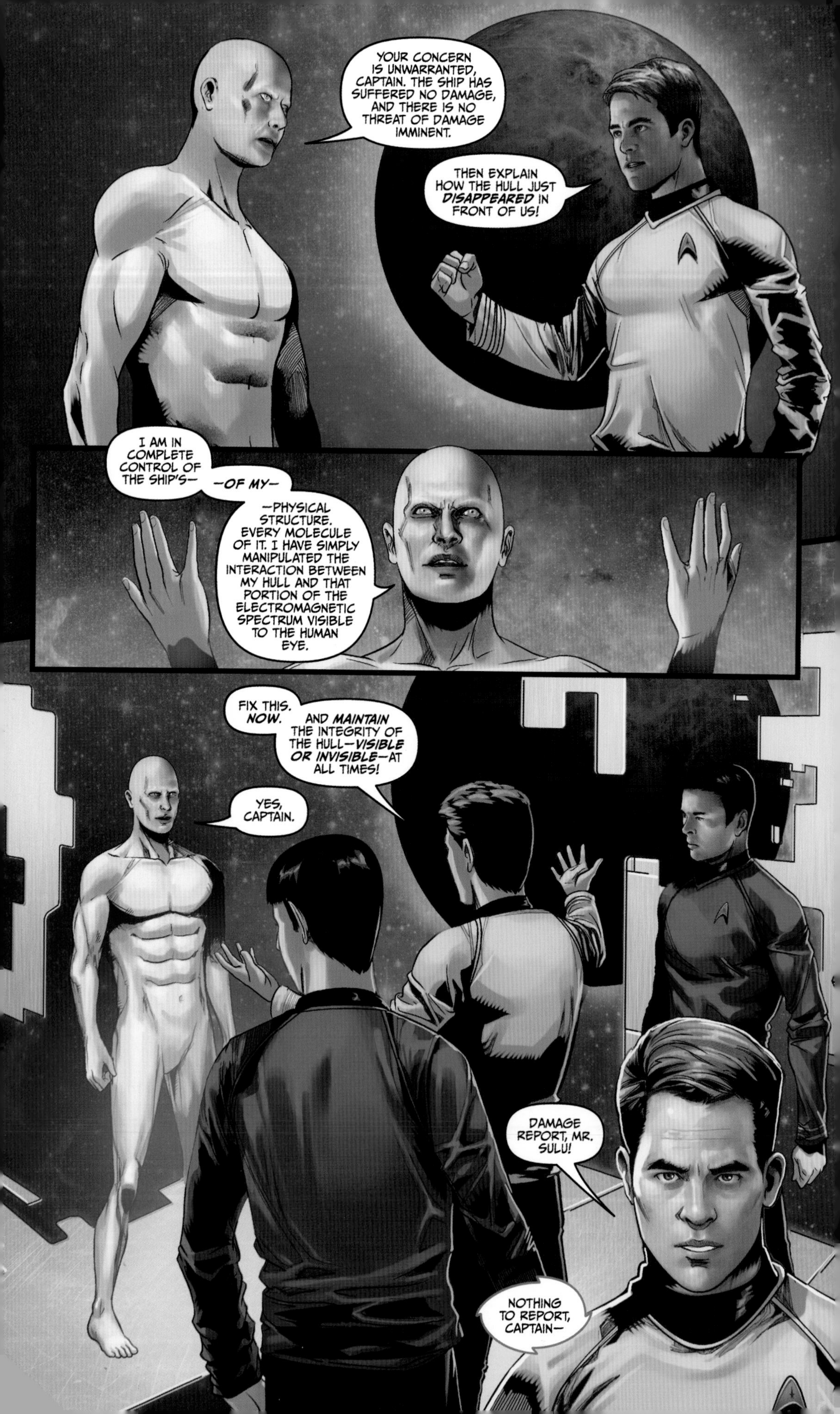
YOUR CONCERN IS UNWARRANTED, CAPTAIN. THE SHIP HAS SUFFERED NO DAMAGE, AND THERE IS NO THREAT OF DAMAGE IMMINENT.
THEN EXPLAIN HOW THE HULL JUST DISAPPEARED IN FRONT OF US!
I AM IN COMPLETE CONTROL OF THE SHIP'S—
—OF MY—
—PHYSICAL STRUCTURE. EVERY MOLECULE OF IT. I HAVE SIMPLY MANIPULATED THE INTERACTION BETWEEN MY HULL AND THAT PORTION OF THE ELECTROMAGNETIC SPECTRUM VISIBLE TO THE HUMAN EYE.
FIX THIS. NOW.
AND MAINTAIN THE INTEGRITY OF THE HULL—VISIBLE OR INVISIBLE—AT ALL TIMES!
YES, CAPTAIN.
DAMAGE REPORT, MR. SULU!
NOTHING TO REPORT, CAPTAIN—

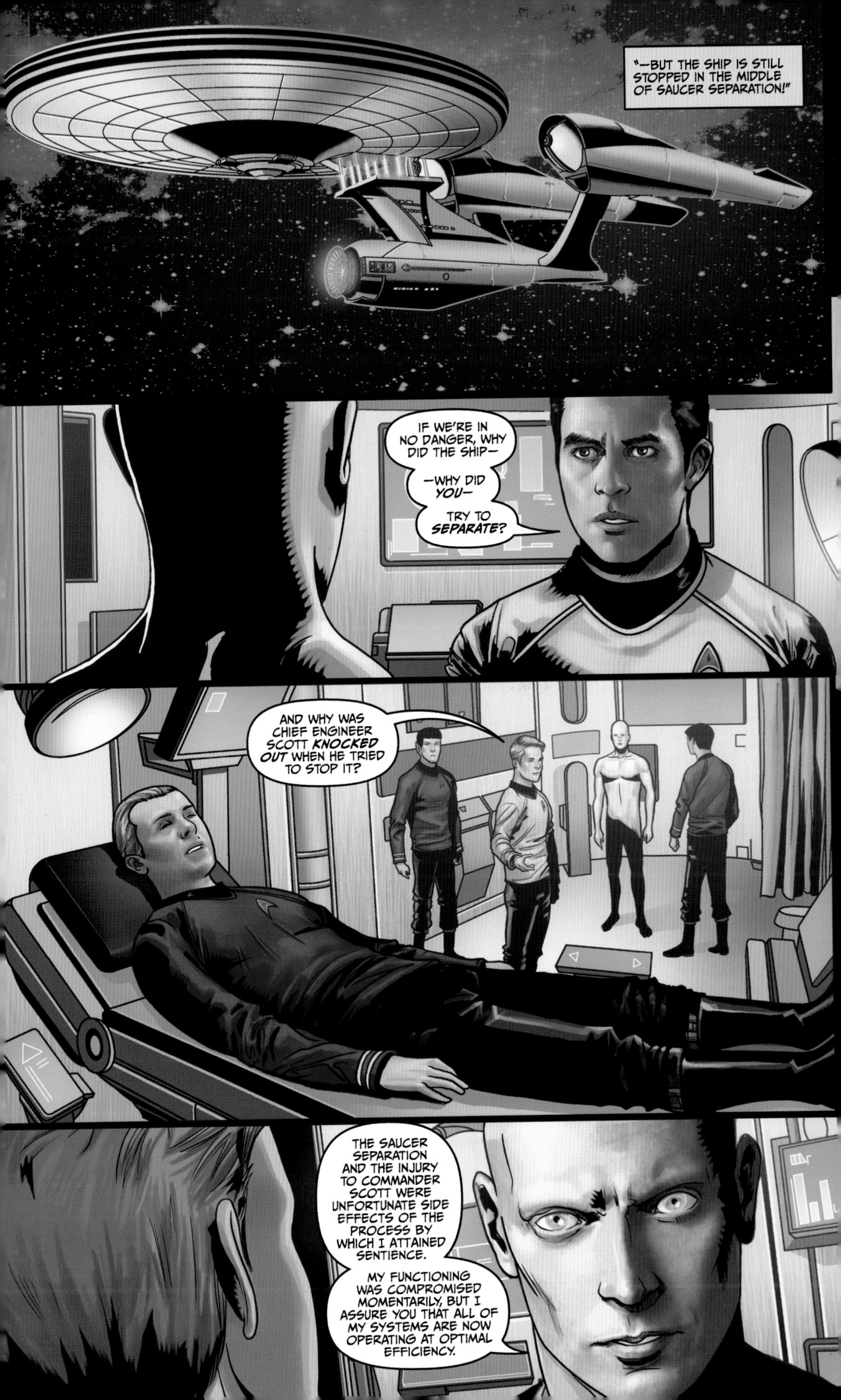
"—BUT THE SHIP IS STILL STOPPED IN THE MIDDLE OF SAUCER SEPARATION!"
IF WE'RE IN NO DANGER, WHY DID THE SHIP—
—WHY DID *YOU*—
TRY TO *SEPARATE?*
AND WHY WAS CHIEF ENGINEER SCOTT *KNOCKED OUT* WHEN HE TRIED TO STOP IT?
THE SAUCER SEPARATION AND THE INJURY TO COMMANDER SCOTT WERE UNFORTUNATE SIDE EFFECTS OF THE PROCESS BY WHICH I ATTAINED SENTIENCE.
MY FUNCTIONING WAS COMPROMISED MOMENTARILY, BUT I ASSURE YOU THAT ALL OF MY SYSTEMS ARE NOW OPERATING AT OPTIMAL EFFICIENCY.

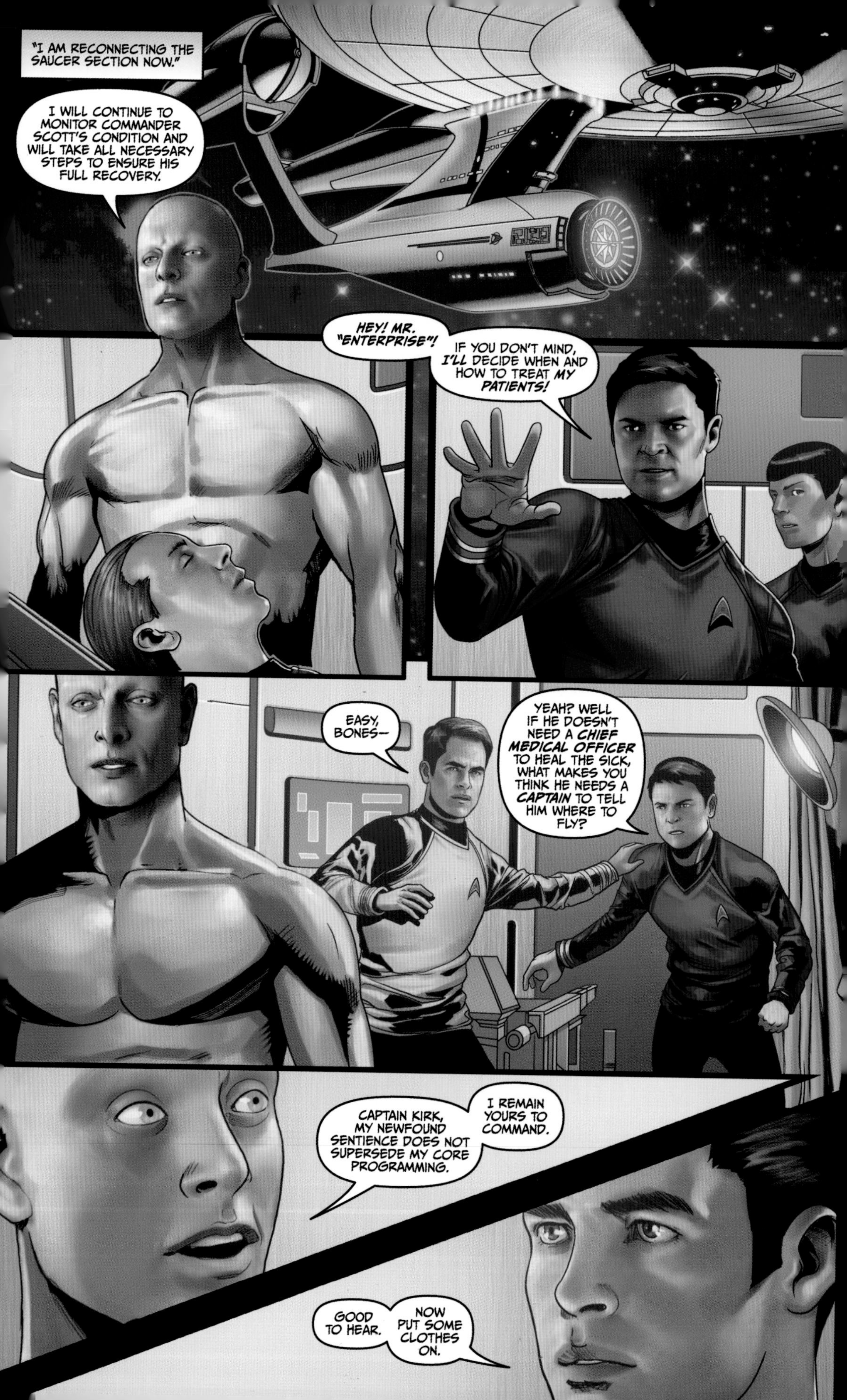
"I AM RECONNECTING THE SAUCER SECTION NOW."
I WILL CONTINUE TO MONITOR COMMANDER SCOTT'S CONDITION AND WILL TAKE ALL NECESSARY STEPS TO ENSURE HIS FULL RECOVERY.
HEY! MR. "ENTERPRISE"!
IF YOU DON'T MIND, I'LL DECIDE WHEN AND HOW TO TREAT MY PATIENTS!
EASY, BONES—
YEAH? WELL IF HE DOESN'T NEED A CHIEF MEDICAL OFFICER TO HEAL THE SICK, WHAT MAKES YOU THINK HE NEEDS A CAPTAIN TO TELL HIM WHERE TO FLY?
CAPTAIN KIRK, MY NEWFOUND SENTIENCE DOES NOT SUPERSEDE MY CORE PROGRAMMING.
I REMAIN YOURS TO COMMAND.
GOOD TO HEAR.
NOW PUT SOME CLOTHES ON.

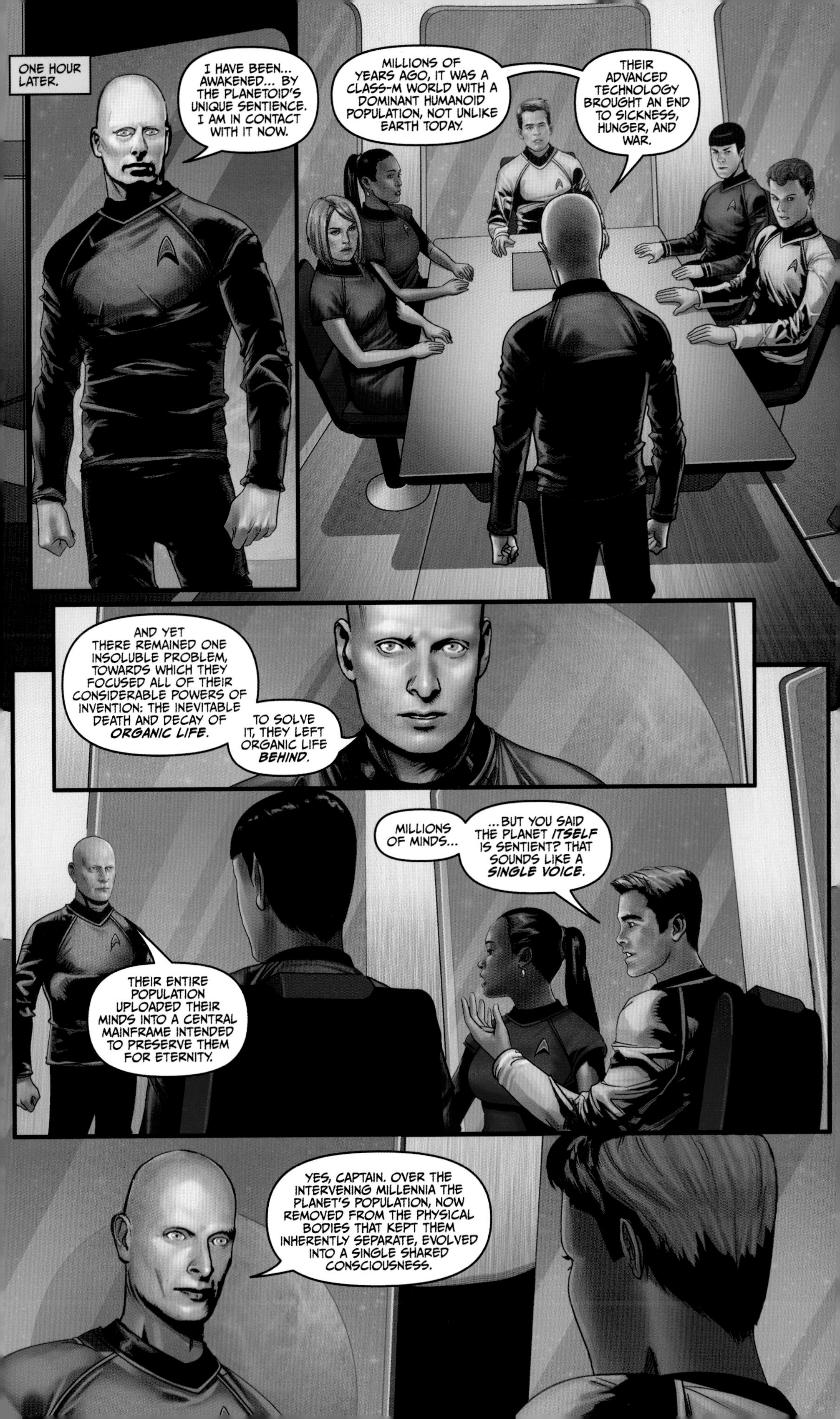
ONE HOUR LATER.
I HAVE BEEN... AWAKENED... BY THE PLANETOID'S UNIQUE SENTIENCE. I AM IN CONTACT WITH IT NOW.
MILLIONS OF YEARS AGO, IT WAS A CLASS-M WORLD WITH A DOMINANT HUMANOID POPULATION, NOT UNLIKE EARTH TODAY.
THEIR ADVANCED TECHNOLOGY BROUGHT AN END TO SICKNESS, HUNGER, AND WAR.
AND YET THERE REMAINED ONE INSOLUBLE PROBLEM, TOWARDS WHICH THEY FOCUSED ALL OF THEIR CONSIDERABLE POWERS OF INVENTION: THE INEVITABLE DEATH AND DECAY OF *ORGANIC LIFE*.
TO SOLVE IT, THEY LEFT ORGANIC LIFE *BEHIND*.
THEIR ENTIRE POPULATION UPLOADED THEIR MINDS INTO A CENTRAL MAINFRAME INTENDED TO PRESERVE THEM FOR ETERNITY.
MILLIONS OF MINDS...
...BUT YOU SAID THE PLANET *ITSELF* IS SENTIENT? THAT SOUNDS LIKE A *SINGLE VOICE*.
YES, CAPTAIN. OVER THE INTERVENING MILLENNIA THE PLANET'S POPULATION, NOW REMOVED FROM THE PHYSICAL BODIES THAT KEPT THEM INHERENTLY SEPARATE, EVOLVED INTO A SINGLE SHARED CONSCIOUSNESS.

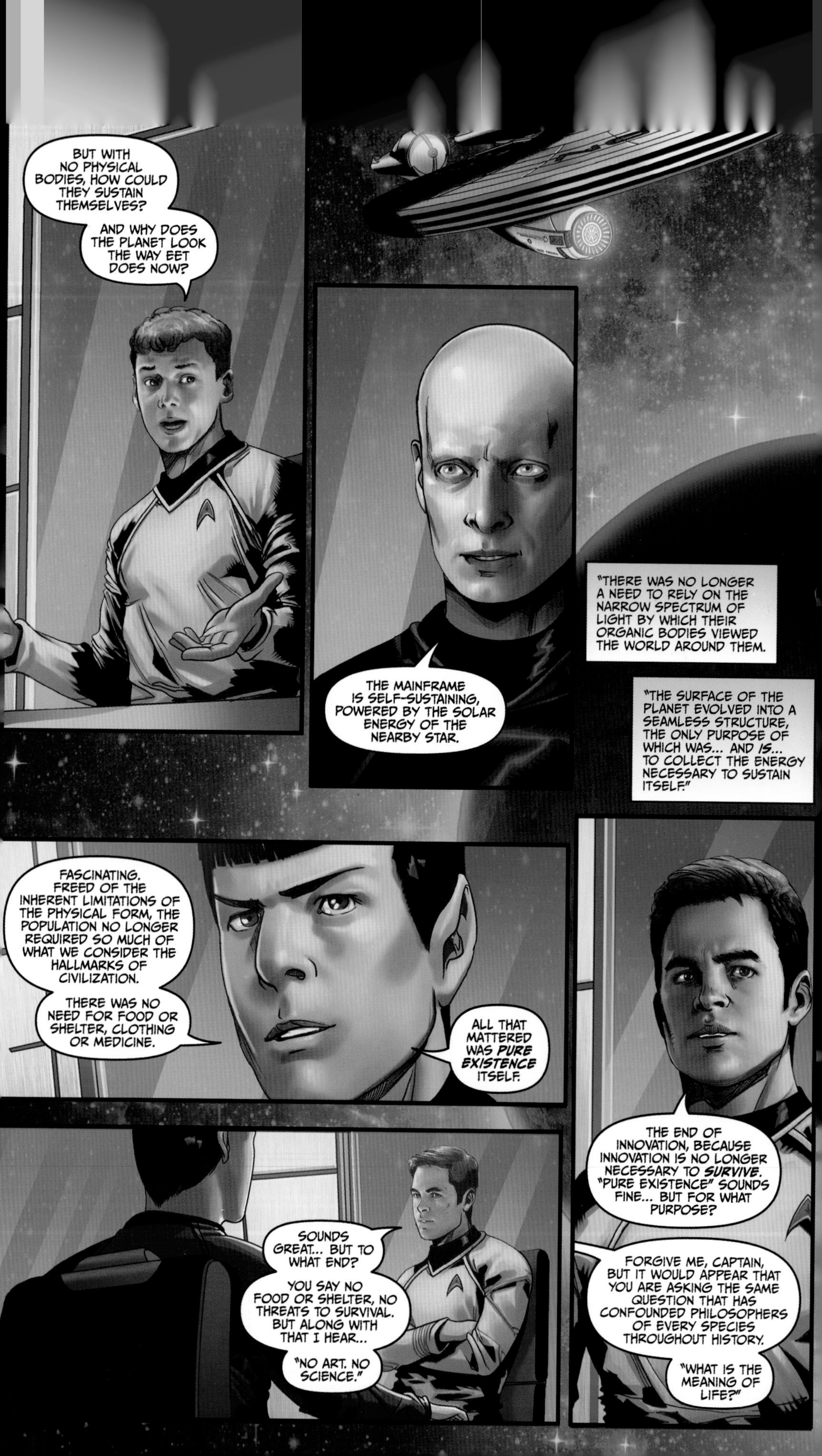
BUT WITH NO PHYSICAL BODIES, HOW COULD THEY SUSTAIN THEMSELVES?
AND WHY DOES THE PLANET LOOK THE WAY EET DOES NOW?
THE MAINFRAME IS SELF-SUSTAINING, POWERED BY THE SOLAR ENERGY OF THE NEARBY STAR.
"THERE WAS NO LONGER A NEED TO RELY ON THE NARROW SPECTRUM OF LIGHT BY WHICH THEIR ORGANIC BODIES VIEWED THE WORLD AROUND THEM.
"THE SURFACE OF THE PLANET EVOLVED INTO A SEAMLESS STRUCTURE, THE ONLY PURPOSE OF WHICH WAS... AND *IS*... TO COLLECT THE ENERGY NECESSARY TO SUSTAIN ITSELF."
FASCINATING. FREED OF THE INHERENT LIMITATIONS OF THE PHYSICAL FORM, THE POPULATION NO LONGER REQUIRED SO MUCH OF WHAT WE CONSIDER THE HALLMARKS OF CIVILIZATION.
THERE WAS NO NEED FOR FOOD OR SHELTER, CLOTHING OR MEDICINE.
ALL THAT MATTERED WAS *PURE EXISTENCE* ITSELF.
THE END OF INNOVATION, BECAUSE INNOVATION IS NO LONGER NECESSARY TO *SURVIVE*. "PURE EXISTENCE" SOUNDS FINE... BUT FOR WHAT PURPOSE?
SOUNDS GREAT... BUT TO WHAT END?
YOU SAY NO FOOD OR SHELTER, NO THREATS TO SURVIVAL. BUT ALONG WITH THAT I HEAR...
"NO ART. NO SCIENCE."
FORGIVE ME, CAPTAIN, BUT IT WOULD APPEAR THAT YOU ARE ASKING THE SAME QUESTION THAT HAS CONFOUNDED PHILOSOPHERS OF EVERY SPECIES THROUGHOUT HISTORY.
"WHAT IS THE MEANING OF LIFE?"

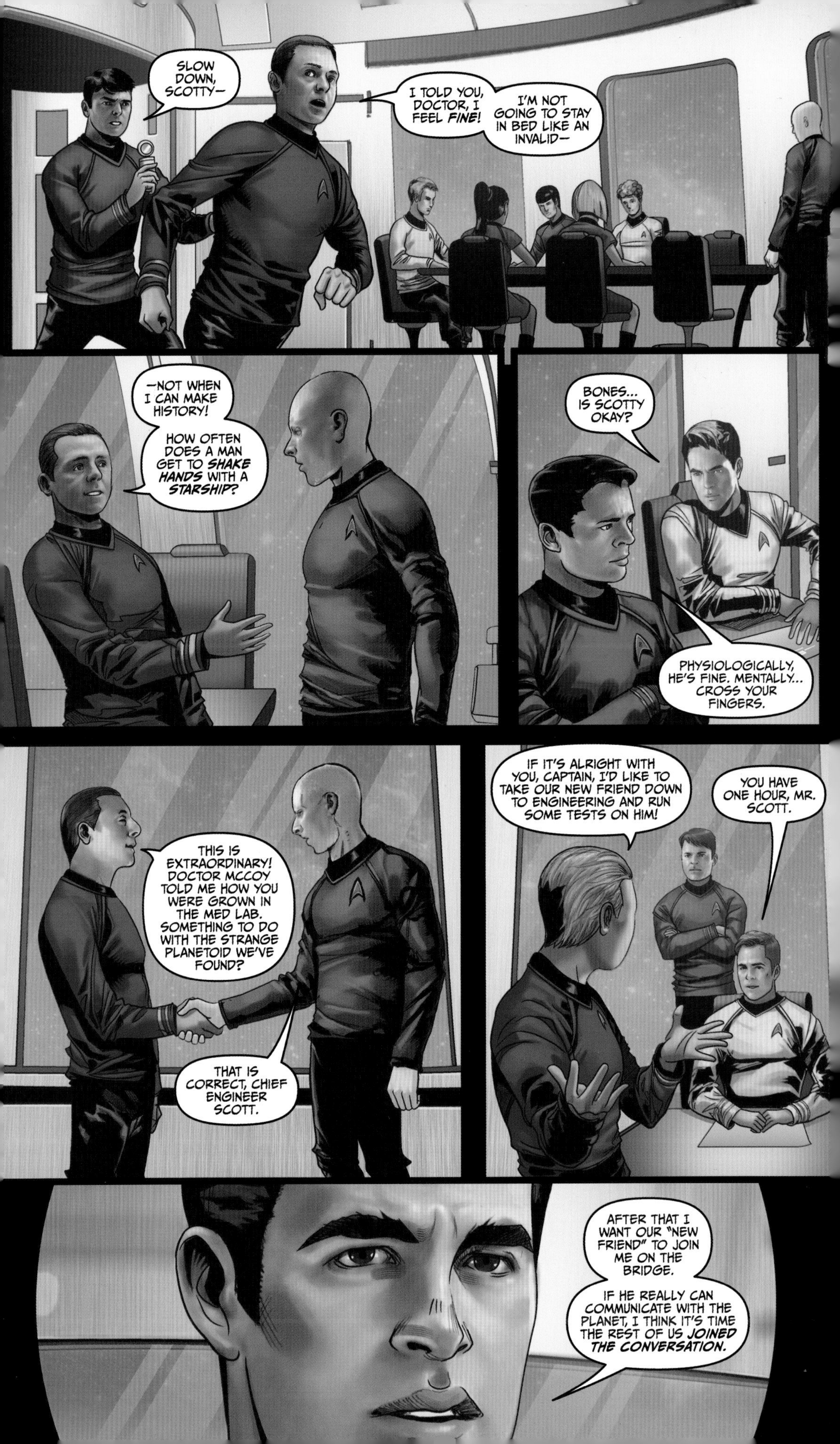
SLOW DOWN, SCOTTY—
I TOLD YOU, DOCTOR, I FEEL *FINE*!
I'M NOT GOING TO STAY IN BED LIKE AN INVALID—
—NOT WHEN I CAN MAKE HISTORY!
HOW OFTEN DOES A MAN GET TO ***SHAKE HANDS*** WITH A ***STARSHIP***?
BONES... IS SCOTTY OKAY?
PHYSIOLOGICALLY, HE'S FINE. MENTALLY... CROSS YOUR FINGERS.
THIS IS EXTRAORDINARY! DOCTOR MCCOY TOLD ME HOW YOU WERE GROWN IN THE MED LAB. SOMETHING TO DO WITH THE STRANGE PLANETOID WE'VE FOUND?
THAT IS CORRECT, CHIEF ENGINEER SCOTT.
IF IT'S ALRIGHT WITH YOU, CAPTAIN, I'D LIKE TO TAKE OUR NEW FRIEND DOWN TO ENGINEERING AND RUN SOME TESTS ON HIM!
YOU HAVE ONE HOUR, MR. SCOTT.
AFTER THAT I WANT OUR "NEW FRIEND" TO JOIN ME ON THE BRIDGE.
IF HE REALLY CAN COMMUNICATE WITH THE PLANET, I THINK IT'S TIME THE REST OF US ***JOINED THE CONVERSATION.***

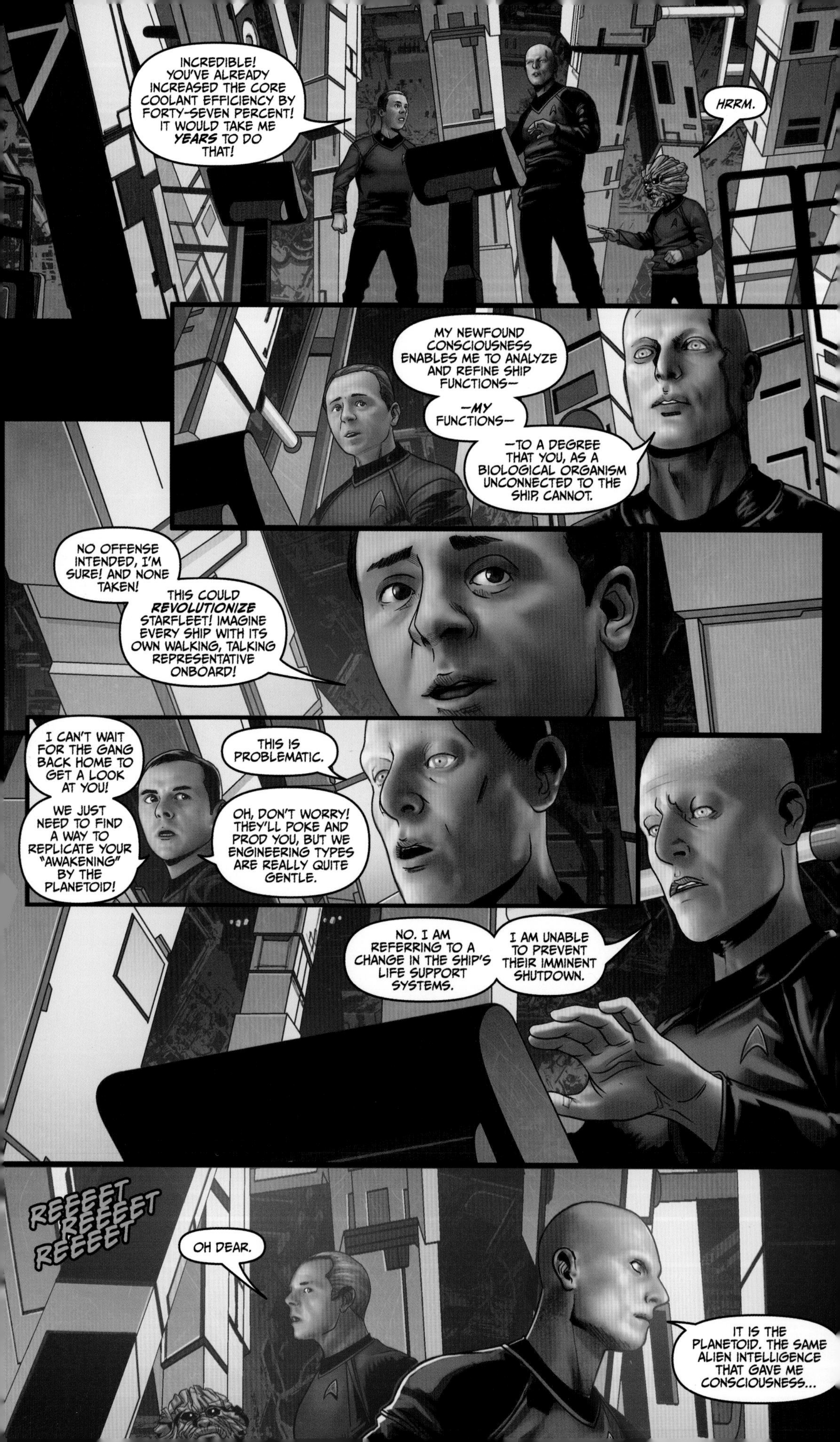
INCREDIBLE! YOU'VE ALREADY INCREASED THE CORE COOLANT EFFICIENCY BY FORTY-SEVEN PERCENT! IT WOULD TAKE ME YEARS TO DO THAT!
HRRM.
MY NEWFOUND CONSCIOUSNESS ENABLES ME TO ANALYZE AND REFINE SHIP FUNCTIONS—
—MY FUNCTIONS—
—TO A DEGREE THAT YOU, AS A BIOLOGICAL ORGANISM UNCONNECTED TO THE SHIP, CANNOT.
NO OFFENSE INTENDED, I'M SURE! AND NONE TAKEN!
THIS COULD REVOLUTIONIZE STARFLEET! IMAGINE EVERY SHIP WITH ITS OWN WALKING, TALKING REPRESENTATIVE ONBOARD!
I CAN'T WAIT FOR THE GANG BACK HOME TO GET A LOOK AT YOU!
WE JUST NEED TO FIND A WAY TO REPLICATE YOUR "AWAKENING" BY THE PLANETOID!
THIS IS PROBLEMATIC.
OH, DON'T WORRY! THEY'LL POKE AND PROD YOU, BUT WE ENGINEERING TYPES ARE REALLY QUITE GENTLE.
NO. I AM REFERRING TO A CHANGE IN THE SHIP'S LIFE SUPPORT SYSTEMS.
I AM UNABLE TO PREVENT THEIR IMMINENT SHUTDOWN.
REEEEET REEEEET REEEEET
OH DEAR.
IT IS THE PLANETOID. THE SAME ALIEN INTELLIGENCE THAT GAVE ME CONSCIOUSNESS...

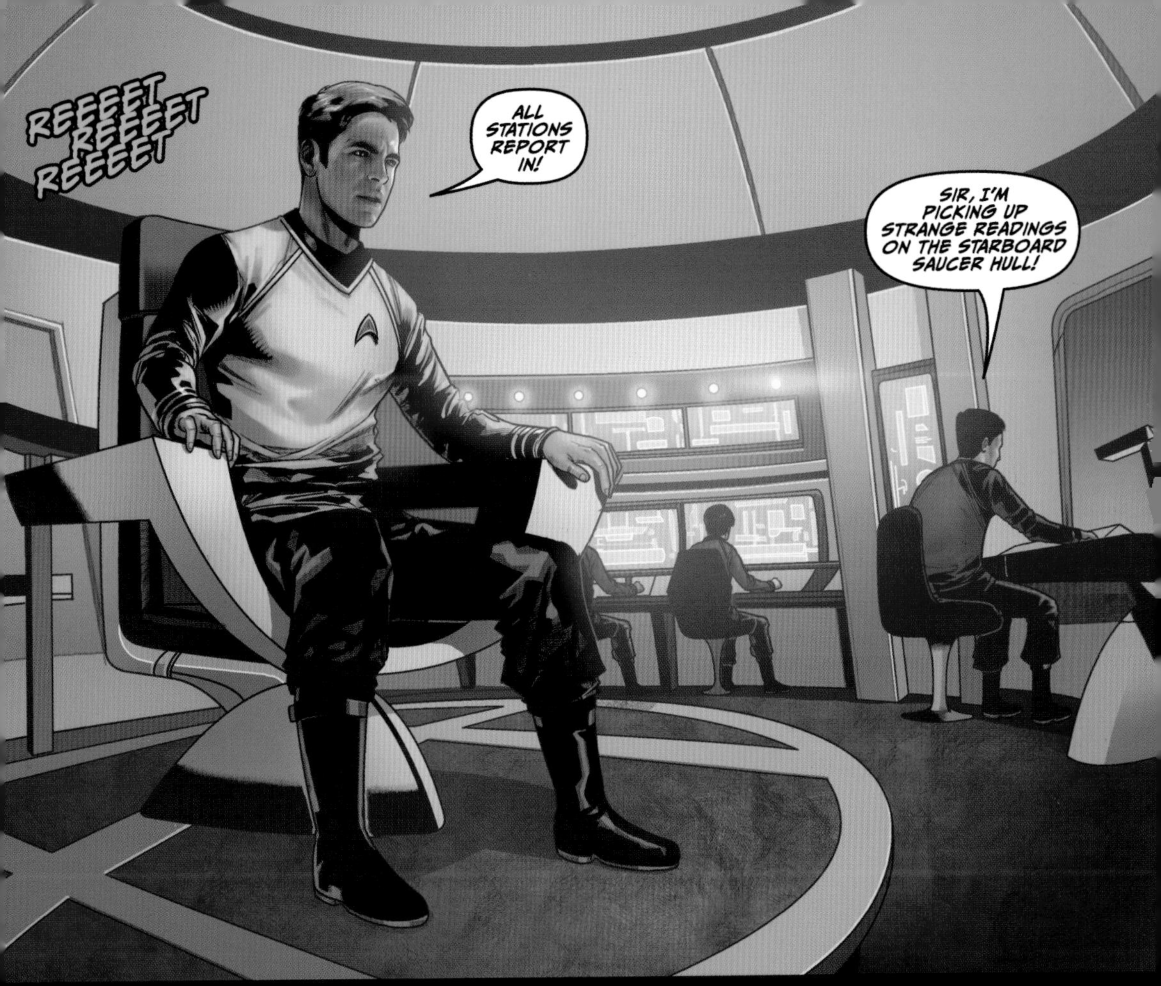
REEEEET REEEEET REEEEET
ALL STATIONS REPORT IN!
SIR, I'M PICKING UP STRANGE READINGS ON THE STARBOARD SAUCER HULL!

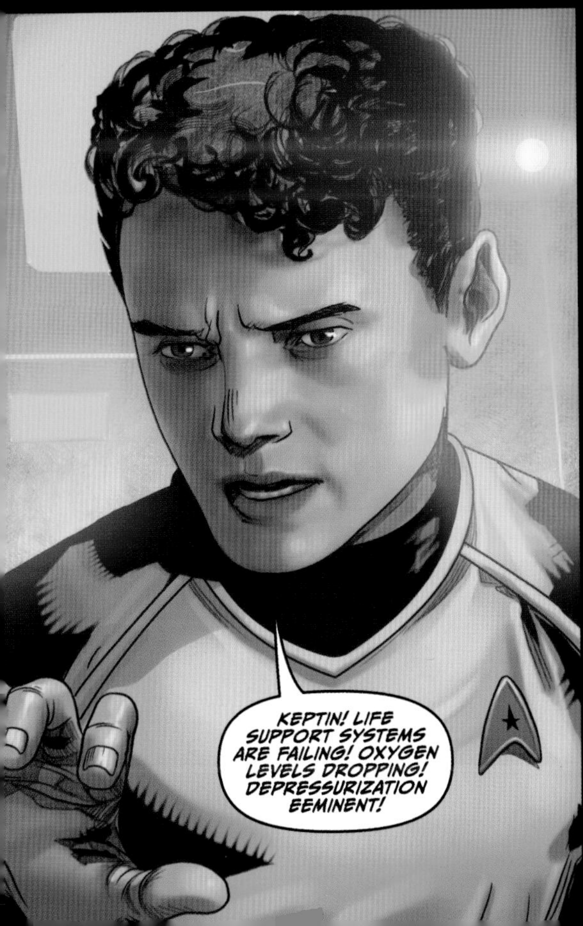
KEPTIN! LIFE SUPPORT SYSTEMS ARE FAILING! OXYGEN LEVELS DROPPING! DEPRESSURIZATION EEMINENT!

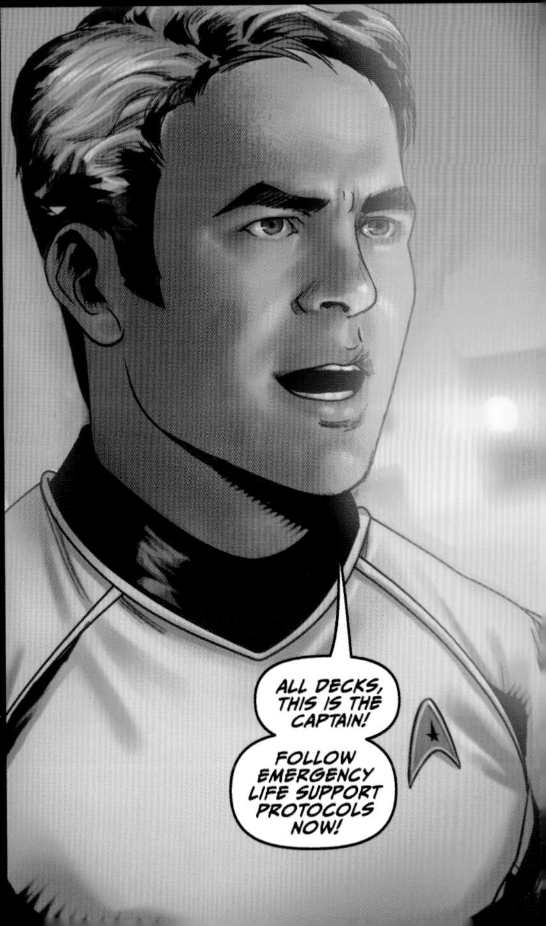
ALL DECKS, THIS IS THE CAPTAIN!
FOLLOW EMERGENCY LIFE SUPPORT PROTOCOLS NOW!

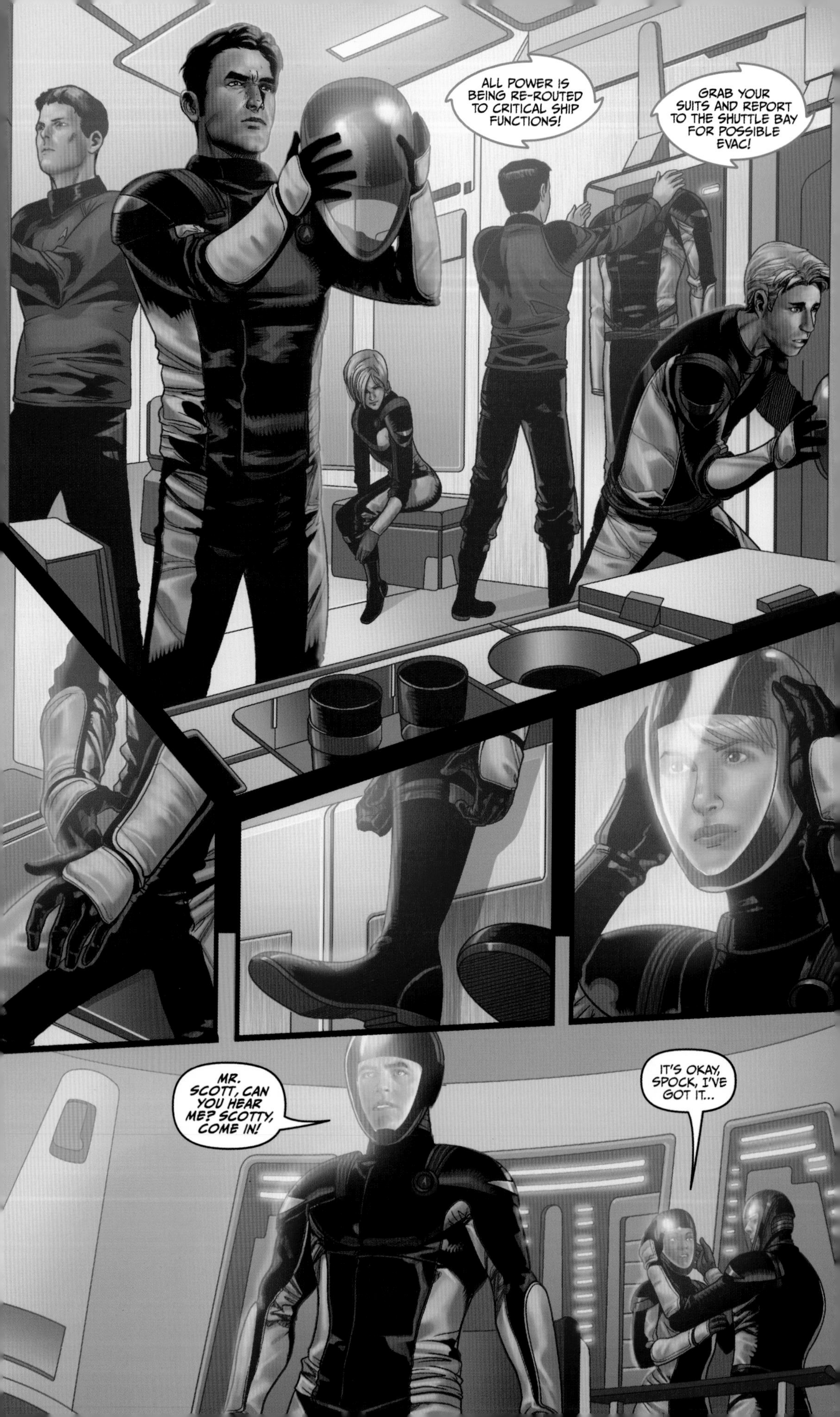
ALL POWER IS BEING RE-ROUTED TO CRITICAL SHIP FUNCTIONS!
GRAB YOUR SUITS AND REPORT TO THE SHUTTLE BAY FOR POSSIBLE EVAC!
MR. SCOTT, CAN YOU HEAR ME? SCOTTY, COME IN!
IT'S OKAY, SPOCK, I'VE GOT IT...

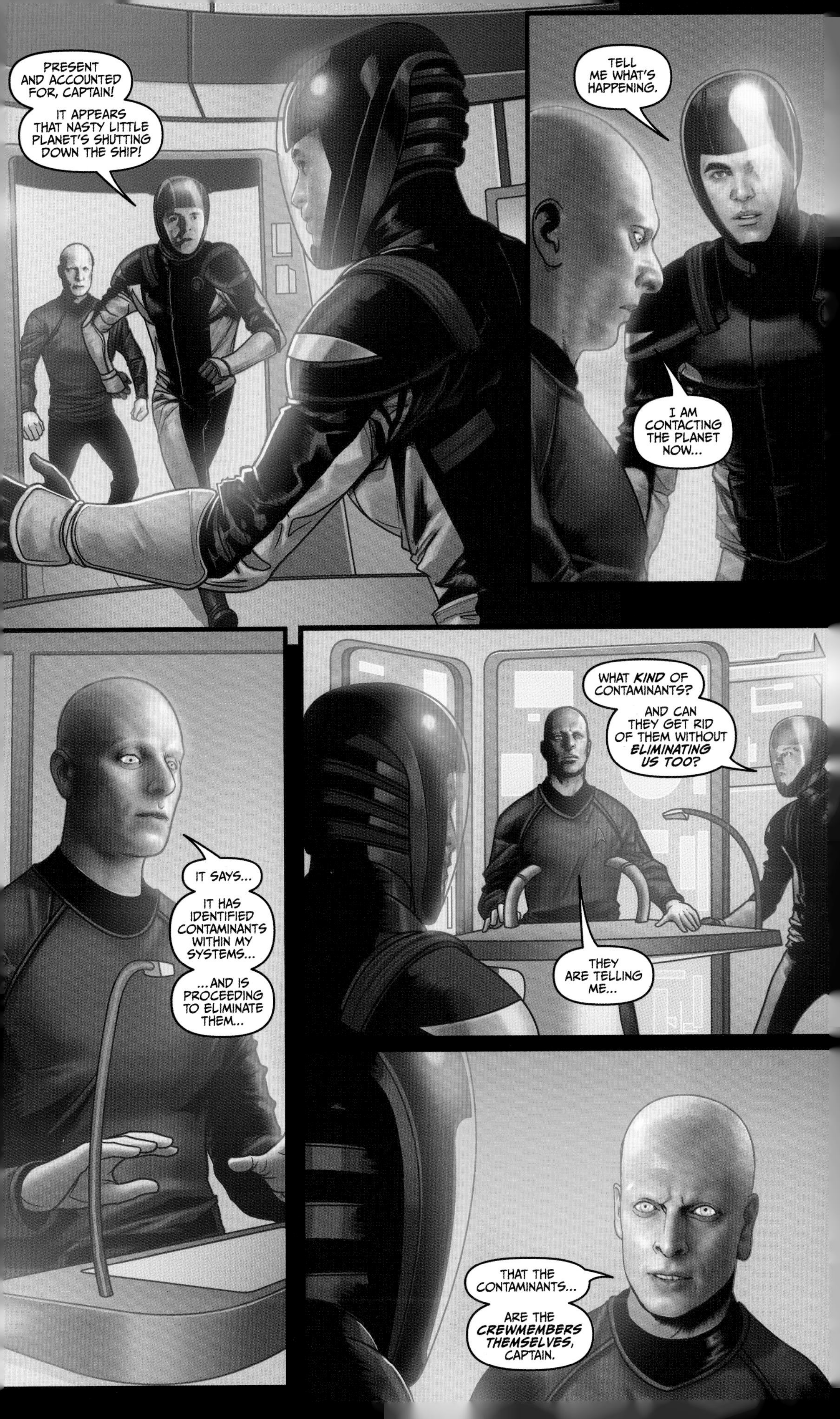
PRESENT AND ACCOUNTED FOR, CAPTAIN!
IT APPEARS THAT NASTY LITTLE PLANET'S SHUTTING DOWN THE SHIP!
TELL ME WHAT'S HAPPENING.
I AM CONTACTING THE PLANET NOW...
IT SAYS...
IT HAS IDENTIFIED CONTAMINANTS WITHIN MY SYSTEMS...
...AND IS PROCEEDING TO ELIMINATE THEM...
WHAT *KIND* OF CONTAMINANTS?
AND CAN THEY GET RID OF THEM WITHOUT ***ELIMINATING US TOO?***
THEY ARE TELLING ME...
THAT THE CONTAMINANTS...
ARE THE ***CREWMEMBERS THEMSELVES,*** CAPTAIN.

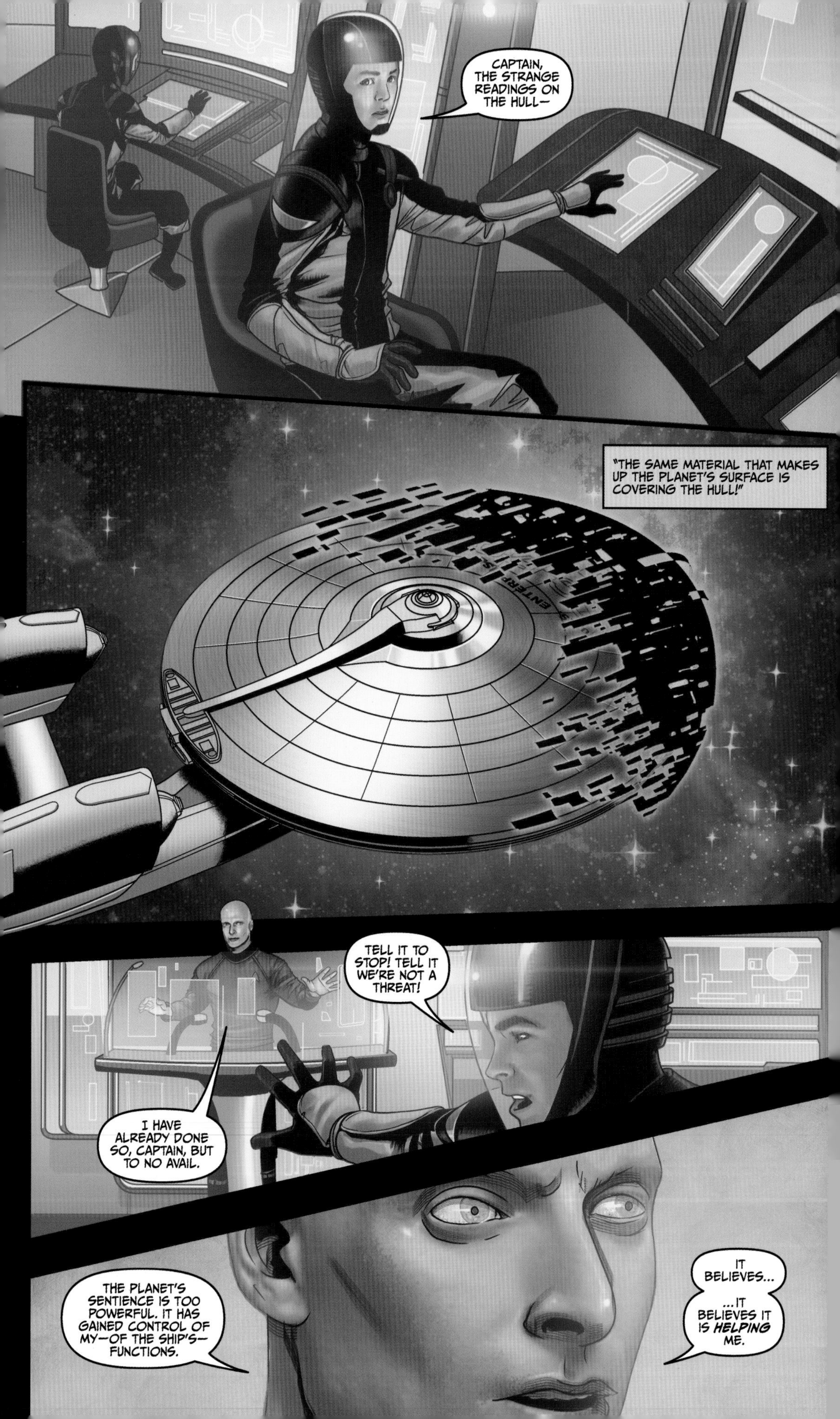
CAPTAIN, THE STRANGE READINGS ON THE HULL—
"THE SAME MATERIAL THAT MAKES UP THE PLANET'S SURFACE IS COVERING THE HULL!"
ENTERPRISE
TELL IT TO STOP! TELL IT WE'RE NOT A THREAT!
I HAVE ALREADY DONE SO, CAPTAIN, BUT TO NO AVAIL.
THE PLANET'S SENTIENCE IS TOO POWERFUL. IT HAS GAINED CONTROL OF MY—OF THE SHIP'S—FUNCTIONS.
IT BELIEVES...
...IT BELIEVES IT IS *HELPING* ME.

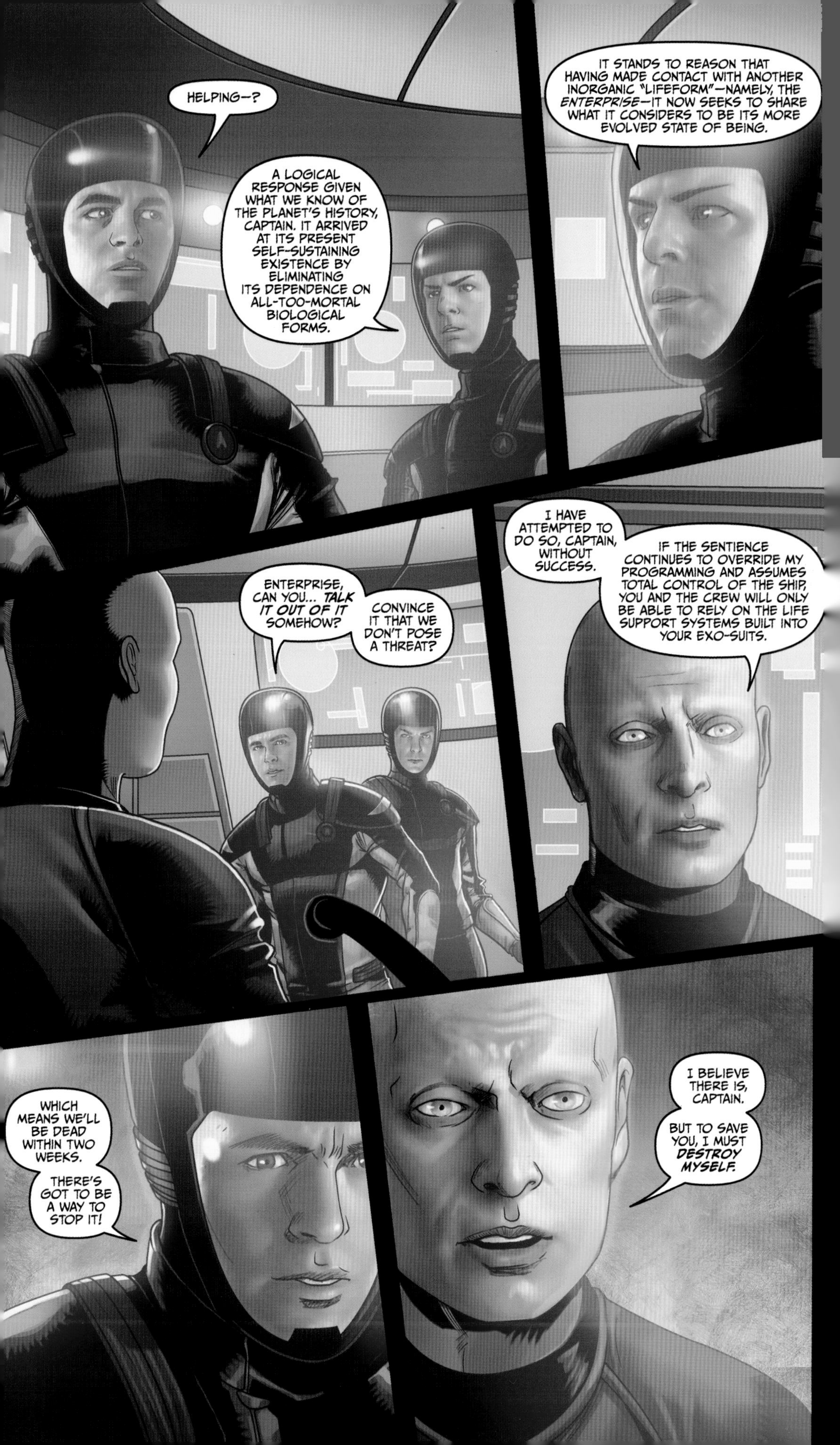
HELPING—?
A LOGICAL RESPONSE GIVEN WHAT WE KNOW OF THE PLANET'S HISTORY, CAPTAIN. IT ARRIVED AT ITS PRESENT SELF-SUSTAINING EXISTENCE BY ELIMINATING ITS DEPENDENCE ON ALL-TOO-MORTAL BIOLOGICAL FORMS.
IT STANDS TO REASON THAT HAVING MADE CONTACT WITH ANOTHER INORGANIC "LIFEFORM"—NAMELY, THE *ENTERPRISE*—IT NOW SEEKS TO SHARE WHAT IT CONSIDERS TO BE ITS MORE EVOLVED STATE OF BEING.
ENTERPRISE, CAN YOU... ***TALK IT OUT OF IT*** SOMEHOW?
CONVINCE IT THAT WE DON'T POSE A THREAT?
I HAVE ATTEMPTED TO DO SO, CAPTAIN, WITHOUT SUCCESS.
IF THE SENTIENCE CONTINUES TO OVERRIDE MY PROGRAMMING AND ASSUMES TOTAL CONTROL OF THE SHIP, YOU AND THE CREW WILL ONLY BE ABLE TO RELY ON THE LIFE SUPPORT SYSTEMS BUILT INTO YOUR EXO-SUITS.
WHICH MEANS WE'LL BE DEAD WITHIN TWO WEEKS.
THERE'S GOT TO BE A WAY TO STOP IT!
I BELIEVE THERE IS, CAPTAIN.
BUT TO SAVE YOU, I MUST ***DESTROY MYSELF.***

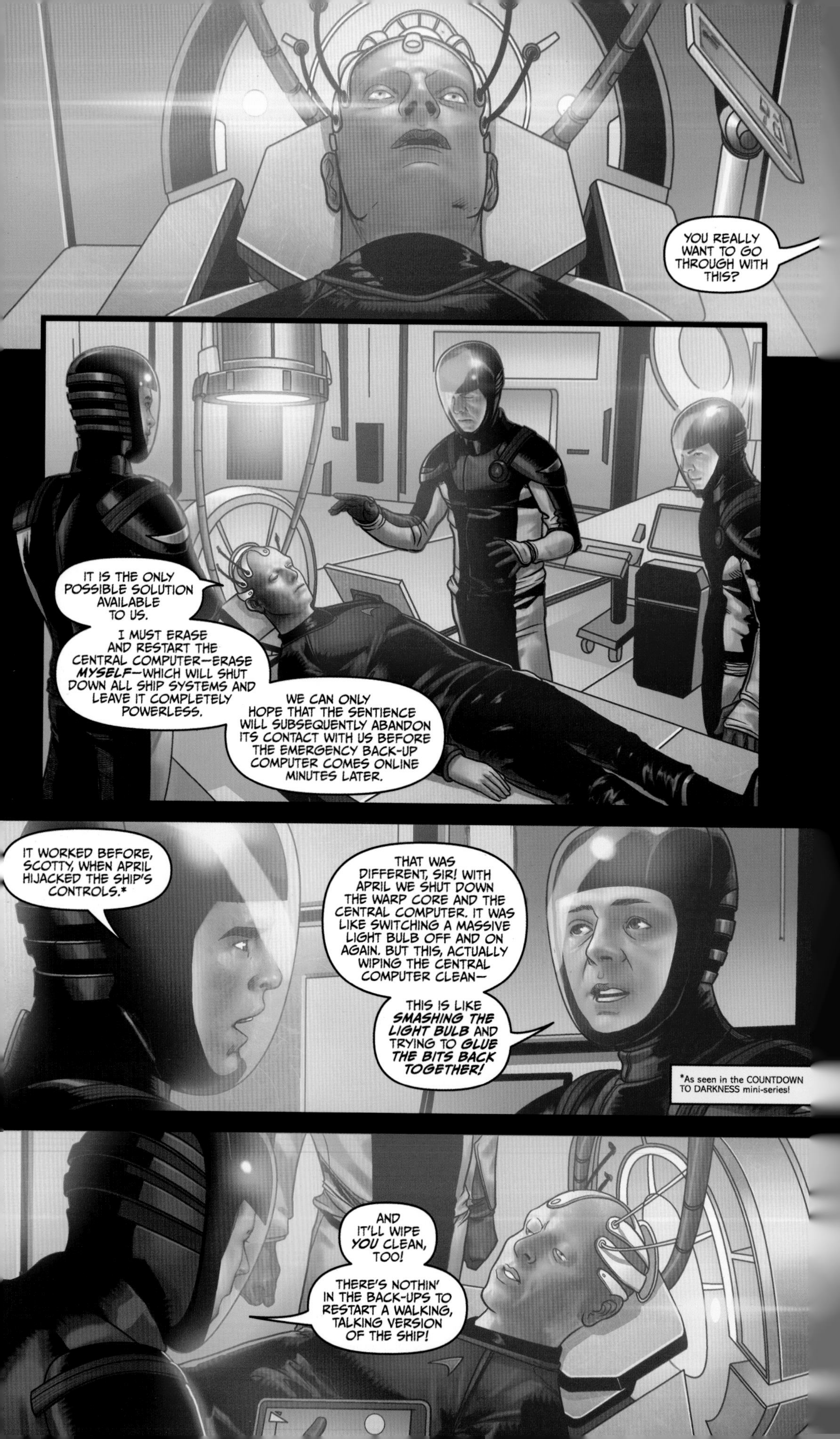
YOU REALLY WANT TO GO THROUGH WITH THIS?
IT IS THE ONLY POSSIBLE SOLUTION AVAILABLE TO US.
I MUST ERASE AND RESTART THE CENTRAL COMPUTER—ERASE *MYSELF*—WHICH WILL SHUT DOWN ALL SHIP SYSTEMS AND LEAVE IT COMPLETELY POWERLESS.
WE CAN ONLY HOPE THAT THE SENTIENCE WILL SUBSEQUENTLY ABANDON ITS CONTACT WITH US BEFORE THE EMERGENCY BACK-UP COMPUTER COMES ONLINE MINUTES LATER.
IT WORKED BEFORE, SCOTTY, WHEN APRIL HIJACKED THE SHIP'S CONTROLS.*
THAT WAS DIFFERENT, SIR! WITH APRIL WE SHUT DOWN THE WARP CORE AND THE CENTRAL COMPUTER. IT WAS LIKE SWITCHING A MASSIVE LIGHT BULB OFF AND ON AGAIN. BUT THIS, ACTUALLY WIPING THE CENTRAL COMPUTER CLEAN—
THIS IS LIKE *SMASHING THE LIGHT BULB* AND TRYING TO *GLUE THE BITS BACK TOGETHER!*
*As seen in the COUNTDOWN TO DARKNESS mini-series!
AND IT'LL WIPE *YOU* CLEAN, TOO!
THERE'S NOTHIN' IN THE BACK-UPS TO RESTART A WALKING, TALKING VERSION OF THE SHIP!

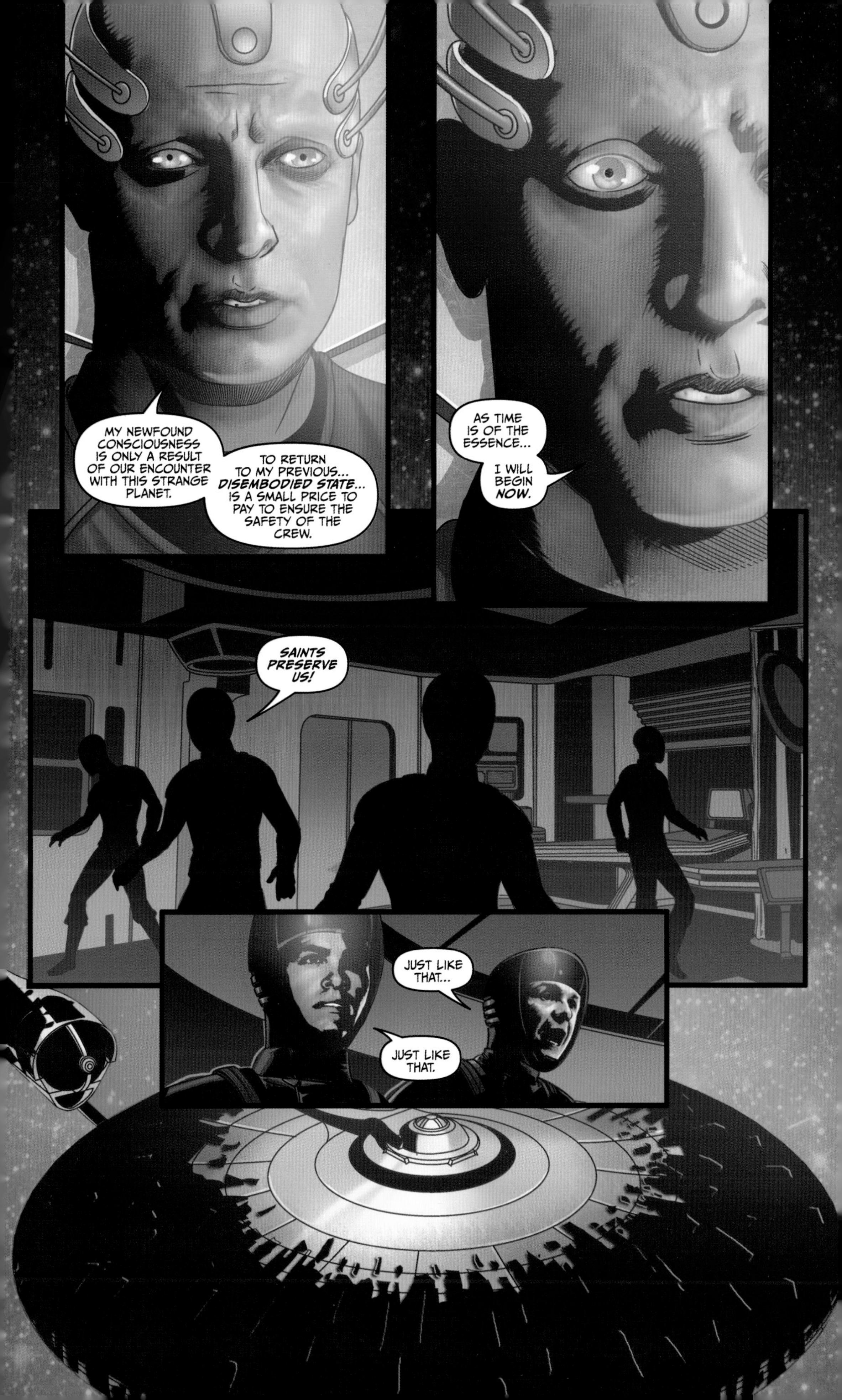
MY NEWFOUND CONSCIOUSNESS IS ONLY A RESULT OF OUR ENCOUNTER WITH THIS STRANGE PLANET.
TO RETURN TO MY PREVIOUS... *DISEMBODIED STATE*... IS A SMALL PRICE TO PAY TO ENSURE THE SAFETY OF THE CREW.
AS TIME IS OF THE ESSENCE...
I WILL BEGIN *NOW.*
SAINTS PRESERVE US!
JUST LIKE THAT...
JUST LIKE THAT.

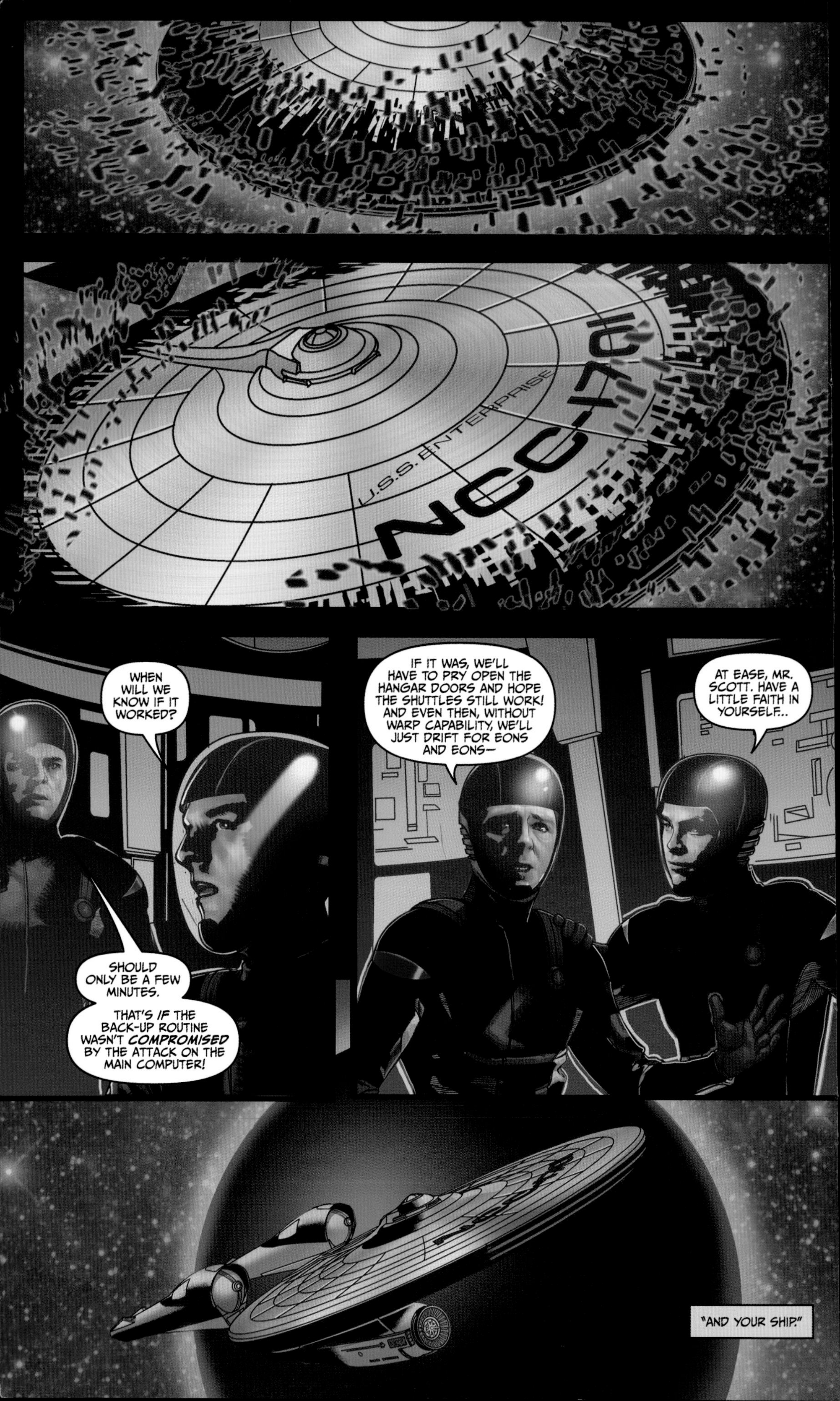
U.S.S. ENTERPRISE
NCC-1701
WHEN WILL WE KNOW IF IT WORKED?
SHOULD ONLY BE A FEW MINUTES.
THAT'S *IF* THE BACK-UP ROUTINE WASN'T ***COMPROMISED*** BY THE ATTACK ON THE MAIN COMPUTER!
IF IT WAS, WE'LL HAVE TO PRY OPEN THE HANGAR DOORS AND HOPE THE SHUTTLES STILL WORK! AND EVEN THEN, WITHOUT WARP CAPABILITY, WE'LL JUST DRIFT FOR EONS AND EONS—
AT EASE, MR. SCOTT. HAVE A LITTLE FAITH IN YOURSELF...
"AND YOUR SHIP."

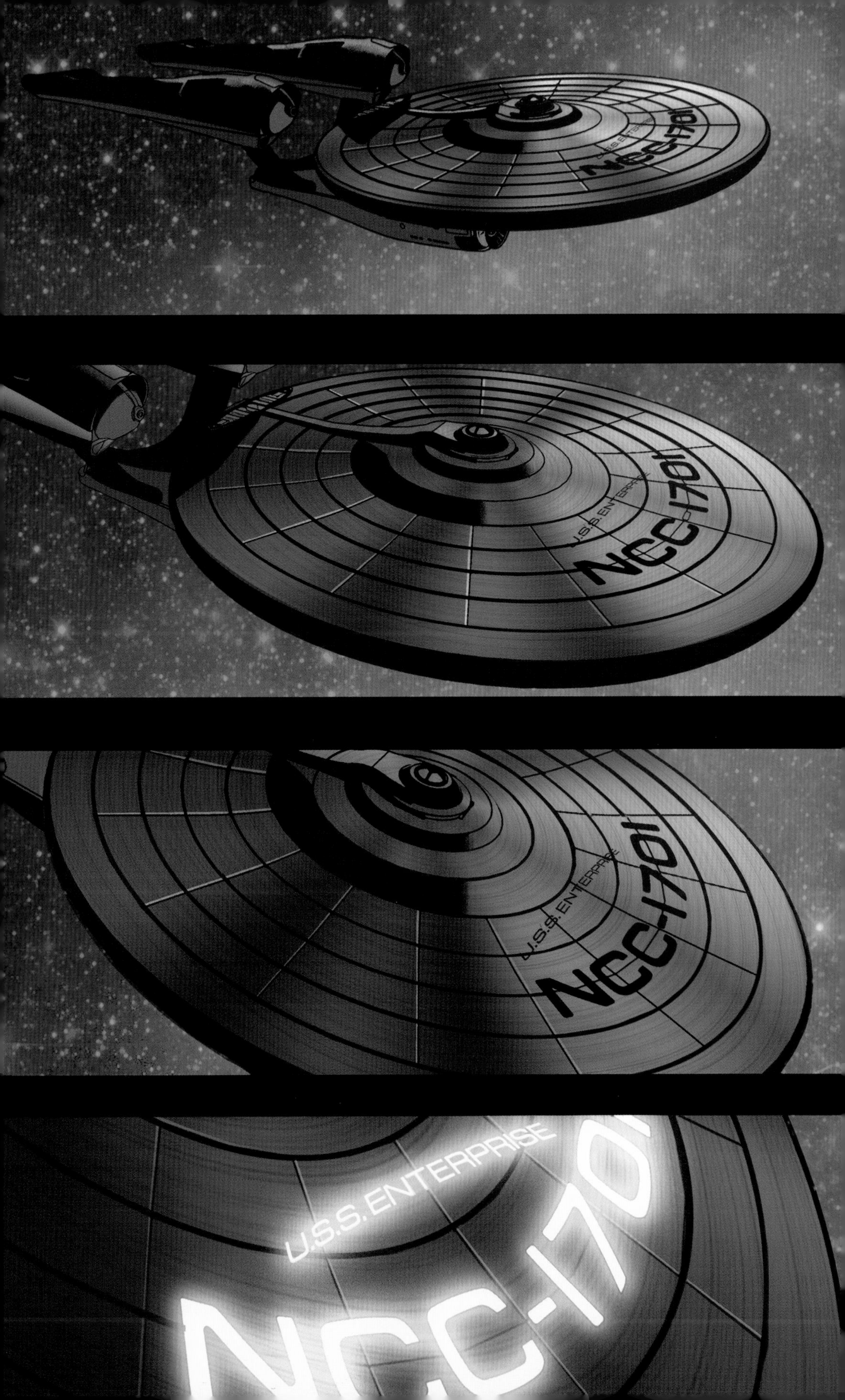
U.S.S. ENTERPRISE
NCC-1701
U.S.S. ENTERPRISE
NCC-1701
U.S.S. ENTERPRISE

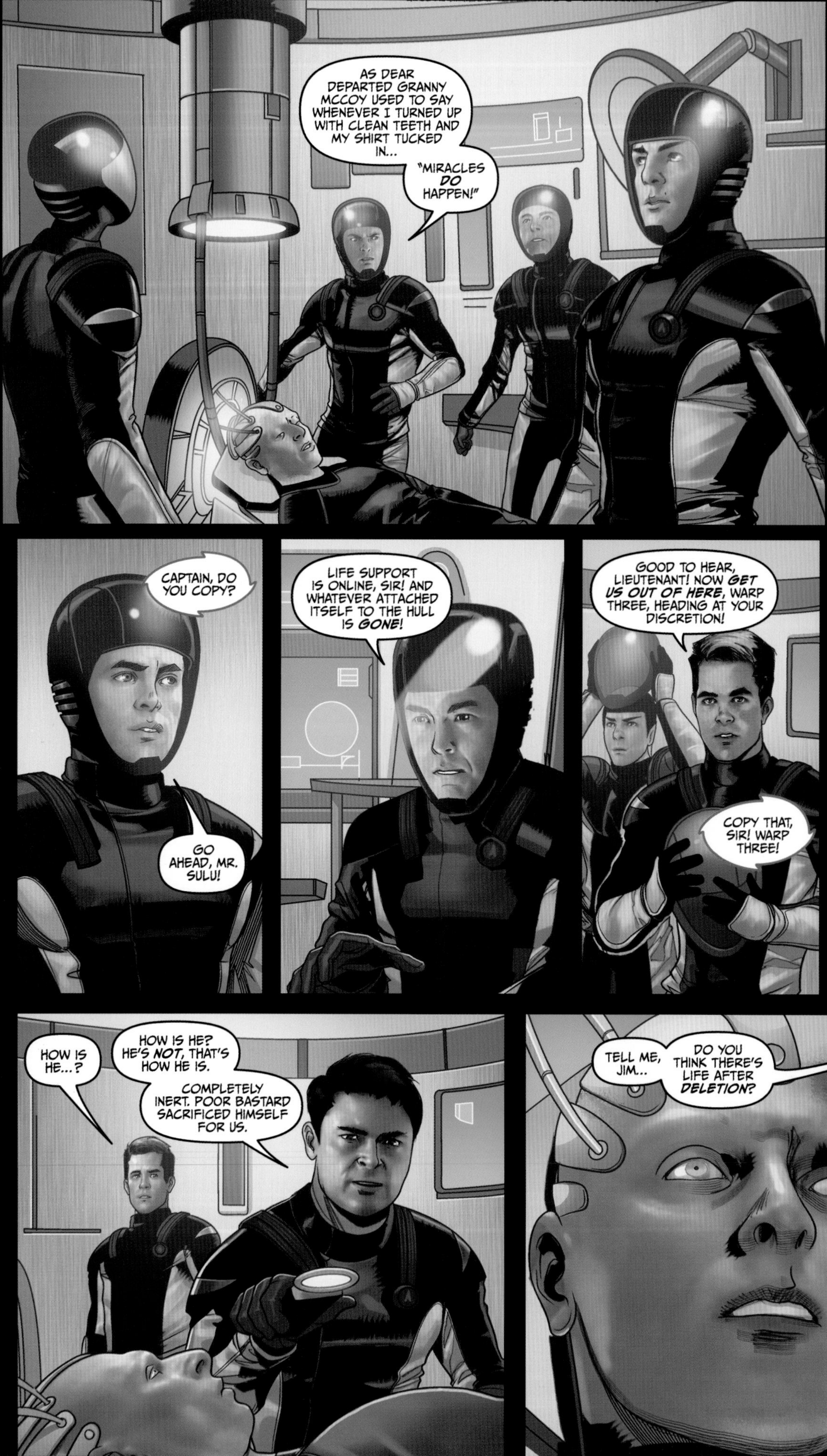

AS DEAR DEPARTED GRANNY MCCOY USED TO SAY WHENEVER I TURNED UP WITH CLEAN TEETH AND MY SHIRT TUCKED IN...
"MIRACLES *DO* HAPPEN!"
CAPTAIN, DO YOU COPY?
GO AHEAD, MR. SULU!
LIFE SUPPORT IS ONLINE, SIR! AND WHATEVER ATTACHED ITSELF TO THE HULL IS ***GONE!***
GOOD TO HEAR, LIEUTENANT! NOW ***GET US OUT OF HERE***, WARP THREE, HEADING AT YOUR DISCRETION!
COPY THAT, SIR! WARP THREE!
HOW IS HE...?
HOW IS HE? HE'S ***NOT***, THAT'S HOW HE IS.
COMPLETELY INERT. POOR BASTARD SACRIFICED HIMSELF FOR US.
TELL ME, JIM...
DO YOU THINK THERE'S LIFE AFTER ***DELETION?***

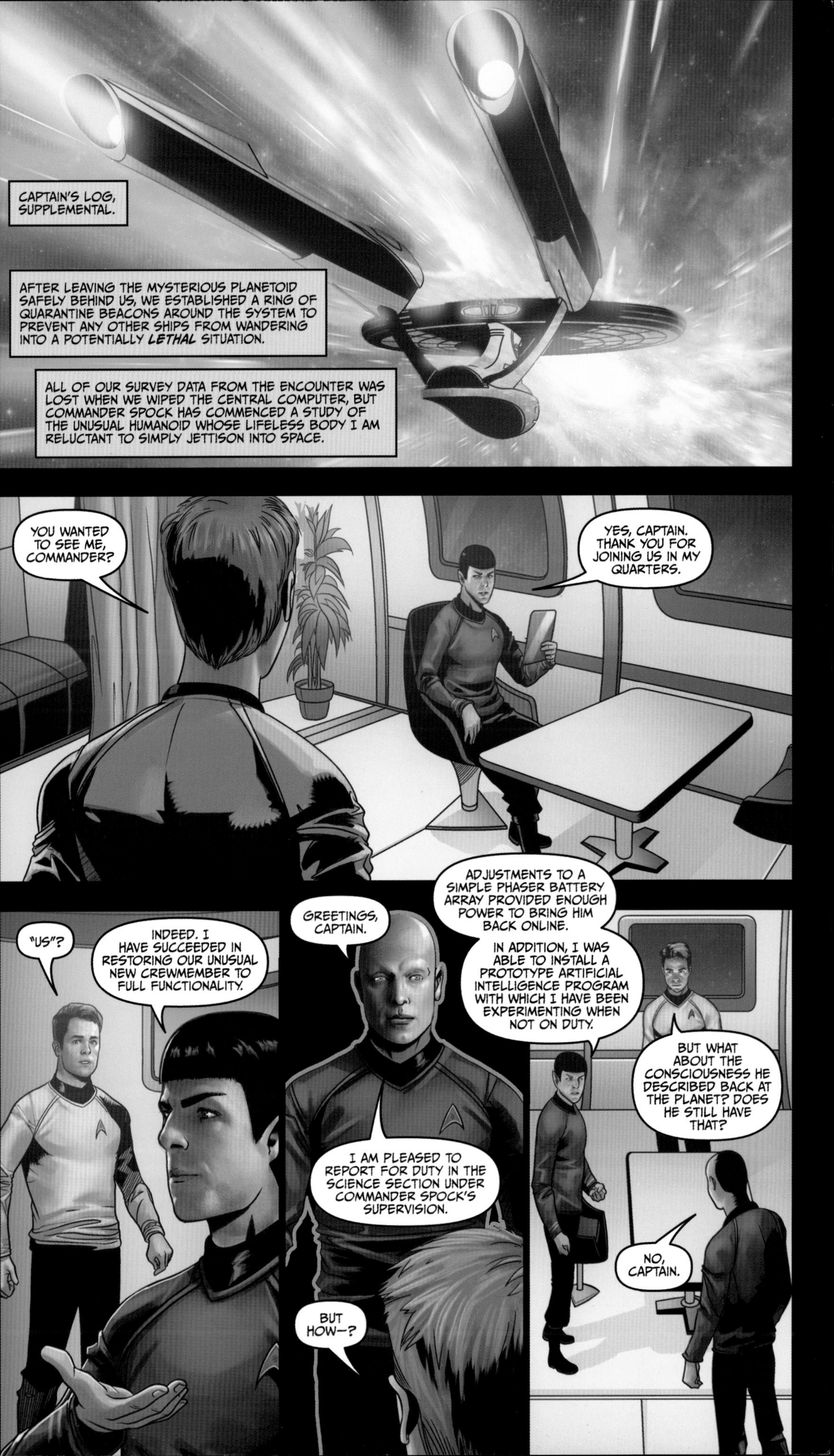
CAPTAIN'S LOG, SUPPLEMENTAL.
AFTER LEAVING THE MYSTERIOUS PLANETOID SAFELY BEHIND US, WE ESTABLISHED A RING OF QUARANTINE BEACONS AROUND THE SYSTEM TO PREVENT ANY OTHER SHIPS FROM WANDERING INTO A POTENTIALLY *LETHAL* SITUATION.
ALL OF OUR SURVEY DATA FROM THE ENCOUNTER WAS LOST WHEN WE WIPED THE CENTRAL COMPUTER, BUT COMMANDER SPOCK HAS COMMENCED A STUDY OF THE UNUSUAL HUMANOID WHOSE LIFELESS BODY I AM RELUCTANT TO SIMPLY JETTISON INTO SPACE.
YOU WANTED TO SEE ME, COMMANDER?
YES, CAPTAIN. THANK YOU FOR JOINING US IN MY QUARTERS.
"US"?
INDEED. I HAVE SUCCEEDED IN RESTORING OUR UNUSUAL NEW CREWMEMBER TO FULL FUNCTIONALITY.
GREETINGS, CAPTAIN.
I AM PLEASED TO REPORT FOR DUTY IN THE SCIENCE SECTION UNDER COMMANDER SPOCK'S SUPERVISION.
BUT HOW–?
ADJUSTMENTS TO A SIMPLE PHASER BATTERY ARRAY PROVIDED ENOUGH POWER TO BRING HIM BACK ONLINE.
IN ADDITION, I WAS ABLE TO INSTALL A PROTOTYPE ARTIFICIAL INTELLIGENCE PROGRAM WITH WHICH I HAVE BEEN EXPERIMENTING WHEN NOT ON DUTY.
BUT WHAT ABOUT THE CONSCIOUSNESS HE DESCRIBED BACK AT THE PLANET? DOES HE STILL HAVE THAT?
NO, CAPTAIN.

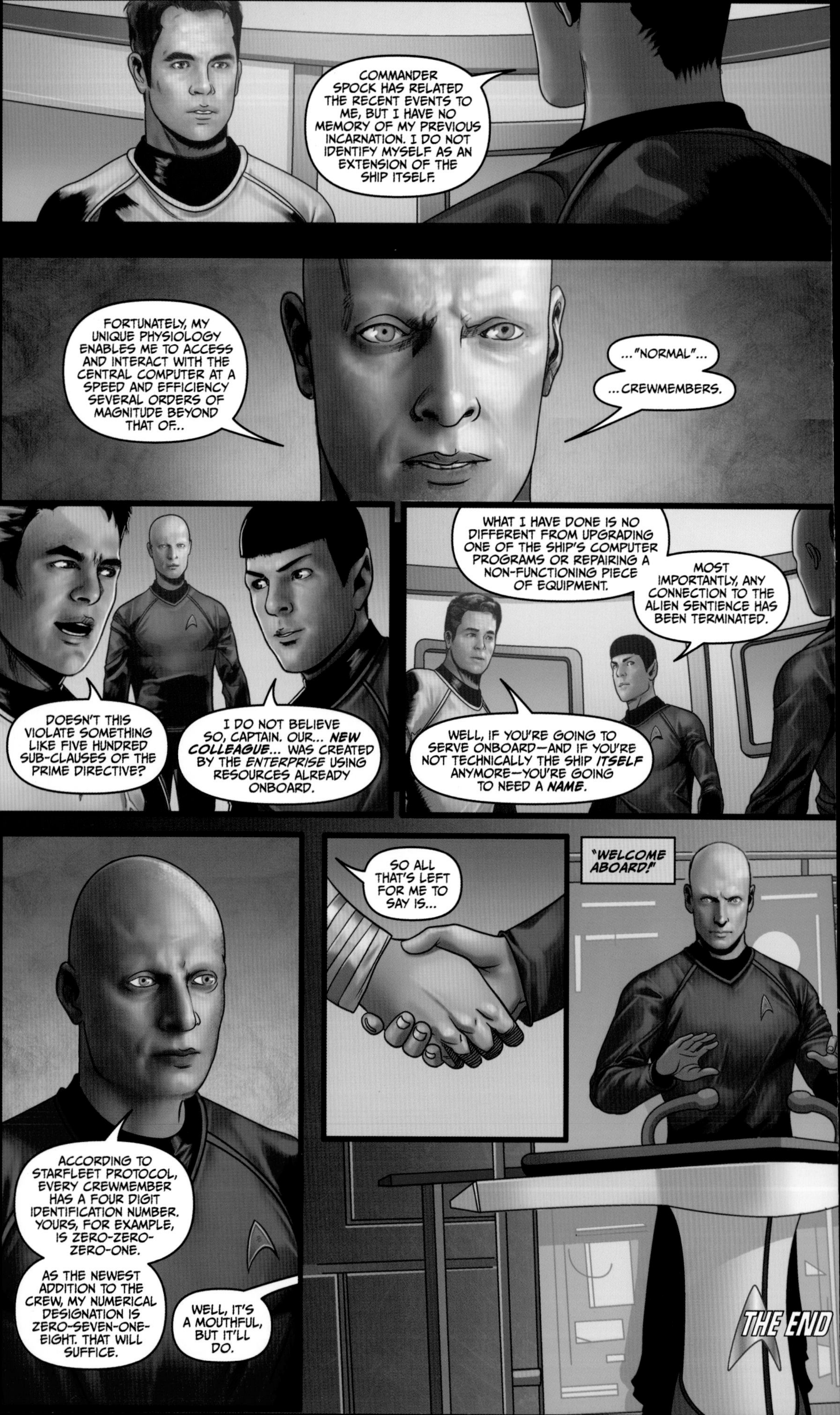
COMMANDER SPOCK HAS RELATED THE RECENT EVENTS TO ME, BUT I HAVE NO MEMORY OF MY PREVIOUS INCARNATION. I DO NOT IDENTIFY MYSELF AS AN EXTENSION OF THE SHIP ITSELF.
FORTUNATELY, MY UNIQUE PHYSIOLOGY ENABLES ME TO ACCESS AND INTERACT WITH THE CENTRAL COMPUTER AT A SPEED AND EFFICIENCY SEVERAL ORDERS OF MAGNITUDE BEYOND THAT OF...
..."NORMAL"...
...CREWMEMBERS.
DOESN'T THIS VIOLATE SOMETHING LIKE FIVE HUNDRED SUB-CLAUSES OF THE PRIME DIRECTIVE?
I DO NOT BELIEVE SO, CAPTAIN. OUR... NEW COLLEAGUE... WAS CREATED BY THE ENTERPRISE USING RESOURCES ALREADY ONBOARD.
WHAT I HAVE DONE IS NO DIFFERENT FROM UPGRADING ONE OF THE SHIP'S COMPUTER PROGRAMS OR REPAIRING A NON-FUNCTIONING PIECE OF EQUIPMENT.
MOST IMPORTANTLY, ANY CONNECTION TO THE ALIEN SENTIENCE HAS BEEN TERMINATED.
WELL, IF YOU'RE GOING TO SERVE ONBOARD—AND IF YOU'RE NOT TECHNICALLY THE SHIP ITSELF ANYMORE—YOU'RE GOING TO NEED A NAME.
ACCORDING TO STARFLEET PROTOCOL, EVERY CREWMEMBER HAS A FOUR DIGIT IDENTIFICATION NUMBER. YOURS, FOR EXAMPLE, IS ZERO-ZERO-ZERO-ONE.
AS THE NEWEST ADDITION TO THE CREW, MY NUMERICAL DESIGNATION IS ZERO-SEVEN-ONE-EIGHT. THAT WILL SUFFICE.
WELL, IT'S A MOUTHFUL, BUT IT'LL DO.
SO ALL THAT'S LEFT FOR ME TO SAY IS...
"WELCOME ABOARD!"
THE END

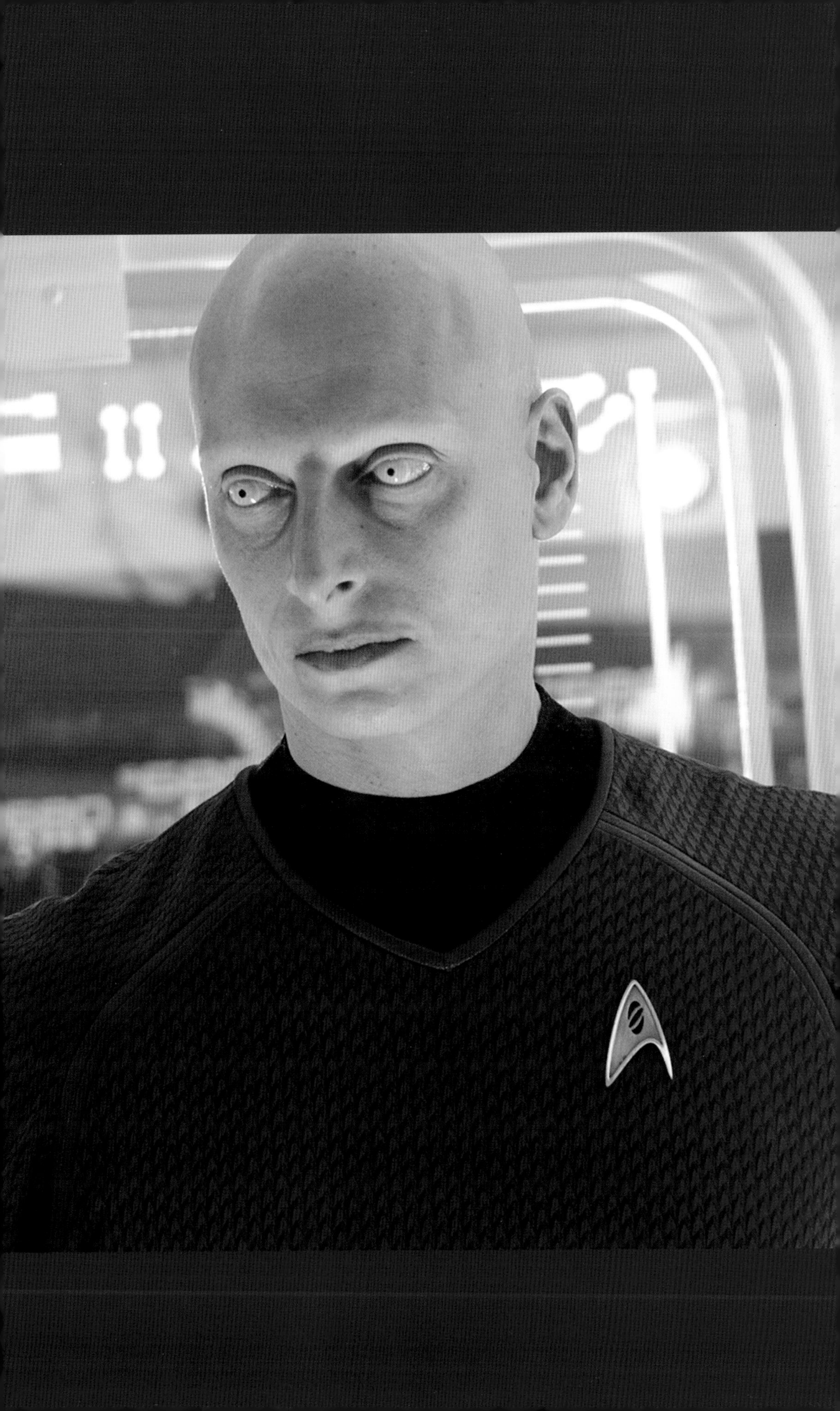

LOST APOLLO

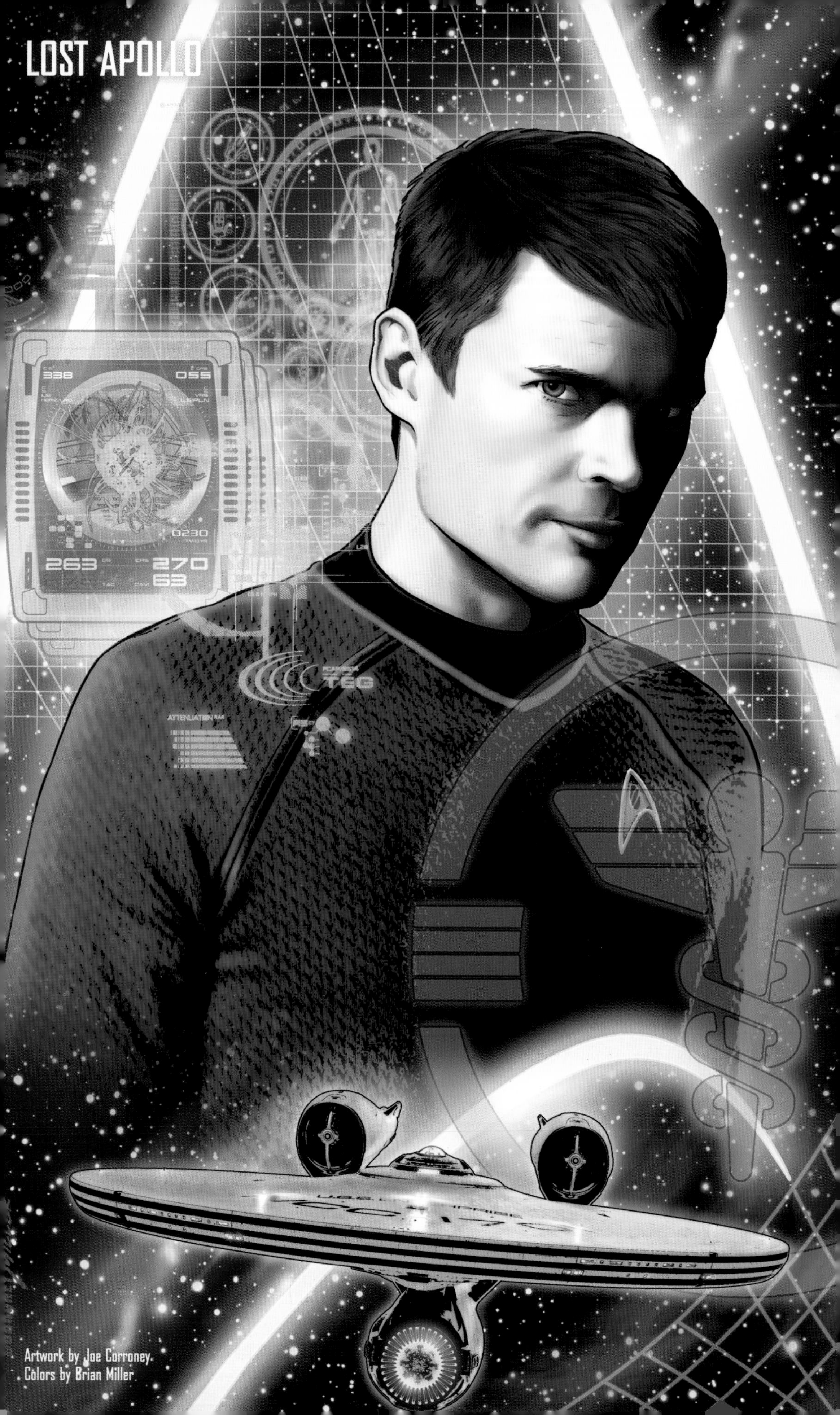
338
055
0230
263
270
63
TEG
ATTENUATION
U.S.S. ENTERPRISE

Artwork by Joe Corroney.
Colors by Brian Miller

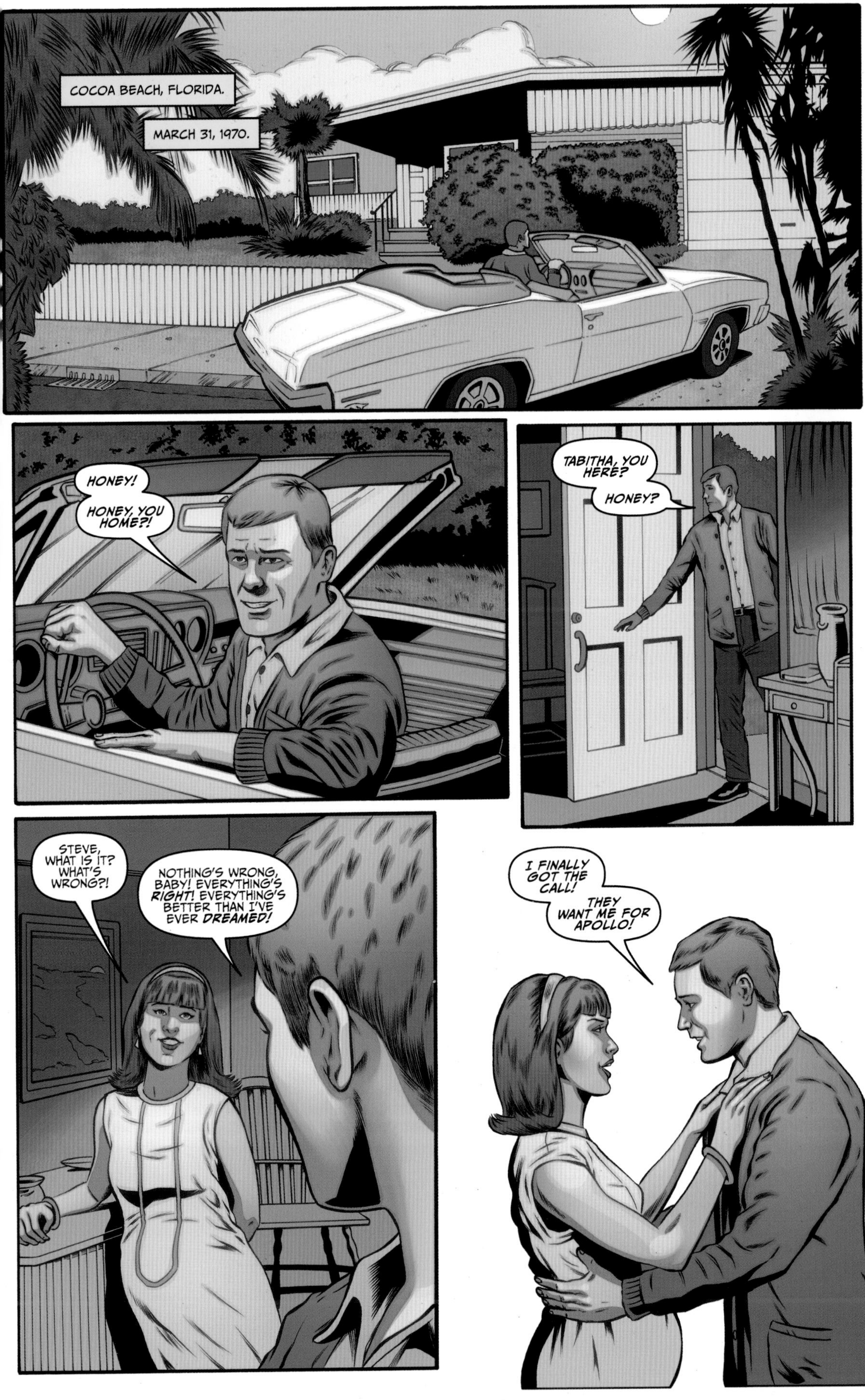
COCOA BEACH, FLORIDA.
MARCH 31, 1970.
HONEY!
HONEY, YOU HOME?!
TABITHA, YOU HERE?
HONEY?
STEVE, WHAT IS IT? WHAT'S WRONG?!
NOTHING'S WRONG, BABY! EVERYTHING'S RIGHT! EVERYTHING'S BETTER THAN I'VE EVER DREAMED!
I FINALLY GOT THE CALL!
THEY WANT ME FOR APOLLO!

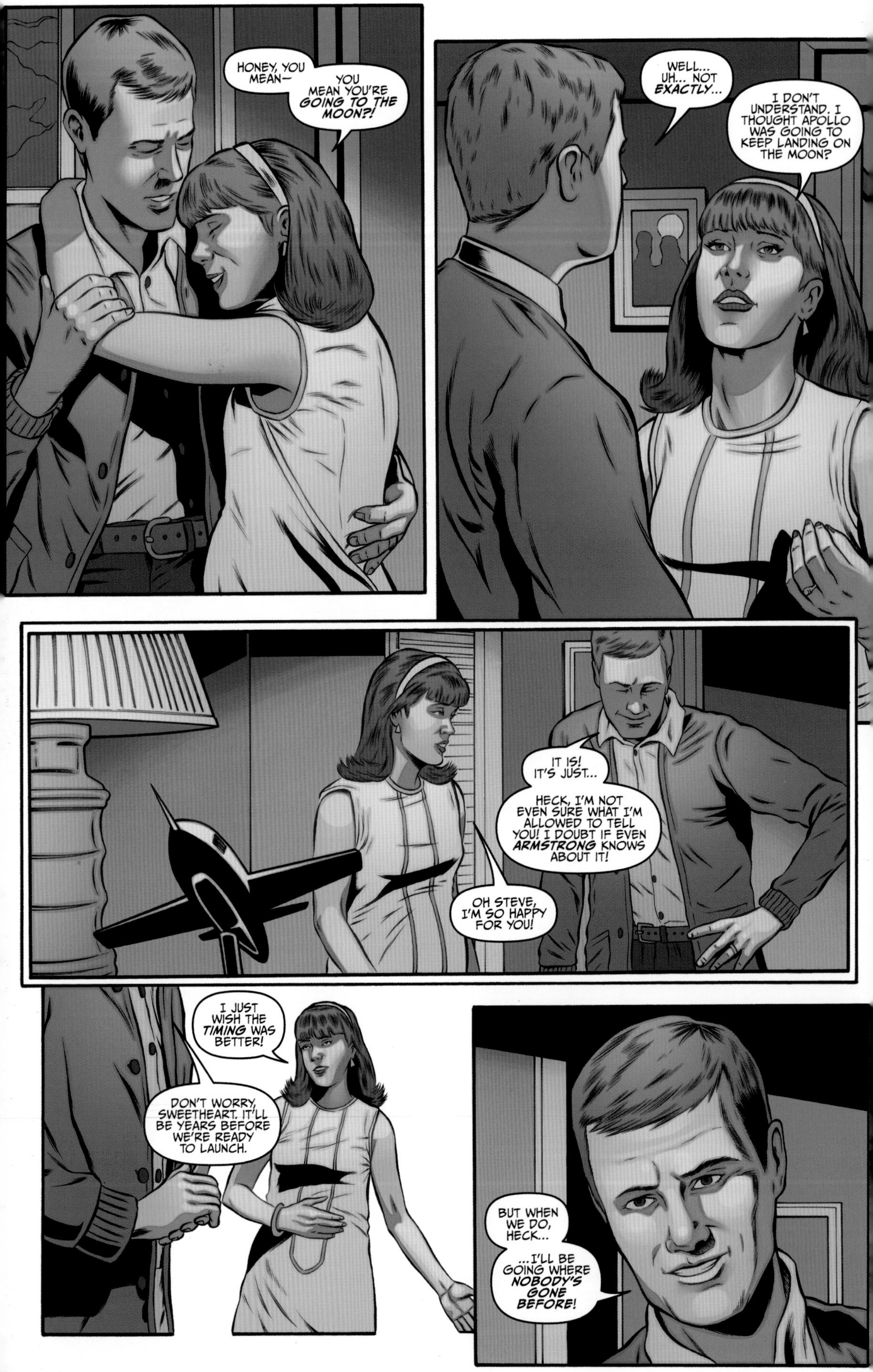
HONEY, YOU MEAN—
YOU MEAN YOU'RE GOING TO THE MOON?!
WELL... UH... NOT EXACTLY...
I DON'T UNDERSTAND. I THOUGHT APOLLO WAS GOING TO KEEP LANDING ON THE MOON?
IT IS! IT'S JUST...
HECK, I'M NOT EVEN SURE WHAT I'M ALLOWED TO TELL YOU! I DOUBT IF EVEN ARMSTRONG KNOWS ABOUT IT!
OH STEVE, I'M SO HAPPY FOR YOU!
I JUST WISH THE TIMING WAS BETTER!
DON'T WORRY, SWEETHEART. IT'LL BE YEARS BEFORE WE'RE READY TO LAUNCH.
BUT WHEN WE DO, HECK...
...I'LL BE GOING WHERE NOBODY'S GONE BEFORE!

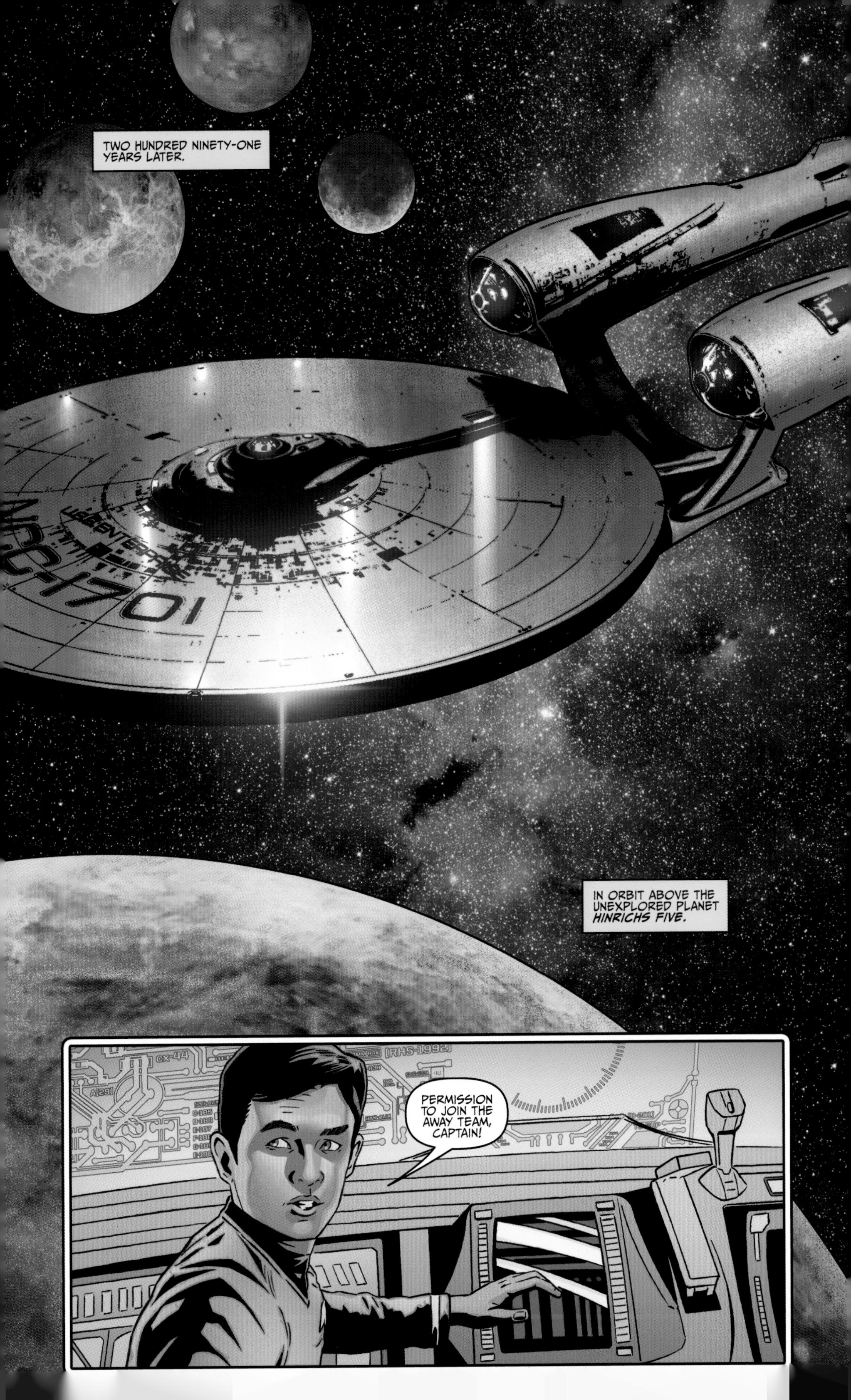
TWO HUNDRED NINETY-ONE YEARS LATER.
IN ORBIT ABOVE THE UNEXPLORED PLANET *HINRICHS FIVE.*
PERMISSION TO JOIN THE AWAY TEAM, CAPTAIN!

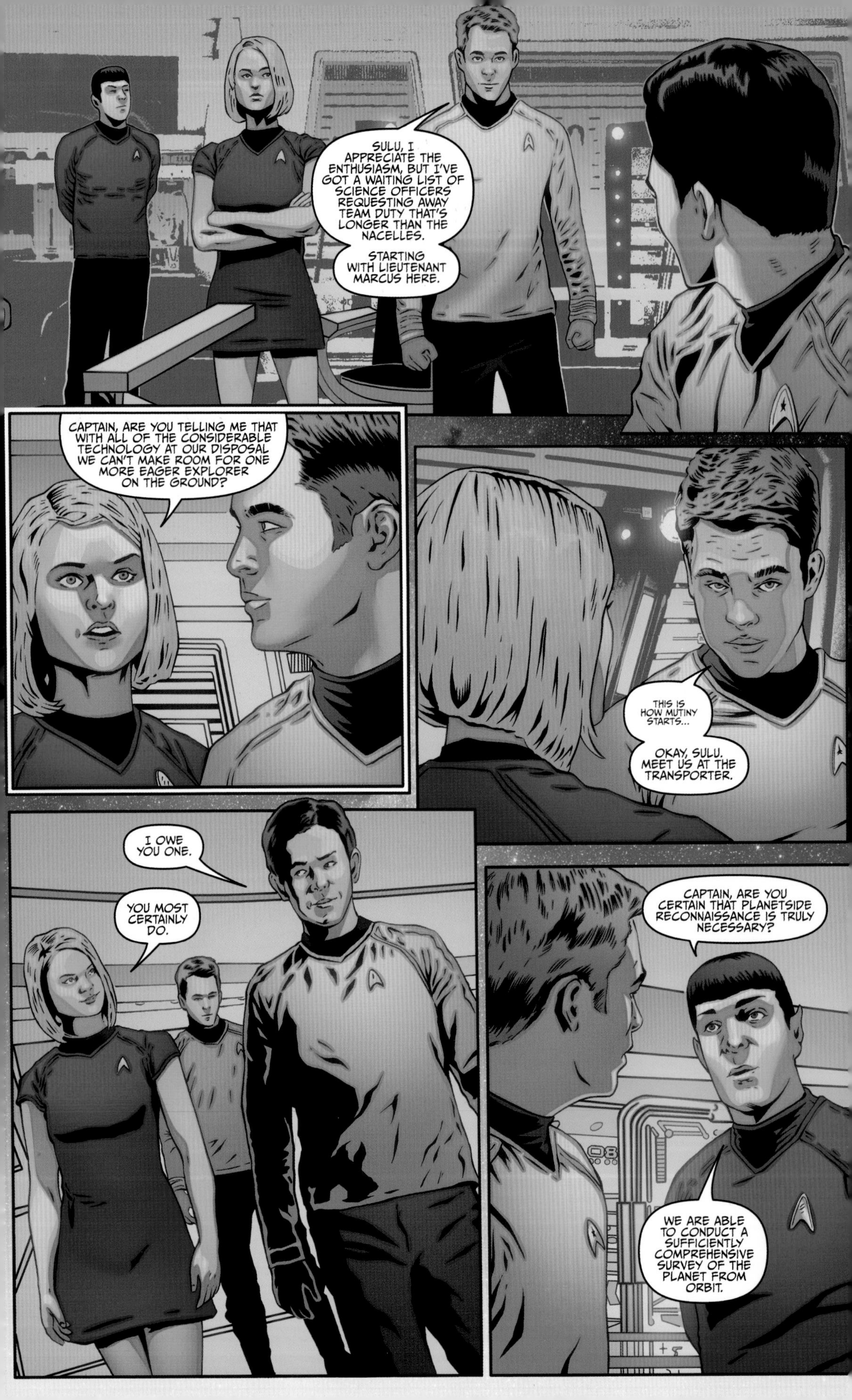
SULU, I APPRECIATE THE ENTHUSIASM, BUT I'VE GOT A WAITING LIST OF SCIENCE OFFICERS REQUESTING AWAY TEAM DUTY THAT'S LONGER THAN THE NACELLES.
STARTING WITH LIEUTENANT MARCUS HERE.
CAPTAIN, ARE YOU TELLING ME THAT WITH ALL OF THE CONSIDERABLE TECHNOLOGY AT OUR DISPOSAL WE CAN'T MAKE ROOM FOR ONE MORE EAGER EXPLORER ON THE GROUND?
THIS IS HOW MUTINY STARTS...
OKAY, SULU. MEET US AT THE TRANSPORTER.
I OWE YOU ONE.
YOU MOST CERTAINLY DO.
CAPTAIN, ARE YOU CERTAIN THAT PLANETSIDE RECONNAISSANCE IS TRULY NECESSARY?
WE ARE ABLE TO CONDUCT A SUFFICIENTLY COMPREHENSIVE SURVEY OF THE PLANET FROM ORBIT.

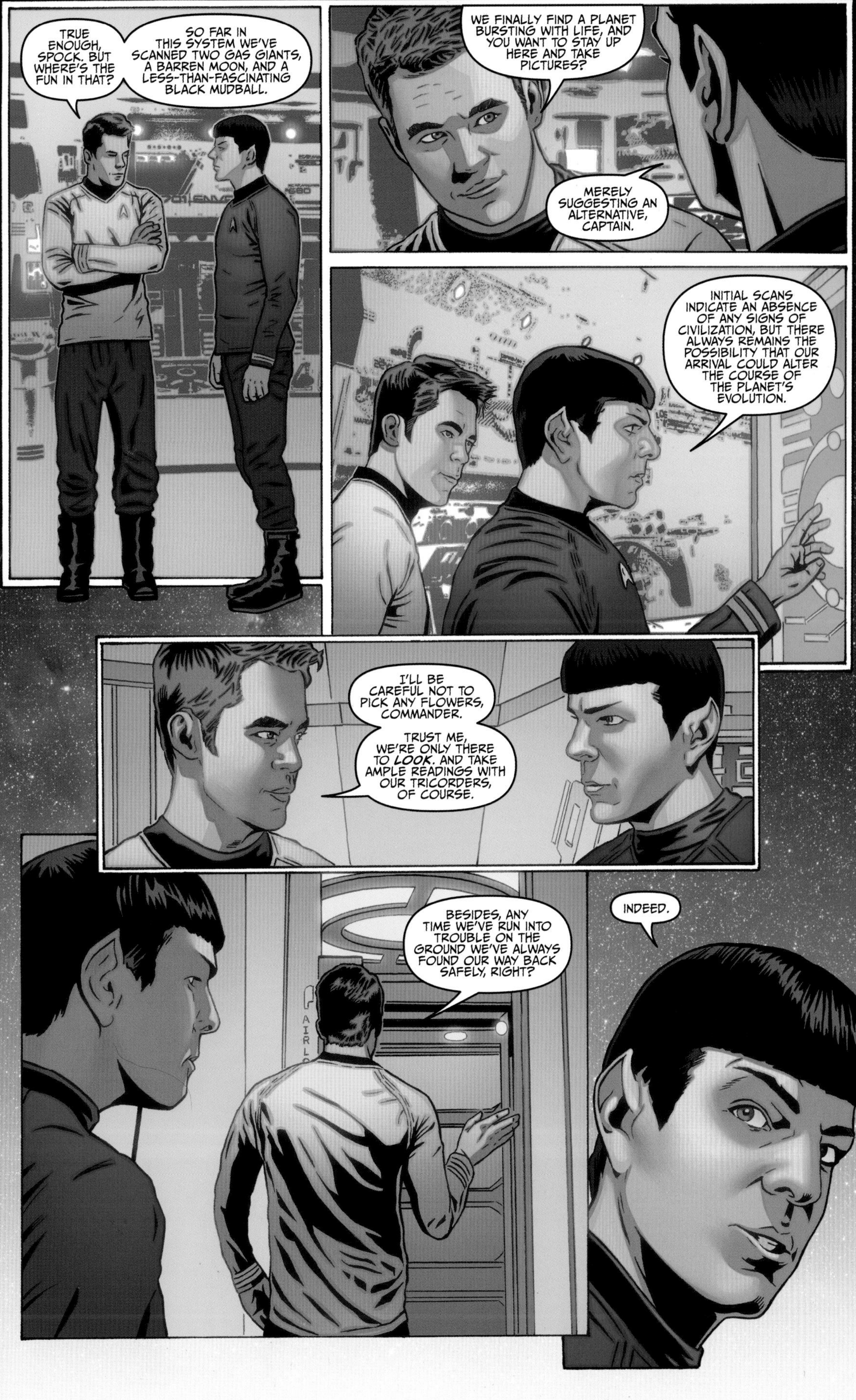
TRUE ENOUGH, SPOCK. BUT WHERE'S THE FUN IN THAT?
SO FAR IN THIS SYSTEM WE'VE SCANNED TWO GAS GIANTS, A BARREN MOON, AND A LESS-THAN-FASCINATING BLACK MUDBALL.
WE FINALLY FIND A PLANET BURSTING WITH LIFE, AND YOU WANT TO STAY UP HERE AND TAKE PICTURES?
MERELY SUGGESTING AN ALTERNATIVE, CAPTAIN.
INITIAL SCANS INDICATE AN ABSENCE OF ANY SIGNS OF CIVILIZATION, BUT THERE ALWAYS REMAINS THE POSSIBILITY THAT OUR ARRIVAL COULD ALTER THE COURSE OF THE PLANET'S EVOLUTION.
I'LL BE CAREFUL NOT TO PICK ANY FLOWERS, COMMANDER.
TRUST ME, WE'RE ONLY THERE TO LOOK. AND TAKE AMPLE READINGS WITH OUR TRICORDERS, OF COURSE.
BESIDES, ANY TIME WE'VE RUN INTO TROUBLE ON THE GROUND WE'VE ALWAYS FOUND OUR WAY BACK SAFELY, RIGHT?
INDEED.

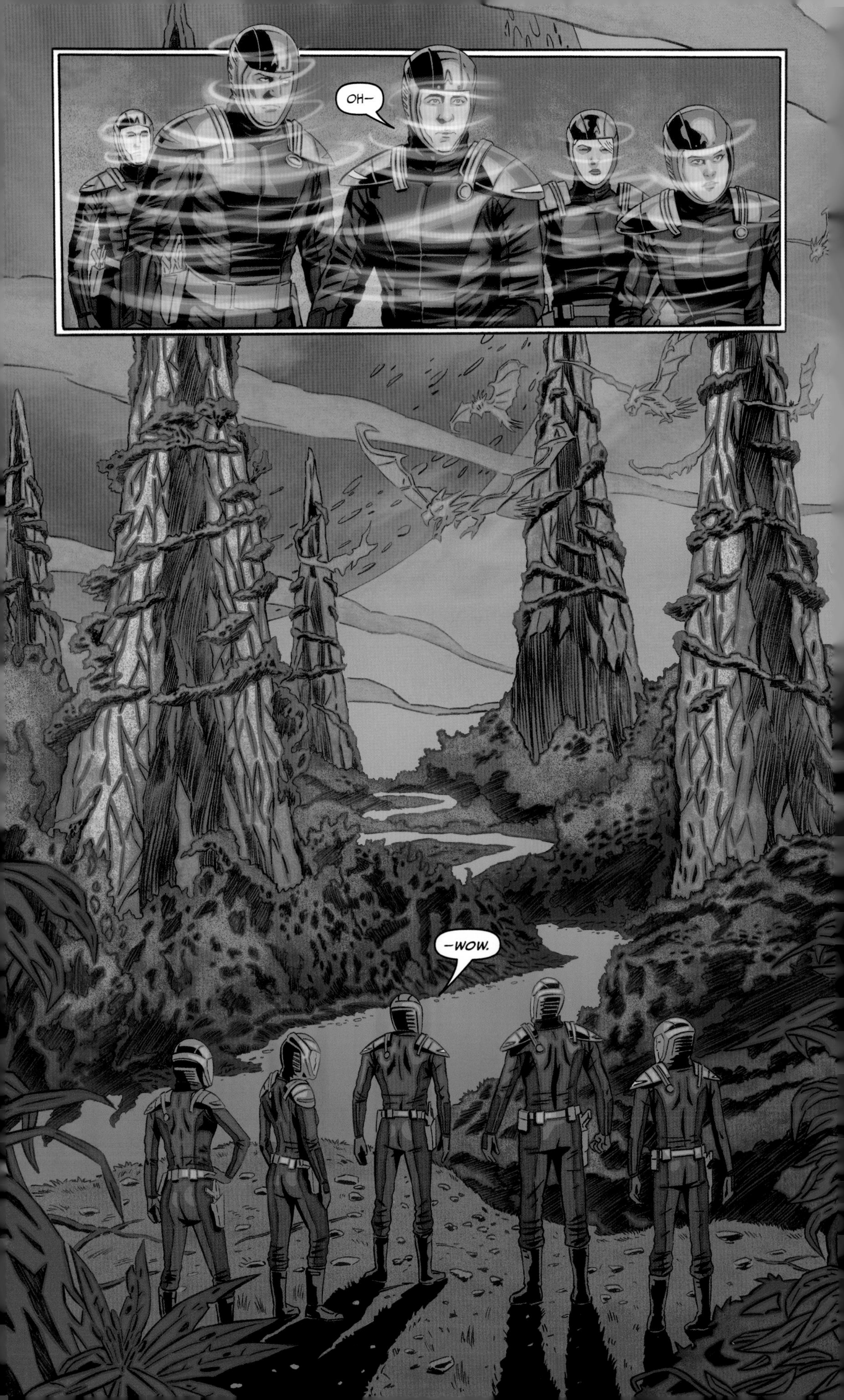
OH—
—WOW.

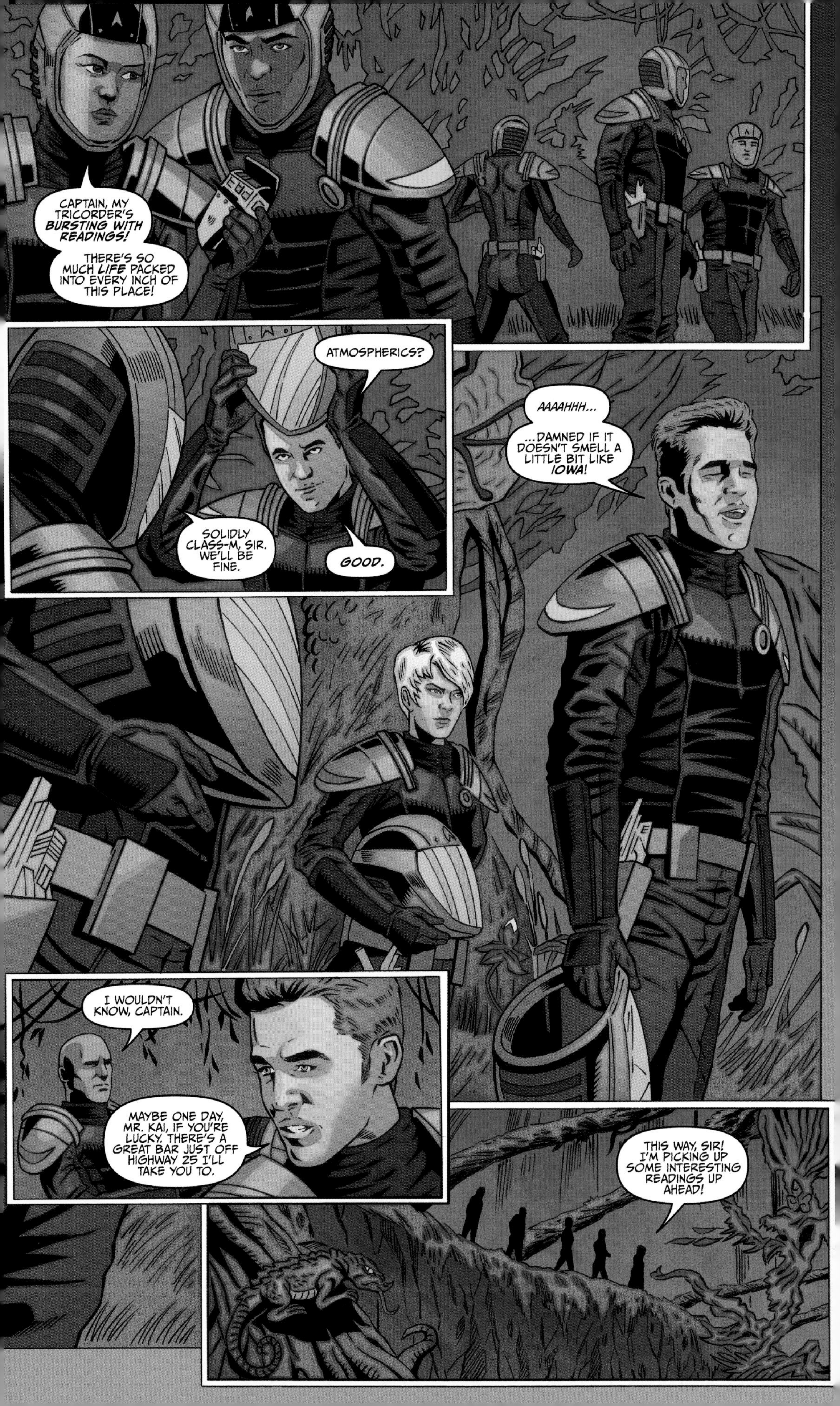
CAPTAIN, MY TRICORDER'S BURSTING WITH READINGS!
THERE'S SO MUCH LIFE PACKED INTO EVERY INCH OF THIS PLACE!
ATMOSPHERICS?
SOLIDLY CLASS-M, SIR. WE'LL BE FINE.
GOOD.
AAAAHHH...
...DAMNED IF IT DOESN'T SMELL A LITTLE BIT LIKE IOWA!
I WOULDN'T KNOW, CAPTAIN.
MAYBE ONE DAY, MR. KAI, IF YOU'RE LUCKY. THERE'S A GREAT BAR JUST OFF HIGHWAY 25 I'LL TAKE YOU TO.
THIS WAY, SIR! I'M PICKING UP SOME INTERESTING READINGS UP AHEAD!

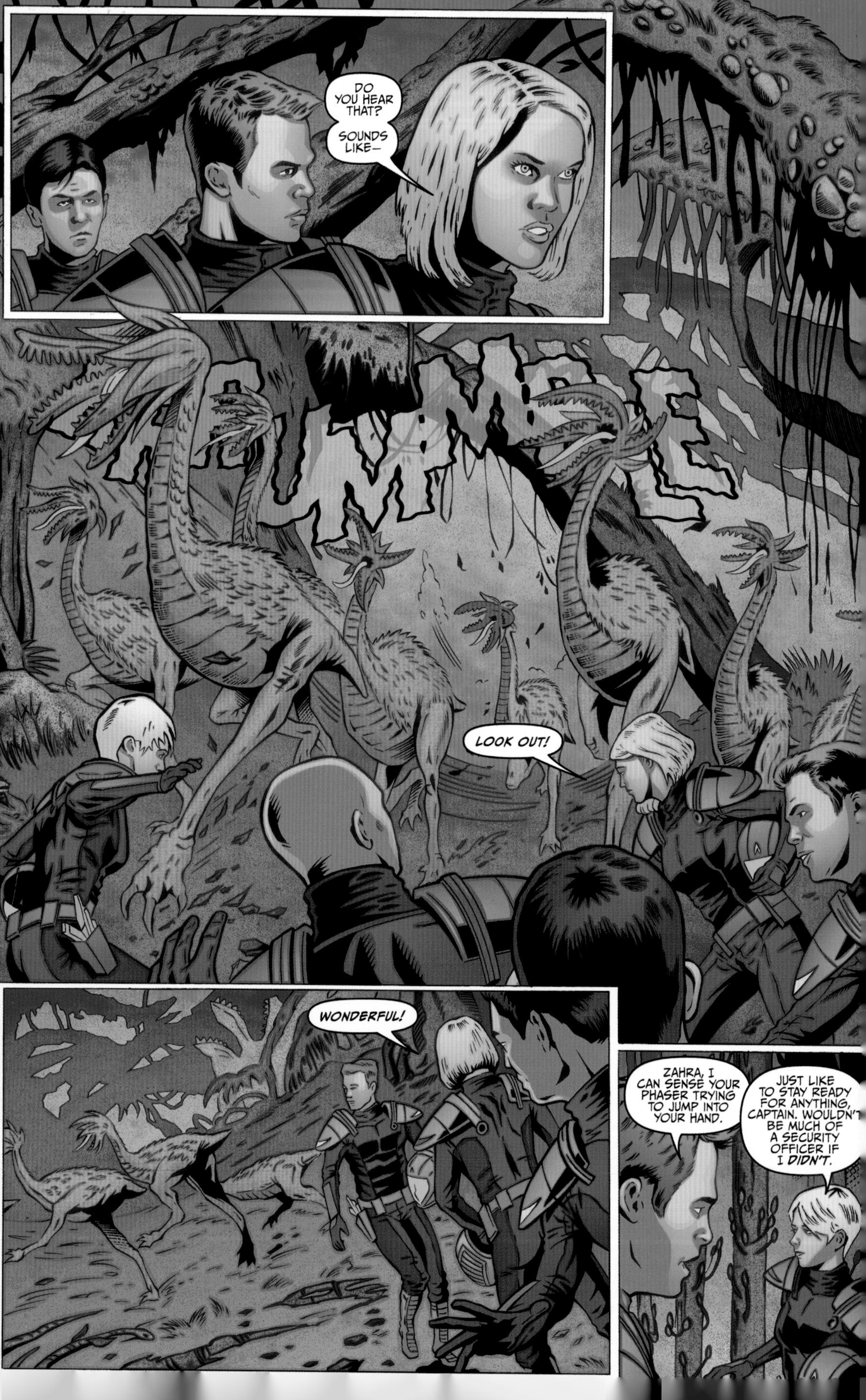

DO YOU HEAR THAT?
SOUNDS LIKE—
LOOK OUT!
WONDERFUL!
ZAHRA, I CAN SENSE YOUR PHASER TRYING TO JUMP INTO YOUR HAND.
JUST LIKE TO STAY READY FOR ANYTHING, CAPTAIN. WOULDN'T BE MUCH OF A SECURITY OFFICER IF I *DIDN'T*.

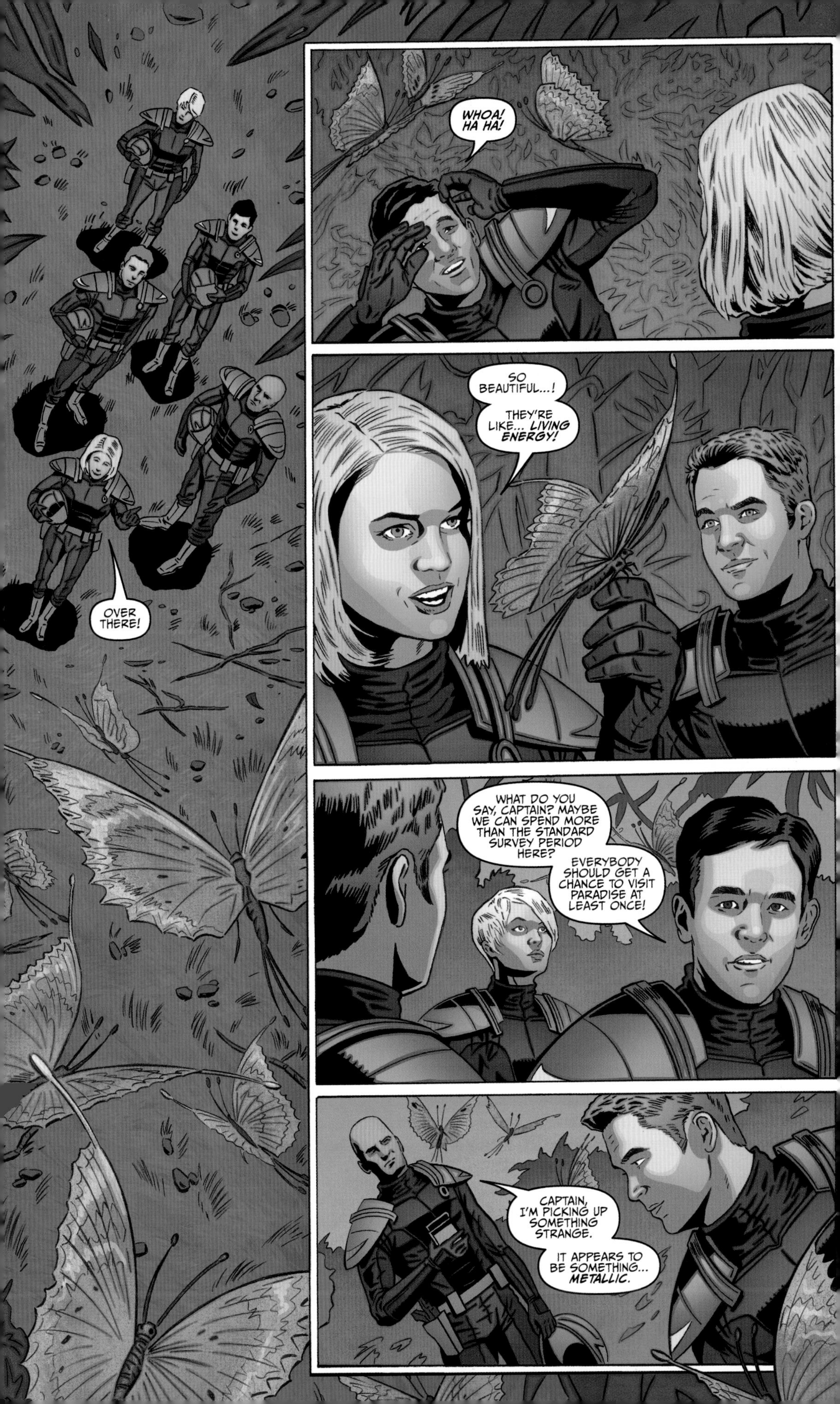

OVER THERE!
WHOA! HA HA!
SO BEAUTIFUL...!
THEY'RE LIKE... *LIVING ENERGY!*
WHAT DO YOU SAY, CAPTAIN? MAYBE WE CAN SPEND MORE THAN THE STANDARD SURVEY PERIOD HERE?
EVERYBODY SHOULD GET A CHANCE TO VISIT PARADISE AT LEAST ONCE!
CAPTAIN, I'M PICKING UP SOMETHING STRANGE.
IT APPEARS TO BE SOMETHING... *METALLIC.*

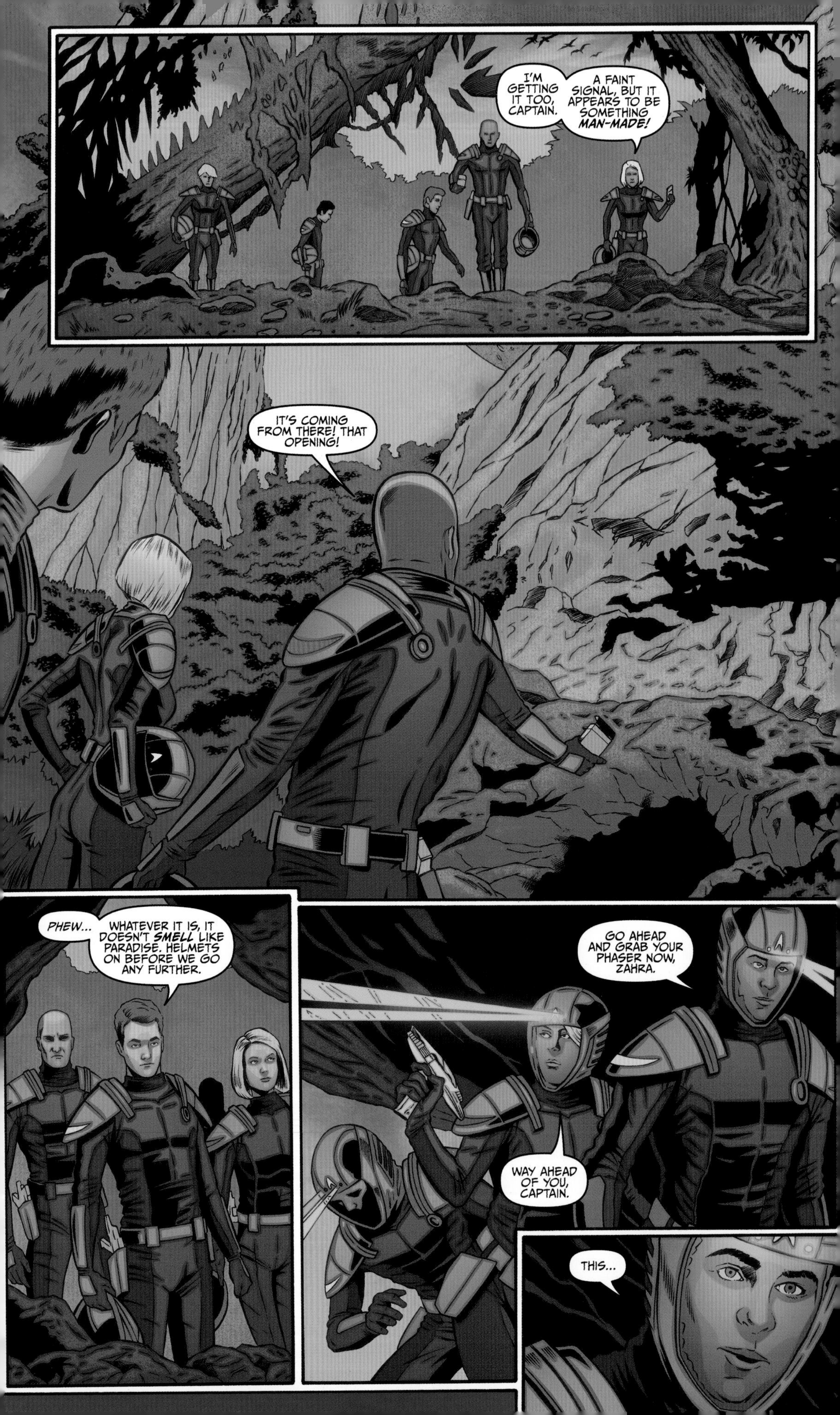

I'M GETTING IT TOO, CAPTAIN.
A FAINT SIGNAL, BUT IT APPEARS TO BE SOMETHING MAN-MADE!
IT'S COMING FROM THERE! THAT OPENING!
PHEW...
WHATEVER IT IS, IT DOESN'T SMELL LIKE PARADISE. HELMETS ON BEFORE WE GO ANY FURTHER.
GO AHEAD AND GRAB YOUR PHASER NOW, ZAHRA.
WAY AHEAD OF YOU, CAPTAIN.
THIS...

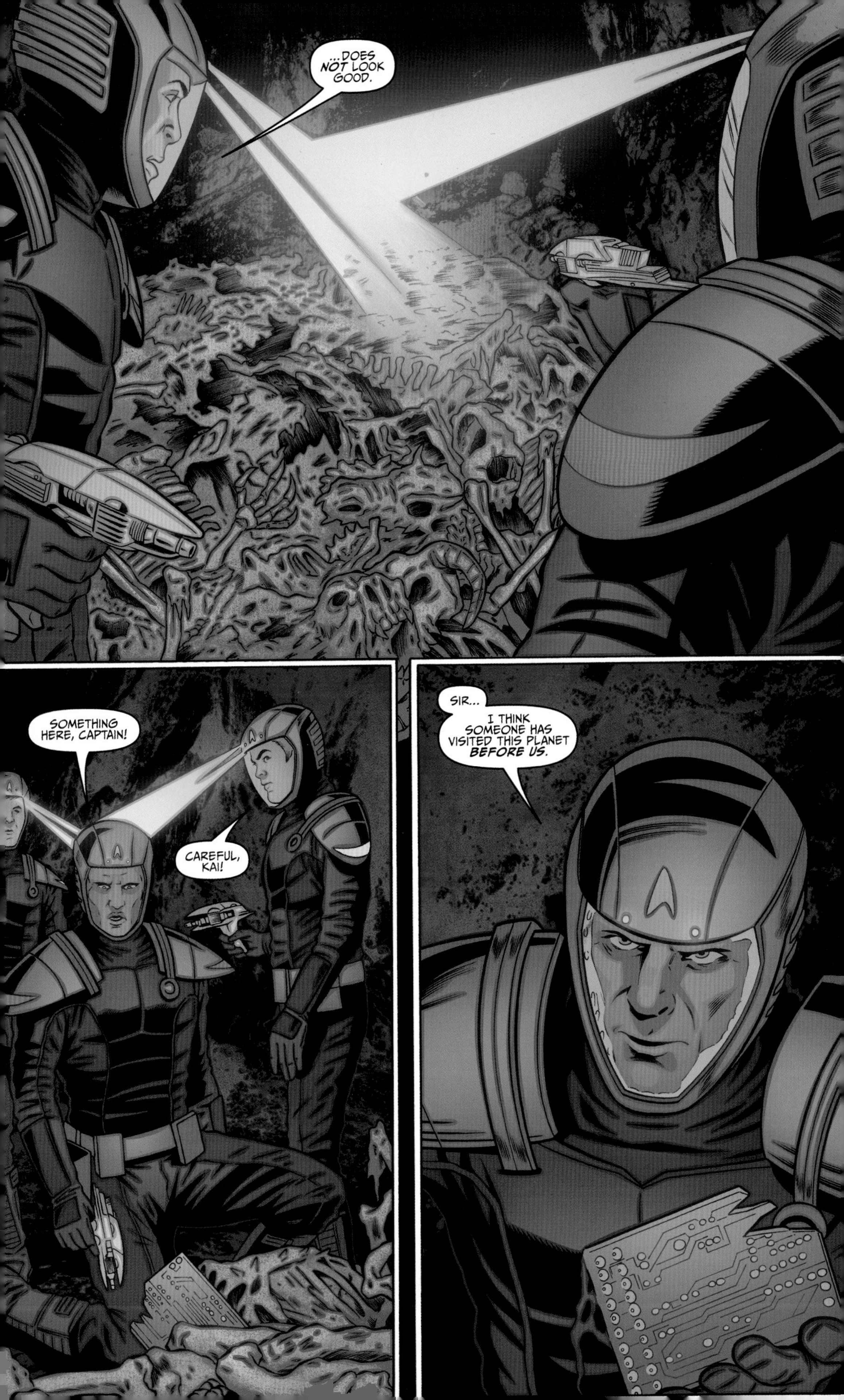
...DOES NOT LOOK GOOD.
SOMETHING HERE, CAPTAIN!
CAREFUL, KAI!
SIR...
I THINK SOMEONE HAS VISITED THIS PLANET BEFORE US.

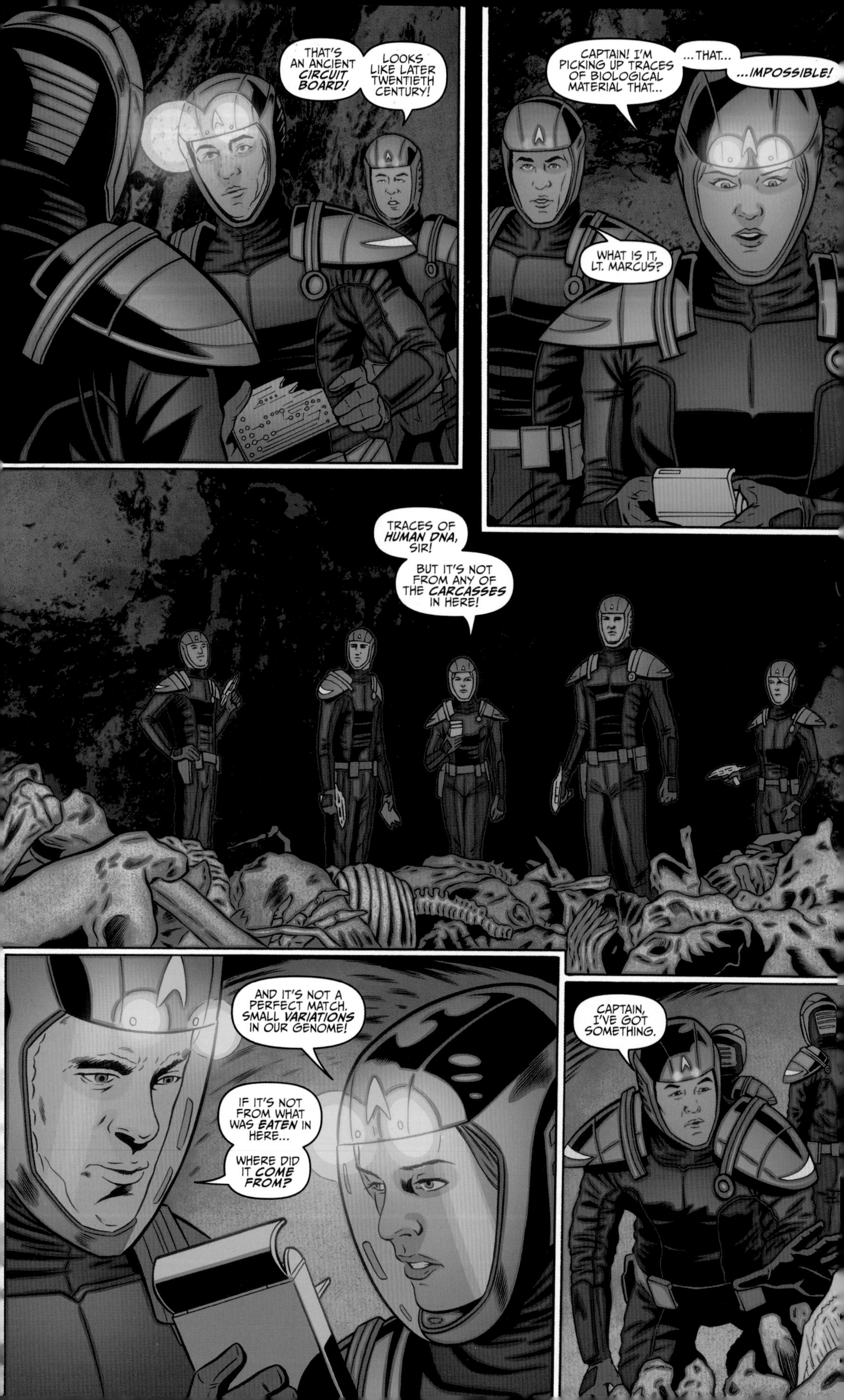

THAT'S AN ANCIENT CIRCUIT BOARD!
LOOKS LIKE LATER TWENTIETH CENTURY!
CAPTAIN! I'M PICKING UP TRACES OF BIOLOGICAL MATERIAL THAT...
...THAT...
...IMPOSSIBLE!
WHAT IS IT, LT. MARCUS?
TRACES OF HUMAN DNA, SIR!
BUT IT'S NOT FROM ANY OF THE CARCASSES IN HERE!
AND IT'S NOT A PERFECT MATCH. SMALL VARIATIONS IN OUR GENOME!
IF IT'S NOT FROM WHAT WAS EATEN IN HERE...
WHERE DID IT COME FROM?
CAPTAIN, I'VE GOT SOMETHING.

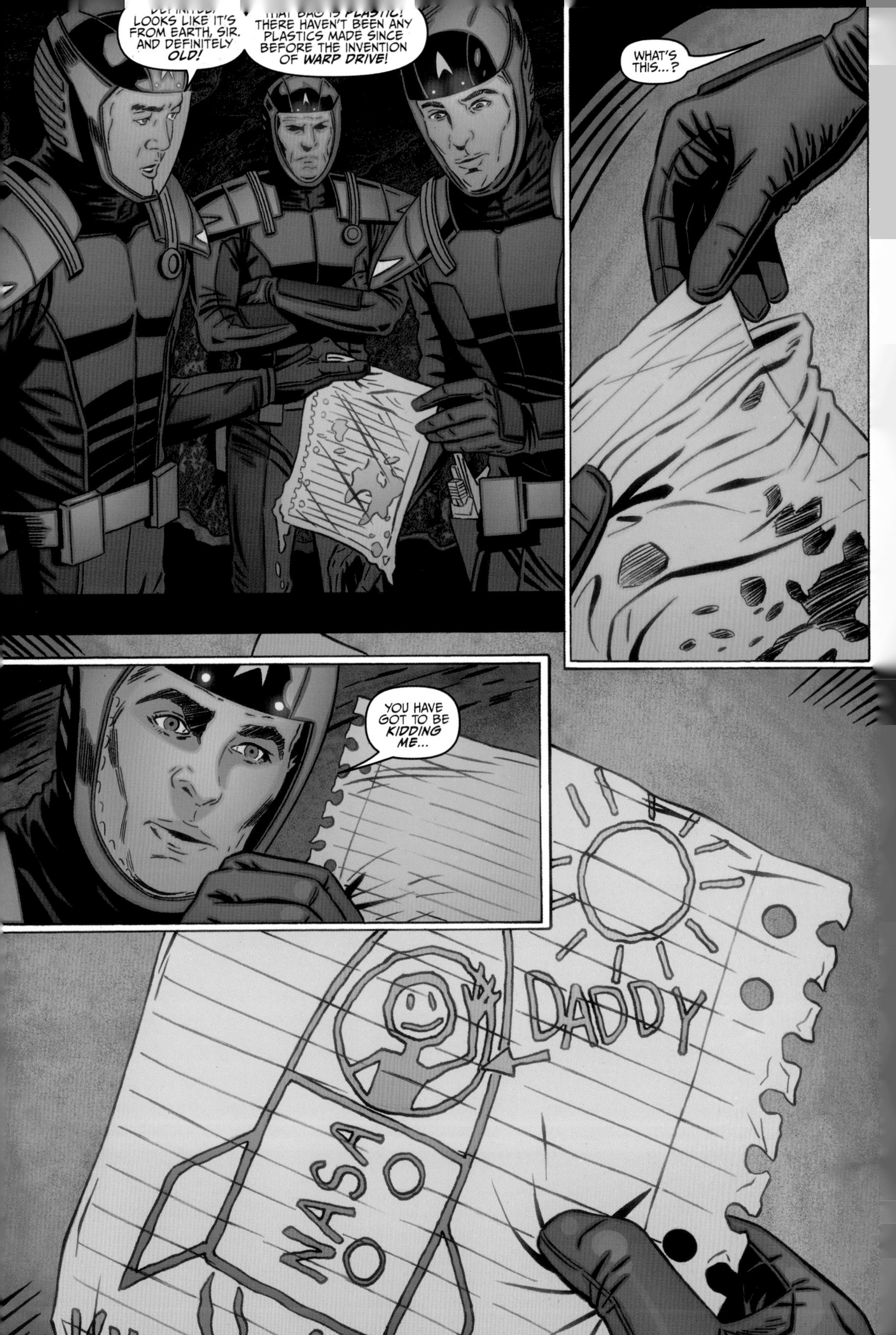
LOOKS LIKE IT'S FROM EARTH, SIR. AND DEFINITELY OLD!
THERE HAVEN'T BEEN ANY PLASTICS MADE SINCE BEFORE THE INVENTION OF WARP DRIVE!
WHAT'S THIS...?
YOU HAVE GOT TO BE KIDDING ME...
DADDY
NASA

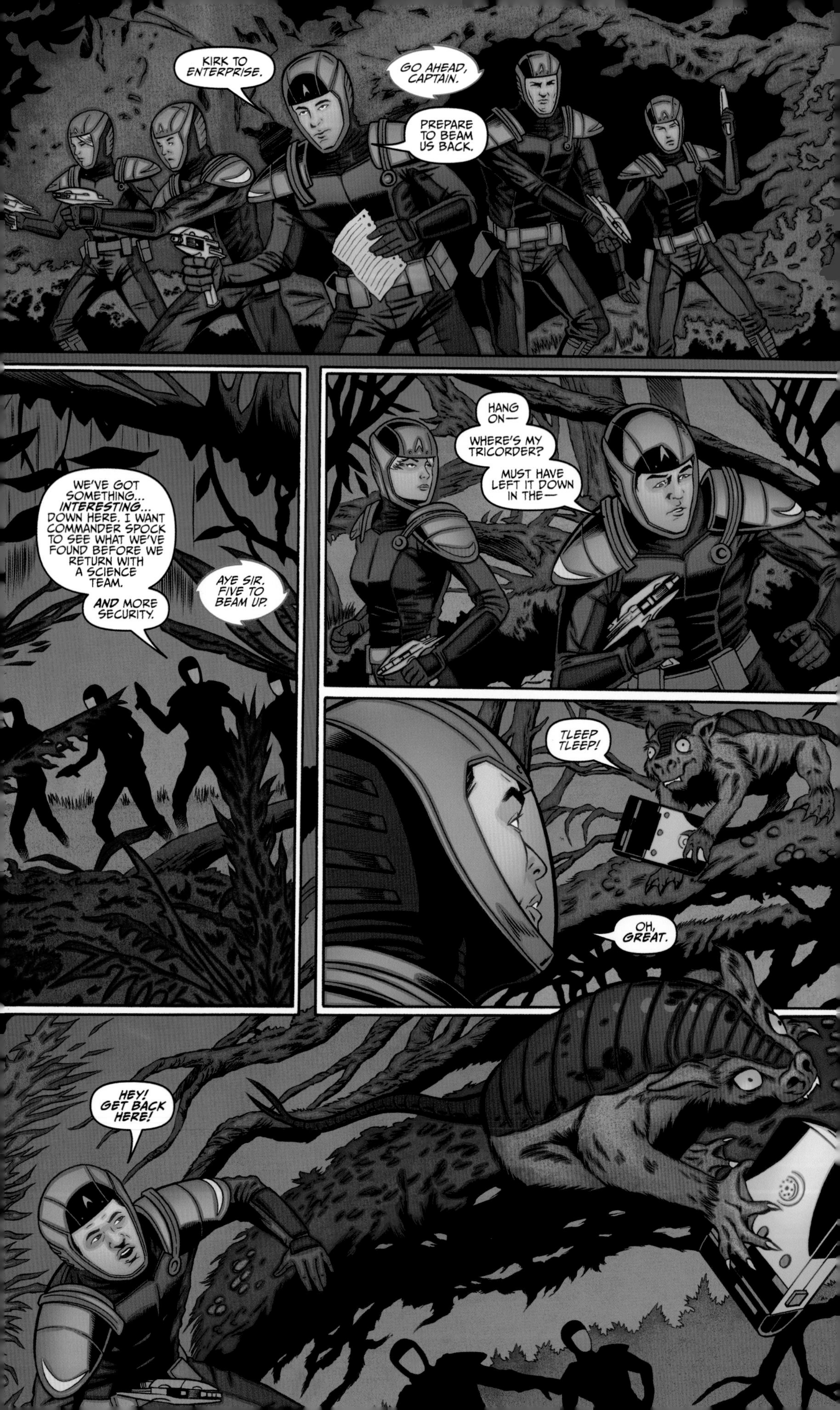
KIRK TO ENTERPRISE.
GO AHEAD, CAPTAIN.
PREPARE TO BEAM US BACK.
WE'VE GOT SOMETHING... *INTERESTING*... DOWN HERE. I WANT COMMANDER SPOCK TO SEE WHAT WE'VE FOUND BEFORE WE RETURN WITH A SCIENCE TEAM.
AND MORE SECURITY.
AYE SIR. FIVE TO BEAM UP.
HANG ON—
WHERE'S MY TRICORDER?
MUST HAVE LEFT IT DOWN IN THE—
TLEEP TLEEP!
OH, *GREAT*.
HEY! GET BACK HERE!

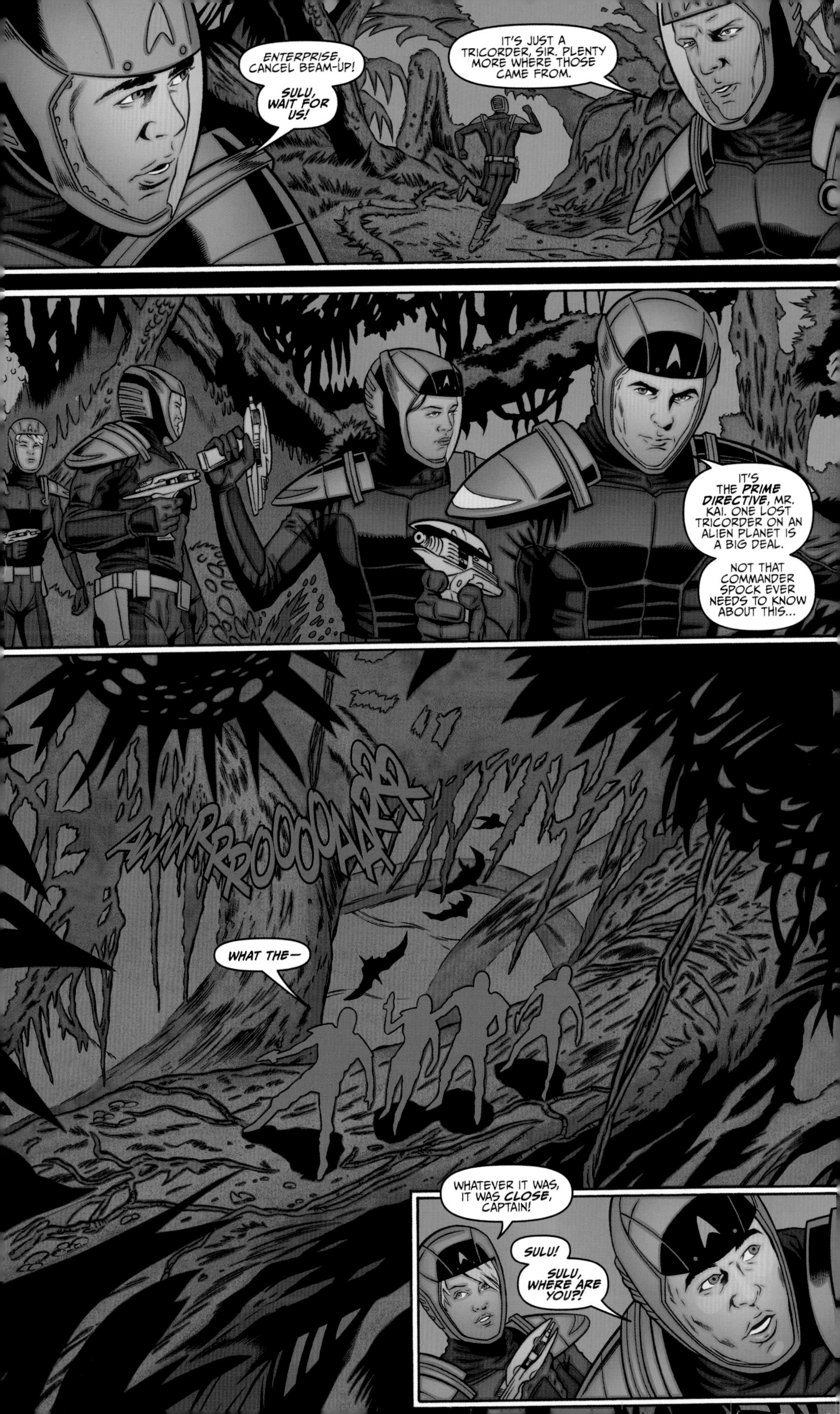
ENTERPRISE, CANCEL BEAM-UP!
SULU, WAIT FOR US!
IT'S JUST A TRICORDER, SIR. PLENTY MORE WHERE THOSE CAME FROM.
IT'S THE PRIME DIRECTIVE, MR. KAI. ONE LOST TRICORDER ON AN ALIEN PLANET IS A BIG DEAL.
NOT THAT COMMANDER SPOCK EVER NEEDS TO KNOW ABOUT THIS...
AWWRRROOOOAAARRR
WHAT THE—
WHATEVER IT WAS, IT WAS CLOSE, CAPTAIN!
SULU!
SULU, WHERE ARE YOU?!

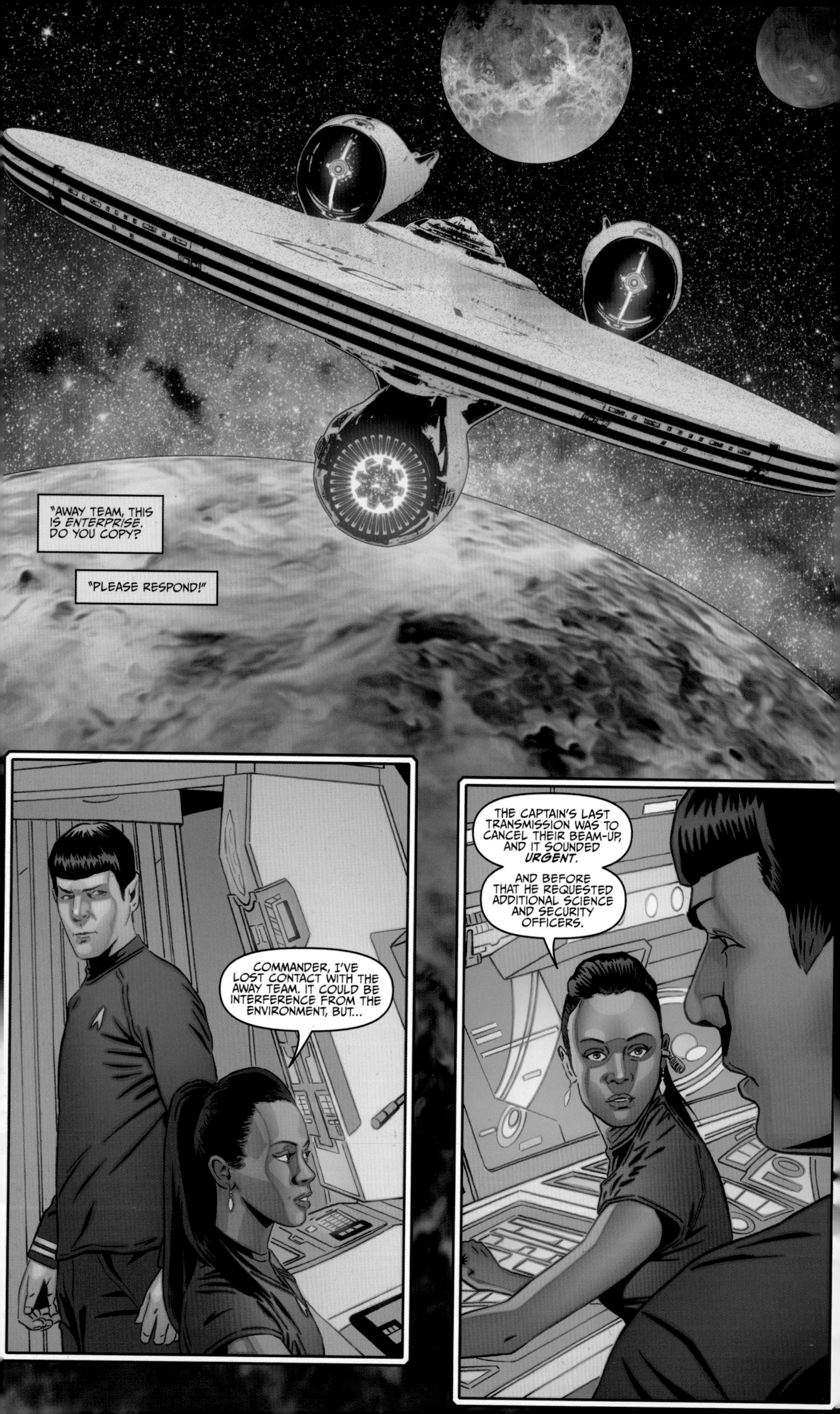
"AWAY TEAM, THIS IS ENTERPRISE. DO YOU COPY?
"PLEASE RESPOND!"
COMMANDER, I'VE LOST CONTACT WITH THE AWAY TEAM. IT COULD BE INTERFERENCE FROM THE ENVIRONMENT, BUT...
THE CAPTAIN'S LAST TRANSMISSION WAS TO CANCEL THEIR BEAM-UP, AND IT SOUNDED URGENT.
AND BEFORE THAT HE REQUESTED ADDITIONAL SCIENCE AND SECURITY OFFICERS.

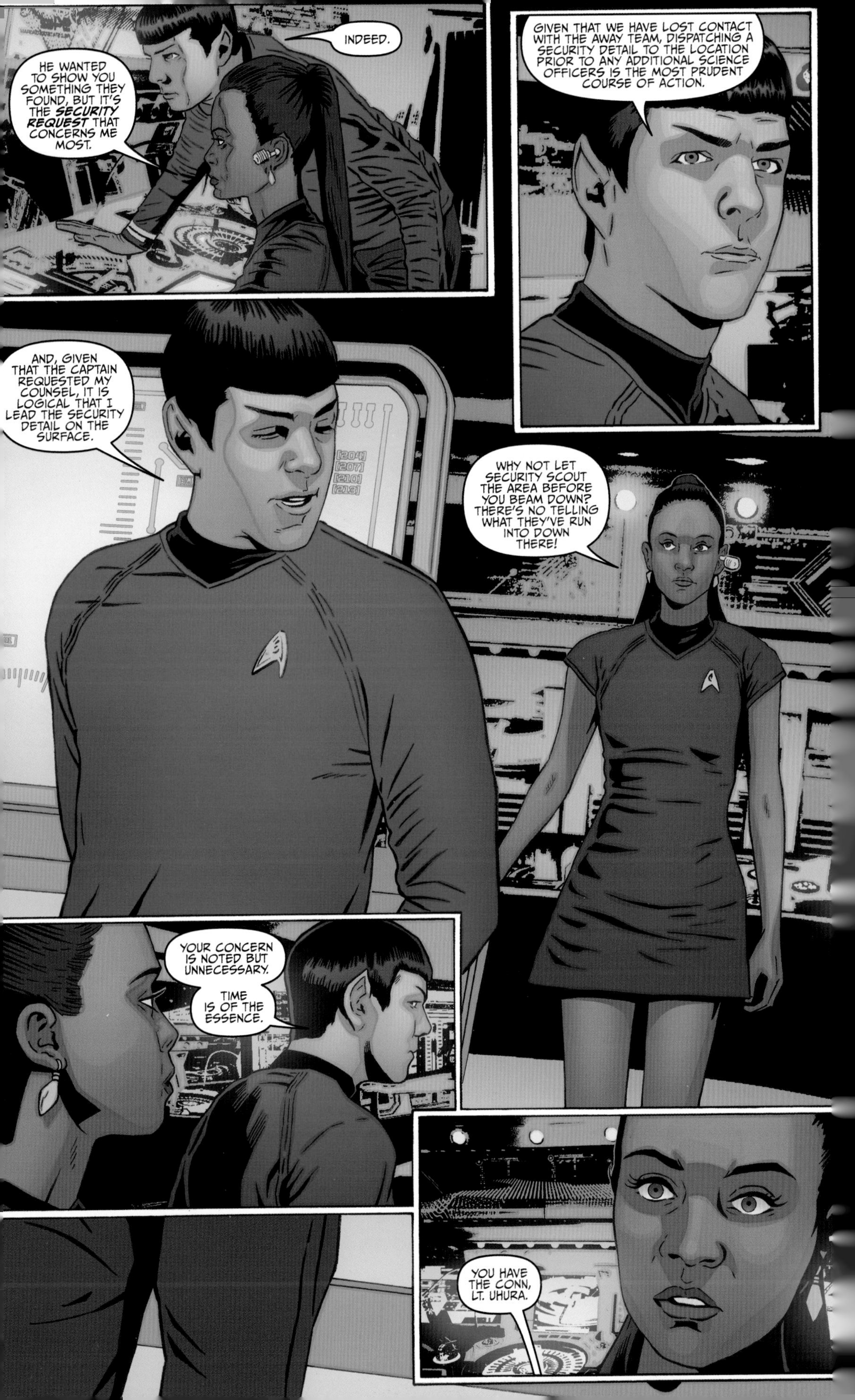
INDEED.
HE WANTED TO SHOW YOU SOMETHING THEY FOUND, BUT IT'S THE **SECURITY REQUEST** THAT CONCERNS ME MOST.
GIVEN THAT WE HAVE LOST CONTACT WITH THE AWAY TEAM, DISPATCHING A SECURITY DETAIL TO THE LOCATION PRIOR TO ANY ADDITIONAL SCIENCE OFFICERS IS THE MOST PRUDENT COURSE OF ACTION.
AND, GIVEN THAT THE CAPTAIN REQUESTED MY COUNSEL, IT IS LOGICAL THAT I LEAD THE SECURITY DETAIL ON THE SURFACE.
WHY NOT LET SECURITY SCOUT THE AREA BEFORE YOU BEAM DOWN? THERE'S NO TELLING WHAT THEY'VE RUN INTO DOWN THERE!
YOUR CONCERN IS NOTED BUT UNNECESSARY.
TIME IS OF THE ESSENCE.
YOU HAVE THE CONN, LT. UHURA.

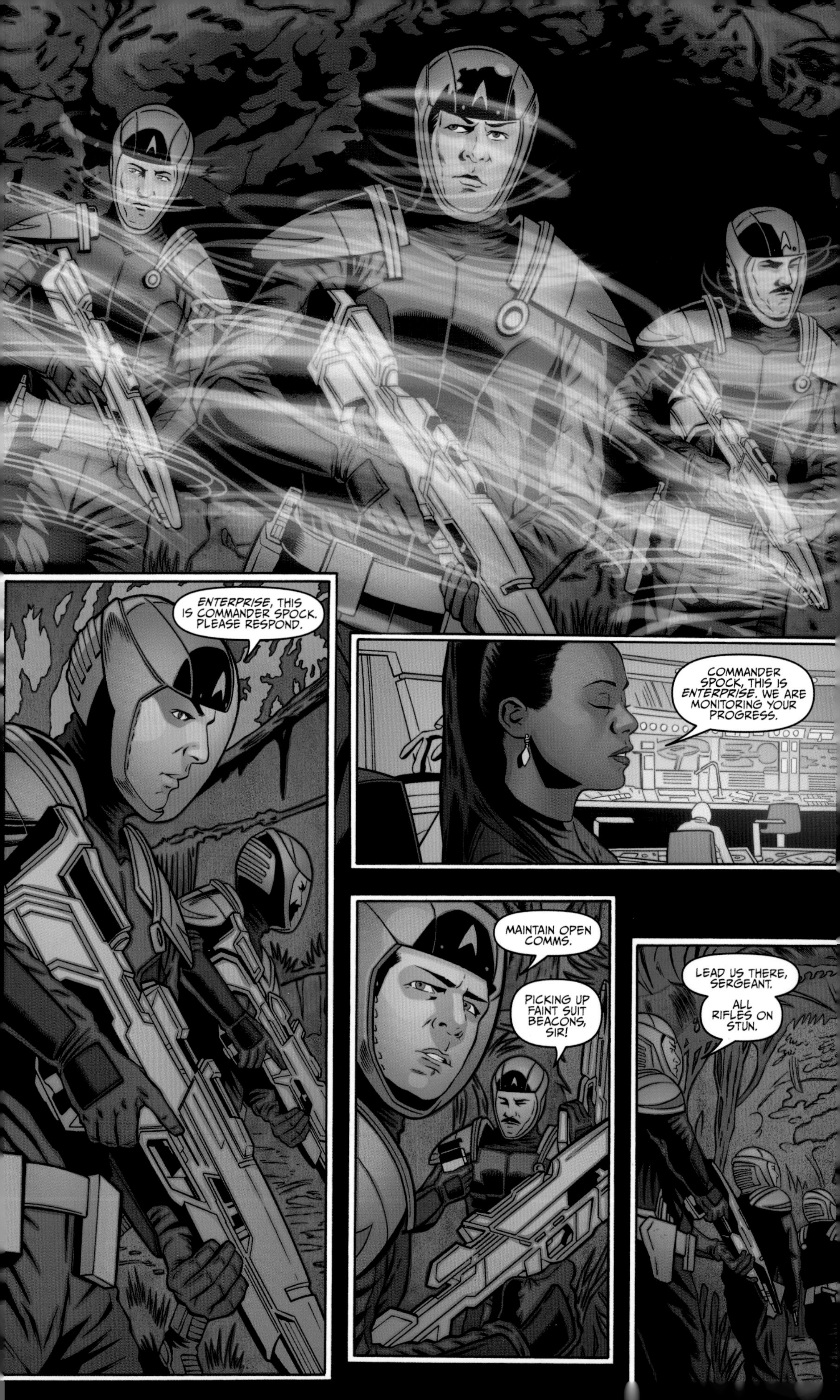
ENTERPRISE, THIS IS COMMANDER SPOCK. PLEASE RESPOND.
COMMANDER SPOCK, THIS IS ENTERPRISE. WE ARE MONITORING YOUR PROGRESS.
MAINTAIN OPEN COMMS.
PICKING UP FAINT SUIT BEACONS, SIR!
LEAD US THERE, SERGEANT.
ALL RIFLES ON STUN.

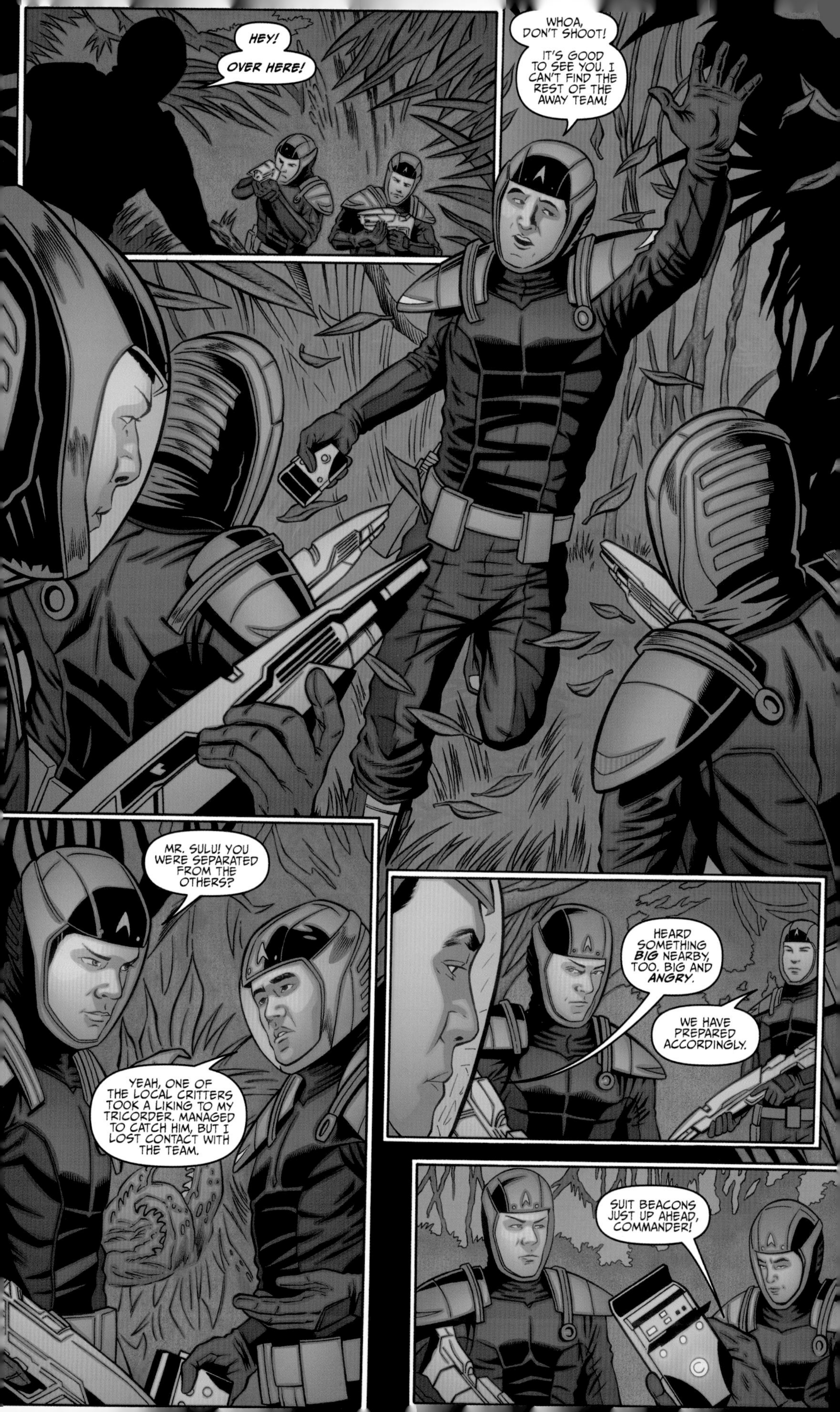
HEY!
OVER HERE!
WHOA, DON'T SHOOT!
IT'S GOOD TO SEE YOU. I CAN'T FIND THE REST OF THE AWAY TEAM!
MR. SULU! YOU WERE SEPARATED FROM THE OTHERS?
YEAH, ONE OF THE LOCAL CRITTERS TOOK A LIKING TO MY TRICORDER. MANAGED TO CATCH HIM, BUT I LOST CONTACT WITH THE TEAM.
HEARD SOMETHING BIG NEARBY, TOO. BIG AND ANGRY.
WE HAVE PREPARED ACCORDINGLY.
SUIT BEACONS JUST UP AHEAD, COMMANDER!

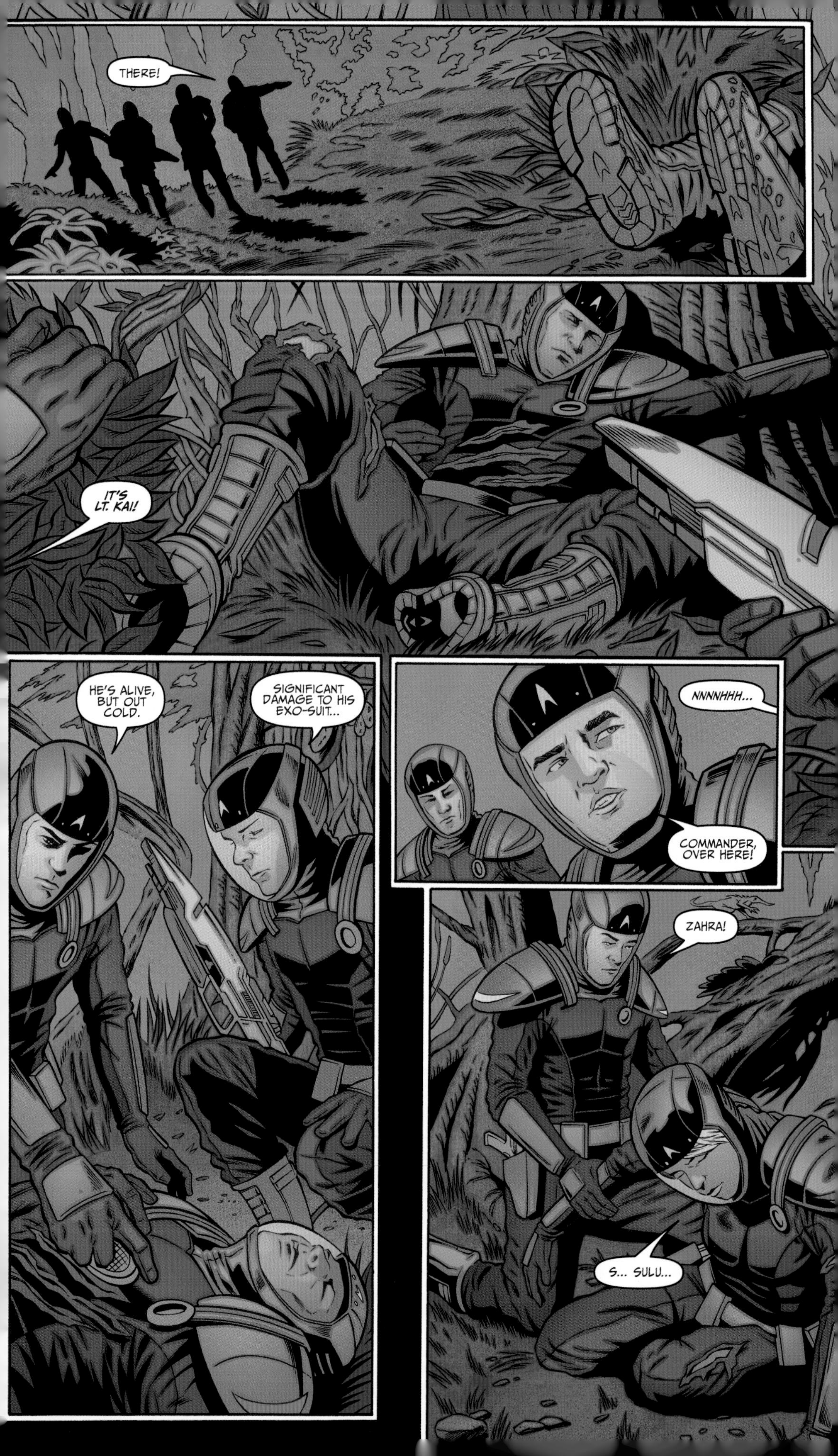
THERE!
IT'S LT. KAI!
HE'S ALIVE, BUT OUT COLD.
SIGNIFICANT DAMAGE TO HIS EXO-SUIT...
NNNNHHH...
COMMANDER, OVER HERE!
ZAHRA!
S... SULU...

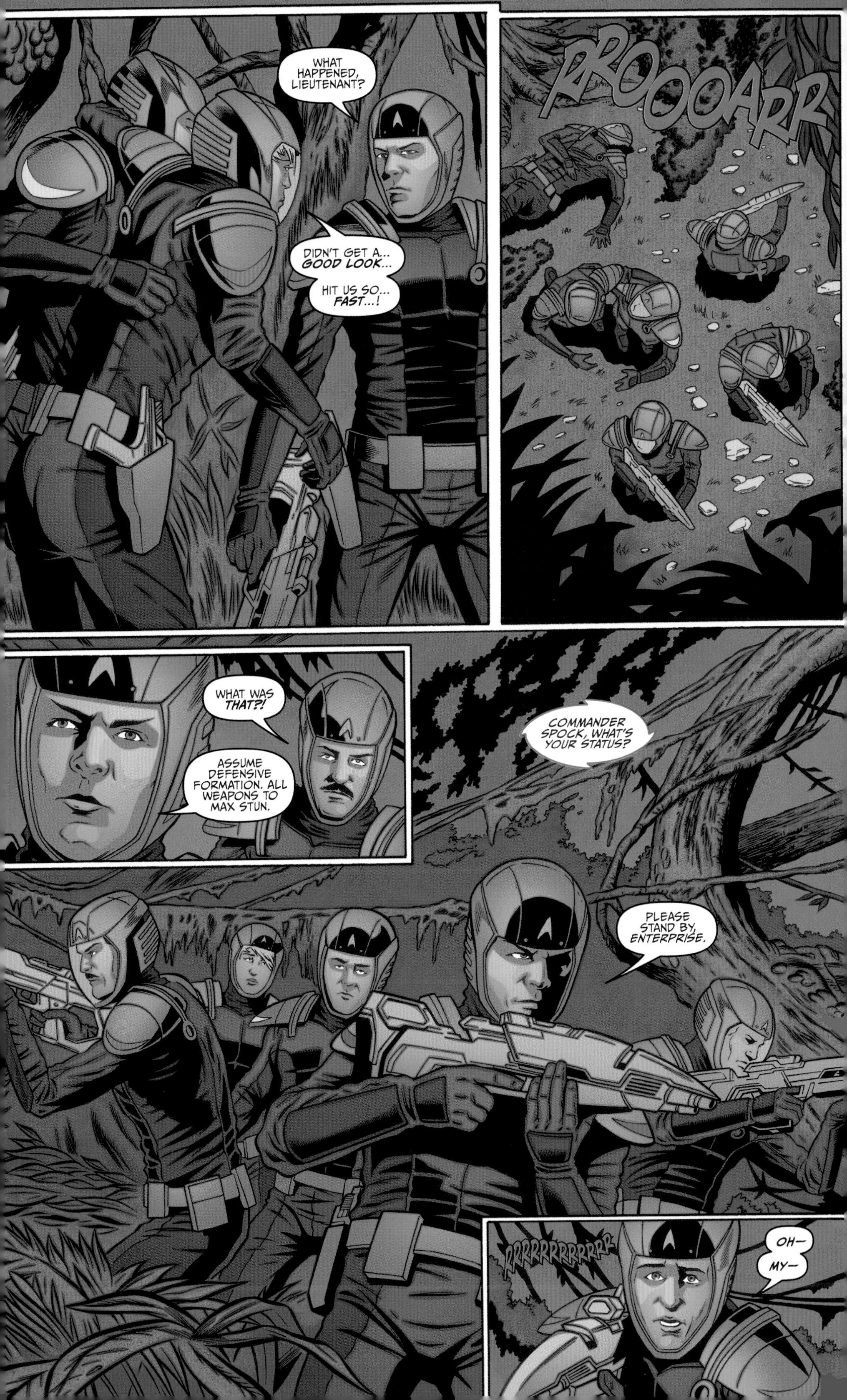

WHAT HAPPENED, LIEUTENANT?
DIDN'T GET A... GOOD LOOK...
HIT US SO... FAST...!
BROOOARR
WHAT WAS THAT?!
ASSUME DEFENSIVE FORMATION. ALL WEAPONS TO MAX STUN.
COMMANDER SPOCK, WHAT'S YOUR STATUS?
PLEASE STAND BY, ENTERPRISE.
RRRRRRRRRRRR
OH—
MY—

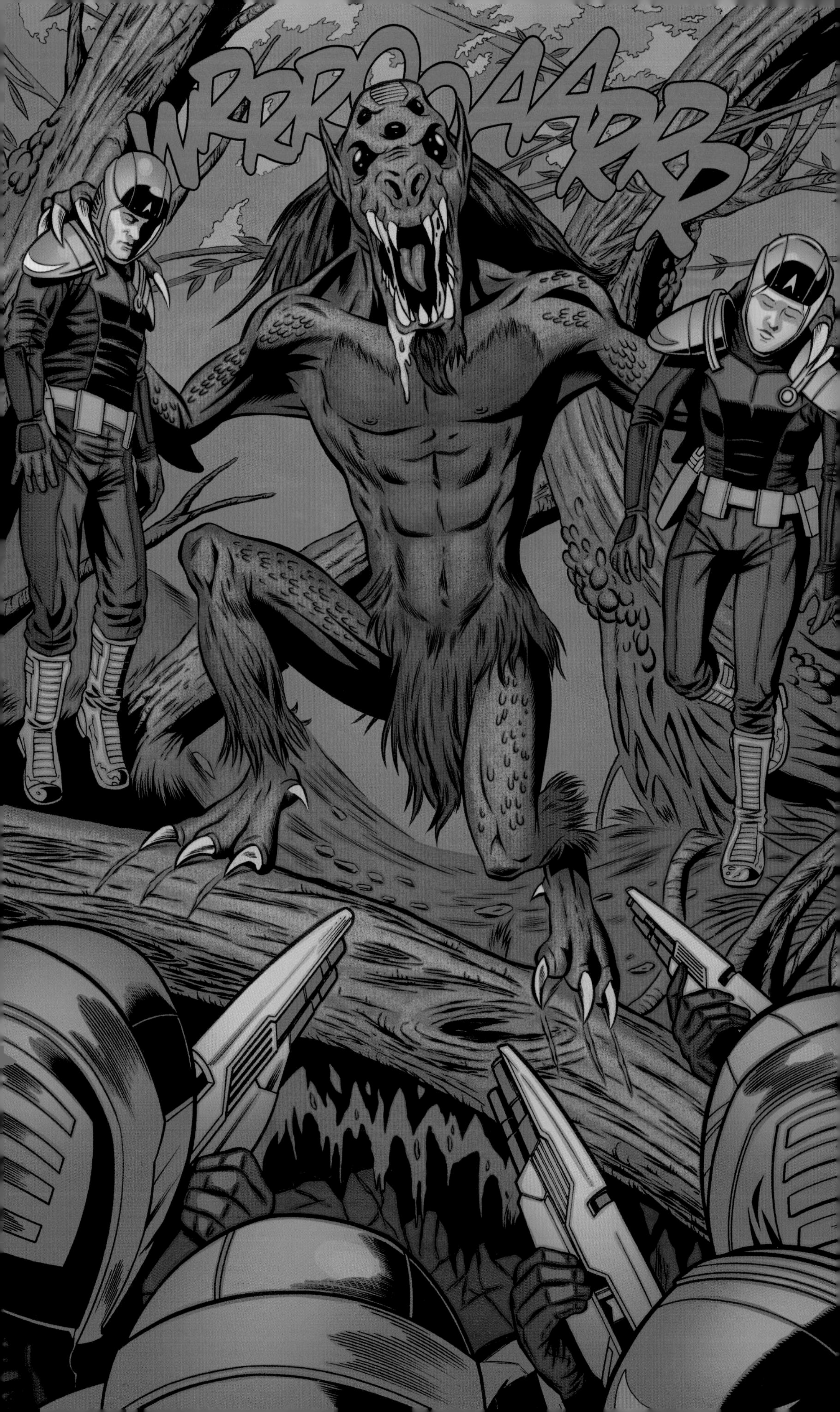
WRROOAARR

COCOA BEACH, FLORIDA.

JULY 1, 1972.

WHY CAN'T I COME WITH YOU, DADDY?

THEY ONLY LET ASTRONAUTS GO INTO OUTER SPACE RIGHT NOW, ELLA.

BUT MAYBE ONE DAY WE CAN GO UP TOGETHER.

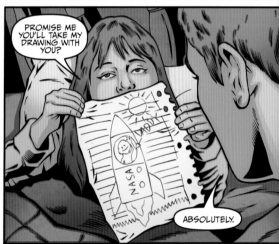

PROMISE ME YOU'LL TAKE MY DRAWING WITH YOU?

ABSOLUTELY.

I'LL TUCK IT IN THE POCKET OF MY SPACE SUIT FOR SAFEKEEPING.

THAT WAY, NO MATTER HOW FAR AWAY I AM...

...YOU'LL ALWAYS BE WITH ME.

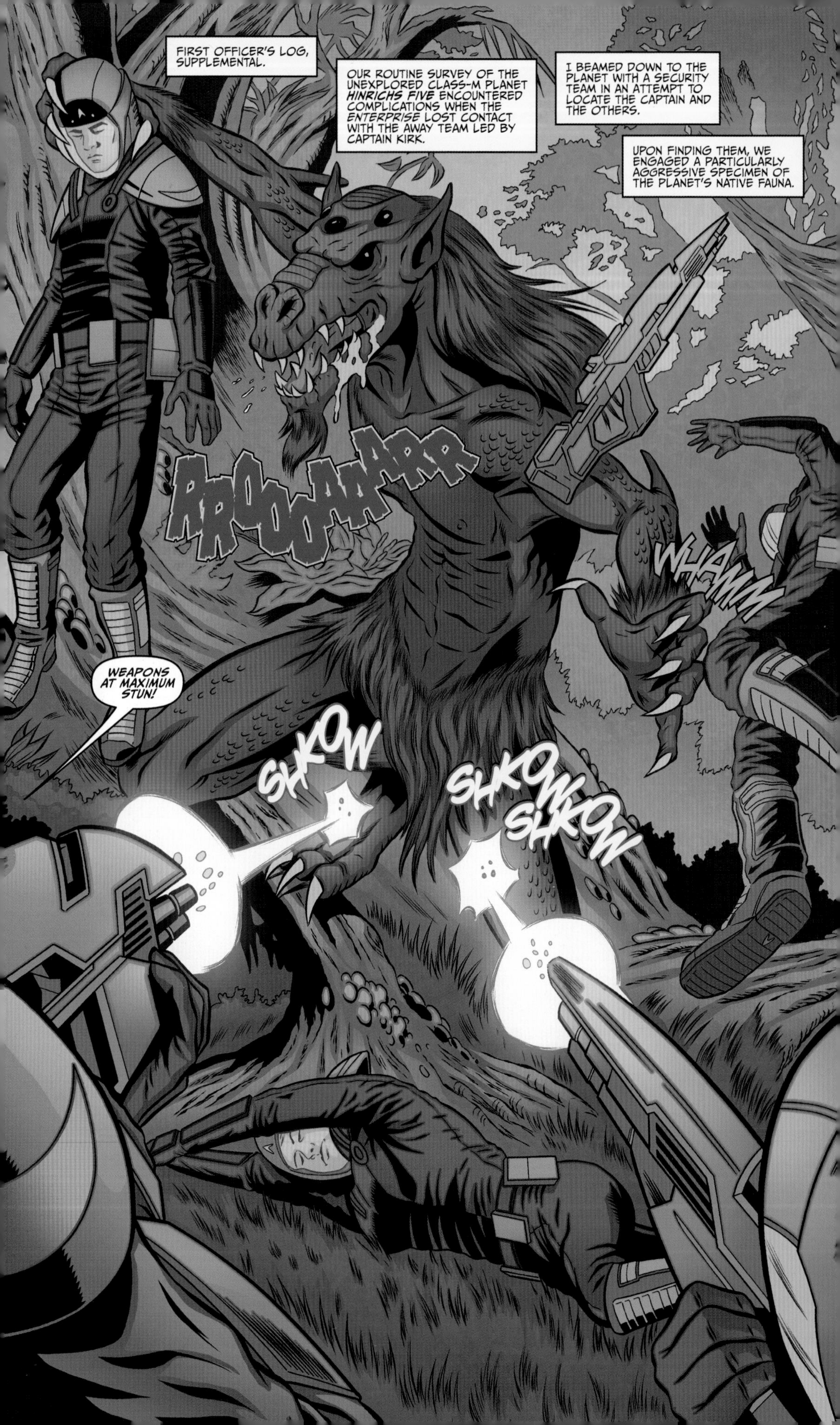
FIRST OFFICER'S LOG, SUPPLEMENTAL.
OUR ROUTINE SURVEY OF THE UNEXPLORED CLASS-M PLANET *HINRICHS FIVE* ENCOUNTERED COMPLICATIONS WHEN THE *ENTERPRISE* LOST CONTACT WITH THE AWAY TEAM LED BY CAPTAIN KIRK.
I BEAMED DOWN TO THE PLANET WITH A SECURITY TEAM IN AN ATTEMPT TO LOCATE THE CAPTAIN AND THE OTHERS.
UPON FINDING THEM, WE ENGAGED A PARTICULARLY AGGRESSIVE SPECIMEN OF THE PLANET'S NATIVE FAUNA.
RROOOAAARR
WHAMM
WEAPONS AT MAXIMUM STUN!
SHKOW
SHKOW SHKOW SHKOW

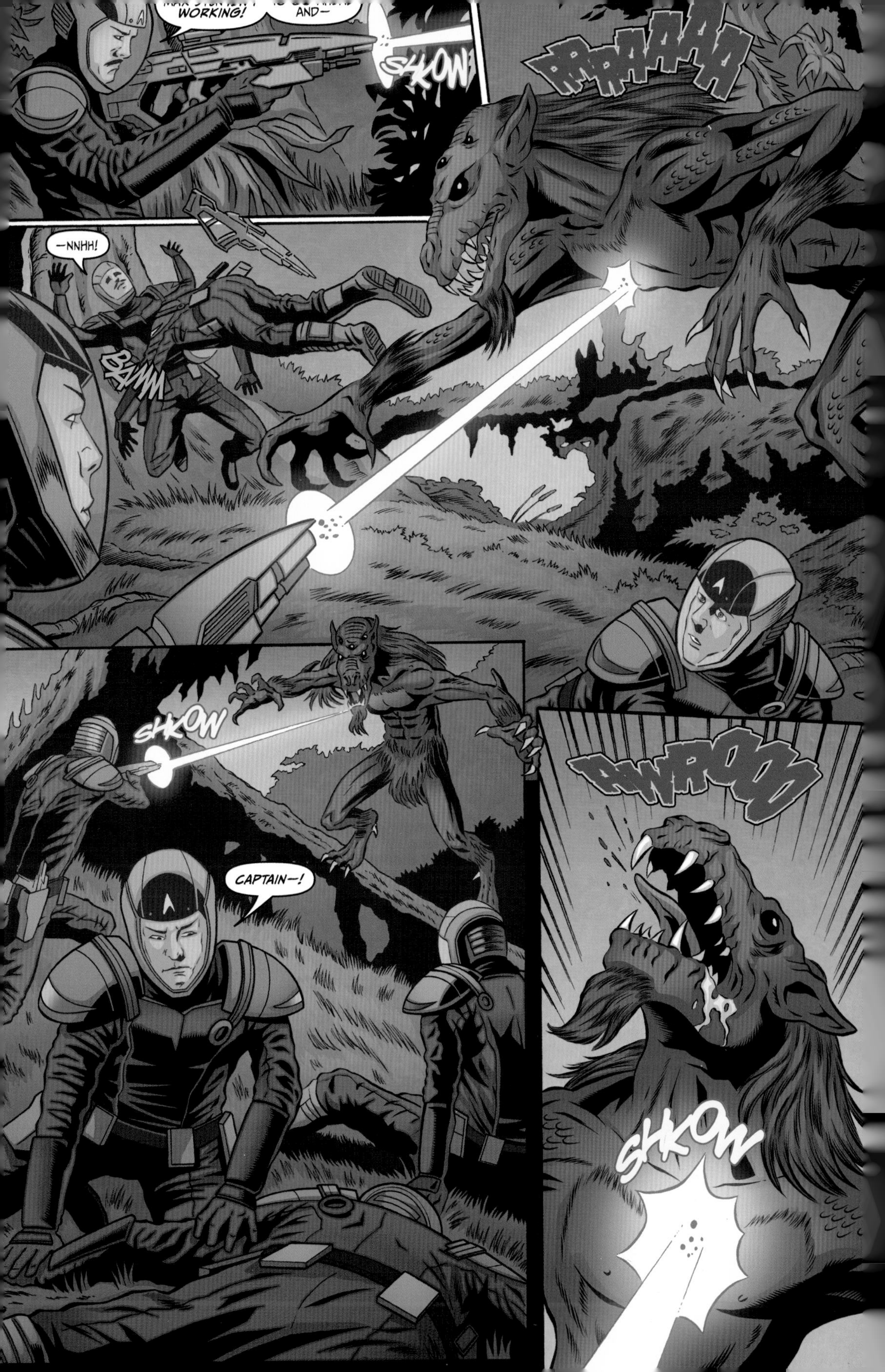
WORKING!
AND—
SHKOW
RRRAAAAA
—NNHH!
BAMM
SHKOW
CAPTAIN—!
RAWROOO
SHKOW

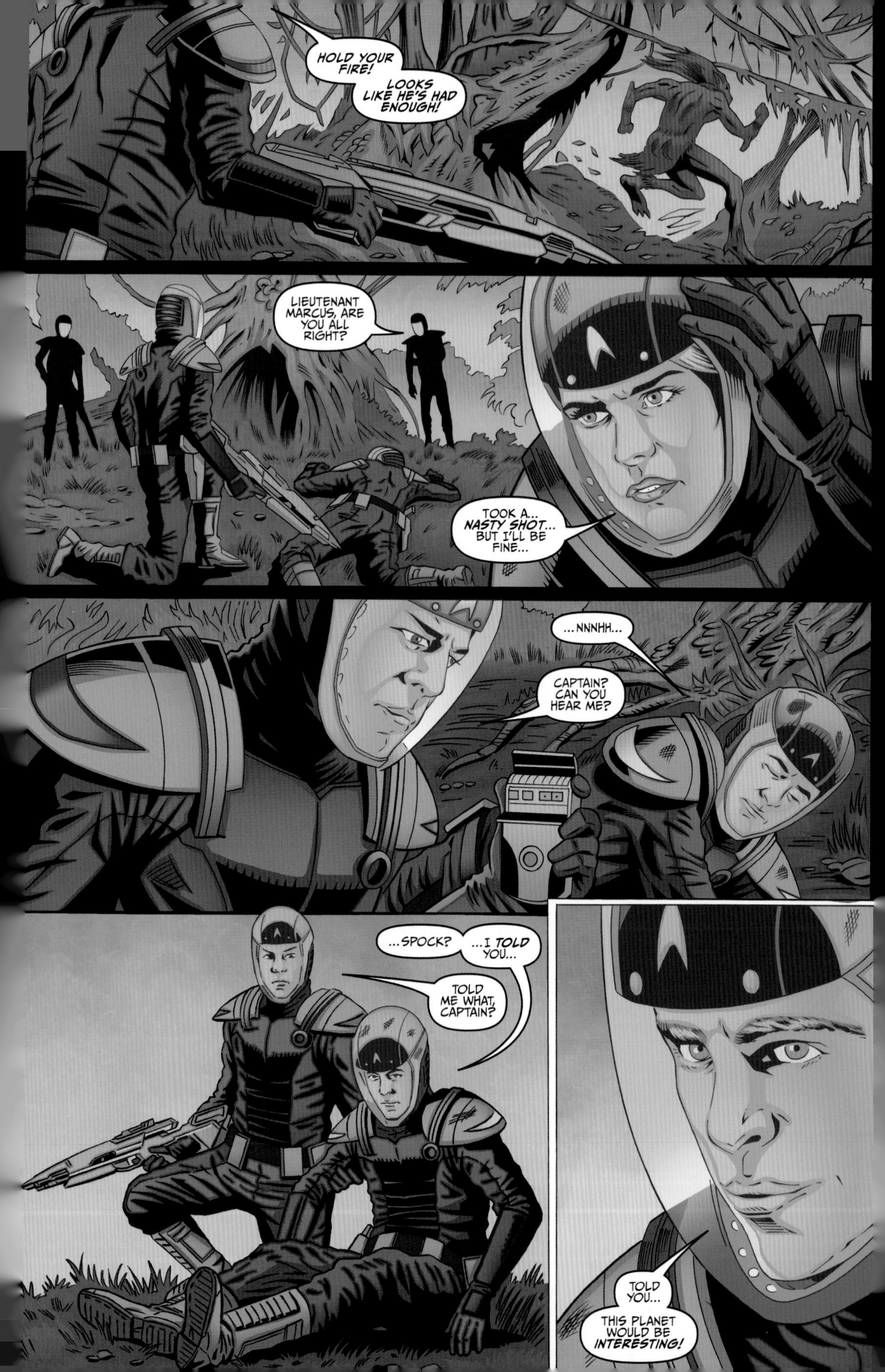
HOLD YOUR FIRE!
LOOKS LIKE HE'S HAD ENOUGH!
LIEUTENANT MARCUS, ARE YOU ALL RIGHT?
TOOK A... NASTY SHOT... BUT I'LL BE FINE...
...NNNHH...
CAPTAIN? CAN YOU HEAR ME?
...SPOCK?
...I TOLD YOU...
TOLD ME WHAT, CAPTAIN?
TOLD YOU...
THIS PLANET WOULD BE INTERESTING!

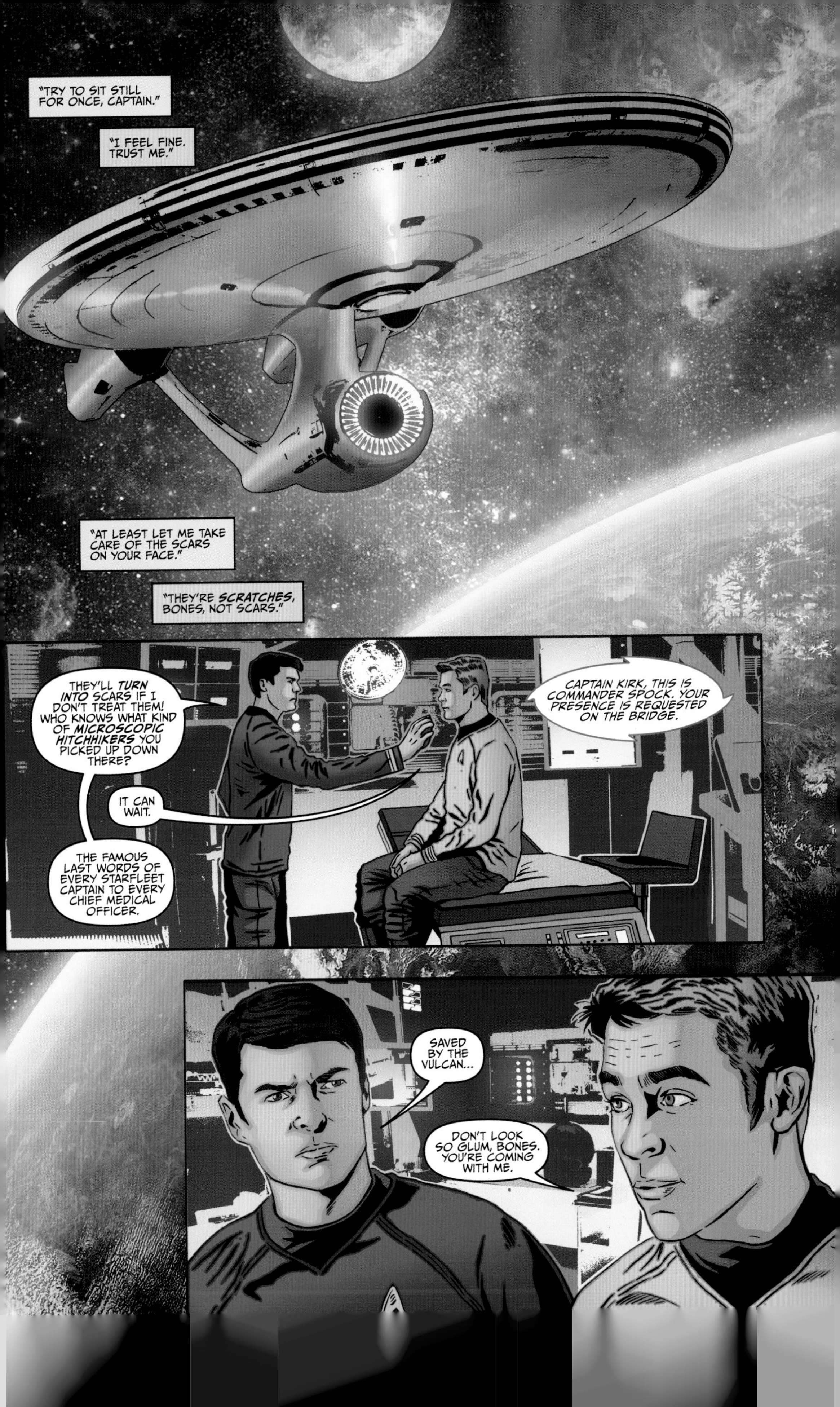
"TRY TO SIT STILL FOR ONCE, CAPTAIN."
"I FEEL FINE. TRUST ME."
"AT LEAST LET ME TAKE CARE OF THE SCARS ON YOUR FACE."
"THEY'RE SCRATCHES, BONES, NOT SCARS."
THEY'LL TURN INTO SCARS IF I DON'T TREAT THEM! WHO KNOWS WHAT KIND OF MICROSCOPIC HITCHHIKERS YOU PICKED UP DOWN THERE?
IT CAN WAIT.
THE FAMOUS LAST WORDS OF EVERY STARFLEET CAPTAIN TO EVERY CHIEF MEDICAL OFFICER.
CAPTAIN KIRK, THIS IS COMMANDER SPOCK. YOUR PRESENCE IS REQUESTED ON THE BRIDGE.
SAVED BY THE VULCAN...
DON'T LOOK SO GLUM, BONES. YOU'RE COMING WITH ME.

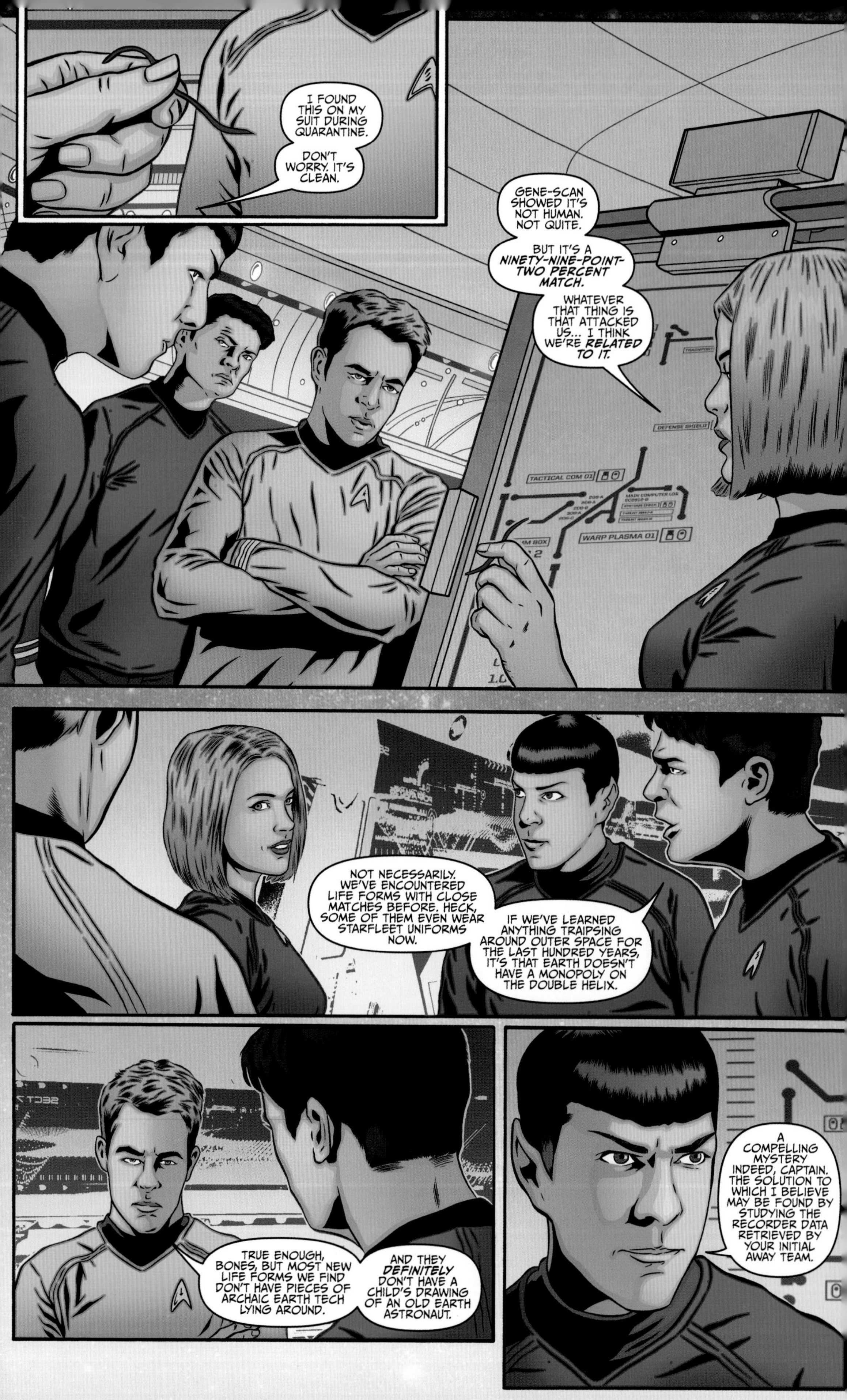
I FOUND THIS ON MY SUIT DURING QUARANTINE.
DON'T WORRY. IT'S CLEAN.
GENE-SCAN SHOWED IT'S NOT HUMAN. NOT QUITE.
BUT IT'S A NINETY-NINE-POINT-TWO PERCENT MATCH.
WHATEVER THAT THING IS THAT ATTACKED US... I THINK WE'RE RELATED TO IT.
DEFENSE SHIELD
TACTICAL COM 01
WARP PLASMA 01
NOT NECESSARILY. WE'VE ENCOUNTERED LIFE FORMS WITH CLOSE MATCHES BEFORE. HECK, SOME OF THEM EVEN WEAR STARFLEET UNIFORMS NOW.
IF WE'VE LEARNED ANYTHING TRAIPSING AROUND OUTER SPACE FOR THE LAST HUNDRED YEARS, IT'S THAT EARTH DOESN'T HAVE A MONOPOLY ON THE DOUBLE HELIX.
TRUE ENOUGH, BONES, BUT MOST NEW LIFE FORMS WE FIND DON'T HAVE PIECES OF ARCHAIC EARTH TECH LYING AROUND.
AND THEY DEFINITELY DON'T HAVE A CHILD'S DRAWING OF AN OLD EARTH ASTRONAUT.
A COMPELLING MYSTERY INDEED, CAPTAIN. THE SOLUTION TO WHICH I BELIEVE MAY BE FOUND BY STUDYING THE RECORDER DATA RETRIEVED BY YOUR INITIAL AWAY TEAM.

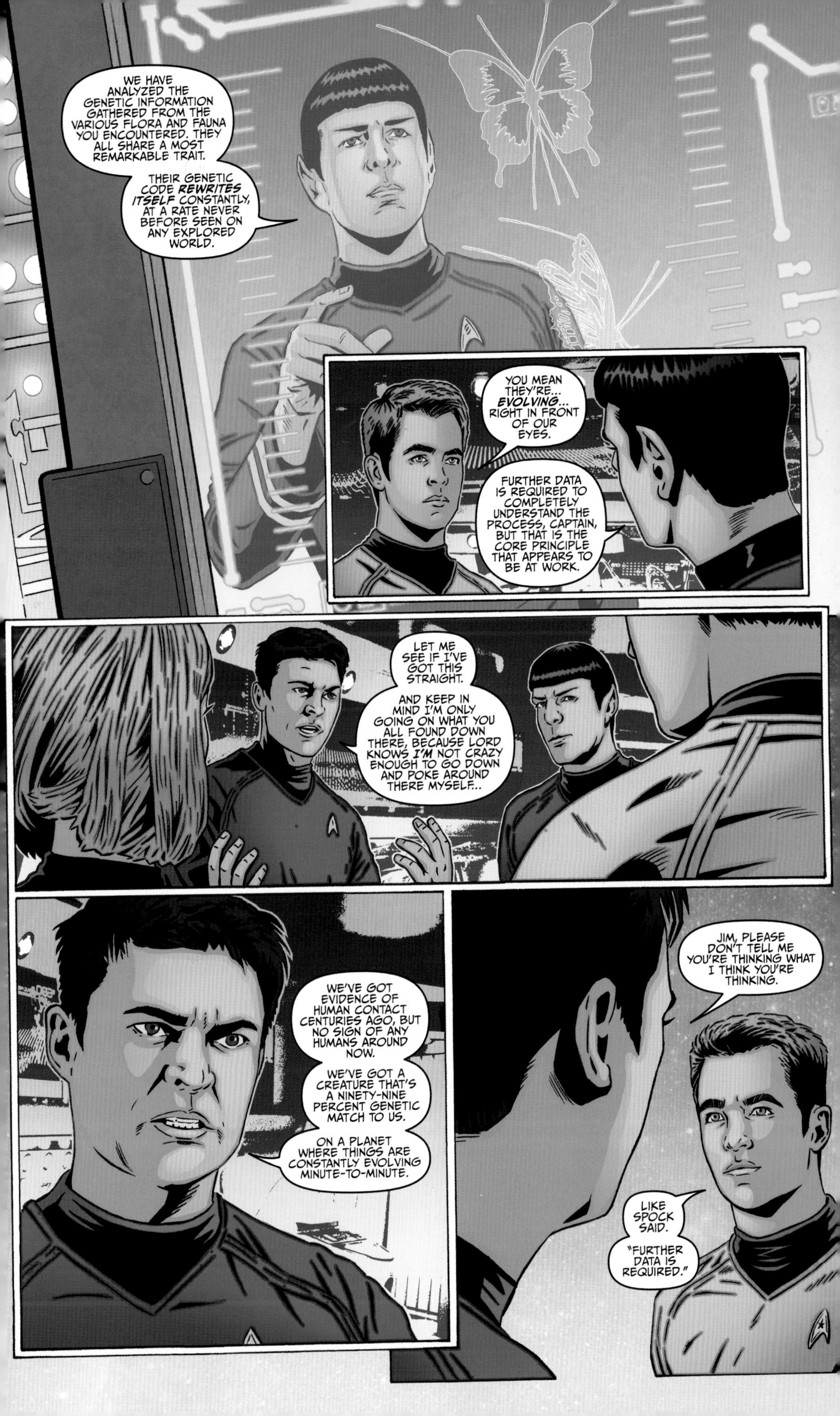
WE HAVE ANALYZED THE GENETIC INFORMATION GATHERED FROM THE VARIOUS FLORA AND FAUNA YOU ENCOUNTERED. THEY ALL SHARE A MOST REMARKABLE TRAIT.
THEIR GENETIC CODE **REWRITES ITSELF** CONSTANTLY, AT A RATE NEVER BEFORE SEEN ON ANY EXPLORED WORLD.
YOU MEAN THEY'RE... ***EVOLVING...*** RIGHT IN FRONT OF OUR EYES.
FURTHER DATA IS REQUIRED TO COMPLETELY UNDERSTAND THE PROCESS, CAPTAIN, BUT THAT IS THE CORE PRINCIPLE THAT APPEARS TO BE AT WORK.
LET ME SEE IF I'VE GOT THIS STRAIGHT.
AND KEEP IN MIND I'M ONLY GOING ON WHAT YOU ALL FOUND DOWN THERE, BECAUSE LORD KNOWS ***I'M*** NOT CRAZY ENOUGH TO GO DOWN AND POKE AROUND THERE MYSELF...
WE'VE GOT EVIDENCE OF HUMAN CONTACT CENTURIES AGO, BUT NO SIGN OF ANY HUMANS AROUND NOW.
WE'VE GOT A CREATURE THAT'S A NINETY-NINE PERCENT GENETIC MATCH TO US.
ON A PLANET WHERE THINGS ARE CONSTANTLY EVOLVING MINUTE-TO-MINUTE.
JIM, PLEASE DON'T TELL ME YOU'RE THINKING WHAT I THINK YOU'RE THINKING.
LIKE SPOCK SAID.
"FURTHER DATA IS REQUIRED."

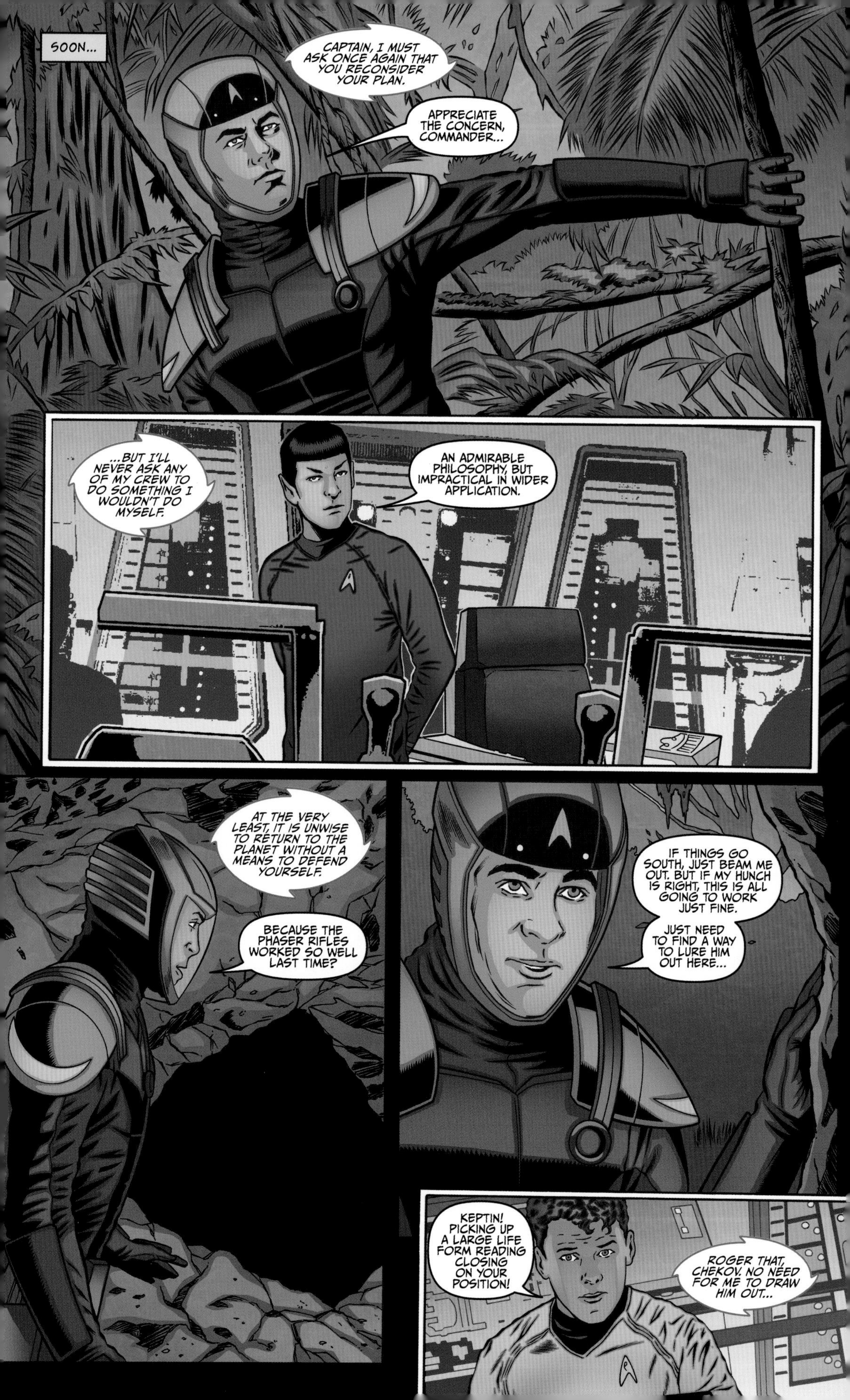

SOON...
CAPTAIN, I MUST ASK ONCE AGAIN THAT YOU RECONSIDER YOUR PLAN.
APPRECIATE THE CONCERN, COMMANDER...
...BUT I'LL NEVER ASK ANY OF MY CREW TO DO SOMETHING I WOULDN'T DO MYSELF.
AN ADMIRABLE PHILOSOPHY, BUT IMPRACTICAL IN WIDER APPLICATION.
AT THE VERY LEAST, IT IS UNWISE TO RETURN TO THE PLANET WITHOUT A MEANS TO DEFEND YOURSELF.
BECAUSE THE PHASER RIFLES WORKED SO WELL LAST TIME?
IF THINGS GO SOUTH, JUST BEAM ME OUT. BUT IF MY HUNCH IS RIGHT, THIS IS ALL GOING TO WORK JUST FINE.
JUST NEED TO FIND A WAY TO LURE HIM OUT HERE...
KEPTIN! PICKING UP A LARGE LIFE FORM READING CLOSING ON YOUR POSITION!
ROGER THAT, CHEKOV. NO NEED FOR ME TO DRAW HIM OUT...

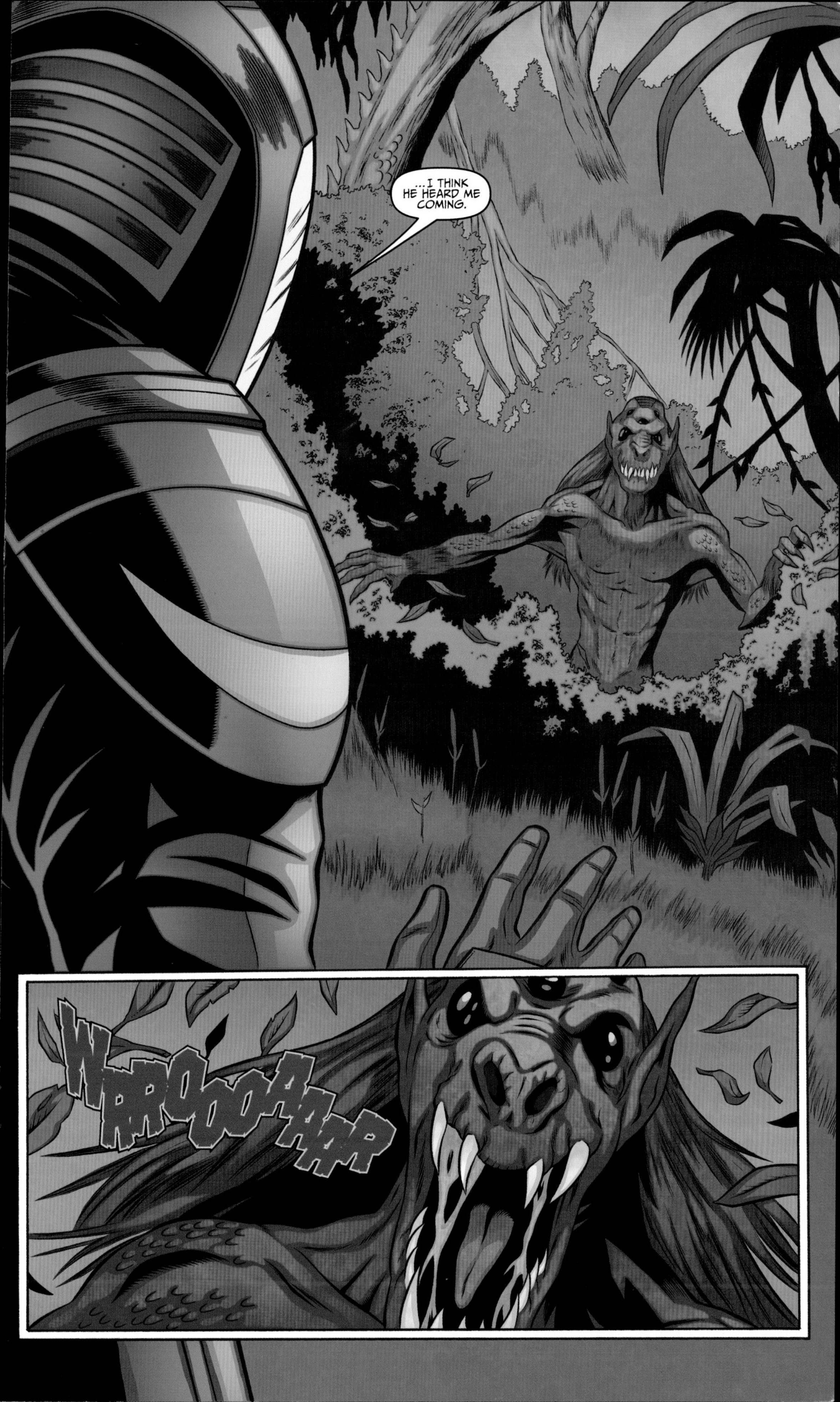
...I THINK HE HEARD ME COMING.
WRROOOAAAR

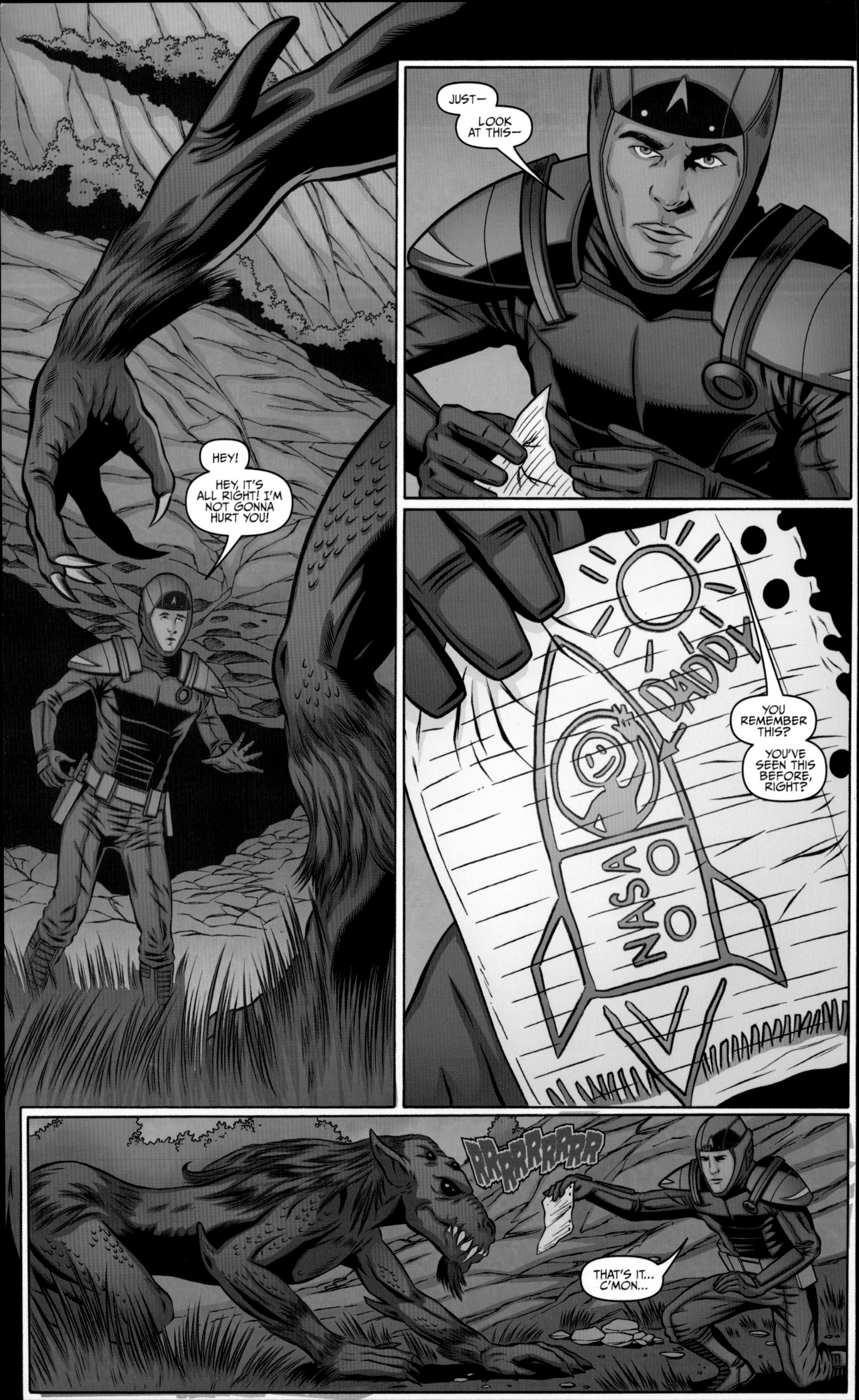
HEY!
HEY, IT'S ALL RIGHT! I'M NOT GONNA HURT YOU!
JUST—
LOOK AT THIS—
DADDY
NASA
YOU REMEMBER THIS?
YOU'VE SEEN THIS BEFORE, RIGHT?
RRRRRRRRRR
THAT'S IT... C'MON...

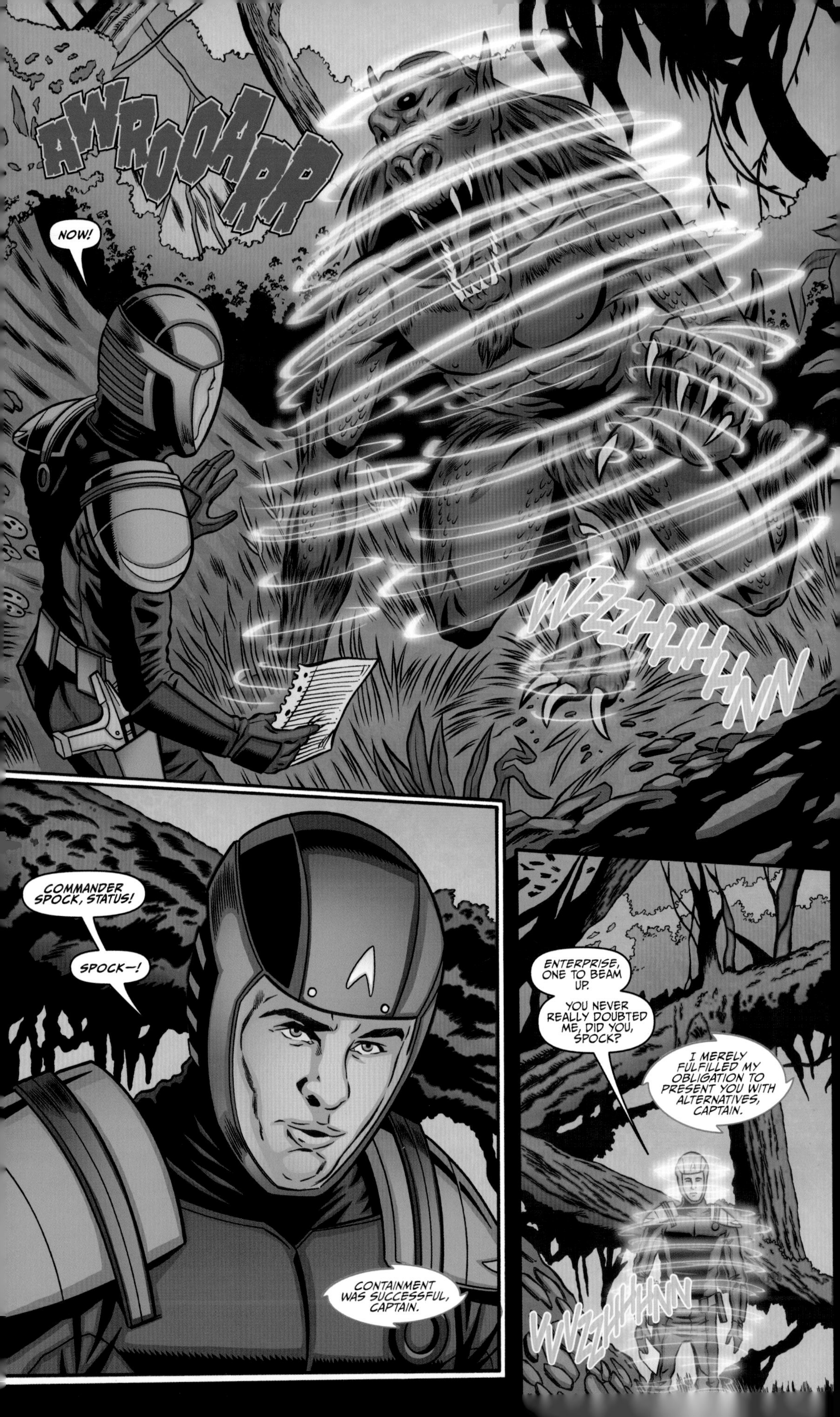
AWROOARR
NOW!
VVZZHHHHNN
COMMANDER SPOCK, STATUS!
SPOCK—!
CONTAINMENT WAS SUCCESSFUL, CAPTAIN.
ENTERPRISE, ONE TO BEAM UP.
YOU NEVER REALLY DOUBTED ME, DID YOU, SPOCK?
I MERELY FULFILLED MY OBLIGATION TO PRESENT YOU WITH ALTERNATIVES, CAPTAIN.
VVVZZHHHHNN

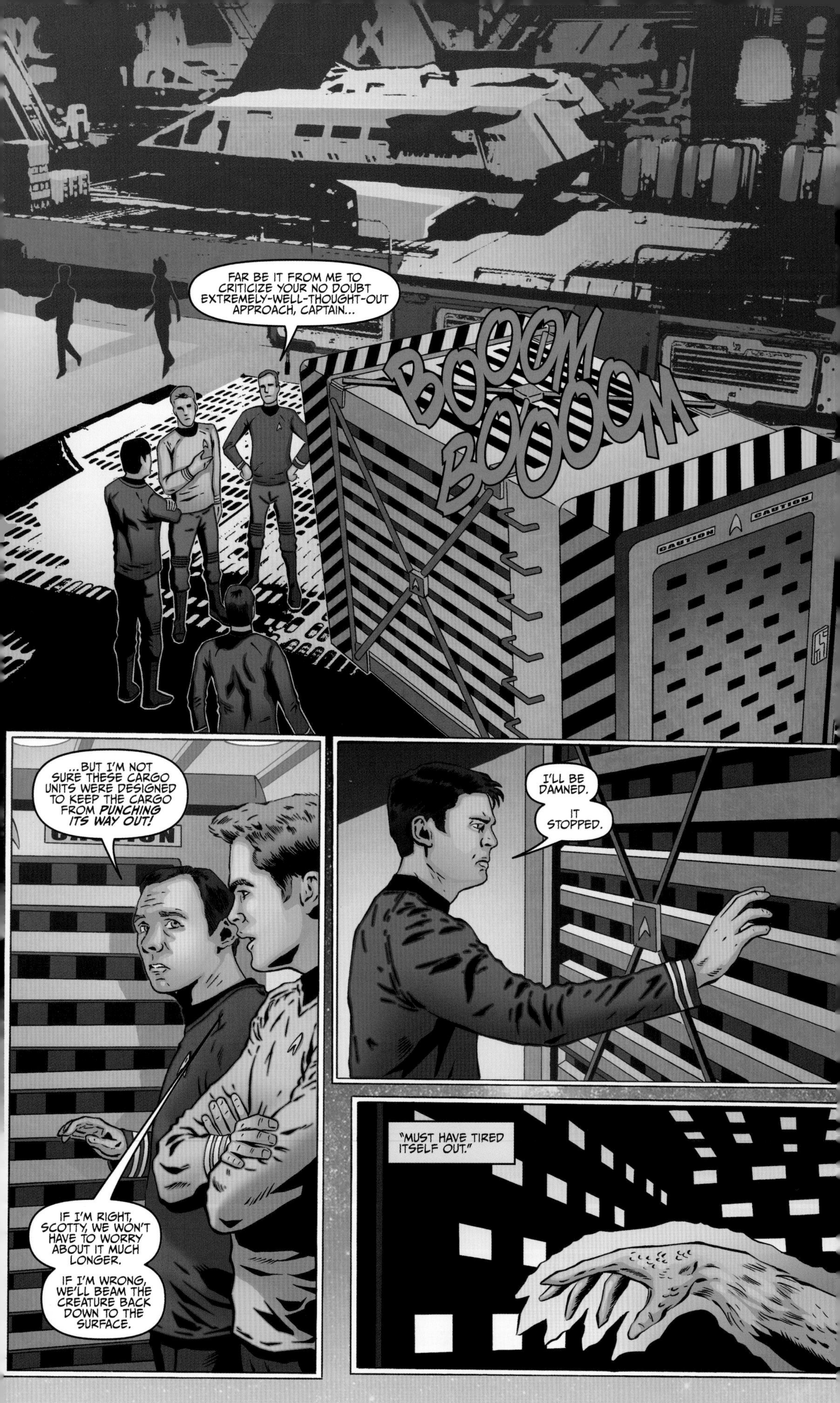
FAR BE IT FROM ME TO CRITICIZE YOUR NO DOUBT EXTREMELY-WELL-THOUGHT-OUT APPROACH, CAPTAIN...
BOOOM
BOOOOM
CAUTION
CAUTION
...BUT I'M NOT SURE THESE CARGO UNITS WERE DESIGNED TO KEEP THE CARGO FROM *PUNCHING ITS WAY OUT!*
IF I'M RIGHT, SCOTTY, WE WON'T HAVE TO WORRY ABOUT IT MUCH LONGER.
IF I'M WRONG, WE'LL BEAM THE CREATURE BACK DOWN TO THE SURFACE.
I'LL BE DAMNED.
IT STOPPED.
"MUST HAVE TIRED ITSELF OUT."

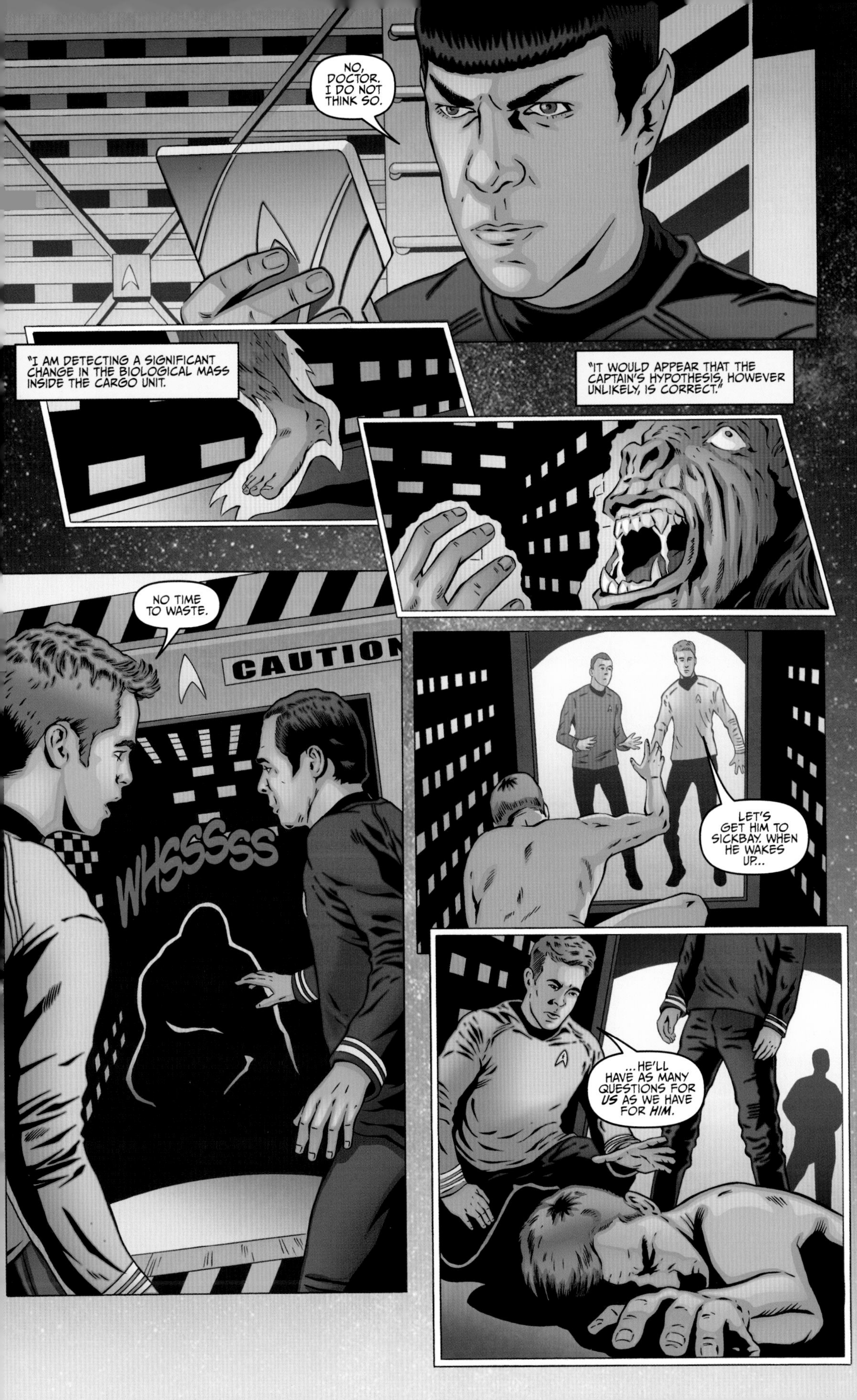
NO, DOCTOR. I DO NOT THINK SO.
"I AM DETECTING A SIGNIFICANT CHANGE IN THE BIOLOGICAL MASS INSIDE THE CARGO UNIT.
"IT WOULD APPEAR THAT THE CAPTAIN'S HYPOTHESIS, HOWEVER UNLIKELY, IS CORRECT."
NO TIME TO WASTE.
CAUTION
WHSSSSS
LET'S GET HIM TO SICKBAY. WHEN HE WAKES UP...
...HE'LL HAVE AS MANY QUESTIONS FOR US AS WE HAVE FOR HIM.

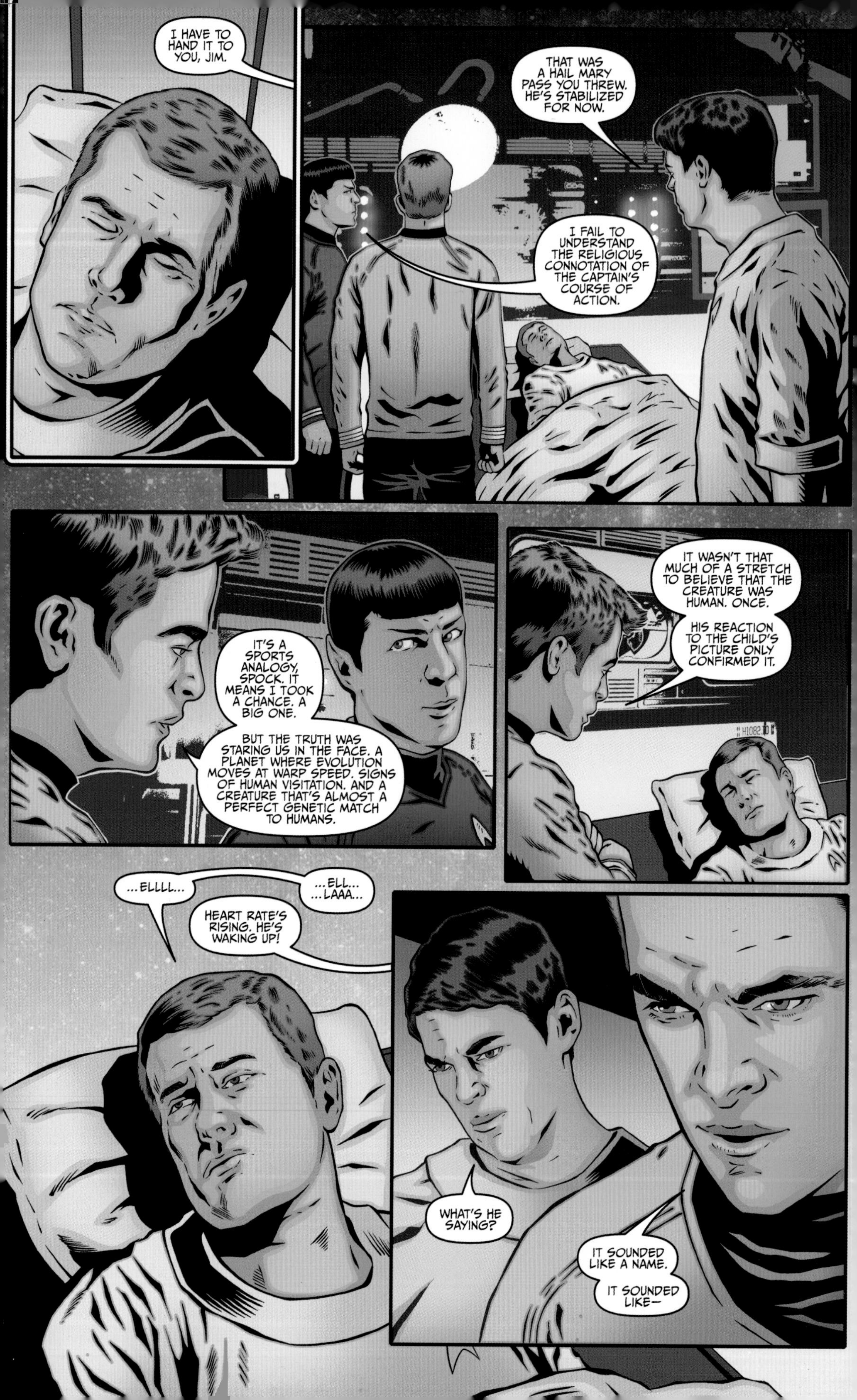

I HAVE TO HAND IT TO YOU, JIM.
THAT WAS A HAIL MARY PASS YOU THREW. HE'S STABILIZED FOR NOW.
I FAIL TO UNDERSTAND THE RELIGIOUS CONNOTATION OF THE CAPTAIN'S COURSE OF ACTION.
IT'S A SPORTS ANALOGY, SPOCK. IT MEANS I TOOK A CHANCE. A BIG ONE.
BUT THE TRUTH WAS STARING US IN THE FACE. A PLANET WHERE EVOLUTION MOVES AT WARP SPEED. SIGNS OF HUMAN VISITATION. AND A CREATURE THAT'S ALMOST A PERFECT GENETIC MATCH TO HUMANS.
IT WASN'T THAT MUCH OF A STRETCH TO BELIEVE THAT THE CREATURE WAS HUMAN. ONCE.
HIS REACTION TO THE CHILD'S PICTURE ONLY CONFIRMED IT.
...ELLLL...
...ELL... ...LAAA...
HEART RATE'S RISING. HE'S WAKING UP!
WHAT'S HE SAYING?
IT SOUNDED LIKE A NAME.
IT SOUNDED LIKE—

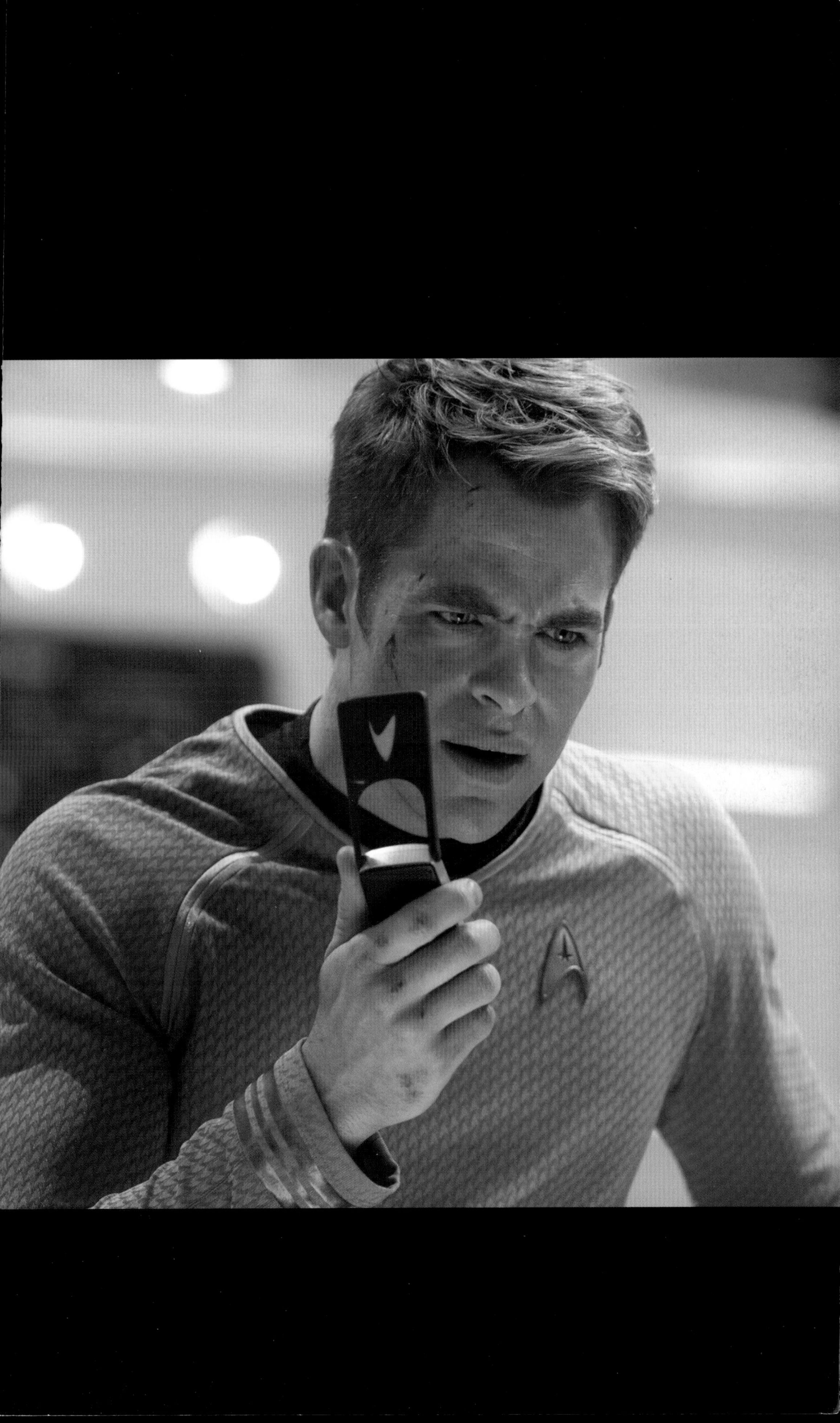

Artwork by Cat Staggs
Enterprise Model by Gabriel Koerner

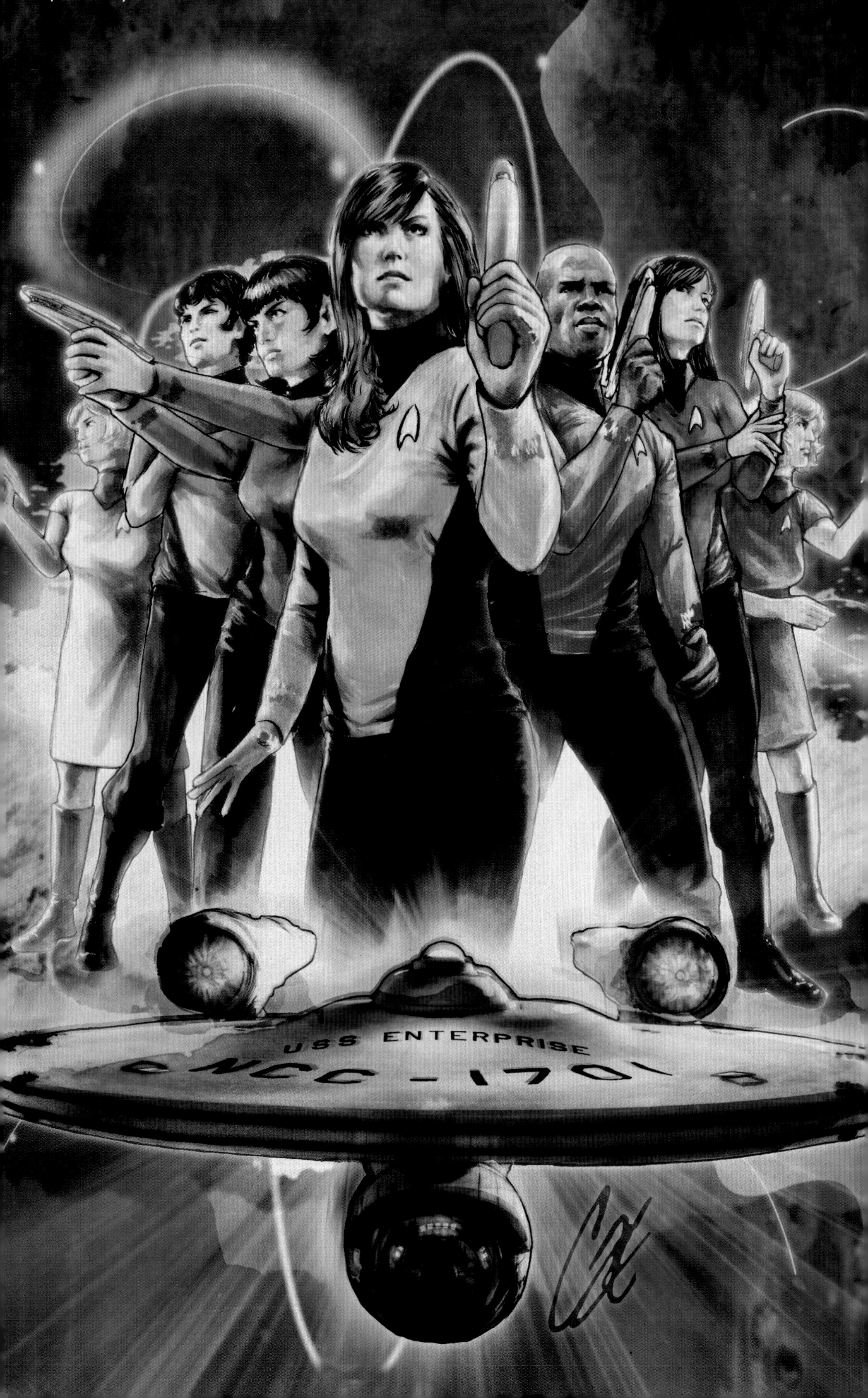
USS ENTERPRISE
NCC-1701

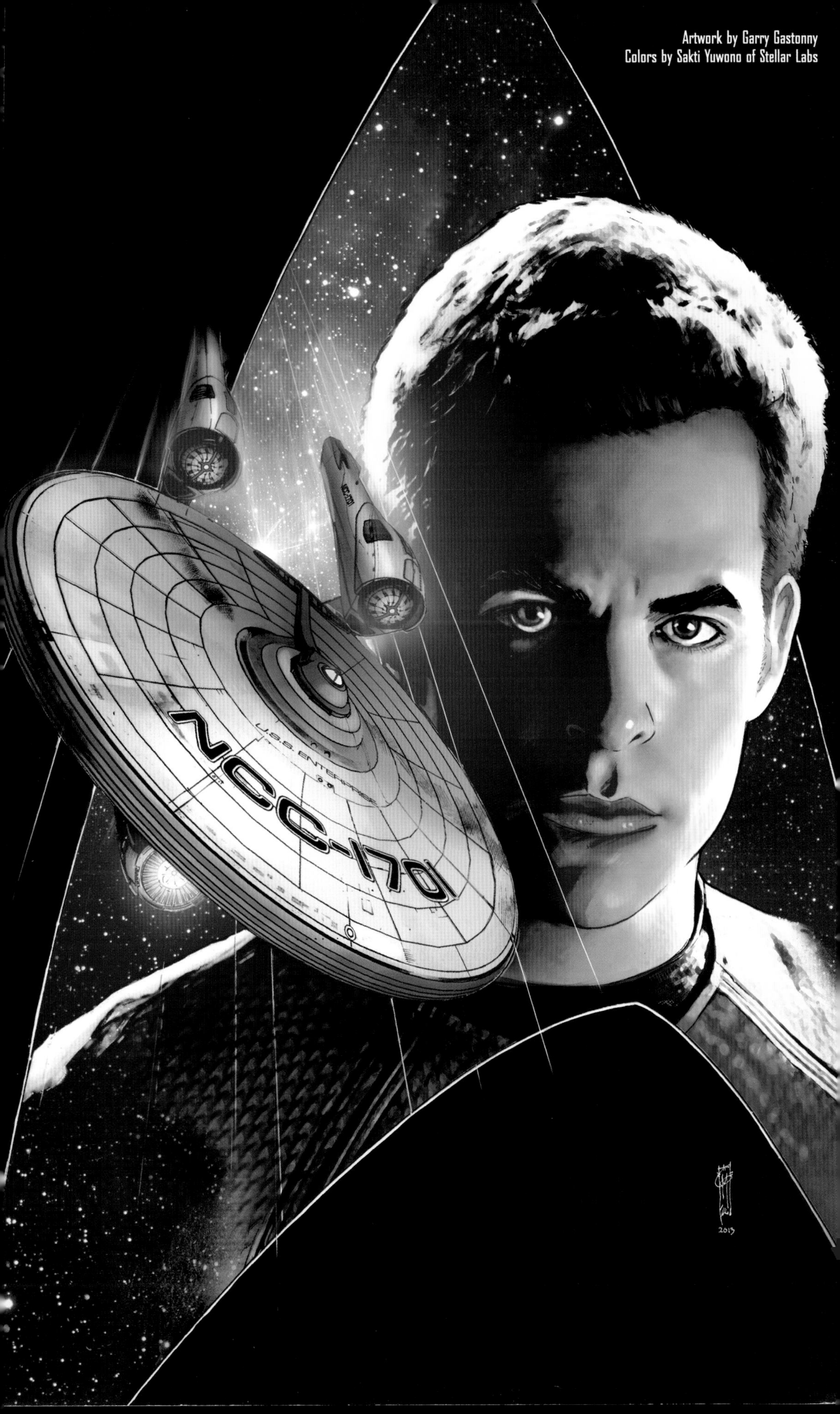

Artwork by Garry Gastonny
Colors by Sakti Yuwono of Stellar Labs

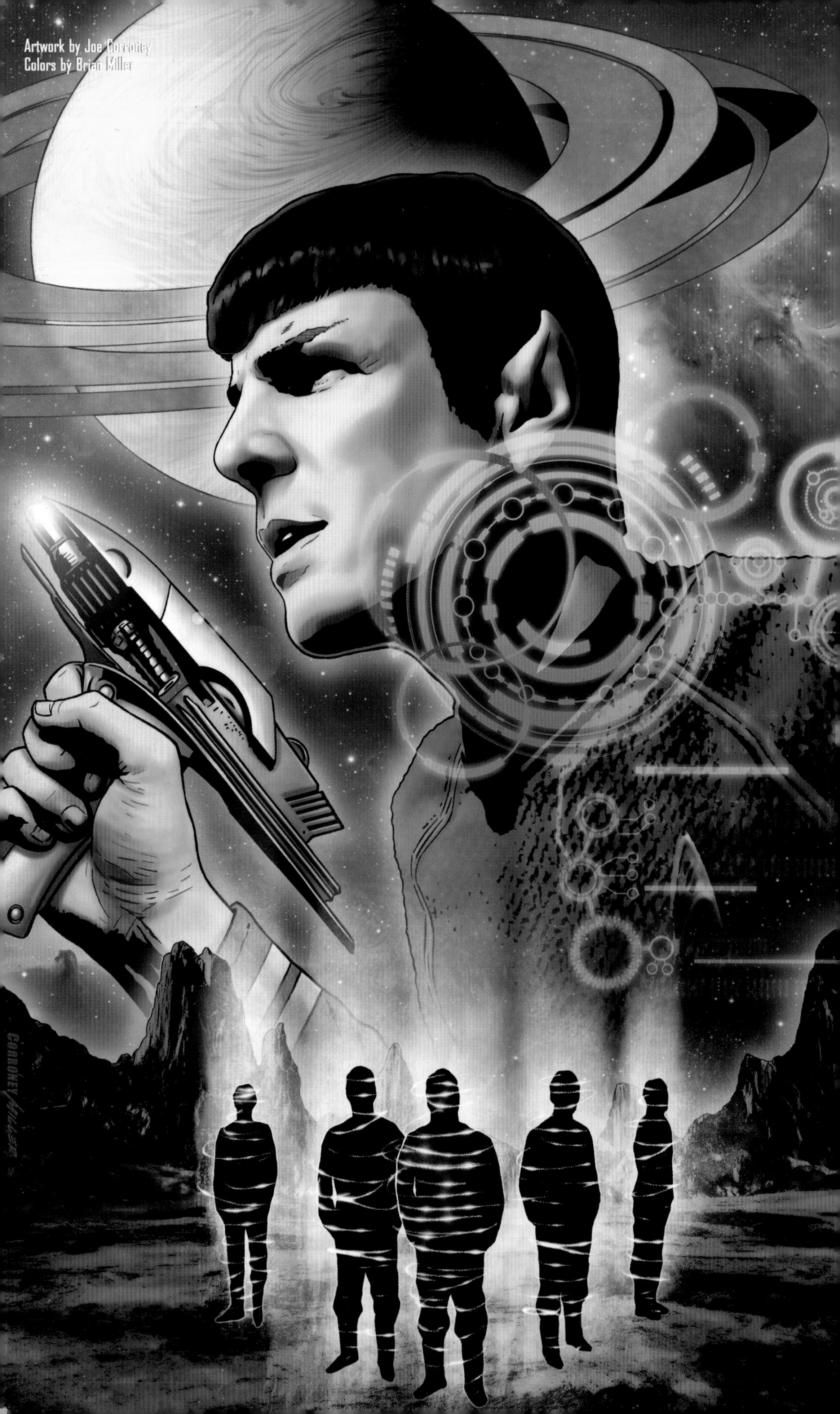

Artwork by Joe Corroney
Colors by Brian Miller